The Stardom Affair

OTHER FIVE STAR TITLES BY ROBERT S. LEVINSON

The Evil Deeds We Do
Finders, Keepers, Losers, Weepers
Phony Tinsel
A Rhumba in Waltz Time
The Traitor in Us All
In the Key of Death
Where the Lies Begin
Ask a Dead Man

A NEIL GULLIVER & STEVIE MARRINER NOVEL

The Stardom Affair

Robert S. Levinson

FIVE STAR

A part of Gale, Cengage Learning

GALE
CENGAGE Learning

Farmington Hills, Mich • San Francisco • New York • Waterville, Maine
Meriden, Conn • Mason, Ohio • Chicago

GALE
CENGAGE Learning

Five Star™ Publishing, a part of Cengage Learning, Inc.

LIBRARY OF CONGRESS CATALOGING-IN-PUBLICATION DATA

Names: Levinson, Robert S., author.
Title: The stardom affair : a Neil Gulliver & Stevie Marriner novel / Robert S. Levinson.
Description: First edition. | Waterville, Maine : Five Star, A part of Gale, Cengage Learning, [2016]
Identifiers: LCCN 2015049810| ISBN 9781432831608 (hardcover) | ISBN 1432831607 (hardcover)
Subjects: LCSH: Gulliver, Neil (Fictitious character)—Fiction. | Marriner, Stevie (Fictitious character)—Fiction. | Private investigators—California—Los Angeles—Fiction | Murder—Investigation—Fiction. | BISAC: FICTION / Thrillers. | FICTION / Mystery & Detective / Hard-Boiled. | GSAFD: Mystery fiction. | Suspense fiction.
Classification: LCC PS3562.E9218 S73 2016 | DDC 813/.54—dc23
LC record available at http://lccn.loc.gov/2015049810

First Edition. First Printing: April 2016
Find us on Facebook– https://www.facebook.com/FiveStarCengage
Visit our website– http://www.gale.cengage.com/fivestar/
Contact Five Star™ Publishing at FiveStar@cengage.com

Printed in the United States of America
1 2 3 4 5 6 7 20 19 18 17 16

FOR SANDRA
and for
DEBORAH and DAVID
Always the brightest stars in my galaxy

Chapter 1

SLUG LINE: HOT RODDY

By Neil Gulliver

It was a long time ago, more than a decade ago, a lifetime ago, several lifetimes, in a galaxy not so far away from anything but the real world, Hollywood by name, show biz capital of the solar system, where the movie stars are also famous for confusing themselves with the center of the universe.

Roddy Donaldson, for example.

Movie Star Supreme.

He of the sunshine smile.

Roddy Donaldson.

Acknowledged leader of the "Diapered Dozen," the bumper crop of teenage movie stars whose every nose-picking escapade back-when routinely sold trillions of copies of the weekly tabloid scandal sheets that turn supermarket checkout counters into libraries for our gossip-drenched society.

Roddy Donaldson.

People magazine's choice as "Sexiest Man of the Year" two years running, whose adoring armada of young and not-so-young female fans, the heralded "Rod Squad," staged a mass protest demonstration at the Chinese Theater on Hollywood Boulevard the year he lost the glittering crown to Sean Connery.

Roddy Donaldson.

The guest insiders said Carson wanted most before he willingly disappeared into the anonymity of retirement (and tracked down by phone with a personal invitation, not Johnny's usual M.O., something he did about as often as he forgot to tap his coffee mug).

That Roddy Donaldson.

Entertainment Tonight's Mary Hart reported breathlessly the night after Roddy's appearance how Carson had compared the young man's hauntingly blue eyes with the violet majesty of Miss Elizabeth Taylor's royal gaze and gone on to ask, "How blue are they? . . . They're so blue, so blue, Paul Newman checked himself into the Betty Ford Clinic with a case of eyeball deprivation."

Nobody laughed louder than Roddy, and what a laugh: Appreciative. Ingratiating. As frisky as his Cuisinart voice.

Nineteen-year-old Roddy reveling in the fun and attention with graciousness and the public good manners that supposedly had gone away with the old studio star system.

Somebody had taught him well.

Show your dazzling orthodonture.

Pose for the photographs.

Sign the autographs.

Do the endless premieres, benefits, fundraisers, and personal appearances, even the sporadic opening of a manhole cover, to remind the fans how much you appreciate them, so they'll be understanding of your occasional "bummers," the infrequent dark moods and bad moments that can't be hidden from a world media that covers scandal the way chimps relish bananas.

The media sponsored an international headline festival after I found those two girls sprawled out naked and in bed with Roddy.

Underage and overdosed.

Their static eyes singing the too-late blues.

Dead.

Murdered.

Lifeless coming attractions for more death, what the movie business refers to as "trailers," before a climax as shattering as any of those in the films that brought an easy, early stardom to Roddy Donaldson.

Death in the real world of Hollywood.

Where hundreds of people arrive every day to live out their stardust fantasies, unaware Hollywood is actually a town where dreams come to die.

All those years ago, the night I found the girls dead and Roddy clinging to life in his apartment climaxed the kind of day that, had it been a pack of cigarettes, would have come with a warning label printed on the back.

More than ten years ago, but—

—the details as vivid as ever whenever I think back to Stardom House and so much else unthinkable that began and ended with Roddy Donaldson, the stuff of nightmares that continue to haunt me.

Chapter 2

What kind of a day was it? you ask.

Don't ask.

It was the kind of gut-wrenching day that kept me on the go until almost midnight, getting too emotionally involved in a story I'd be cranking out for "On the Go," the column I've been doing six days a week for the *Los Angeles Daily* since I was promoted out of the crime beat a few years ago.

An eight-year-old boy on the edge of death at the City of Hope in Duarte, a last haven for hopeless cancer victims. Little Pedro Cisneros, his frail, failing body a pincushion for the finest needles modern medicine had to offer, his stagnant brown boulder-sized eyes staring at the hospital ward ceiling for signs of angels.

His parents, Pedro senior and Maria Elena, at his bedside. Pedro, who'd already cried beyond tears and now was onto a catalog of grunts and groans that translated into despair in any language. Maria Elena, working her beads in silent prayer. And working them and working them and working them.

I'd sat with them for hours, smiling a smile I didn't mean and feeding them dream words about possibilities for little Pedro that we all knew were no possibilities whatsoever, but me needing to say something, do something, anything, trying to shoulder some of the load they were no longer able to hoist for themselves. It was me being a lousy reporter, unable to remain subjective and distanced from the story—victimized by an unquenchable need to be a good human being.

Not the first time.

Not the last time.

Later, finally, an escape to home.

Off the freeways into a slow ride through the dimly lit, mostly empty streets of downtown and midtown to my part of town, a trip made by memory, my mind too busy suffering through words and phrases I might want to use in describing for my readers the kid and a death worse than dying, most inadequate, making me feel more inadequate than usual.

I owe my condo at the Heathcliffe Arms in Westwood to my ex-wife, Stephanie Marriner. Stevie, still the "Sex Queen of the Soaps," not yet the major movie and stage star she'd go on to become, loaned me the money I needed to buy the place after she dumped me. She called it an act of generosity. I still don't know if Stevie meant the divorce or the loan.

Mine is the smallest of the one-bedroom apartments in the three-story, two hundred and fifty-six unit complex below Wilshire Boulevard on Veteran. The Heathcliffe is not as tony as the high-rises that stand sentry on both sides of the Wilshire corridor between Beverly Hills and Westwood Boulevard. You wouldn't know it from the average high-six figures it costs to get into something like my six hundred and ninety square feet castle.

I grumbled trying to get the keypad to the underground parking garage entrance to accept the date code, cursed the black iron gate for refusing to budge until I remembered the code had been changed yesterday from 1914 to 1690, the year William of Orange had maneuvered the Boys Brigade into the Irish Sea. The gate slid back and I sailed through. I navigated a deliberate turn off the steeply inclined ramp and, moments later, angled the old Jag into my assigned space by mindless rote.

I hoofed the stairs to the third floor rather than risk the elevator, which lately was breaking down with irritating regularity, and was out of my tie and sports jacket before I double-locked the apartment door behind me. I liberated the last cold Heineken from the fridge and checked for messages on the machine from habit, no intention of making any callbacks before morning.

It didn't work out that way.

Among five calls and three hang-ups was one logged around ten o'clock from the Heathcliffe Arms' resident manager, Sharon Glenn.

There was an unusual urgency in her chronically calm voice, which resembles the sound I imagine someone would make buttering a pane of glass: "Neil, it's Sharon. Call me back, please. No matter what time you hear this, okay? Okay? Call me back."

I punched in her number on the automatic dial.

Sharon answered with my name before the first ring finished.

"Not too late?"

"I said so," she said, sounding relieved at hearing my voice. Before I could ask, she said, "It's Roddy Donaldson again."

"Of course."

"Roddy's mother has been after me for the last two hours to go over and check up on him. I didn't want to do anything without you, you know?"

"I know."

As well I should have.

Roddy Donaldson.

There were a half dozen or so recognizable celebrities resident at the Heathcliffe, including a former sitcom regular and a two-time All-America on Bruins teams that went to the Rose Bowl back-to-back and got clobbered by Ohio State and Michigan State front-to-rear, but Roddy was the only movie star. In this town that's like the pearl in the oyster.

The entrance directory listed him by the name of the character he'd played in a lush remake of *Captains Courageous,* opposite the illustrious Brian Armstrong (in the role that won a second Oscar for Spencer Tracy). *Lush* remake. How Freudian a choice of word.

Shortly after Roddy moved in about eight or nine months ago, Sharon learned the kid was an alcoholic. Certified and chronic. A kid who couldn't handle one step, much less try for twelve, but discreet in his staggering; savvy enough to avoid being spotted by other residents and abetted by our building security guards, who guided him upstairs and through the right doors like they were auditioning for a part in Roddy's next buddy movie.

The first time the kid's mother called, asking Sharon to check out the apartment and confirm Roddy's presence, Sharon discovered him sprawled half on and half off his bed in a stupor. Smelling like a distillery. Using his puke for a pillow.

She was on the phone to me immediately.

We got the kid cleaned up.

And again the next time.

And several times after that.

It became obvious without Melba Donaldson telling us that her megabucks movie star son was nineteen going on early liver problems.

Last Christmas, as an expression of her gratitude, Mrs. Donaldson sent Sharon a gift basket containing VHS copies of all his movies.

Her note, hand-printed in large capital letters on an embossed notecard that reeked of money as well as perfume, said: THANKS FOR KEEPING YOUR EYES OPEN. (Had it been a larger card, she might easily have added: AND YOUR MOUTH SHUT.)

One early-morning alert, Sharon found Roddy snoring off a hangover with a small American flag dragging at half-mast from his cock. I admired Roddy's patriotism, but all Sharon could think to do was blush. That's one reason I keep getting Sharon's calls asking me to join her and go inside the apartment first. Like was happening now.

I pushed out a sigh and said, "I'll meet you at your place in two minutes."

"Two minutes, great . . . Neil!"

"Yes?"

"Thank you."

"You're welcome."

"I mean it, Neil. Thank you."

"I mean it, too. You're welcome. Does this mean we're friends again?"

Sharon let the question marinate for several moments before answering with one of her own: "Were we ever never?"

"Two minutes," I said.

Chapter 3

There are some people around the Heathcliffe Arms who'd bet something is going on between Sharon Glenn and me: hanky, as in panky. Absolutely not. We'd developed a nice social relationship as well as a business relationship since Sharon came to work here a couple years ago, but manage to share mutual good times without trading away our private lives, like strangers on a ship's cruise. Most of the time, but not yesterday.

Yesterday, we'd had an argument that dissolved into a Cold War when I broke a movie date because of Stevie, my ex. We'd planned on catching a Truffaut double-bill at the Monica, *The Bride Wore Black* and *Such a Gorgeous Kid Like Me,* followed by pasta, fresh hot bread dripping in garlic, and cheap vino that somehow tasted like a million bucks at Mateo's.

"Are you aware how you're always letting Ms. Marriner treat you like some pet," Sharon said, like she'd seen one courtroom movie too many. "She calls, 'Here, boy, here, boy,' and you come running."

"That's not entirely fair, Sharon. Sometimes I walk."

"In the divorce, did Ms. Marriner get custody of the leash?"

"That's not fair, either."

"What it's truly not is any of my business anyway."

"Stevie has an emergency, a family emergency."

"Then shouldn't she be calling John Gotti?"

"She's desperate for my help, Sharon, or you know I wouldn't do this to you. Do it to us. I'd been looking forward to you and me—"

Sharon pushed a *shut up* palm at my face. "I said it's none of my business, Mr. Gulliver." She rose imperiously from her desk and stalked out of the office like some Prussian general off to lead the troops into battle. Left me sitting there wondering why I cared. Hell, I knew why.

When Sharon isn't trying to hide her sense of humor, as if having one is a capital offense, she's quite capable of a sardonic wit and a conversational satire to be envied and appreciated. I doubt she's as tough as she makes out, but she's prettier than she knows—or lets on.

Sharon has a curiously distant face, an ethereal quality Whistler would have begged to capture on canvas. Yet, it's not my kind of beauty. That may be a reason we get along so well, except for infrequent times like the present. No pressure in the relationship. Only the simple pleasures of true friendship and good company.

For more than that, I'm invariably attracted to a woman with an indefinable inner spark, with a certain verve generating a cosmic connection that forces me to get up from wherever I am, walk over to her, and—

—usually make a fool of myself.

That kind of woman. The kind of woman Picasso was likely to paint. A woman full of color and movement, surprising flashes of excitement. A woman more apt to be found in a carnival than a cathedral.

A woman like—

Stevie.

My ex.

Stevie Marriner.

Let's be honest about this.

My ex marks that spot.

And damn few others before or since.

Sharon's one-bedroom is in the building adjacent to mine, one of three structures comprising the Heathcliffe Arms complex.

I passed through the connecting fire doors, took the auxiliary elevator to five, and hurried along the corridor analyzing the distinctive smells of last night's meals that hadn't already commingled with the stale, perpetual odor of public use clinging to all the public areas. Someone had had barbecued chicken and ribs. Someone else, Pizza Man. Was that Mrs. Polonsky's goulash I smelled? Twice in one week?

Sharon was double-checking her doorknob as I passed through the last fire door. I returned her wave and doubled my pace. She had on a thick chenille wrap robe over her floor-length, floral-patterned hostess robe. She cinched it tighter as I approached.

Her shoulder-length auburn hair was wrapped in a single-strand braid that reached almost to her trim waist. In her fur-lined slippers she looked shorter than the five-seven in stocking feet she claimed. Apart from a touch of magenta lip gloss, she wore no makeup, and the zoo of freckles on her round, rose-complexioned face seemed to be painted in place.

Even dressed like this, she appeared a good ten years younger than the thirty-five years she admits to routinely and with a great degree of pride, where I look every day my thirty-three years on the good days—forty-three or more on all the rest.

Downstairs, around her office, she demonstrates a flair for dressing to look good, not to satisfy some current whim of fashion. Even her no-nonsense business outfits hint at the well-defined, nicely proportioned body lurking inside. She bounces around wearing a scuffed pair of Nikes, but switches to two-inch heels for meetings or business trips away from the building.

Sharon caught me admiring her and turned her head aside. Studied the off-white, spray-flecked ceiling for earthquake damage. Decided to give the doorknob another twist.

"How was Ms. Marriner?"

"How were the movies?"

We stumbled over our questions, Sharon seemingly as anxious as me to put our personal problems behind us.

"Her crisis a damn party, can you believe that? I couldn't escape fast enough."

"Just okay. They won't ever be among my favorite Truffauts."

We laughed at the chaos of our words, but the laughter was not registering in her veiled green eyes, luminous even in the shadowed hallway light as Sharon fought to resist any sign of vulnerability and get back to the cool efficiency that marks her working hours and carries over into the playtime we spend together.

"Thanks again for coming."

"I live for these magical moments," I said. She tried not to let me see a tick of a smile. "How long has Roddy been among the missing this time?" I took her by the elbow as we started for the stairwell.

She nudged loose and jammed her hands inside her robe pockets, instant body language that said she really wasn't ready to forgive or forget. She tried to step ahead of me. I hid my disappointment and kept pace.

"Mrs. Donaldson told me it's been about seventy-two hours," she said. "Since Sunday night."

"You mean the estimable Show Business Mother from Hell waited all that time before putting in her frantic call to have you check?" Sharon shrugged. "What's her old record?"

"Two days, a little less."

"You suppose she's planning to submit the kid for a new category in the *Guinness Book of World Records*? The Longest

Period a Kid Movie Star Successfully Hides from His Mama?"

"Neil, come on. Don't play the sarcastic newspaper guy who's seen it all with me, okay? I'll appreciate it if you save the act for someone who doesn't know better."

Definitely not ready to make peace, this one.

"But I have seen it all," I said.

"You're not funny."

"I save the A material for my column."

"He could be dead inside there," she said, and caught her breath.

"Not if it isn't in the script."

"Neil!"

"He could not be in there at all, but chances are good he'll be there the way he's always there when you answer Mother's cry and go looking. As soused as a skunk. Four hundred sheets to the wind. Not the first time I've seen this, you know?"

"Of course, I know. You've *seen* everything, haven't you, Neil? But do you *feel* anything?"

I hadn't intended to antagonize her. "I don't mean to be insensitive, Sharon, only realistic. The problem, pure and simple: our frequently absent Roddy Donaldson should be the poster boy for Alcoholics Invisible. His mama shouldn't be calling you. Melba should be calling someone who can really help her child clean up his act, not just his vomit, but God forbid she do anything that might draw public attention to the problem or rescue her son at the expense of his image. *Sic transit* stardom."

Sharon skipped down the stairwell. She took the steps two and three at a time. She almost slipped once or twice and grabbed the rail to keep from tumbling as she increased the distance between us.

By the time I reached the door to the courtyard, she was entering Roddy's building on the far side of the pool.

I caught up with her at the door to his second-floor unit. She was arched against the wall, struggling to catch her breath. I held out my hand. She reached into her pocket for the key and handed it over. I didn't need it. The door was not entirely shut. The security chain hung uselessly. I told Sharon to wait in the hallway and entered the apartment. I called for Roddy twice, getting nothing in return either time. I snapped on the overhead light in the entry hall and moved forward, calling out his name again.

Roddy Donaldson and I shared the same floor plan and not much else.

My place is furnished in traditional Divorced Male, clean, neat, and lonely. Roddy's decorator had surrounded him in red-rouged luxury inspired by some picture-book notion of a bordello around the turn of the century, the eighteenth.

The parlor, to the right of the flocked wallpaper, had everything but a leather-bound guest book, an upright piano, and assorted ladies of the moment lined up in various states of undress and enticing postures. Thick, drawn velvet drapes in an off-shade of purple. The famous Andy Warhol silkscreen on canvas of Brian Armstrong, a serial image as widely known as his Marilyns, Jackies, and Elvises. Dominating another wall, a David Hockney oil I didn't recall seeing in his LACMA retrospective: a nude sunbathing on a diving board who bore an uncanny resemblance to Roddy. An extravagant, glistening English Regency crystal chandelier that belonged downtown at the Ahmanson or over a winding staircase in one of those sumptuous Pasadena mansions.

Where the whorehouse piano should have been was a table draped in quilted satin, on top of which was spread a computer setup, video and sound equipment, assorted gear I had never seen outside a recording studio or didn't recognize well enough to give a name; in all, by my casual estimate, worth a hundred thou minimum.

Music was pouring through recessed speakers that tracked to a perfectly balanced ear-boggling stereo system buried inside one of two remarkable matched armoires that had to date back to one of France's Louies. Their customized interiors held a supply of liquors, half the Tower Records CD inventory in all flavors, and more electronic gear. What began on top as rows of neatly lined and labeled, magnificently fitted shelves dissolved halfway down into a jumble and, at the base, a mountainous mess. I knew this from surveys during prior tours of Donaldson duty, the unwritten "Right to Snoop" commandment that's among the first thing reporters learn, intuitively if they're any good at all, the same way they learn to read correspondence on somebody's desk upside down.

Once certain Roddy was not tanked out on the chaise lounge large enough to sleep four and drowning in Brunschwig & Fils fabric that competed with the intricate patterns of a Persian rug, I retreated from the room, across the entry hall, past the guest bathroom, to the closed bedroom door.

The heavy odor of incense was leaking over the baseboard, along with a splinter of light and the sensation newspapermen develop working the crime beat, that headlines were lurking on the other side of the door. I called Roddy's name again. I got no response to my cautious rapping. I turned the knob and carefully pushed open the door.

I saw the black girl first.

She was propped up against one of the posts at the foot of the king-sized, canopied bed. Her left arm hung uselessly by her side. A needle was stranded in her vein, just inside the elbow. Her black hair streamed down the back of her naked, distended body. Her wide mouth was open and her eyes stared blindly, welcoming a stranger to the rest of her life.

I judged her to be younger than Roddy, who was on his back,

naked, pinned by the weight of the other girl, white, whose own nude form smothered him at a diagonal angle. All over her body, bloated similarly to the black girl's, more tracks than a hen house. The tattoo across her buttocks was a tabernacle of meaningless designs and colors.

I smelled a grass residue inside the perfumed radiance of rectangular candles tall enough to burn for three or four more days. I spotted empty booze bottles, one on the bedside table, another on the floor, Roddy clutching a third bottle in his clenched right fist. Scotch. Gin. Vodka.

I crossed to the bed, reached over, and tried to pry the white girl off Roddy, but I couldn't work it from that angle. I climbed onto the mattress, on my knees, and wedged both hands solidly between her and Roddy, like I was getting ready to open a window. I lifted hard, harder and—heaved, feeling a sharp sting of regret in my left testicle as she rolled off and onto her back.

She was surprised to see me.

Only she didn't know it.

Another damned kid to remember longer than she'd remember me, which was not at all.

I heard something that sounded like a gurgle. I heard it again.

I pressed two fingers to Roddy's neck, checking for a pulse, but expecting to feel another death. The noise again. The noise was coming from him. So was a pulse, faint as a falling leaf.

I shouted, "Sharon, get in here!"

I heard her hasty feet padding along the carpeting. I heard her painful gasp, then another, before she slid to a tripping halt behind me. I stopped administering mouth-to-mouth to Roddy long enough to shoot her a look over my shoulder and order, "Call nine-one-one."

Sharon was frozen in place, her transparent green eyes glazed by disbelief, a fist pressed to her mouth.

"Now, Sharon. Now! Pick up the phone over there and dial

nine-one-one."

Seconds later I heard her shouting the address at someone while I worked to pump any sign of life back into the poor stupid bastard, wondering how many years it would be before I would be able to go to sleep and not expect to see the two dead girls frolicking in my dreams with all the others who had come before them.

Wondering why some days happen at all.

Chapter 4

In the dark and the damp of the pre-dawn hours, about two hours after I found the movie star and the dead girls, I stood outside the Heathcliffe with Det. Sgt. Jimmy Steiger and watched the ambulance carrying Roddy Donaldson go whoop-whooping up Veteran and across Wilshire, its red turret trailblazing to the UCLA Medical Center. The county medical examiner's meat van was double-parked out front with a parking lot of squad cars from the West End Station and Jimmy's unmarked Chevy, creating an obstacle course for the occasional vehicle cautiously lumbering by. A couple television news crews were still hanging around. Small clusters of the neighborhood curious remained across the street or behind the yellow investigation tape that kept the Heathcliffe sidewalk and entranceway clear, most of the people mesmerized by thc sights and sounds they probably knew best from the Dirty Harry movies.

Jimmy and I go back to my earliest days on the police beat at Parker Center, me being tutored in the ways of big-city crime by my predecessor and self-appointed mentor, A.K. Fowler, Jimmy still in blue and pumping up his jacket with busts designed to get him a detective rating faster than his sizeable, equally hungry competition within the rank and file. We wound up helping each other. We wound up liking each other even more than that.

We're about the same age, only Jimmy doesn't show the wear and tear of the cops and robbers business as much as I was feeling it right now, except for a modest softening of his sharply etched features and, between thick brows, a thicker crevice of concern that belies the quotation marks tilting at the corners of his warm whale-gray eyes and handsome mouth on a frat-house face.

He's packing about twenty pounds more than when he was hustling into end zones in his linebacker days with the USC Trojans, but he covers it well on his six-foot frame, in off-the-rack suits that hang from his broad shoulders like custom jobs.

Next to him I look positively anemic. And antique, my receding hairline no match for the golden bowl of hair he wears pulled back in a tight pigtail the LAPD brass stopped trying to regulate years ago, recognizing Jimmy was too good a cop to keep on permanent suspension.

It's not all roses to go with the guns, though.

Jimmy is still covering street crime, while his peers are beginning to jockey desks at Police Central, behind doors that carry titles like lieutenant and captain, commander and even one deputy chief. He maintains that he doesn't care. Maybe he doesn't, but sometimes I can spot the hurt breaking past his jaunty laugh.

The ambulance disappeared. Jimmy slapped an arm across my back and said, "Shall we rejoin the M.E.? It'll be another hour at least before the lab guys finish up and the body bags come downstairs."

I icked and shrugged and told him there wasn't much blood and gore I could use at this late hour. My story was already pumped into my computer and uploaded to the *Daily.* I'd batted it out under the deadline wire, in time to make the home edition replate for L.A. County subscribers, who'd now have more than Mother Russia's political and geographical facelift to take with their morning toast and coffee.

I had me an Exclusive, clean and neat and hard to come by in this dawning age of electronic immediacy. The topper: I was an eyeball witness. No question, this was a first-class beat that would be getting the banner on page one.

My detective pal was being all business, the best way to be when your business is death. I was pretending I hadn't been affected by my discovery of those sad child-women, the kind of lying you learn to do on the crime beat, or you graduate to bargain-basement burnout and hiding bottles in the bottom drawer under unwieldy files and used snot rags nobody would want to touch. Every murder takes a tiny piece of you, until the day there's so little of you left you're routinely confused with a Giacometti sculpture.

I don't hide it so well anymore, less and less well since I scrammed the crime beat for the column. Nowadays it takes less than blood and guts and gore to make my stomach do the tango. It was doing that while I was managing Sharon through the initial stages of her own emotional chaos.

Sharon's office was to our immediate right, off the second set of glass entrance doors and across from the security guard station that looked like a movie theater candy counter castoff. It's small, but comfortable, crammed with some of the cheap furniture left behind by the builders when they closed the sales showroom. An outdated word processor sits on a rickety typewriter stand behind her schoolteacher desk. Two unmatched visitors' chairs barely fit the space in front of the desk. A copier, a fax, and a coffeemaker are on top of the tan file cabinets, and orderly piles of olive and tan manila folders occupy most of the other flat surfaces. Inexpensively framed museum and movie posters are the only touch of personality on display and clues to Sharon's life outside of business.

She was standing by the window fronting Veteran, the blinds

open enough for her to survey the street. She had the phone in her hand, the receiver cradled between her neck and shoulder, and was reassuring another resident. The inquiries had been ringing in ever since the first squad cars arrived. She caught our reflection in the glass, indicated the fresh pot of coffee. Answered my wave with a ruffle of fingers.

I mouthed the words: *Are you okay?*

She nodded and broke out an expression thanking me for my concern.

I was concerned.

Since shortly after the first sirens pulled up, without a break, she had been on the phone or over in the lobby area dealing with the nosy and the noisy, tired, cranky, curious people who had gravitated there demanding answers. Whenever I tuned in, I heard Sharon fielding the inquiries in the calm, confident, patient manner that characterized all her work.

She clicked down the disconnect and was about to say something, but the phone rang again. She motioned us to help ourselves and fell into the soft patter of a consoling parent.

Jimmy filled a mug and passed it over to me. He filled his own halfway and added three spoonfuls of powdered milk and three packets of sweetener before sinking into the other visitor's chair. He studied Sharon as she moved from the window to her swivel chair behind the desk, gave me a wink of approval. I shook my head and made a mental note to add him to the list of people who will never understand that a man and a woman can be Just Friends. He grimaced in disbelief. I rewarded him with that universal sign of affection, a middle finger.

Sharon turned back to us and cradled the phone. By the way she explored our faces I was certain I hadn't made my finger disappear fast enough, but Jimmy had his choirboy deadpan in place. She pulled her robe tighter across her chest and looked for traces of dust on her impeccably neat desk before asking

Steiger, "Roddy's all right?"

"The medics are calling his condition critical, Miss Glenn, but I'd log his chances at better'n fifty-fifty. It would have been a different story if Neil hadn't acted quick as he did."

Sharon showered me with an appreciative look and lowered her eyes. They were underlined by crescents of black. "I don't believe I'll ever forget the sight of those poor, poor girls," she said, wiping a speck from the desk's surface and rubbing it between her finger and thumb.

Jimmy said, "Makes you want to go out and break some face, them damned drug pushers."

Sharon looked up, surprised. "Drugs?"

"For these four walls until it becomes official . . . It looks to me like an OD times two. Heroin, probably, judging by the swollen nature of the bodies."

She appeared overwhelmed. "Roddy?"

"Smelled to holy hell from alcohol. What probably saved his life. Must've slowed down his intake enough to keep him from bailing out with the Jane Does. Maybe doing a little blow to go with the H. There were traces."

"You don't know who the girls are, Sergeant? Were?"

"Probable make on the black girl in the oven now. The other . . . ?" He shrugged. "A good set of prints can solve that riddle quick enough. If she's a runaway, not a local, we'll send them out for a scan on the national database. Doesn't add more than a few minutes to the search. This technology crap is just the damnedest." He rinsed his mouth with coffee and fixed on the ceiling. "Meanwhile, you're still certain you never saw the deceased before this? Maybe here to visit Roddy some other day, or the three of them lounging around that pool outside there in the courtyard?"

I jumped into his laid-back debriefing, suggesting, "Jimmy, maybe you could save all this for later? One look tells you how tired Ms. Glenn is." Anybody could see it. The drag of emotion was playing out in unseemly puckers on Sharon's face. Short circuits in her body movement. Nervous bursts of energy offsetting the invisible emotions replaying the spectacle of horror she had walked in on. I recognized Jimmy was doing his job, but I resented it all the same, for her sake.

Sharon said, "Thank you, Neil, but it's fine." She turned back to Jimmy. "The only time I remember him being at the pool, Roddy created a panic among the UCLA kids who live here. They went ballistic. He hasn't been back since."

"I suppose it has something to do with his image up there on the silver screen?"

"In person, Roddy exudes even more sex appeal. Have you ever really looked into his eyes?"

"Can't say that I have, Miss Glenn."

I said, "Me, neither."

"Then take my word for it, both of you," Sharon said.

Jimmy shot me a glance, hoping to catch some jealousy. When I didn't react, he cleared his throat and asked her, "What's the likelihood Roddy was dating one of them, with the other along for the joy ride?"

"I suppose . . . Except for the tabloids at the market, the closest I ever get to one of his dates is when the stretch limo pulls up to take him to some ritzy premiere or party. His dates don't get out even then. His date waits for him inside the limo and the driver buzzes upstairs to let Roddy know the car's here."

"The last time you saw a stretch?"

Sharon thought about it. "Maybe last month. I was working late, finishing up the agenda and minutes the day before the board of directors meeting. The president of the Heathcliffe Arms Homeowners Association was anxious to review them."

I answered her look with a tip of my invisible hat.

That's me, the president. The Prez. *El presidente.*

It had become my lot a year ago through every fault of my own, when I agreed to run in the annual election, at Sharon's urging. It made sense at the time, less sense after I found my life infested with a constant parade of resident oddballs, terminal loudmouths, occasional perverts, busted plumbing, bad security, creative vandalism, car burglaries and garage thefts, and the occasional lusty old dame who, unable to compete poolside with the UCLA coeds in their string bikinis, took creative approaches to seducing the hired help.

The phone rang as Jimmy started to ask Sharon another question, something about who else in the building might be able to talk about Roddy. Tired as she was, she managed to put some false cheer in her voice acknowledging a troublesome tenant I knew by name. She sent a helpless motion across the desk and launched into another explanation of what all those policemen were doing in the building.

Jimmy watched her with stakeout eyes, nodded approvingly, flashed me a thumbs-up sign out of her sightline. Definitely, I would have to set him straight about Sharon and me at first opportunity.

I shifted my eyes to Sharon and said, "It's beginning to sound to me like the lady is needed upstairs."

Jimmy said gently, his voice as mellow as a jazz riff by Wes Montgomery, "Ease up, pard. The lady will tell me when she's had enough."

Sharon had been half-listening. She nodded agreement.

I made a gesture of surrender, eased out of the chair, and mumbled a few words about dragging my own tired bones upstairs.

Jimmy aimed and fired a stubby finger gun. "Catch you later."

Sharon gave me a tired smile and a wave that almost worked.

I made a mental note to get her some overtime bucks, not

called for in her contract, or compensatory time off, which Sharon rarely took, at the next board of directors meeting. The members were about as generous as a hooker's kiss, but I'd get it approved somehow. It's never a sin to let someone know she's appreciated.

I popped two Advil and flopped into bed, immediately feeling the dull, familiar ache of muscles relaxing. I began wrestling the slow assassin of sleep. I lost. Six hours later, I awoke and clicked on the TV to a head-and-shoulders shot of Roddy Donaldson, sexy eyes and all.

The CNN Hollywood correspondent standing under the Heathcliffe canopy in the sunrise hours was quoting liberally from the *Daily* story I'd filed and giving the breathless impression she was the one who had stumbled onto Roddy and the two dead girls, layering in none of the obligatory warning labels, like *asserted, allegedly, reportedly, according to informed sources.*

For a minute I let myself be angry at her theft of my exclusive, while she moved ahead to the penalty phase of Roddy's trial. She had already personally convicted him of Murder One, based on some vague, supercharged innuendo recited darkly from a notepad, quoting the feckless mouth of a politically astute but otherwise asinine assistant D.A., Hapgood Harris, a man whose lust for power didn't always allow for justice and for whom I enjoy a certified contempt.

I hit the remote and found a local station talking news headline between reruns of *I Love Lucy* and *Gilligan's Island.*

The screen filled with a shot of the *Daily*'s front page. The headline made me smile. Seventy-plus point splattered across the page, type so large they'd had to go down to paste-pot hell in the storage basement to find the old wood trays for a handset job that gave my story the splinter-edged feeling of immediacy:

MOVIE STAR DONALDSON A KILLER?

For a moment I ignored that the paper was doing its own take on tying Roddy to the murders, the headline based on nothing that could have been pulled from the story I filed. Maybe a little shamefacedly, I was pleased to see my byline on something besides my "On the Go" column:

By Neil Gulliver

It had been a long time.

My delight was short-lived.

Chapter 5

When the phone rang, I'd just stepped out of the shower and was toweling down.

It was the *Daily*'s M.E., Chet Wilkins. I don't like Chet Wilkins, never have, but it's balanced by Chet's burning dislike of me. He got there first, and to this day I don't know why. I don't care, either. Chet's the kind of guy who goes to bed in his suit jacket and tie. Doesn't that tell you something?

Now, Chet Wilkins telling me: "You got any Donaldson skinny you didn't file, upload it to Buster Byrd. Listening?"

"Thanks for the kind words on my exclusive, Chester."

"The paper's exclusive, you mean. Check the header on your paycheck next week. You get me about Buster?"

"You think you're taking me off the story?"

"I don't think, I know."

Tell him, *I don't think you know, either.*

No, no, no.

Too cheap a shot.

I said, "I don't think you know either, Chester."

"Hah-hah-hah. As funny and original as anything I've caught in your column lately. When you're through amusing yourself, Gulliver, go and check the mast for who's the boss here."

"Check and double-check, Chester. I planned on staying on the story—"

"The best laid plans."

"How wise is this? I know Roddy. He lives here in my building. I—"

"Right. Conflict of interest. We need Buster's objectivity on this story."

"Buster can't hold a candle to me."

"Why would he want to? I don't want to. Stick to your column, Gulliver, and leave covering the news to key-burners who would never think once about leaving the news side of the plant."

"And somebody on the copy rim who lays on a head that makes Roddy out to be a murderer, nothing that stems from my file." I crushed my teeth to keep from spilling any of the anger building inside me.

"You saw the question mark I also had dropped in the headline? Roddy Donaldson is fair game and the question mark is the offset. Besides, my little birdie inside the district attorney's office tells me it's not as far-fetched a possibility as you might suppose."

"Your little birdie have a name?"

"Yes. Little Birdie."

I made a leap of faith. "Hapless Hapgood Harris. He's all over CNN this morning. The usual Hapless Harris grandstanding before he lives up to the rumors and jumps into the race for the governor's mansion."

Silence on the other end, long enough to let me know it was a gold medal leap of faith, before Chester said: "Anybody *hapless* right now, it's definitely you, Gulliver. Just be a good little boy and upload anything more you have to Buster. You dig?"

"I dig, Chester."

"Just make sure you steer clear after that or it'll be your own grave you're digging."

★ ★ ★ ★ ★

I had barely clicked off when the doorbell chimed. I padded over, figuring to find someone from the building. Strangers don't get past the sentry phone in the small outer island of a lobby between the entry doors without a key, a buzz-through, or a bulldozer.

Jimmy Steiger yawned back at me through the spy hole.

I opened the door and ushered him inside. "You still here?"

He dragged his disheveled presence past me, his neck lost inside his shoulders, hands jammed inside his trouser pockets. "No. I'm the ghost of Christmas past. Think I could borrow the use of a shower?"

I made a show of sniffing after him. He smelled like a locker room. "It's either that or a gallon of extra-strength roll-on-everywhere . . . What time was it when you finally showed Sharon some mercy?"

He checked his watch and shrugged. "Half an hour ago."

"What? No time off for good behavior?"

"I asked her if somebody could show me around the place, one of your guards or someone, and she insisted on handling it herself. Nice person. She's got the hots for you, you know that, pard?"

"Give. Me. A. Break."

"Mean it. Spotting hots was one of the items on the written exam for detective one, and I finished on top in that category. Not that Miss Glenn said anything, but it was written all over her face. Trust Dick Tracy here on this one . . ."

"Sharon is not my type."

He raised an eyebrow ridge, gave me the one-eyed onceover. "Funny, how I would have sworn she was breathing. Hasn't that always been your criterion?"

"Why are we still friends?"

"Reminds me—how's Stevie?"

"She and I are still divorced."

Jimmy made a vertical chalk mark in space. "Weren't you telling me something before about seeing her a couple of nights ago?"

"Run out of questions for Sharon, so now it's my turn?" There was something in the way Jimmy kept ducking my eyes that told me the reason for his drop-in was not all soap and water. It's a Jimmy tic, like his buckets of cold sweat whenever he latched onto three of a kind or better in the old floating press room poker sessions at Police Central. "What really brings you to me, Det. Sgt. Steiger?"

Jimmy humped his shoulders and looked around, like he was investigating enemy territory, although nothing had changed in the year since his last visit. Same secondhand furniture. Same framed movie posters on the wall, except for one on loan to Sharon. Still the same kind of standard one-bedroom that's stamped out by cookie cutter for just about every condo and co-op in town. Two thousand square feet of living in six hundred ninety square feet of living space.

"See you still haven't shaken the neat fetish," Jimmy said, taking charge of the conversation again. "A place this size doesn't give you a choice, I suppose. Either you clean mean or you drown in your own doo-doo." He draped his jacket over the back of a breakfast counter barstool, dug into the fridge, and pulled out two Heinekens. Liberated a half-finished package of Fritos while angling back around to my side of the counter. "My house over in Glendale is five times larger than this here rabbit hutch."

"You still have a wife. And three kids."

"And one in the oven." He tossed a beer can to me. I barely managed a left-handed catch at one o'clock.

Pop.

"What am I, the last to know?"

Pop.

"Why not? What are friends for? It's usually me who's last. I think my little momma keeps getting it off with some mad scientist who's running illegal sperm bank experiments. *Skoal!*" He toasted the air, took a swallow, and patted his stomach. "Sure hits the G-spot after a hard day's night at the crime scene." He worked off his shoes and settled onto the couch with his head on the arm rest.

"Will you remember to send my love to Margie?"

"Hell no. It's bad enough with just the mad scientist." He planted the Heineken can on his belly, a modest mound of evidence that he'd abandoned the daily workouts that once were ritual, and threw a question at the ceiling. "What, pray tell, my man, is with this bird, Buster Byrd?"

"What, pray tell, makes you ask? You clairvoyant all of a sudden?"

"Let's cut out the horseshit and pray together . . . Got a call from downtown. Deputy chief in charge of hemorrhoids, saying Byrd'll be on the Donaldson story for the *Daily* and instructing me to extend cooperation in a way that'll appear to demote you to hind tit, pard. I've been ducking this guy Byrd's calls all a.m., waiting for your input."

"An all-field no-hit cityside guy that my M.E. is grooming for bigger things, in spite of Byrd's Achilles heel."

"Which is?"

"There's more life in our obits than in anything he's ever pumped out for the paper. He writes like he thinks the five Ws is some group that used to sing for Motown."

Jimmy braced the sky with his eyes and gestured for more.

I told him about Wilkins's call.

When I finished, Jimmy sat up. He finished the Heineken in a swallow and put the can on the coffee table. He ran one hand and then the other over his mouth from opposite directions, clasped them in his crotch while drinking me for a chaser. Finally, he said, "I suppose you'll be asking me to join you in some devious and crafty plan that'll keep you in the loop and let you one-up Buster Byrd?"

I showed him a clean palm and shook my head. "I don't have a plan, Jimmy."

"Because you haven't had time to work one out?"

"You could say that."

Steiger checked over both shoulders. "Think I just did . . . Good, though, 'cause it's a no-can-do with the marching orders I got from on high. You, especially and in particular, Mr. Neil Gulliver, are *persona non grata* anywhere near the official LAPD investigation."

"Understood."

"Shame, too, pard. I know what fun you could've had with some of the stuff our prelim has turned up. So, please, don't ask me anything about any of it, like about how I guessed right on the heroin. Guessed right on the coke. And a whole lot of speed-ballin' going on."

"I wouldn't think of it, Sgt. Steiger."

"A lesser man wouldn't even hesitate to put me on the spot."

Rising, he crossed the room to study my prized four-by-six-foot framed poster for *Casablanca* that dominated the hallway wall. Bogart embracing Bergman in Technicolor, under the patriotic eye of Paul Henried.

He said, "A nice print lifted from the needle you saw in the black girl? I can't tell you it belongs to Roddy Donaldson."

"If you could, I've have to say I was sorry to hear. Roddy seemed like a decent kid, and straight, the time or two we met. Nothing major. A few nods and trading some brief, polite dialogue. That and Sharon's seal of approval. I'd have to say the print on the needle probably makes Roddy your primo suspect."

"Is that a question?"

"Negative."

"If it were and coming from Buster Byrd, I'd have to tell him off the record that we have even better, a witness who says he eyeballed the movie star arriving here with both of the victims a few hours in front of the time you and Miss Glenn reported stumbling into the bodies. That's more than enough reasonable cause to hold in any man's police department."

"I doubt Buster would remember that one of the W's is 'who' and pinned you down on whether your eyeball is a Heathcliffe Arms resident."

Jimmy shook his head like he was clearing his ears. "He did, I've have to set him straight, tell him it's one of the security guards, the one on the overnight shift. One whose name is a corker. Scandinavian." He gave me a look over his shoulder.

"Gustav Ljung."

"Gesundheit."

"Thank you."

"Anyway, it's that one-plus-one that makes it pretty certain Hapgood Harris will go after a bill of particulars from the grand jury on Murder One, something we're not ready to release to this Byrd bird or anyone." He stepped back from the wall and resumed his study of the poster.

I said, "Buster may be stupid, but he's not exactly Charlie McCarthy. Without the one-plus-one, even Buster would see it as involuntary manslaughter, *prima fascia.* Maybe Murder Two on a stretch, but—Murder One?"

"Would he see Hapgood Harris's finger in the pie, the way you would if you knew any of this, so good thing for us you don't."

"A famous movie star and two dead teenage girls—"

"One of them under the legal age of consent—"

"One of them under the legal age of consent?"

Jimmy ignored me. "A natural Murder One for anyone hosting political ambition, like old Hapless Harris, who'll hardly need any sleight of hand to pull off his trick with the grand jury."

Jimmy was right, of course.

It wouldn't be the first time a reputation was enhanced at the expense of truth. The system wasn't invented by Hapgood Harris.

I saw Harris pull the stunt shortly after settling his ambitious ass behind a desk in the D.A.'s office. He was a corpulent conviction machine, whose small, black, and devious ball-bearing eyes were always fixed on the prize. A straight-arrow kid from Korea Town found himself facing hard time on Murder One off a playground fracas that should have gone down as self-defense, but the young D.A. was eager for conviction and the other guy, the gang-banger who'd started it, was too dead to oblige. Less than a week into his cell, the kid refused to bend over and earned himself a few lines in the obits.

The clips and the obit are in my active file. They're what first got me wise to Harris. He manages to stay a step ahead of me, using the system as well as he plays the media, but retribution—like Murder One—has no statute of limitations.

I said, "Sgt. Steiger, I suppose you'll give Buster the names of the victims?"

"He asks, but not you. In that category, he gets same as everybody else, except you, soon as the next of kin are notified. One we're doing now, the black girl. Hope Danbury is who she is." He spelled the last name. I committed it to memory. "Local. Down Crenshaw district. The other one?" A shrug. "We have her logged as 'Janie Doe.' "

"No input from any ID in the apartment? A purse or a wallet? Driver's license?"

Jimmy wagged a finger at me and started for the kitchen. "Even if the crime scene boys had, all you'd be getting from me is a 'no comment, smart guy.' " He helped himself to a fresh Heineken, came around and perched on a breakfast barstool. "And no way you get to hear what Donaldson says, not that he's said squat so far."

"Not news anymore, anyway. I saw it on CNN. Roddy is still unconscious and his condition listed as 'critical.' "

"You were still on the scent instead of the shit list, I'd have to laugh in your face, buying into that leak. Cosmetic, to keep people like you out of our assholes. No percentage blabbing to the world that Donaldson's condition's been upgraded from 'critical' to 'serious.' He's awake and coherent off and on, but no access for nobody until tomorrow earliest, his private room up there, the fourth floor, and then access only after we finish running all our questions. Before then, nobody gets by the guards except for family. Not even the Byrd bird, no matter how much pressure hits the department from your paper."

Jimmy shifted his gaze past me to Bogie, Bergman, and Henreid. "Well, pard, now it's my own nose telling me it's time to take that shower we talked about." He saluted me with the Heineken and lumbered off for the bedroom.

Under my breath, I answered his salute. "Here's looking at you, kid," I said, and began counting the minutes before he'd be out of my way and I'd be on my way to UCLA Medical Center and Roddy Donaldson.

Chapter 6

Some of my best friends are actors, only they're called "reporters."

It's a lesson you learn, a knack you pick up, a trick you turn into perfection with practice, going from one story scenario to another, one interview to the next.

If you're any good, you develop a sixth sense that turns you chameleon-like into a friend, brother, preacher, teacher, whatever the target needs you to be in order for him to spill his guts.

You're convincing enough, a good enough actor, what you hear is usually mostly the truth. "Mostly," because the biggest truth of all is that everybody lies. They lie to look better, more honest, more sympathetic, more innocent. You're convincing enough, a good enough actor, you learn to read through the lies, maybe not necessarily to the whole truth and nothing but, but to enough of the truth to know there's more to the story than the story, and where the rest of it, the rest of the truth, might be located.

I like to think I'm as good an actor as I am a liar.

I was about to be both, again, navigating my way into Roddy Donaldson's room at the UCLA Med Center.

Not just there.

I knew where else I'd be heading when Jimmy Steiger said Roddy was awake and coherent, but, *before then, nobody gets by the guards except for family.*

I would be heading straight into a role I'd first played ten years ago in New York. It got me an exclusive, a reputation, an award or two, and a crime beat desk at the *Daily.* First of all, it got me to Mark David Chapman, the twisted bad seed who, in an insane desire for fame, gunned down the great John Lennon.

The role, passing myself off as Chapman's uncle, got me to Chapman past the tightest, toughest of police security in the jailhouse section of the psychiatric ward at Bellevue Hospital. This time, by comparison, dressed for the role, getting in to Roddy would be as simple as tying shoelaces.

I glided my untrustworthy dust-crusted Jag near the terrace-level elevator and followed the foot path up to the entrance of the Jules Stein Eye Clinic. Using a house phone and passing myself off as a direction-challenged cop, I pulled Roddy's exact location from a switchboard op whose frazzled inquisition spoke to the hundreds of calls she'd been getting from unsavory news people trying to pry information from her. Using back stairways—certain there would be checkpoints anywhere more direct to Roddy—I made it to the fourth floor and across to the main building, where Roddy was under watch.

The uniform outside his room had his chair tilted against the wall and was dozing. My grunts and heavy-legged shuffle down the empty corridor snapped him to attention. He cocked his bald head and gave a curious red eye to this approaching derelict, who appeared to have taken a bad turn off Skid Row and was now hunting after his shopping cart.

I stopped in front of him and said, "You Shannon?"

"Haywood," he said, getting past the surprise on his face. He tapped the name tag below his badge. "Who the fuck are you and how'd you get up here anyway, dirt bag?" he said, his voice rising with him. His gun hand shifting onto his holster.

I tapped a grubby finger to my lips and gave him two

animated *take it easy* palms.

I said, "Name's Donaldson, same as my nephew the other side of the door. Come to check on him for the rest of the family. A whole lot of worrying going on right now about the kid."

He gave me another onceover. It did nothing to dispel the doubt pouring from his hardboiled squint. His fingers played nervously with the release on the holster. "Nobody gets in there, family or nobody, today. You still haven't answered my question. And how do you know Shannon?"

"I don't, dickhead. Who Steiger said would be guarding the bedpans, this Shannon. Nothing about a shift change."

"Steiger?"

"Steiger. Lead detective on this case? Detective sergeant out of West End, same as my own home plate?" The uniform chewed this news without swallowing. "Steiger said he would call ahead to Shannon with a green light on me. I guess the word wasn't passed on before Shannon hit the trail."

"Wasn't Shannon working the last shift?"

I wasn't about to confess to Shannon as my invention. I feigned surprise and, after another moment, showed him a smile that could raise the saints. "The name Steiger came up with, pal, not me."

"Show me your badge, Donaldson. Some ID."

"This might shock you, but carrying a badge, ID, doesn't exactly go with working undercover vice."

"Undercover vice?" Sounding like he'd never heard of it.

"Look, Haywood, I don't want you losing sleep over maybe getting found out and reprimanded for disobeying an order." I pointed to the voice mic clipped to his collar. The rest of his two-way was attached to his belt. "Call me in to Steiger."

The uniform stared hard at me. I gave him the saintly smile again, trying not to let him recognize that my pulse was destroying my temples while I waited out his answer.

Unless the rules around here had changed since a column I did on the med center about a year ago, I knew what it would be. It was, Haywood saying, "The squawker's off-limits up here. Interferes with whatever."

"Maybe why Steiger couldn't get the word to Shannon or whoever?"

"Braithwaite. Like me on short-term loan from Hollywood Division, the troops from West End down on the ground level keeping the fucking news ghouls in their place."

"I've been on that detail myself, before I got bumped into plainclothes . . . So, what say, Haywood? A fast five or ten with my family's favorite movie star? That's all I need, while you go down the hall and grab a coffee break. I'll owe you one."

Haywood played with the concept like he was determining the fate of the world, until, at last: "No can do, Donaldson. No can do. Nope. Negative."

It wasn't the answer I expected.

I felt a mountainous migraine on its way to full gestation.

"Tell you why?" the uniform said, sounding like he wasn't just following the book, but had written it.

"I'm all ears."

"Coffee, as little as a cup, it gives me tremendous gas. It'd get me to farting up a storm, make the hall a danger zone, maybe even send over the edge some of the patients currently tottering on the brink." His head bobbed up and down, agreeing with his words, which he delivered like a funeral oration, until—

His body began shaking from a gargantuan laugh that bounced off the opposite wall and gave his mottled cheeks a glow richer than a summer sunset.

"Just playing with your head, Donaldson." The words coming out hard, his laughter refusing to make way for them. He clutched a palm to his chest and got his breathing back to normal after another minute or two. He said, "I'm dying desperate for a smoke, which also they don't allow up here. Too many oxygen masks, oxygen tanks, and them doctors fearing a big kaboom somebody's lit cigarette gets too close. What say you hold the fort while I take five or ten?"

He tugged at a lower eyelid, wheeled around, and grunted out a noxious smell that exploded like a Bronx cheer delivered by all of the Bronx. "That's without any coffee at all," he said, and followed his new burst of laughter down the corridor.

I was in Roddy Donaldson's room the second Haywood turned out of sight.

Chapter 7

Roddy's room was lit for *film noir.*

Daylight filtered in through the blinds and decorated the quiet figure in the bed closest to the window in a thin, diagonal series of mousy gray and less-gray stripes. The familiar smells of a hospital—medicinal, sterile—overpowered the red and yellow roses on the dresser and a smaller bowl of pink and white carnations on the sill.

A trail of tubes and wires led to the figure angled under the thin sheet in a fetal position: Roddy, looking smaller than life.

The orange glow of a cigarette specked his inquisitive eyes trying to make out my shadowed figure. I wanted to tell him to put out the cigarette, but it wasn't my call. I said, "Neil Gulliver, Roddy."

He analyzed the announcement, then gave a little grunt of recognition and stole the butt from his mouth.

"Hey, Prez, come on in," he said in the coarse nicotine-tarnished voice that always made me think of Jack Nicholson. Fragments of odorless smoke trailed the invitation. He moved the cigarette to a collection of butts in the ashtray on the rolling nightstand and adjusted the bed into a lounging position. His head went up and down as he looked me over. "How'd you manage to get past Robocop at the door?"

"Tricks of the trade."

"Take a load off," he said, accepting the answer. He pushed his thick hair to the back of his neck. "Here ain't the Georges V, but then what is?" He pronounced the hotel *George Sink.* He was improvising charm, the way he must have charmed the nurses into bending a rule and letting him smoke.

I took a chair from the wall, settled to the side of his bed, and tried not to stare too hard in the bad light. His complexion was sallow. No sparkle in his eyes. Certainly none of the sex appeal Sharon swore to, but his boyish grin was intact. So was the pocket dimple it caused inside one cheek, as much a part of Roddy's mass appeal as an outward manner that made him as warm and accessible as homemade apple pie.

With an actor's awareness, he recognized he was being examined.

I've examined enough of them to know an actor's ego begins where his ego lets off.

He said, "I look for shit, don't I?"

"I've seen better-looking shit." He liked that. The grin sprang to life again. "But the shit you're in, I've rarely seen shit that deep." The grin disappeared again.

"Fried chicken shit," Roddy said. He made a face at the empty cardboard packet of Players, tossed it into the wastebasket, and recruited a butt from the ashtray. He lit it with a lighter that gleamed enough to be eighteen carats. Wisps of smoke trailed upward from his nostrils. "You here to fry some more?"

"What do you think?"

"Well, I don't suppose the president of my homeowners association's here on no goodwill mission. I don't see no pot of chicken soup." He arched an eyebrow. "So, maybe it has something to do with the story you wrote, Herman Hero, smack on page one of the newspaper my mother brought along with my lawyer."

"Could it be both?"

"When they make the movie, I'll be the one huffing and puffing into *your* mouth. That's how it always gotta be when art imitations life. I'm the hero, man, so gotta be me kissy-mouthing the artificial respiration. Don't you never go to the movies? You go to the movies, you'd know that."

Roddy wasn't fooling me with his bravado. Right now the movie star could have been any scared nineteen-year-old kid, or was it the actor acting? I wasn't here to call a bluff. "Anything else I should know?"

"Yeah. Thank you. You should know that, too. Whatever abuse I'm giving you, Prez, I really appreciate how you went and saved my life, you know?" Roddy verged on tears. They may have been real.

I fidgeted in my seat. Praise makes me uncomfortable. "Yes," I said, ever the master of words.

It was clear Roddy wanted to tell me something, by the way his eyes searched mine. We looked at one another for another minute before he spoke: "Off the record?"

"I'll put away my notepad," I said.

His gaze dropped down to my hands, folded in my lap, then he gave me a questioning look. In fact, I had trained myself years ago to memorize an interview in progress. Absent note-taking or a tape recorder, a subject is more likely to relax his guard and sprinkle truth dust in and around his propaganda.

Satisfied, Roddy said, "Didn't do it, Mr. Gulliver."

"Didn't do what, Roddy?"

"Any of it."

"The cops and the district attorney think you did."

"Yeah. Bummer. But that doesn't change the truth."

"What's your truth?"

His eyes wandered the walls. "You know Nicky Edmunds?"

Nicky Edmunds. Like Roddy, one of the Diapered Dozen, who leaves a trail of gross narcissism at all the current and trendy nightspots. Like Roddy, always followed by the paparazzi who live off the tabloids. He'd recently slugged a photographer who ignored Nicky's drunken warnings and came too close to his Cherokee. Sharon had mentioned him to me once or twice; he'd visited Roddy at the Heathcliffe.

"Nicky's my best friend," Roddy said, not waiting for confirmation. "We're making a picture together right now, *Tough Times Two,* and it's got a nasty, nasty budget; you'll see. Something blows up every five minutes. Eat your heart out time for Bruce Willis." He wanted to make a point, but didn't quite know how to get there. I waited. "What I mean, I was with Nick that night. Nick will tell you that."

"What night?"

"Three nights ago. Monday. We had ourselves a great day and we celebrated in my Winnebago by finishing a fifth of tequila, then moved next door to Nick's Winnie, where we vanquished a bottle of Stoli. Party openers, because we had scored invites to a raucous private gig being tossed by Maxie Trotter at the Roxy."

"Is that where you met the girls, the Roxy?"

"That's just it, Mr. Gulliver. I don't remember a thing after being in Nick's Winnie. Nothing at all until I woke up here in the hospital."

Roddy gave me a blank, almost desperate look and let his mind follow his eyes around the room. Abstractly, he reached for the remote and turned on the TV mounted in the corner by the window.

I said, "The police have identified one of the victims, the black girl. Her name was Hope Danbury. The police don't have a name yet for the other girl."

"Me, either." He muted the sound, switched from channel to channel until satisfied there was nothing worth watching. He clicked off the set and said, "Mr. Gulliver, I don't know who she is any more than I knew this Hope Danbury. I don't know where I could've met them. I don't know even if I met them.

I'd tell you if I did."

"The evidence tends to bear out that part, Roddy. You met them long enough to get them up to your apartment. You were seen arriving. Your print is on the needle they found in Hope Danbury's arm. The story is all about to come out."

His flashpoint was lower than mine. "It can come out your ass all I care. And, you know what you can do with your goddamned evidence."

"Not me, Roddy. They. The cops. The D.A. I'm trying to be on your side, but I can't do it without help from you."

Roddy started crying, choking on his words, making them unintelligible. I poured him some water. He accepted the glass gratefully and emptied it in a swallow. If it was a performance, I was convinced. He replaced the glass on the roller table and tried his voice again.

"Mr. Gulliver, you know I drink. You know what a bad drunk I can be. Primo bad. How many times has Mom asked Miss Glenn and you to make certain her little boy isn't napping face down in his own puke? You keep count? You asked me, I would tell you to never start. But, something else, Prez. I do not ever do narcotics. Not coke. Not crack. Not H. Not nothing. Not never in this bod. Booze is my drug of choice, my only drug of choice. I don't never have anything else up to my place. Or needles. You are looking at one rank dude who is scared shitless it comes to needles. Go ask my mother. Go ask Nick." Roddy pointed at the IV needle in his arm. "I been awake I got here, this never would've happened in my arm, as God is my witness . . ."

"What else should I ask?"

Roddy began shaking visibly.

I said something about calling for a nurse.

He waved me off.

When he could speak again, he said, "Mr. Gulliver, please. I want you to give me your word that what I'm about to tell you is confidential. Strictly."

I saw it was the only way I was going to get it out of him, whatever *it* was.

"My word."

"I'm sure I can trust you . . . Can't I?"

"Yes."

He took a deep breath and said, "Those two girls, they had absolutely no business being in my pad, because—" He exhaled. Stopped breathing altogether until: "I'm gay, Mr. Gulliver."

Surprised? Me? Roddy Donaldson wasn't a name anybody had ever dragged from the closet within my earshot. At once, I felt sorry for the kid. Not because he was gay, but because he was playing hide and seek with a fact of life that was nobody's business but his own.

Roddy's cheeks did a little jig and his look became one of quiet resolution before he averted my gape. "So, now you know something not even my mother knows. Will you help me anyway, Mr. Gulliver? Help get to the truth and get me out of this mess?"

I said, "Even if you were straight." A smile flickered like a silent two-reeler at the edges of his mouth. "I'll check out the truth, Roddy, that's the best I can promise. I'll write the truth and, if whatever I find out works for you, then both of us will have something to celebrate."

"And we definitely will celebrate," Roddy said, his old enthusiasm joining him out of the closet. Resurrecting his boyish grin. Showing his dimple. "You'll see, Mr. Gulliver. Thank you. Miss Glenn, too, you see her." Appreciation mounting across his photogenic face.

Before I had a chance to respond, the door swung open, patching us into the stark fluorescent lighting of the corridor and the bulky outline of Haywood, the uniform from Hollywood Division.

He aimed an arthritic index finger at me and said, plainly annoyed, "Please step out here, Donaldson, or whoever you are."

Roddy gave me a quizzical look.

"Not you. He means me. Has this crazy notion we're somehow related."

I shrugged, used the bed to push myself up from the chair, captured Roddy's hand in mine for an encouraging squeeze, then joined the cop.

Haywood pressed a hard palm against my shoulder blade and directed me to the elevator, his rubber soles squeaking the route. "Sgt. Steiger, we connected, wise guy. He didn't understand one word what I was talking about. Said he never heard of you and give you the bum's rush, you bum."

"Early Alzheimer's? Poor guy. It wouldn't be unusual."

Haywood's fists were tense little balls by his side. He used his neck to diffuse the rest of his anger. His neck was red with strain, except for two veins popping varicose blue. Waiting for the elevator, he ticked off the time lobbing mad glances at me and, when the elevator door opened, he flung me inside.

I stepped out onto the entrance level. Tracking the exit signs to the Jules Stein wing, I saw a press conference in progress across the wide marbled floor.

I recognized the woman in charge. Her name was Jayne Madrigal. I had met her for the first time two nights ago. Our crossing paths again so soon, here and now, I wanted to believe it was kismet.

Chapter 8

My first encounter with Jayne Madrigal—

For that, credit my ex—

Credit Miss Stephanie Marriner, the inimitable "Sex Queen of the Soaps," who had pleaded "family emergency," wheedling and cajoling me into breaking my planned Truffaut doubleheader with Sharon Glenn.

"Well, we used to be family and that counts for something," Stevie had wailed into the phone. "I'm sitting on my ass here by my lonesome at Spago and need rescuing, honey. This bad news bum actor I've been media-dating just said the wrong words to me over our spumoni pizza, so I fractured his ego with some café au lait to his garbanzos."

"And he walked out on you."

"And the tab. Cheap SOB."

"Like you walked out on me."

"That was a long time ago—"

"—In a galaxy far, far away."

"Huh-neee, be serious. Besides, it wasn't café au lait then. It was orange juice and it was in that scrumptious Tiffany's crystal pitcher my producers gave me for Christmas."

"It wasn't orange juice, it was the pitcher, and you beaned me with it . . . I have plans for tonight, Stevie. I have a date."

"A date?" For a moment or two all I heard was the crackle of empty space, like the woman who didn't want me anymore was having trouble understanding why, then, anyone else would want me. Then she was back onto her favorite subject: herself.

She said, "I'd head the limo back home, my darling angel, only I'm on the superstar advisory board of this magazine, or something, so it's an image thing and a commitment on top of that. Army Archerd will be there. They even have *Entertainment Tonight* and *People* on the case, you know what I mean?"

"Don't I always, Stevie?"

"Anyway, honey, I'd much, much rather be seen with you," she said, ignoring the question, her every word a purr.

"Since when?"

"Since when was the last time you ever tried cheating me out of a close-up and then have the balls to deny it, the way that SOB lousy actor just tried?" She had me there. "And besides—there is something I must, must talk to you about."

"You're talking now. I recognize your voice."

"If I hadn't left you because of all the gambling you did, the horses and the cards, it would have been because of your snotty attitude, do you know that?"

"I do now, babe."

"You called me 'babe.' "

"To your face. Don't look behind your back."

"You don't really mean that. I know that, honey. But I do mean it when I say I truly, truly need your help. A major crisis like even President Nixon never had. Serious stuff, and I am madly desperate for your help." She inhaled a quart of breath. "A family emergency."

"Tell me."

"Thank you, thank you, thank you. It's black tie. The Palladium." She rattled off the details. "I'll put your name on the list when I get there."

"Don't go cute on me. You know I mean about this so-called 'family emergency.' "

"I hope and pray it won't be that old *schmatta* of a tux you refuse to admit you won in a Goodwill lottery," Stevie said, and—

Cut me off as easily as she'd quit our marriage.

Confession: I'm like all the other poor saps who don't get over a wife any easier than they ever get over a love affair, especially when both revolve around the same woman.

How I came to be at the Hollywood Palladium for a third-anniversary celebration for a magazine called *Stardom.*

I tracked the revolving klieg lights dividing a light-bulb sky down Sunset to Argyle, where a left turn delivered me to one of dozens of red-jacketed parking attendants, whose wandering eyes speculated past my press ID to the twenty I flagged at his hungry face. He rolled aside the sign that said *Parking Lot Full.*

The theater marquee over the entrance spelled out in block letters three feet high:

TONIGHT: STARDOM!

It was typical Hollywood, where nobody who has really made it gives failure a second glance or tomorrow a second thought.

I steered into the Palladium lobby, around mixed sets of attractive, animated young men and women in rented tuxes and evening gowns, to the gold cloth-draped registration table set up for PRESS AND VIP, where a young brunette promptly tried putting a name to my face. Behind her, hundreds of manicured guests milled in the spacious vestibule outside the ballroom doors.

The brunette's voice was as eager as her chest, heaving high and mighty inside the v-cut neck of a red velvet dress and flashing pink nipples as she leaned forward, gave me a gooey wide-eyed stare, and said, "You're somebody, aren't you? Sure you are. Yes. Yes. I do recognize you." She contorted her kewpie doll lips into an off-kilter smile she probably thought looked sexy, but only disorganized her cheeks.

I indicated the PRESS sign. "Neil Gulliver. The *Daily.*"

She struggled with herself, unsure whether or not to believe me. I turned her list around and ran my finger down it until I located my name. I pointed it out.

She twisted her body to check, giving me another flash of nipple leaning closer to the table surface. Her head started bobbing with recognition. "From the buses!" Her voice became loud enough to turn heads. Her accent sounded Carolinas. "That's why I recognize you! Your photograph? It's on all them buses?"

"That's me," I said, wondering why it sounded like an apology.

"You're that somebody. Yes!" Her smile grew warmer and more grotesque while she checked my pores. "I see you every Tuesday and Thursday, when my roomie has the Honda for scene interpretation." She studied the list again. I tried not to linger on the flash of pink. "There's a note here added, says you're the special guest of Stephanie Marriner?" She said the name the way I might say *Michelle Pfeiffer.*

"That's me, too," I said, slightly less apologetically.

"She's one of my favorites."

"One of mine."

"And you're her friend?"

"Used to be her husband."

The brunette's eyes squeegeed. "You're putting me on."

I pledged the truth at the same time I heard a female voice calling out my name from somewhere beyond the brunette. Its owner saw me searching and waved. Except for Stephanie Marriner, nobody here tonight was going to be more beautiful. She reached the top step, slipped between two of the tables, and thrust out her hand. "I'm Jayne Madrigal, Mr. Gulliver. I don't know if Stevie has mentioned me to you." Her hand was warm and comforting, in no more a hurry than mine to pull away. I used the time to memorize her sultry presence.

Jayne Madrigal had on an open-shouldered embroidered and beaded silk bustier tied to a matching collar in layered, swirling Technicolor patterns of blue, green, red, and gold that couldn't compete with her face. A high forehead. Cheekbones of a high fashion model tapering into a perfect chin. The hint of a cleft to go with broad-set hazel eyes betraying a vulnerability behind her assertive manner. Straight nose in perfect pitch with the rest of her face. Modigliani neck. Dark hair piled on top of her head, a single strand falling below her cheek and curved into a *J* by sensuous bee-stung lips.

I was seeing Jayne Madrigal for the first time and already I knew how anxious I was to see her again. The last time I'd had this kind of reaction was for a sixteen-year-old kid at a rock festival who turned out to be Stevie, who went on to become my wife, who—

I suspected Jayne Madrigal had read my mind by the way she laughed, an elegant series of punctuation marks sounding just right for the throaty quality of her voice, and no way she could miss the sight of my cheeks turning hellfire crimson. Before I could invent something charming or clever or witty to say, she gently withdrew her hand.

"Stevie is waiting for us, Mr. Gulliver, and you certainly must know it's never wise to keep Stevie waiting."

Jayne Madrigal led me past the vestibule to a padded leather door at the end of the corridor. A discreet hand-printed placard said this was the *Green Room, Admission Only By Invitation.* The beefy guard wearing a black t-shirt buttered over his muscles gave me a sturdy onceover before opening the door, as if he were heat-sensitive to celebrities.

"Just another somebody," I said, trying to sound believable

while inching ahead of Jayne Madrigal.

There were maybe two hundred people in a room meant for half that many. As I looked around heads and shoulders for the Scarlett O'Hara of the Soaps, my eyes started smarting from the heady mixture of cigarette smoke and sweet perfumes, accented by a smell I remembered as Chasen's standard party catering. A few TV news crews, a team from *Entertainment Tonight,* and a dozen freelance photographers were working the room.

I recognized a handful of the faces getting the most attention, the ones with sagging chins, faded movie careers, and canceled television series, perennial celebrities who could always be counted on at the drop of an invitation.

An exception was a small, skinny black kid in a black satin outfit straight out of the French Revolution, who even at this hazy distance had to be Maxie Trotter of rock-and-roll fame. Maxie had one arm cinched around the waist of a scantily clad blonde the size of an L.A. Laker, who towered over him by a foot. His other hand gripped the leash attached to the apathetic leopard in repose at his feet.

Jayne steered me along the perimeter of the room to an interior door marked *Private* and rapped a few times, one of those bump-umpa-bump-adump kinds of signals. At once, the door opened wide enough and long enough for us to pass through. A different beefy guard snapped the lock behind us. We were in a private lounge about twenty by forty feet, full of upholstered armchairs and plush divans pushed together for fifty or so people deep into the status game. They were using real silverware to sample delicacies from Chasen's A-menu on bone china and utilizing two sweating bartenders, who seemed to be pouring doubles automatically at the small, overstocked service bar. A lone photographer I recognized from *People* magazine, Porky Pigue, was working the room.

Jayne caught me straining to locate Stevie. She whispered just loud enough to be heard above the din, "She's in the powder room getting ready." For what? For me? Before I could ask, Jayne said, "I'll fetch her and be back. Make yourself to home." She gave me a last reassuring look and left.

I was starving. Except for the aging ruins of a Subway tuna I'd devoured before leaving the Heathcliffe, I hadn't eaten since breakfast. I inched across to the buffet table, intending to bottom out on the imported caviar and hamburger miniatures I preferred to Chasen's heralded chili.

A dapper Hollywood type in a hand-stitched tux and red carnation boutonniere broke loose from a small circle to block my way and inspire a handshake.

I figured him to be in his late forties. He was tall and lean, well kept, and wore a mane of prematurely snow-white hair slicked straight back from one of those rugged lived-in faces full of pock-marked character and confidence. His customized teeth were the size of mah johngg tiles, the better to greet you with.

He said, "Eugene Coburn, Mr. Gulliver. Gene to my many friends. Can't thank you enough for joining us tonight." He paused as if I were supposed to know the name. I didn't. He showed off more tiles and said, "I'm your biggest fan. Every morning, your column is as much a part of my breakfast as my vitamins and oatmeal." I mumbled thanks and gave him my best Steve McQueen grin, wondering to myself how many used cars he had sold so far this month. "In fact, I hear you might even be inclined to write about our little magazine and I could not be more thrilled, Mr. Gulliver."

Before I could set my new friend Gene straight, we were joined by somebody else from the circle, a bald-headed gnome of a man who peered at us on shaky legs like a puppy begging a snack. Coburn tried not to show his annoyance. "Roscoe, I suppose you already enjoy the acquaintanceship of Neil Gulliver.

The distinguished columnist for the *Daily*?" He identified me as if he were sending up a flare.

"Only by osmosis, Gene. . . . Roscoe Del Ruth, Neil, purveyor to the stars and a legend in my own mind." He withdrew his hand when he saw Coburn was not about to let go of mine and toasted me with his martini. I saw his disappointment that I hadn't laughed uproariously at his joke, so I forced a smile. His Statue of Liberty pose almost threw him off balance and a few drops splashed onto his head.

"Whoops." Cautiously, Del Ruth lowered the glass, navigated it carefully to his mouth, and emptied it in a swallow. "AA is for sissies," he said. He wiped his mouth with his fingers, traded the empty for another martini from the sterling silver tray of a strolling waiter. I liberated a diet Pepsi with a lemon twist.

"Roscoe does enjoy his booze," Coburn said.

"No argument from me, Baby Cakes. No argument from me."

"Roscoe, my spies report Mr. Gulliver is thinking seriously about writing one of his *Daily* columns on my little magazine." Coburn sneaked a wink.

"No argument from me," Del Ruth assured us. "I, too, also know a good story when I hear one. Gene here, he's a good one, Neil. He went and dug himself a gold mine with his *Stardom* magazine. You only have to count the pages in the latest issue. At an average of six thou a pop?" His eyebrows reached the moon.

"Now, now, Roscoe," Coburn said, his frozen smile offsetting the anxiety of his stare. "I wouldn't want you to be giving Mr. Gulliver the wrong impression—that I'm in it solely for the money." Another wink.

Del Ruth looked from me back to Coburn. " 'Course not, Baby Cakes, but you gotta answer me something first. What 'zactly is the wrong impression you don't want me to give him?"

He bit his lower lip, again blasted off his eyebrows, and watched as the crimson tide inched up Coburn's cheeks before cackling with bloodshot-eyed delight. He took another swallow and informed me with mock seriousness, "Of course Gene's not in it *solely* for the money." Cackle. "It's also a great way to meet the broads."

"Roscoe!" Coburn fiddled with his carnation and shot me a looked that begged for understanding. I gave it to him in a gesture. No problem, considering I didn't intend to do a piece about Eugene Coburn or *Stardom* magazine.

Whatever gave him the idea? Something Stevie said? Stevie knew better than to donate my column without permission—most of the time, anyway. Nothing about doing a column when she torpedoed me here with her "family emergency." She wouldn't—

Cuh-lick.

Porky Pigue had worked his way to us and grabbed a shot. He gave me a nod of recognition before aiming the Canon again.

Cuh-lick.

"Just one more, please. And, Neil—you move in a little tighter to Mr. Coburn this time? No, that's okay, Mr. Coburn. You're fine. Just look over my left shoulder. All of you. Mr. Del Ruth, you, too."

"You got it, Baby Cakes."

"Swell, Mr. Del Ruth, but this time could you just put the glass down away from your face, maybe behind your back? And look over my shoulder. That's it . . . That's it . . ."

Cuh-lick. Cuh-lick. Cuh-lick.

Over Porky's left shoulder, as he knocked off three quick shots, I spotted Stevie heading for us, a path opening on some silent cue as people stepped aside to let her pass. She seemed to glide three inches above the worn carpeting, looking neither left nor right, responding to murmurs of recognition with an automatic, delicate Queen Elizabeth wave. Jayne Madrigal was two steps behind her.

"Honey!" Stevie called loudly, reaching out for me. "How positively grand to see you!"

Cuh-lick. Cuh-lick. Cuh-lick.

I explored Stevie's hypnotic face, counting the freckles I adored, that no amount of makeup ever obscured entirely. A few new laugh lines book-ending her incandescent eyes, somehow enhancing her kittenish appeal. She was the complete incendiary blonde again, but I saw through the coloring job to the redhead that went with the good times we shared.

Stevie glanced away to be certain Porky was getting it all, weaving like a boxer as he shifted angles and went from horizontal to vertical. She pushed her boobs harder into me. Clutched me in an embrace like she meant it to last forever or at least until somebody yelled *Cut!* She shifted us around to give Porky a better view of her profile.

Porky called, "Hold it, that's just great, Stevie, great. Now, maybe, you could plant one on Neil's cheek?"

Stevie pulled her face from mine. "Of course, Porky Pie. Just call your shots." She grazed my cheek, then slid her mouth over to mine, locked on like a penny arcade clamp, and shoved her tongue down my throat, like the old days. I heard delight filtering through the crowd.

She came up for air and moved back to my ear, taking the one closest to Porky's lens, cooing, "How do the boobies feel?"

"Six inches larger."

"Don't be silly, honey. It's the same old me . . . and I can feel it's the same old you. Still miss me, don't you?"

"I've been taking acting lessons."

She pressed tighter against my body and did a vague gyration. "Your acting lessons certainly have been paying off . . .

Getting any lately?"

"None of your business."

Porky called, "Got it, Stevie."

At once, she released her hold and stepped away.

Jayne Madrigal moved closer. "Now, maybe, a setup with all of you. What do you say to that?"

Gene Coburn nodded his agreement and Roscoe Del Ruth toasted her.

She moved around Porky and began arranging the shot, centering on Stevie. She wedged Coburn between us and, after taking away his martini, put Del Ruth on Stevie's other side. Stevie licked her lips and restored her smile, ran her arms onto their shoulders, giving greater exposure to what the fan magazines called "The Chest That Won the West." From this angle her boobs definitely seemed to have grown larger than the state's homeless rate.

Cuh-lick. Cuh-lick. Cuh-lick.

Jayne pressed down on Porky's shoulder and decided, "Now, maybe one of Stevie with Mr. Coburn and Mr. Del Ruth, if you don't mind Mr. Gulliver?"

Her smile was almost as gratuitous as Stevie's as she dismissed me with a gesture.

I stepped out of the shot.

"Best damned press agent in the business," Del Ruth called to no one in particular. "Worth every penny."

Press agent.

Jayne Madrigal. Jayne Madrigal. Jayne Madrigal.

The name was suddenly familiar.

Jayne Madrigal had been on to me a few times over the last year or so, pitching clients for an interview, getting the polite pass I usually give to anything with a show-business twist. It wasn't my territory of choice. Stevie recently had said something about getting new PR, but hadn't attached any name to the announcement.

Jayne may have sensed me studying her again. She answered me with a flash of eyebrow before turning to the lithe young woman who had lapped up to her side like a wave hitting the shore. The woman was the color of Ovaltine, body barely into a black vinyl swimsuit cut thigh-high, zipped down to her belly button; metal-studded boots that quit midcalf. They exchanged quiet words.

Jayne gave the photographer's shoulder another tweak. Porky rose from his crouch and turned to her for new instructions. She excused herself and Porky, explaining, "Maxie Trotter needs us over there. I'll be back in five minutes, tops." She held up as many fingers extended wide.

Stevie nodded. "Perfect, darling. That's how much time I need alone with my man Neil." She stepped away from Coburn and Del Ruth and to me as Porky fell in step behind Jayne and Miss Ovaltine.

Del Ruth called sharply after them, "Hold on there a second, Baby Cakes." They stopped. Jayne gave him a tolerant look and was about to say something. Del Ruth was quicker. "I want you to take one more picture first," he said.

"Your client needs me out there, Mr. Del Ruth."

"Pshaw and pshit," Del Ruth said. "Let the fucker wait. 'Member it's my signature on the big fat checks you get every month, Baby Cakes."

He reached them in a series of cautious steps. He got behind Miss Ovaltine and strapped her in his arms with hers trapped to her side. Miss Ovaltine rotated her neck and shook her head to add spring to her hair. Del Ruth peeked around her and directed Porky Pigue to shoot.

Cuh-lick. Cuh-lick. Cuh-lick.

From the sidelines, Jayne Madrigal sent me a look that could mean anything I wanted it to mean.

Chapter 9

Putting aside my memory of that night, I found a men's room, ditched the jumpsuit, and did some heavy scrubbing, then wandered over to the med center lobby area where Jayne Madrigal was conducting her press conference. Her clients were the two men fielding questions inside a semicircle of camera gear, lights, and microphones. I remembered them from the Palladium: Cleveland Buntine and Jack Zipper, Jr., the producers of the new Roddy Donaldson–Nicky Edmunds movie, *Tough Times Two.* She had brought them over for introductions and I'd taken slick Hollywood handshakes from both of them.

My eyes wandered the crowd, looking for somebody else, Chet Wilkins's fair-haired boy, Buster Byrd. I found him poking out behind the Eyewitness News sound tech holding the boom mic. Furiously scribbling down questions being asked by the rest of the news gang, not him. It was like Buster was afraid of embarrassing himself if he asked the wrong questions the wrong way, something I'd heard about him from day-room veterans.

He had this scared-rabbit look on his gaunt face, which might have been okay if he was the new kid being tested on his first major story. Maybe fifteen or twenty years ago, but not now. Buster was verging on forty or forty-five, although there wasn't much more than startup sags here and there, and modest patches of skin peeking through a head of hair yellow enough to stuff an Iowa scarecrow. Word was he was kin to some power brokers in Sacramento who were owed favors by the publisher.

Buster spotted me staring. He adjusted his Coke-bottle lenses and made sure who I was before acknowledging me with a limp two-fingered salute and a dead smile. Nothing in his expression suggested any curiosity or concern about me being here. The message he seemed to be sending back was *Good luck.* Good luck? Like Buster already had it figured, or he figured what was mine was going to be his anyway.

The banks of camera lights clicked off. The conference had run out of steam in time to catch the early news. Jayne took charge of Buntine and Zipper, guiding them to an exit, talking animatedly before she gave each a hug and air kisses, waved them off, brushed a hand through her hair, headed back.

Her turn to spot me.

She started in my direction, pausing en route to chat with some of the familiar TV faces or to give up another press handout.

She was all legs in a full-sleeved gray chemise that stopped eight inches from her knees. They were slender and firm, sheathed in matching gray hose and heels. Their effect on me was disconcerting. My pulse rate flashed a warning that she might be the Newly Anointed One, who could measure up to Stevie.

"Mr. Gulliver." She pushed her hand at me. I took it delightedly. I could tell by the look she returned that she knew what I was thinking. Do they? Don't they always? "It is so nice to see you again so soon. So unexpectedly."

Today she was wearing her hair pushed to one side. Her only jewelry was a pair of interwoven circle earrings in sterling silver. I told myself, *Be careful around her, Neil. You have been doing perfectly swell without a regular woman in your life.* I told myself, *Shut up, Neil.* I told her, "Since *Stardom* magazine at the Palladium," fearing that was about as clever as I'd be able to get with her. "Couple nights ago."

"I remember," she said, making a *get-away-from-here* gesture. "How's Stevie?"

"I've talked Geraldo into inviting her with Calypso, Maxie Trotter's pet leopard, for a special about sex queens and sexual fetishes." She aimed a sexy, playful growl at me and clawed the air, her long nails perfectly shaped, crimson-colored to match her lipstick.

"Let me guess. She refused to share billing."

"But I'm working on her." Jayne's laugh sounded like an orgasm echoing from the base of her throat. "And what are you working on?" I put my hand over my mouth. "I know it's not my press conference got you here, was it?" She surrendered one of the handouts. "So, maybe it was the chance to see me again?"

"Yes." Like that. I couldn't believe I hadn't even the smarts to pretend to having to think about it.

Jayne took a step away and arched backward. She studied me over her nose before dismissing the idea with a flamboyant gesture. "Hardly, not if only half of what I've heard about you from my fabulous client, Miss Marriner, is true."

"What's she tell you?"

"Everything. She's not just my client. Stevie and I are also pals."

"What does she say about me?"

Jayne weighed the question. "She says you're carrying a torch for her. She says you have it on long-term loan from the Statue of Liberty. True?"

"In a manner of speaking."

"What manner?"

"Truthfully . . . But, that's only sometimes."

"And other times?"

"Can I plead the fifth, Ms. Jayne Madrigal?"

"Is hiding behind the Constitution allowed for somebody without a Declaration of Independence?" She was clever and smart, this press agent. She sensed my discomfort and changed the subject. "May I thank you for the way you handled your story about my other client, Roddy Donaldson? Very straightforward, very fair."

"Just the facts, ma'am. Do you represent everybody?"

"Not yet . . . You came here to see him, didn't you?"

"I beg your pardon?"

"You came to the hospital to see Roddy," she said, smiling like a Cheshire cat. "Were you able to slip past the guard?" Too clever and smart. "I'm wagering you were."

"It's not my story anymore."

"I know. Mr. Byrd made a point of telling me that before my press conference. What a shame. The *Daily* trading in a winner like you for an obvious loser." Nothing wrong with being too clever and smart. "If it were still your story, maybe I could have helped."

"You? Why would you want to do something like that?"

"Roddy needs help. He's innocent."

"He hasn't been charged with a crime yet."

"We both know he will be, don't we? You fertilize and water grass seed, it grows. Roddy needs help and maybe you could use some yourself, Mr. Gulliver?" A stare-down. "I can help. Really. No obligation. I promise."

The three biggest lies in the world: The check is in the mail. The BMW is paid for. No obligation. Well, two out of three. *No obligation* didn't sound right, but there was also something about the way she made the offer that didn't sound right, either.

I said, "You have time for a cup of coffee?"

Jayne said, "No . . . But let me make a call. After, I might have time for a margarita."

I read the handout while waiting for her at Stratton's Grill down in the Village.

Six paragraphs on the letterhead of Jayne Madrigal Public Relations, well written as those things go, tight and to the point. A declaration of faith in Roddy Donaldson by Cleveland Buntine and Jack Zipper, Jr., executive producers of *Tough Times Two,* a $45-million motion picture nearing completion at the historic Grenedier & Grimm Studios, co-starring Nicky Edmunds and featuring an original musical score composed and performed by international idol Maxie Trotter, soundtrack LP to be released on Sumo Records.

Jayne had worked in enough plugs for a hair transplant. I assumed these were all client references, certainly the tag paragraph reference to the Donaldson character's team of "Oomph Girls" cast from the pages of *Stardom* magazine. If she was charging only half of what I'd heard was the current fee at places like PMK and R&C, I knew she could afford to dress as expensively as she did without worrying about interest payments.

"Couldn't find parking," she said apologetically as she slid into the booth across from me and reached hungrily for the waiting margarita. "I'm two blocks away in a yellow. I could have just stayed in the med center lot and walked."

That's what I had done, a decorated veteran of the Westwood Village parking wars. I'd left the Jag in its six-dollar space and hiked the half mile down here, enjoying the warm sky stirred by a modest breeze creeping in from the ocean, using the time to sort out what Roddy had told me and how his press agent might be helpful.

I toasted Jayne with my Heineken, barely aware of the noisy bar action drifting upstairs to our corner booth in the back, the one I request whenever I want conversation without distraction. I led off with a compliment, saying how well I thought she'd handled the media.

She accepted it graciously. "More crisis management than

your basic press agentry, Mr. Gulliver, given what we hear about Roddy being charged with first-degree murder and the D.A. pressing for him to be held without bail. *Tough Times Two*'s already five mil over budget and three weeks behind schedule. Roddy is in almost all the scenes remaining to be shot. No Roddy—" She studied the margarita. "No Roddy and the picture shuts down. The picture shuts down, Cleve and Jack lose a bundle."

"What about insurance, the completion bond company?"

"You ever take a contract to the observatory and read the fine print? You'd see that everybody else gets paid, but not the producers. *Tough Times Two* goes on the shelf, there is no guarantee it will ever get finished. All the rights would revert. Cleve and Jack might have to think seriously about stealing two shopping carts. This is Hollywood, Mr. Gulliver, where your failure is your best friend's excuse to tell you to go fuck off."

"My goodness, where did you ever find such skepticism?"

"At the intersection of Show Business and Reality, and as the late Miss Mae West once observed, correctly, 'Goodness has nothing to do with it.' " She finished the margarita. "I'd like another one of these. My treat." I signaled our waitress. "What I'm hoping is to get public opinion rolling on Roddy's side. That can go a long way toward convincing a judge to keep Roddy out of jail long enough to finish the picture for Cleve and Jack."

"Maybe the charge will be second or manslaughter. Bail comes with either. Maybe Roddy won't be charged at all."

She gave me a funny look. The waitress showed up with our refills and took away her empty. I still had half a live Heineken and now two Diet Coke chasers. Jayne used a finger to sample the salt clinging to the rim of her glass. She asked, "Why say that? When you cracked Roddy's room at the med center, did he tell you something?"

"I remember your asking that question about me stealing time with Roddy. I don't recall responding in the affirmative. Or the negative."

"The answer was all over your face."

"Were you looking that closely?" There it was. Finally. I was flirting with her. I heard it in the way I peeled the words.

Jayne stopped leaning across the narrow marble table, leading with her chin. She sat up straight, pushed against the high back wall, and stroked her long neck delicately. "Yes. I was looking that closely and it's exactly as Stevie predicted. I liked what I saw."

I almost coughed out the swallow that was halfway down my throat. The beer dribbled down my palm as I reached for the napkin. "Stevie 'predicted'? What exactly is that supposed to mean?"

"It's supposed to mean Stevie predicted. She saw the party I organized for *Stardom* as a great place to throw the two of us together, after weeks of selling me on your virtues; her version of a blind date. A small, intimate opportunity to get acquainted, just you, me, and three or four thousand people panting to be stars. She predicted I'd like what I saw. And I liked what I saw." Jayne's eyes gleamed wickedly. "And I like what I see now." I had no idea if it was her speaking or just the second margarita kicking in. "Tell me. What is it I can do for you, Mr. Gulliver?" Her tongue roamed her lips.

I wanted to ask her if she knew how bothered I was by Stevie still trying to control my life. I asked, "You know Nicky Edmunds?"

"In the Biblical sense?" I shot her a sour look. Jayne squeezed her mouth shut and slapped the back of her hand. "Nicky Edmunds is the Crown Prince of Troublemakers. He is loud, vulgar, demanding, and has an ego on loan from Saddam Hussein, but he always pays my fee on time and he never gets in front of me on expenses."

"I understand Roddy and Nicky are best friends."

She didn't try suppressing a smirk of triumph, recognizing that tidbit had to have come from Roddy. "Uh-huh. The best of best friends."

"I understand the last time they were together was the day after Melba Donaldson checked up on Roddy. Monday. He was in his trailer at the studio . . . with Nicky."

"Uh-huh." She stared into her drink. "Monday was also the last time I spoke with him before the—before the incident. I had a limo organized to pick them up and take them to a gig I had put together for Maxie, Maxie Trotter. Nick called and told me to cancel the limo. Then Roddy came on, sounding smashed to the gills. He told me a dirty joke." Up went one of her tantalizing eyebrows. "Dirtier than usual."

"I'd like to meet Nicky."

Jayne thought about it briefly. "Tomorrow soon enough?"

"Tell me where and what time. Day or night, I'll make myself available to you."

"Tell me something first—does that mean we're beyond foreplay?" Was it the tequila and Triple sec hitting home or that the wheels of her agile mind never stopped spinning games? "You expect me to behave myself, Mr. Gulliver, you must stop feeding me straight lines."

Jayne had gone from reminding me of Stevie to reminding me of myself. I was about to get myself in deeper with her than two meetings and a couple drinks suggested, and—

So what?

I said, "You have to stop calling me *Mr. Gulliver.* The name is Neil."

She smiled, shook her head, and draped a hand across a delicious breast. "No."

"No?"

"Me Jayne, so you Tarzan."

I waited until I was sure I could get the words out. "Let's take it a step at a time. Right now I have to see a computer about a deadline."

The corners of Jayne's mouth curled upward. She spilled across the table to stroke my cheek and had me blushing even before she pressed her fingers to her lips, first, and then to her heart.

We let mood do most of the talking after that, until I was satisfied Jayne was sober enough to drive.

We'd been so lost in each other that, outside, the sky had aged to darkness. Heading for her car, she locked her arm onto mine and used me as a shoulder brace, but kept to generally good behavior after I resisted her unsubtle invitation to fetch my Jag and follow her Beamer home—

Except for her kiss.

A sneak attack.

A fleeting thank-you on the lips just before she slid behind the wheel.

I watched her drive off, thinking how good she tasted. I was smitten by fantasy, yet bothered by an annoying suspicion she was playing some other game with me.

By the time I pulled into my space at the Heathcliffe, I had abandoned it as the old caution of a crime reporter who had learned too early and too well to trust nothing but the truth and, that lacking, his instincts.

It was more fun reflecting on the way Jayne smiled, the way she smelled; trying to put a name to the scent.

Chapter 10

I changed into a reasonably fresh pair of work pajamas and settled down in front of the computer. I had the makings of another story no one else had and I was going to bat it out, ship it downtown to the *Daily*, and—

What was Chet Wilkins going to do?

Spike my copy for spite or run it, because deep down under his resentment toward me still beats the heart of a newspaperman?

Fire my ass for being a better reporter than his error apparent?

Been there.

There and back.

Been pissed on by bigger dogs than Chet Wilkins.

The stain washes off.

Truth is, it would not be much of a story. I had to be careful how I used Jimmy Steiger's information, and what I learned from Roddy Donaldson, for now anyway, was off the record and confidential. There was enough, though, to show the M.E. and Buster Byrd how a major story is supposed to be handled in the big leagues.

The words I fed across my monitor added up to one of those in-depth superficial yarns that stalk the facts without ever going into detail, quoting highly placed officials and unnamed reliable sources.

I disclosed the probability of Assistant District Attorney Hapgood Harris asking the grand jury to hand him a Murder One indictment while resisting defense lawyers' attempts to secure bail with Roddy. I revealed that police had discovered a witness who saw Roddy with the two dead girls only hours before their bodies were discovered and were also about to cite drugs as the cause of both deaths.

I didn't ID the witness. I didn't reveal the names of the victims. I was ambiguous about the kinds of drugs, because the department's crime lab hadn't finished the posts or the blood analysis that would confirm cause and also pinpoint the times of death.

I sent my story on its electronic flight.

Almost at once the phone rang, the direct line, Nate Walpow on the city desk, volunteering, "If you have any idea where you might've lost your mind, I'll be happy to come try and help you find it."

"It's an exclusive, Nate."

"You don't know about the memo everyone on the desks got from Wilkins?"

"He saved on paper and called me with the gospel."

"I can't let it run without running it past him, Gully. I needed to let you know."

"On your mark, get set, go."

Nate was gone after the usual family and Lakers small talk.

I drew Pedro Cisneros's phone number from my memory bank and dialed.

Little Pedro's mother answered and, when she heard it was me, burst into tears.

"The words you wrote about our son, so nice, so wonderful," Maria Elena said. "God bless you, *Señor* Gulliver."

Then it was the boy's father on the line, choking on his words: "For my son, cards and letters by the hundreds since your story. Even money to help us out, you know? Even phone calls from complete strangers with their prayers."

"How's little Pedro?" Too much silence. "Mr. Cisneros? You there?"

"Maybe the prayers will help," he said, finally.

"For what they're worth, I'll add mine."

"You do believe in God, yes?"

"Sometimes, I think, more than He believes in me."

"Then, me and Maria Elena, we'll add you to our prayers, *Señor* Gulliver."

There were eighteen messages on the answering machine, the regular blend of calls. Fans of the column, who'd found something special to like. Readers who hated the column and had to tell me why in pinched, hurrying voices anxious to flee before someone picked up and demanded a name. People with ideas to give away, or press agents with something to sell, like Jayne Madrigal.

The worst of the messages hurt me sometimes, but I never get so angry I have to answer them. I nurse my wounds like a hunted wolf and convince myself I'm right—not them, me. Have these misguided people ever seen what I've seen? Sometimes I wished I had pictures to show them and to burn, instead of memories that never go anywhere but to the next thought.

One message among the eighteen stood out.

The woman's voice was graying at the edges, her conversation hesitant, sorrowful, reluctant to share, disjointed and confusing, yet determined.

I only half-listened until I recognized the significance of her name: Danbury.

"I just learned about my baby from the call," she said in a tone almost inaudible. "The police called and it's my baby girl. It's my Hope, the little black girl you got no name for in your newspaper story. My name is Mrs. Pearl Danbury, sir. I have read your story in the newspaper and you ought to be telling the truth about my baby, but what the police are saying and what you already wrote up so far is a pack of lies."

Pearl Danbury had left a number.

I tried it at once and several times afterward, but got no answer, the last time before I dragged off to bed and wrestled sleep to a draw before drifting into a dream about Jayne Madrigal and me, the kind you never want to end, but they do.

They always do.

I was up at seven-thirty.

I threw on a robe and headed downstairs to the security desk for the copies of the Home and Street Final editions a runner from the plant drops off every day, anxious to see how the Donaldson story had played. The papers weren't there. Neither was the guard.

Fifteen minutes later, I was in my sweats and halfway through my regular morning jog into the Village. The morning sun was invisible behind the last dull gray layers of night and the sidewalks were empty. I'd found an easy stride by the time I reached the Westwood and Wilshire intersection, pumping in place while dredging up coins for the news rack.

A whimpering sound turned me around. In a crevice of the marble high-rise, barely out of sight, an old man in a pauper's hand-me-downs sat guarding a shopping cart piled full of his life. I trotted over and offered him the change, something I've been doing ever since the helpless and the homeless crowded onto the streets, guided by a selfish need to prove there are people who care and are trying to make a difference.

Up close, I saw through his sunbaked grime and a jungle of coarse black whiskers that he was probably my age, maybe even a few years younger. He studied me with eyes too proud for the reality of the moment, but took the coins anyway, shoved them inside a torn pocket of his gutter jacket, and turned away.

"You know I didn't ask for anything?" he said. His deep baritone was demanding, sharp as shrapnel.

I had no answer for him, except for the uncomfortable feeling he had brought on.

It could have been what he wanted—some small token of victory in a life of defeat.

I started back for the racks.

"Hey!" His voice stopped me and spun me around. He pressed a crooked hand to his mouth and flung it at me; a kiss or a kiss-off. I wasn't sure which, until he said, "For you, mister. May the grass always be green, the skies always blue, and the rivers always flow."

There was a problem with the page one story in the street edition I pulled from the *Daily* rack: It wasn't mine.

It was most of the story I'd written last night, with all of the qualifiers removed, under a banner head reading:

MURDER 1 - DONALDSON 0

A byline reading:

By B. Keaton Byrd

Assistant District Attorney Hapgood Harris was quoted as saying he had enough evidence on hand to ask for the grand jury's endorsement of first-degree murder charges against "Hot Rod" Donaldson and expressing confidence in winning a quick conviction.

Hope Danbury was identified as one of the victims.

Heathcliffe Arms security guard Gustaf Ljung was identified as Harris's principal eyewitness.

The effects of a compound heroin and coke overdose were described in fervent, microscopic detail; how intravenous injections cause death within a few minutes, where the time lag can be anywhere from two to four hours if the drugs are sniffed or injected subcutaneously.

There was a grocery counter logic to it all, including gratuitous coverage high up of the press conference at UCLA Medical Center. Extravagant expressions by producers Jack Zipper, Jr., and Cleveland Buntine of their belief in Roddy's complete innocence, followed in the next graph by Harris's ridiculing their claim.

I followed the jump to an inside page.

The story was tagged in agate bold:

Neil Gulliver contributed to this story.

Making me look like a damn research librarian or some running-nose cub reporter doing Buster Byrd's bidding.

I called Byrd from a pay phone in the building lobby.

He sounded like he expected the call and listened quietly while I played out my rage.

"You got some ego on you, Neil."

"Worked long and hard for it, Buster. What's your excuse?"

"Excuse? What do I need an excuse for?"

"Your lack of journalism ethics."

"For going your file one better and earning a byline you thought you deserved?"

"You not only ask the questions, you answer them."

"Think and say what you will, Neil. I'm finally fed up with letting you and all those others poke fun at me behind my back. Chet's given me an opportunity and I'm not going to let you or anybody steal it away from me."

"Not when you have my reporting to steal from."

Byrd said, "Keep up the good work, Neil," and was gone.

It must have been then I vowed to make his absence permanent.

Back at the Heathcliffe, the security guard noticed me in a passing glance away from the bank of small TV monitors that took up most of his desk surface. The screens provided a rotating overview of our four garage entrances and other common areas that made the building fair game for illegal entry. He smiled recognition, although his swarthy complexion and heavily bearded face were new to me, and buzzed me through the glass doors.

Stopping inside to do some squats and stretching exercises, I saw Sharon standing outside her office door on the other side of the entry aisle, her back to me, turning the key in the safety lock. A few feet away, two women appeared to be waiting for her. The older of the pair matched perfectly Sharon's description of Roddy Donaldson's mother, Melba. The other woman was Jayne Madrigal.

Jayne saw me and called over, with broad mock astonishment, "Why, Mr. Gulliver, look at you in those spiffy jogging duds. I didn't know you were the athletic type."

Before I could answer, Sharon swiveled around, swept us both in a single glance. "You know each other?"

"Neil and me? Not necessarily," Jayne said. She winked mischievously.

Sharon was not amused. "I know what you mean," she said, like Neil Gulliver was every woman's first choice after boredom.

Jayne did her own swift analysis, studying Sharon, studying me, probably coming to a conclusion no more accurate than the one I figured Sharon had reached about Jayne and me.

They made an interesting combination. Sharon looking attractive in smart, practical business attire highlighted by a simple strand of pearls and matching earrings. Jayne by far the glitzier one in a pure silk floral print chemise that wore its price tag like a pedigree.

Explanations overlapped. Jayne saying, "Besides Roddy, I do PR for the ex-Mrs. Gulliver, Stephanie Marriner." Me saying, "Ms. Madrigal does Stevie's publicity. We just met the other night." Neither of us saying anything about yesterday.

Jayne seemed amused. Sharon less so. Both were smiling, but not really.

Melba Donaldson, who had been staring into space, her foot tapping rapidly, said, "So? Do I have to put up with this fucking small talk all morning or what?" Her jarring voice ensnared us. "Can we get down to business?"

"Mrs. Donaldson and Miss Madrigal are here to pick up some things for Roddy from the apartment," Sharon said. "I checked it out with Sgt. Steiger after Mrs. Donaldson called. He gave us permission. You want to come along? As president of the association—"

"Please do," Jayne chimed in. "President, huh?"

Melba Donaldson said, "Listen, I don't want to sound ungrateful. You always take care of me whenever I call and ask you to go see that Roderick is all right, but I am pressed for time today."

Sharon had often described Melba as a woman used to having her own way. I heard it now in the way she addressed us, like a Marine drill sergeant, only with fewer manners. I didn't find it attractive.

Sharon had failed to prepare me for how much alike mother and son looked. The resemblance was amazing, especially on a squint. Roddy was the prettier, not that Melba was ugly, but the features that gave Roddy allure seemed common on his mother. They made her only ordinary-looking in a business that considers itself much too attractive for anything as ordinary as ordinary.

Her appearance wasn't helped by a catacomb of crevices and creases sun-bleached with years of hard living. Under a tangle of bottled strawberry dangles, the star was harder, the smile less sincere, and her boxer's nose was the kind that came with more bad breaks than she'd likely bargained for, maybe the sign of one ham-handed bad-ass boyfriend too many. She was taller than Roddy by three or four inches, a robust figure in a matching jacket and skirt my eye priced somewhere between the outfits worn by Sharon and Jayne. The exaggerated cross around her neck looked eighteen carat and large enough to cover the down on a new Mercedes.

She caught me studying her. Instead of irritation, she unloaded a Roddy Donaldson smile that exposed a modest overbite. Her teeth were as perfect as her son's and the chin dimple was there, too. I saw clusters of freckles for the first time on her cheeks and the ridge of her sad nose, and at once the woman became human and appealing. Younger than she had looked at first. Possibly the same age as Sharon, thirty-five or thirty-six.

Nobody had bothered, so I introduced myself to her. Melba grew another inch. She snapped her fingers and lit up like a Halloween pumpkin. "Gulliver! Of course! I should've known. Your fans don't come any bigger'n me, especially now that you're gonna help out my boy."

"Help him out?"

"Get to the bottom of all this fucking shit. Write up how he's innocent of all them bullshit charges and make people see the light of day." Speaking like she was leading the longshoremen's charge against Johnny Friendly.

I dug my hands into my pockets. "Where did you hear that, Mrs. Donaldson?"

"Melba. Please. Never one to stand on formality. Where? From Roddy, of course, when me and Jayne went over and seen him at the hospital before coming over here. Soon as we can, we get his ass moved to Cedars. UCLA, ugh! You know what a downgrade that is from Cedars, anyone in the business what knows his hospitals?"

"What else did Roddy say?"

"Only how much he admires and trusts you. So! Me, too!" She gave me the thumbs-up sign. "You got a daughter?"

Melba the Matchmaker? I shook my head.

"A son? Somebody you think deserves the shot? I'm a casting director, you know? Best around today, in this town anyway. I get all the big flicks, like the Brian Armstrong coming up and, of course, Roderick's new one, *Tough Times Two.* You see my name on the big screen all the time. Casting by Melba Donaldson, C.S.A." She zoomed her arms forward and used her thumbs and index fingers to make a Cinemascope screen. "Single card and a hundred percent of the writer, first card position after the stars." I hated myself for understanding what she was telling me. "Well, you got a kid, the least I could do would be to give your kid a shot in the next good flick comes along. Least I could do to pay you back some for what you're doing here for me and Roderick." Melba pushed her face into mine. I caught the twinkle in her eye and smelled the slight odor on her breath, like stale champagne.

Jayne reminded her: "Tight schedule, Melba. Remember? The boys at Paramount, then the trip clear back across town for Lochte at Fox. Then Roddy with the items he was asking for."

Melba acted like she hadn't heard. "Ain't that what the biz is all about? Just like the song says, 'Ain't that what friends are for?' And, just like I say only to my friends, I worked my way to the top by starting out on the bottom."

She pulled back enough to see if I understood what she meant; reared forward and trapped me in a halfback's hug. "Yeah, yeah, yeah, and first chance I could, I begun casting my

Roderick. A shitload of other kids got talent, maybe even one or two close to him, but not one of them also got Melba Donaldson for a mama. Anything you wanna know, you go ahead and ask. I been quoted all the time. *People. Premiere. Entertainment Weekly. Vanity Fair. The Enquirer.* You better believe it."

Jayne stepped in to pry Melba off me. She reminded her again of her appointments and suggested, "Why don't you lead the way, Ms. Glenn?" Sharon started off. Jayne looped her arm through Melba's and, picking up the pace, called, "Coming, Mr. Gulliver?" Turned her head so only I could see what she meant—

A personal invitation more than an inquiry.

Chapter 11

I smelled death still hanging heavy in Roddy's place, but the women didn't seem to notice. Even Sharon had gone right in without reservation, as if her bravery were enough to void the truth of what had happened here.

Melba made a cursory inspection of the parlor, then headed for the bedroom with Sharon in tow. Jayne hung back and gestured for me to wait with her. Certain of privacy, she abandoned her playground pose. "We have to talk about something," she said, at once nervous, like it was a state secret.

"Nicky Edmunds?"

"Not here. Can you meet me for lunch?"

We agreed on a time and place.

Melba returned from the bedroom lugging a Vuitton case. Sharon followed behind, carrying a smaller piece of Vuitton. Melba was disturbed, trying to pretend otherwise, but her voice betrayed her as quickly as her face.

"Roderick's computer, it's missing," she said.

She described a state-of-the-art 486-based portable PC I had been hungry for since reading the specs in *PC World*. The T-980 did more than most of the powerful desktops, as well as some of Superman's tricks and the occasional load of dirty laundry, but at fifteen gees it was strictly a rich man's toy.

Melba said, "Roderick told me I'd find it in the bedroom closet. It wasn't there or anywhere else in the damn bedroom. Help me search for it. A silver metallic case, the size of an overnighter. Heavy. Twenty pounds. Impossible to miss if it's in the apartment."

I helped sort through everything, including the two armoires, while Melba got down on her hands and knees to explore the space below the satin-cloaked table holding other gear. Jayne did, too, starting from the opposite end of the row.

Sharon watched from a chair by the door, the Vuitton bag on her lap. She made a sour face or looked away anytime I smiled in her direction. I interpreted this as her way of telling me off. I knew what she was still thinking, just as I knew what Jayne was thinking. I was wondering when anybody was going to ask me what I was thinking.

Melba inched out from under the table, rose, dusted herself off, and realigned her skirt. Jayne followed her and duplicated the process while Melba walked over to Sharon and asked, "Any other person who got a duplicate key to this place, like the one I give you, Sharon?" By her tone, the implication was clear. She turned to me with an inquiring look, working on a smile that added to the instant menace of her tightly drawn gaze.

Sharon said, "The only spare keys allowed under the bylaws and covenants of the Heathcliffe Arms are sold to owners, Mrs. Donaldson. The owners may do as they choose with them." She'd also heard the accusation. "My rule is never to have a spare key, except when there's a specific request by a tenant or if we need to get into a unit for maintenance work while the tenant is away. The key to your son's unit is the only one I routinely keep in my desk drawer, because of the special nature of your urgent request the first time—"

"I know, I know, I know." Melba wheeled around and pushed her hand at Sharon like a traffic cop. "Nothing personal, Sharon. Believe me. I only asked because Roderick, he's so looking forward to having that damn computer for company."

She glimpsed at me over her shoulder, trying to relax her smile.

I faked one back.

Sharon wasn't satisfied. "Our guards keep a master set of keys, of course, but they are used only for emergencies." She was not going to let her polite nature retard a direct answer. "Our security service is licensed and bonded and we have had no complaints about any improper use for as long as I've been employed here." Melba's anxious wave signaled she understood. "If you're thinking it might be missing because of a break-in, please, let's report it to the police." She turned from Melba to me. "Would you care to make the call, Mr. Gulliver, as president of the homeowners association?"

Before I could answer, Melba yelled, "Jesus fucking enough already! Maybe he just went and loaned it to a buddy or something and forgot. Jaynie, you think he might've loaned it or something to that dumb fuck Nicky?" Jayne answered with a shrug and a polite smile. "Okay, okay," Melba said, looking from one of us to the next. "I'll ask him when I go and see him later at the hospital and then worry over it."

"I'll wait to hear back," Sharon said, the tension easing from her voice. A subtle pink blush of victory spread over her cheeks as she suppressed a smile of satisfaction.

I tried to let her see how proud I was of her.

She stared back at me like she was inventing refrigeration.

The Nickodell was popular in the forties and fifties, sort of an annex to the Brown Derby on Vine Street, a hangout for movie types doing business, trying to do business, or intent on a little funny business in the softly lit bar just off the long stretch of comfortable booths for fours and twos that comprised the main dining room. The Naugahyde was green and the extravagantly framed oil paintings on the walls were almost as lively as the faded wallpaper. The Paramount stars who didn't go to Lucey's down the block would walk here during the lunch break for a few belts or a fast meal while they listened to their agents' lies or told their own being interviewed by some Louella or Hedda. Sometimes the decades of lingering grease smelled better than the freshly prepared meals being served, but nobody ever complained.

Jayne was waiting at one of the fours against the wall about midway, facing the entrance and looking as anxious as Goddard or Stanwyck ever did.

I thanked the maitre d' and slid in alongside her.

Her bag was between us. She moved it to the floor.

She had a Heineken and a Diet Coke chaser waiting for me. Half a margarita was in her glass. We toasted the day, and she said, "Thank you for coming, Neil. I thought how I might have been too forward with you last night and—"

"Absolutely no problem," I said. I felt my disappointment setting in, thinking this was what she wanted to meet about. She wanted to set the record straight. Lucky for me I didn't go and blow it by telling her how glad I was to be here. I faked a smile and started to inch away.

Jayne set down her glass and gently placed a hand on my forearm. "I want you to know I meant it, Neil. I meant every word. I find you extremely attractive." My neck was ballooning with tension. She paused to study me. "I'm sorry, Neil, I didn't mean to—"

I waved her off. "It's this place. They always keep the temperature fifteen degrees higher than anywhere else in the world." I did a thing with shirt collar and jacket.

"Does it bother you, me telling you this?" I shook my head, not trusting myself to speak. "I talked to Stevie this morning, to thank her."

I frowned. "Stevie thinks she has the right to pick her successor the way she used to pick out my suits. She owes me a call. An explanation. An apology."

A flicker of that smile from her. "I was afraid so. Stevie throwing us together the way she did, that does bother you. Yesterday, I knew it was the wrong thing to tell you, after I said it."

"Chalk it up to the margaritas and forget about it."

Her head edged left and right. She pointed to herself. "No, that wasn't it at all. I'm a full-grown adult and I take full responsibility for my behavior. I can't speak for you, Neil, but I grew up not believing in love at first sight. I've found out it's possible."

"If you're trying to flatter me, you're succeeding."

"Do you believe in love at first sight?"

"I did, once upon a time."

"And then what happened?"

"Stevie happened."

"She's still your biggest fan, Neil, but not if you give me a chance."

Before I could answer her inquiring look, the waitress arrived to take our orders. She was a bleached-blonde pixie with legs like telephone poles and a face that fell two years before Rome. She knew Jayne and appeared to like her as much as I did.

She left, and Jayne said, "So, maybe you don't mind telling me something, Neil? Do you have a thing for her?"

"The waitress?"

"Neil . . ."

I considered my answer. "Stevie is still just a kid, in a woman's body. She was astonishingly beautiful. She was love at first sight. I'll probably always have a thing for her."

"Sharon Glenn?"

"People talk where there's nothing to talk about."

"She has the hots for you, you know?" The same words I had heard from Jimmy Steiger. I tossed off a dismissal. "She does,

Neil, so I'm ready to back off if you have the hots for her. Just say the word."

"Sharon and I are just friends. Let's change the subject. Let's talk about Nicky Edmunds."

"Not my type."

"The interview?"

Jayne smiled wickedly and toasted me before announcing, "A problem."

"Nicky won't talk to me?"

"Not that. I told him it was an interview. Nicky hates interviews. It's that stupid Diapered Dozen image he won't come off. I told him the picture needed it, especially with Roddy facing charges. I sold him hard until—"

"Don't say you're about to ask me to do a column on Nicky."

"Not exactly. I'm sure Nicky will manage to piss you off somehow, and that will be my explanation." She put down the glass and ran her fingers through her hair. "It's hard for me to tell you this, Neil."

"Try."

"*Stardom* magazine?" Her eyes shifted as she tried to figure out how to put next whatever she planned to tell me. "Hell, I'll just come right out and say it. Ever since the *Stardom* party, Eugene Coburn, the publisher, has been hounding me on the phone, five and ten times the last couple of days, asking when Neil Gulliver's column is going to run." She made a funny face, somebody's small daughter begging sympathy.

I had an instant picture of Mr. Smooth with the Teeth, his pumping my hand like gas was a dime a gallon and talking about me doing a piece on his *little magazine*.

"Never my intention, Jayne. I was there to attend to her majesty, my ex, that's all." She made a modest gesture of lament. "A column about *Stardom*? I don't think so. Sorry."

"No apologies necessary. I didn't give Gene the idea. I'm

embarrassed by it. I've read 'On the Go' long enough and know it well enough to know you never do that much puff. But, when Gene saw you, he assumed his humble and obedient magician had pulled one out of her hat again."

Jayne shut her eyes and took a deep breath, then exhaled, trying to exhaust her nervousness. I sensed some of the same vulnerability I'd seen in her before. I wanted to take her hand and tell her I was sorry, maybe volunteer to call Coburn and apologize for any misunderstanding.

"Here's the deal," Jayne said suddenly, her voice filled with the cold steel of desperation. "No column about *Stardom,* no meeting with Nick Edmunds."

The waitress had clumped back with our orders.

We waited in silence while she mixed the chef's salad for Jayne and pulled out my cheeseburger and French fries from the warming cabinet of the service wagon. My appetite was gone. I jammed a couple fries in my mouth to keep from saying what I was thinking.

Jayne put her elbows on the table and formed a finger bridge over the salad bowl. She looked away. She said, "I need to keep Gene Coburn's business, Neil. If you want, I can explain."

I cranked my face left and right.

She was determined to tell me anyway. "Gene pays me extremely well. It's his fee that makes the difference between the way I like to work and live and the other way, on the cheap, that has put more than one rising PR star six feet under the ground."

I said, resolutely, "I'll call him and explain what happened. If you think it would make more sense, I'll do it in person."

"You didn't hear me?"

"Loud and clear."

Her eyes misted over. "Mindset, Neil. When he hears no interview, it will be goodbye, Jaynie. Trust me on that." She bit her lower lip and turned her mouth into a tightrope.

"You never told Coburn you could deliver my column?"

"Trust me on that, too. Never. I swear to God."

I wasn't ready to lose her.

I said, "Go call Coburn. Tell him I'd like to see him later this afternoon. Then, call Nicky Edmunds."

CHAPTER 12

Eugene Coburn and I sipped Perrier from long-stemmed crystal and shared a view on the sweeping terrace outside the library of Stardom House. The sight below, through a maze of trees crippled by years of wind, was of distant traffic slipping onto the Hollywood Freeway from Highland Avenue, just outside the Hollywood Bowl's front door.

"Valentino's estate was straight down there," he said. He turned to me and flashed another smile.

"Northbound on the 101?"

"Exactly," Coburn said. "Precisely. Down there where Wedgewood Place once used to be. See that Mercedes jacking off in the fast lane? Now that BMW? Just about there." He pointed as if the tip of his finger was hitting a bulls-eye.

Stardom House occupied one of the myriad multi-story homes built in the twenties to achieve the spectacle of an authentic Mediterranean village in the eccentric hills north of Franklin Avenue, an echo away from the Bowl.

The terraced landscaping at "Whitley Heights" was also designed to meet the developer's extravagant fantasy. When the magic faded and vogue moved movie stars like Swanson, Harlow, and Barthelmess over the ridge to the Valley or east to Beverly Hills, the sculptured trees and brush began to run wild and turned into an overgrown forest of forgotten dreams that sometimes seemed on the verge of overtaking the clusters of tiled roofs and layered picture windows.

"You don't mean Falcon's Lair."

"That came later, when Valentino was trying to keep up with his friends, Mary and Doug. The Sheik came scouting the Heights right after his first big score, they say because it reminded him of home. I tracked the mansion one morning, using plans I obtained from the Department of Building and Safety after moving into Stardom House."

"What's this place add up to? An acre?"

"Maybe two, when you pace back to the old barn," he said. "I'm told Valentino used to march up here to our place every morning decked out in a white turtleneck and jodhpurs, leading a matched pair of Great Danes to their daily poop."

Smile. Wink. Teeth.

Coburn was all happy talk, full of himself, asking the questions and providing the answers while we waited for his partner, Knox Lundigan, to join us. It wouldn't be a tour without Knox, he insisted, trying so hard to impress me or, maybe, coached too well by Jayne Madrigal.

We wandered back inside. I chose an outsized armchair of cracked and faded leather that whooshed noisily when I adjusted my body inside a deep cavity worn by time. Coburn picked its twin and duplicated the sound, pointing to the sterling ice bucket on the low coffee table between us.

I shook my head.

"We can crack the hard stuff if it's not too early in the day for you."

"Perrier is fine," I said, hoisting the goblet. "While we're waiting, why don't you give me some of the background on *Stardom* magazine." He liked that. "Jayne says it's quite a success story," I said, throwing in a plug for his PR lady. He liked that even more. I felt a jealous twinge, sharp enough to wonder if that was causing my increasing dislike for him.

Coburn leaned back, locked his hands behind his thick, white mane, and stared up at the wood-beamed ceiling while reciting with a salesman's charming, precise cadence a story he knew well and clearly had told dozens of times before, as cavalier about his failure as his subsequent success.

Struggling off-Broadway in the years after Nam, he was brought west by a studio to recreate the role that won him an Obie. The picture's failure rubbed off on Coburn, and he scraped around town for a dozen or so years, a face people knew but didn't hire, except for the occasional guest shot on the tube as a gangster or shyster lawyer. Emmy nomination talk for an episode of *Hill Street Blues.* A recurring role on a series about two traveling salesmen and their lovable talking dog, *Rovers,* that didn't get past the pilot.

Coburn paid the rent with temp jobs at the studios, talent agencies, and other offices conducting the business of show business. He was bright and could type a hundred words a minute, and he saw every gig as an opportunity to increase his knowledge of computers.

He learned all the systems, all the programs, and never stopped learning how the town works. He never lost the blind vision of all true believers, that stardom was an agent's call away.

Early one morning, in the cold sweat of an interrupted sleep, he woke up with what he came to call "Coburn's Law": *There will always be as many dreamers as there are dreams.*

Coburn reckoned that the thousands of people who come to Hollywood dreaming of stardom are joined each year by thousands of people who come to Hollywood dreaming of stardom. He reckoned that they represented a pyramid of opportunity for somebody who knew how to serve the dream.

He meant to be that man.

His vehicle became *Stardom* magazine.

For a fee, the hopefuls of Hollywood could put their

photograph in Gene Coburn's upstart publication. The photos ranged from postage stamp size on pages straight out of a high school annual to full-color pages as glitzy as an Oscar reminder in *Daily Variety* and the *Hollywood Reporter.*

In exchange for the investment, Coburn guaranteed his dreamers that a copy would reach the desk of every producer, casting director, mover, and shaker in movies and TV. He always made good, even in the first year, when he was a staff of one and scraped to pay the printing and mailing bills that far exceeded his income.

A ten-year-old boy's photo in *Stardom* got the boy an agent, a lead role in a movie that went on to become one of the highest grossers of the year, and a reported salary of two mil for his next movie.

The kid told his story to Johnny Carson.

Overnight, Coburn's future and fortune were made.

Midway through the second year, the quarterly was a bimonthly and the original two dozen pages on cheap newsprint had become a slick, sophisticated magazine as thick as the Sunday *New York Times.*

Coburn got his own guest shot on Carson and two segments with Robin Leach on *Lifestyles of the Rich and Famous. Newsweek* called him "The Savior of the Star Struck" in a story he now insisted to me was set for a cover until Iraq began playing toy soldiers for real.

Coburn's vision kept pace with his growing empire. He added a video production division that offered the dreamers opportunity to supplement an appearance in *Stardom* magazine with *TalenTapes,* available to executives who preferred to "take a meeting" on video; for an additional fee, of course. The number of TalenTapes, halfway through the second year of operation, was already more than twice the hundreds produced in the first year.

The newest link in his flourishing empire was *BBStardom,* an ultra-sophisticated electronic communications system that allowed subscribing studio executives, producers, personal managers, and agents, using *Stardom* magazine as an index, to scan candidates for stardom via computer, seven days a week, twenty-four hours a day, from anywhere in the world.

"Wait until you see this," Coburn said, checking his watch. He leaned forward, offered me the silver pitcher, and when I declined he helped himself to a Perrier refill. "The other night at the Palladium, you saw the thousands I have tried to help so far?" I nodded. "As you arrived here, you must have seen a dozen or two dozen people entering Stardom House with their career dreams and aspirations tied to a common bond—belief in what we're doing here as the key to unlocking the door to success in an industry that shuts them out. It is this way every day, day in and day out, Neil. Take my word."

Coburn used the table to push himself to his feet. He began pacing, preaching his gospel like Burt Lancaster in *Elmer Gantry,* ever the actor and now his own best audience.

"Are we fulfilling that promise, Neil? Sometimes. As much as we would like? Of course not. But enough so far to know that we have made a difference. We. Have. Made. A. Difference. And we will make a greater difference yet, because of this decade full of the technical marvels that let us launch BBStardom."

Smile. Wink. Teeth.

Behind my own neutral smile, I knew it was more than jealousy that kept me from liking Eugene Coburn. It was distrust. It played to another of the basic commandments I'd learned to live by on the crime beat: "When the trumpet starts sounding too good, pay attention to the brass bassoon." The more he postured and pontificated, the louder I heard Prof. Harold Hill beneath his Billy Graham.

Behind me I heard clapping. Coburn also heard it. He looked

away from the picture window and past me as I turned around.

"You will have to excuse Eugene," the man in the open doorway said. "His strong suit is not understatement."

He was nice-looking in an anonymous way, of average height and build dressed in a colorless tweed jacket, button-down collar open at the neck, yellow cords, and scuffed penny loafers. Early thirties, I judged, with genes that would sustain his boyish appearance for another thirty years—the dreaded Dick Clark Disease.

"Knox!" Coburn's face exploded with new delight. Smile. Wink. Teeth. "There the hell you are, baby, and not a decade too soon. Say hello to Neil Gulliver. You know. He's here to write up that column for the *Daily* that Jaynie told us about."

Knox Lundigan crossed to me, his hand outstretched in anticipation. His grip was indefinite. "I was installing a new program for our BBS and ran into some complications," he said. Not an excuse; a simple declaration of fact. Lundigan didn't quite look at me, but glanced at Coburn, his small eyes as tentative as his voice had become, hardly better than a whisper. I had to strain to hear him.

Coburn joined us. He threw an arm across Lundigan's back and announced, "The real power behind the throne, Neil. Knox here." His other arm closed around Lundigan's narrow chest, and he hugged hard. "I had the idea, but Knox had the brains and he had the bucks. In our civilization ideas are a dime a dozen. Execution is everything."

Lundigan shifted his eyebrows and let a modest smile flicker on his plain-vanilla face. "Serendipity, Eugene."

"That and a wealthy father," Coburn said. Smile. Wink. Teeth. He gave Lundigan another squeeze before letting go. "And P.S., my partner is a computer genius. He would have invented Apple if it hadn't been done already, so you know what I mean. He's light years beyond the Sabaroff EQI."

"Eugene, please." Lundigan's gaze drifted to the floor and he seemed to meditate on the Oriental pattern.

Over the next two hours, Gene Coburn and Knox Lundigan led me through every facet of the Stardom House operation. I saw everything but the ghost of Valentino and his pet Danes. Coburn never stopped talking or lost his effusiveness, conveying the excitement of discovery, as if he also was seeing the wonders of the place for the first time.

The historical, lived-in luxury and ambience of the library did not carry over into public areas, except for architectural delights and inlaid woods that could not be hidden behind portable walls and other practicalities of modern business. There was efficiency to the operation, an unmarked yellow brick road for hopefuls to follow upon arrival, helped along by young, attentive clerks.

Registration led to one of the many doorless rabbit warrens running the perimeter of a spacious room that once may have been for elegant dining. Here, "career counselors" told applicants about the photo opportunities available in *Stardom* magazine. Framed examples hung on the walls, commingled with framed covers from the magazine of major movie and TV stars in inspirational close-up. Stevie. Roddy Donaldson. Maxie Trotter stroking a pig in his lap. Nicky Edmunds, whom I'd be seeing when I left here.

The counselors were all young, stylishly dressed, and as attractive as the clients who filled rows of folding chairs, stealing combative glances at one another while waiting nervously for the next available hutch. They came in all flavors, all topped with the same ambition. The little ones generated the most excitement, as if discovery was through the next door, while their mothers eyed one another suspiciously.

As we kept the leisurely pace through a wing given over to

the magazine's portrait photographers and two-man video crews responsible for TalenTapes, I sensed Lundigan's impatience.

He was harder to figure than his partner. He threw off fewer clues. His infrequent words got lost in a soft mumble. His mind was somewhere else, and I would not have been surprised to see him walk into a wall. He seemed like every father's favorite first date for his teenage daughter, so—

Why did I have the same reservations about him?

Coburn and Lundigan.

One, too good to be true?

The other, too true to be good?

Me, too wary for my own good?

Was this going to be one of those times I wished I could trust the world more than I do my own instincts?

Coburn was saying, "Knox will tell you he considers BBStardom as his ultimate legacy, but TalenTapes is a piece of it the world will treasure after somebody cracks his genius . . . probably those same wonderful folks who gave us Pearl Harbor." His giggle was laced with the same sarcasm and undercut his words.

Lundigan looked away modestly.

Coburn said, "That's your basic video camera over there. It bypasses any need for a tape recorder and plugs directly into Knox's computer circuitry. After the tapes are processed by the magic of BBStardom, they travel up to our communications satellite and back again. Next, the tapes are cataloged and stored for random viewing access or downloading by our subscribers. On floppy or laser disk, or in an exclusive interactive configuration we plan to license out one of these days. Meanwhile, on a lesser level, TalenTapes is the place where professionals can do one-stop computer shopping for the stars of tomorrow, thanks to the day after tomorrow's technology."

All the tape crews were busy, and Coburn noted with a sense of pride that every gallery, on average, was running an hour behind. "I hope you're getting all this, Neil," he said. "So technical and all . . . Stop me anytime it gets too rigorous and I'll slow it down and do some backspacing."

"Sure, Gene." I resented being treated like a computer illiterate, but in my world playing dumb is being smart.

"Shortcut here," Coburn said.

We moved out of a quality control room behind a row of video-editing bays, leaving banks of monitors, a hundred or more, running work in progress or metering the progress of tape copy duplication. Everywhere, technicians performed efficiently at state-of-the-art equipment.

Coburn halted at an unmarked door in the middle of the busy corridor.

He motioned for me to wait while he set aside a small piano bench blocking the way and turned a sculpted glass knob as old as the mansion. The door creaked open. He ushered me through and waited for Lundigan. He closed the door behind us, snapped on a lamp light from the wall switch, and took the lead through a medium-sized room smelling of dust and disuse; once a bedroom and now used for storage. Furniture was covered with old blankets and sheets.

Open-faced metal cabinets and filing shelves taller than me took up almost all the available floor space. They were full of videotapes, hundreds in uniform black boxes, all neatly labeled. Color-coded plastic containers for computer floppies and microfloppies, sundry office supplies.

Coburn cautioned me to watch my step around the precarious stacks of unopened cases of blank computer disks and videotape. I grazed one stack with my arm. It swayed nervously, but didn't tumble. He pushed aside the fallen cases blocking our way, muttering appropriate profanity for the optimistic delivery men who had guessed wrong.

Coburn boasted, "We'll be growing into here next. Knox and

I aren't certain yet if it goes to more editing bays or to expand the physical plant of BBStardom." He swung open the door on the other side of the room and urged me to move ahead. "Speak of the devil," he said. He trilled a musical *duh-dah*!

Lundigan's communications base overpowered my ears even before I stepped into the room and gasped in appreciation as Coburn announced with a carnival barker's reserve, "Knox, baby, you are on. You are on, my man!"

This was Mission Control.

BBStardom.

Later, when my life depended on it, I would remember this visit and pray my memory for detail was as good as I'd always claimed.

The room was about the same size as the bedroom we had just passed through, but the resemblance ended there. The room was spotlessly clean and efficiently organized on a checkerboard tile floor around a console positioned magisterially in the middle. A plush high-backed captain's chair was flanked by lesser seats for ten co-pilots, all of them now occupied by attractive young men and women in fresh, white smocks with the BBStardom logo emblazoned on the back, clickety-clacking out commands on matching keyboards and VGA display monitors. Nobody looked up when we entered, even after Lundigan adjusted the brightness level for more visibility below the drop-ceiling of muted Plexiglas.

I turned to Lundigan and said, "Lot of people for a BBS, no?"

"For a BBS, yes," Coburn said, before Lundigan could answer. "But what we have here is more than a BBS. Not one of those toy systems anybody can operate on the kitchen table or from corporate headquarters. Hands on, Neil. The power of the past restored to the future."

I heard the trumpet, sounding too good again. "What do they do?"

"Knox is our eight-hundred-pound gorilla, Neil. They do whatever it is Knox needs in order to keep his priceless time free for the global intricacies of our system and to chart our course into the future."

Lundigan said, "A clean, dust-free environment. We maintain climate control as well, colder than elsewhere in Stardom House." He seemed to come alive in here. "It's better for our gear and it helps keep my assistants alert."

There was a full wall of terminals and whatever else went into the BBStardom communications system. The opposite wall was lined with metal filing cabinets and shelves that climbed to the ceiling, the top rows reachable only by one of those rolling ladders found in old English estates and serious libraries.

Monitors stretched across the wall directly in front of Mission Control. Fourteen rows of ten across. No two images alike. Words and pictures in fast-changing patterns of high-tech interaction.

Above them, a row of digital clocks ticked off the time, day, and date at a dozen locations around the globe.

The main entrance to the room was off to one side.

On the wall bisected by the door we had entered through, brightly colored pins decorated a detailed map of the world.

The only other adornments were Lundigan's framed Cal Tech diplomas in applied sciences and, in ornate art museum frames with gold-plated identification plates, gigantic oil portraits of a heroic Captain Kirk from *Star Trek* and another of HAL, the computer from *2001: A Space Odyssey.*

My mind wanted to blank out during Lundigan's slow, cautious, excruciatingly detailed explanation of modem communications, but I managed to keep my face a genial mask of interest.

Lundigan beckoned me to join him at the console. He slipped into the captain's chair and I took the seat to his left after he directed the worker bee to take a coffee break.

Lundigan rubbed his hands together, then attacked the keyboard like a virtuoso. I type fast and I know one or two old-timers who can type even faster, full-hand pump or two fingers, but nothing like Lundigan was typing now. His fingers became busy blurs as he brought his screen alive with an elaborately animated version of the BBStardom logo and music reminiscent of a 20th Century Fox newsreel, the stereo sound barreling out of speakers built into the console.

In an instant, our screens filled with the photograph of an attractive woman in her mid-twenties, trying to look like Julia Roberts; coming close. There was an almost three-dimensional quality to the still. It was replaced by a screen that identified her as Laraine Dailey and carded her vital statistics before dissolving into a résumé of professional credits and incidental information.

The concluding screen gave us opportunity to see more of Laraine or wish her well and move on. Lundigan didn't ask for my opinion. He hit a key igniting a preprogrammed macro. Now I was seeing a scene from *Murder, She Wrote,* Angela Lansbury generously giving the close-up to Laraine. Another macro. Laraine doing a singing soft-shoe straight out of the Miss America pageant. Benevolently, Lundigan cut it off.

The next keystroke brought back Laraine's headshot.

Another keystroke and she was as good as alive again, talking to us in a respectful voice full of sultry optimism.

Another keystroke.

The animated still dissolved into a theatrical setting. Laraine sat on an empty stage in a form-fitting white slip that was molded to her curves and cut off just below propriety, the spaghetti straps suffering the enhanced weight of contoured breasts; bathed in a single key light forming a perfect diamond of illumination under one eye.

Quietly, then increasing in intensity and animation, Laraine launched into what the journey line at the base of the screen, moving like a PBS pledge advisory, described as a cold reading from *Cat on a Hot Tin Roof.*

I have seen Maggie the Cats before. Taylor. Ashley. Lange. Dear, brave, hopeful Laraine was no Maggie the Cat, flaunting more tits than talent before Lundigan mercifully zapped her and went back to the opening menu with its animated list of subscriber options.

He said, "And so on," quietly, not entirely unlike a man kissing himself on the back of his neck.

Eugene Coburn proclaimed, "The future, Neil! The future!"

This time I believed him.

It was after seven when I sprinted into the production offices of Cleveland Buntine and Jack Zipper, Jr., at the Grenedier & Grimm Studios in the old Edendale area south of Glendale, where the boy geniuses like Sennett and Disney got started and Keystone Kops can still be heard clanging silently through intersections.

The studio was on Alessandro, a long block south of the sloping dirt hillside where Sennett's Keystone Company once headquartered. It had been converted for sound on top of *The Jazz Singer.* Metropolitan in Burbank had kept the stages upgraded and in constant use since acquiring them during the movie boom of the late thirties.

A secretary with ski slope shoulders, looking like she'd been around the business since before the Paramount Pictures mole became a mountain, was sorting a stack of file folders. Her bosses had left an hour ago, and she made certain I didn't misunderstand her irritation. "I'm late for my bowling league because of you, Mr. Neil Gulliver," she said, using my name like an enema. She gave me directions to Nicky Edmunds's Winnebago. I got lost almost immediately, but was rescued by a shuffling watchman who resembled an overweight Oliver Hardy.

The motor home was parked in a narrow alley across from the soundstage where *Tough Times Two* was shooting. It was the length of an RTD bus, a twin of the one next door, which I figured to be Roddy's.

Nobody responded to my knocking. I tried the door. Unlocked. I stepped inside. The interior lights were on, but no sign of Nicky. Anybody. I called out his name a couple times. A dead fifth of vodka, next to a brown plasticized ice bucket on the kitchen bank. Two glasses. An unmistakable smell, burnt hash, lingering like a lost cloud in the smoky interior.

"Nicky?"

Nothing.

I started a slow walk through the motor home. I figured the bedroom was behind the door at the end of the aisle. I got there and propped my ear against the fake redwood paneling. Feeling like a voyeur, I strained to hear any signs of activity. I thought I did. I called again for Nicky. Nothing.

The door was unlocked. I pushed it open a crack and peeked discreetly.

The naked body sprawled on the bed wasn't moving.

It wasn't Nicky, either.

CHAPTER 13

The comely brunette staring back at me was in her early twenties. She had painted toenails, a freckled chest, and eyes as unfocused as a nightmare. My stomach knotted. I was pinned in place for a minute, flashing on Hope Danbury and "Janie Doe" in Roddy's apartment. I forced myself forward.

I was at her side in two steps. I dropped onto the edge of the narrow bed and in the same motion moved my hand to her neck to check for a pulse, certain there would be none. The smell of hash on her was oppressive. She could have been wearing it for perfume.

I felt the surprise of a slow rhythmic beat under my fingers in the same instant she gripped my wrist and pushed my hand between her slender thighs. Her eyes didn't waver. Her bruised lips barely moved as she mumbled, "Do me good, dude. For starters, a little finger action goes a long way."

She yelped, disappointed, as I pulled my hand away and jumped to my feet.

"C'mon back." A whimper more than words. "Do me like you promised."

I started to answer, but the aggravated voice behind me was unfair competition.

"Who the frig are you to be tampering with my lady? The big bad frigging wolf?"

Nicky Edmunds stood in the altogether, except for a blue rubber at half-mast on his cock. He stared over his nose through half-moon eyes, a vodka bottle in one hand, a .38 automatic in the other, not sure which to aim.

By the way he slurred his words I knew he was loaded.

My immediate concern was whether the .38 was also loaded.

"Man can't take a quiet dump without someone invading his tent," Nicky said. He eased up a leg and farted, then looked for someplace to put the bottle and decided on the vanity shelf. He got a two-handed grip on the .38, spread his legs for balance, and seemed to weave in all directions at once trying to get a bead on me. "Explain yourself in a hurry, Homes, or I'll huff and I'll puff and I'll blow your brains out."

Nicky was a muscular six-footer and had a dark, dangerous edge his pal Roddy lacked.

I believed him, because it was the safe thing to do.

The brunette groaned, "Nicky, come on back here and come on back here." She ran a hand inside her, a finger at a time, reciting "This little piggy," lazy line by lazy line, until the last finger slid out of sight. Wee, wee, wee, all the way home; not one blink of an eye.

I felt my sweat pumping faster than my thoughts about options, no better than they ever are when the finger on the trigger isn't mine. I resisted letting my fright take over and the impulse to do something stupid, instead of nothing, "stupid" being all the excuse a nutcase with a weapon needs to send you passing Go to a plot at Forest Lawn.

"Piggy is right," Nicky muttered, showing his disgust. His eyes momentarily fixed on her wrist. It seemed to grow out of the cloud of puffed brown hair between her thighs. I used the moment to turn stupid anyway. I stepped quickly to my right, grabbed the vodka bottle, and swung.

The bottle landed with a crack against Nicky's cheek. He yelled in pain, dropped the .38. I launched a knee and caught him on the condom. His hands moved from his face to his cock. He bent forward in a half crouch, his chin too good a target to waste. I used it for batting practice with a backhanded whack of the bottle. He tottered, then staggered in reverse down the motor home. He tripped on something and stumble-bummed his way to an abrupt halt face up in the aisle.

"Do I get done or what!?" The brunette had taken her fist out of hibernation and was waving it like a victory salute.

I retrieved the .38 and chased after Nicky, who stopped trying to push himself off the green pile carpeting when he saw the automatic aimed at his broad forehead.

"Hello, Nicky," I said. "I'm Neil Gulliver. Sorry about being late for our interview."

Nicky Edmunds was the surly SOB I'd heard about, not so much as a smile or a nod of understanding, no apology, of course, to go with his disclaimer: "I thought you could've been her old man. Anything's possible anymore with these Stella Starlets."

"I'm not old enough to be her old man."

"You are in my eyes, Pops."

Surly SOB.

He farted again, and this time it was stronger than the hash smell and potentially more damaging than the .38. He smirked, setting up his high cheekbones and a strong jaw line that was swelling and turning purple where I had scored. He touched the spots gently and didn't try to hide the meanness.

"Shoot, Pops."

"Don't tempt me."

"Your questions, funny man. You should know I'm only doing this for Jaynie." He stretched his arms like some tinhorn Jesus waiting for the cross.

"Me, too." I held out a hand to help him up.

He waved it off. "Here is fine, Pops, ready for action whenever

Stella can slither over." He called, "Stella," doing a passable Brando. "She still owes Sr. Wences a polish," he said, pointing to his cock. "She's not so good, *mi dolce amor,* but what's a hot-blooded Latin lover to do? She's the one who's here." He saw my disapproval and smiled heroically. "You feel like getting off, just say the word."

"Tell me about Roddy Donaldson."

The demand surprised him. "Interview's about me, Pops."

"Roddy remembers the two of you partying here first of the week. That's the last he remembers until he woke up a couple days later at the UCLA Medical Center as the prime suspect in a homicide investigation."

I read a new look on Nicky's face. He muttered something about being had by his PR bitch. He gestured helplessness. Behind me, Stella Starlet yelped support for multiple orgasms, like it was a campaign issue.

Nicky said, "Roddy is my best friend. We run together."

"I know."

"He's no frigging murderer."

"I don't think so, either. He asked me to talk to you."

"Because he doesn't remember?"

"Because he doesn't remember."

Nicky sat up, his arms around his knees, and hid his face against his thighs. He quietly began telling me what he knew, sounding not quite so out of it as he had a few minutes ago. I leaned over and stashed the .38 on the edge of the buffet counter, a peace offering. Nicky started talking. He had a better memory than Roddy.

Yes, they had partied Monday after the shoot. The tequila. The Stoli. The same as Roddy remembered. Roddy gets drunk enough to launch an ocean. Nicky calls Jayne and cancels the limo to Maxie Trotter's super-exclusive party at the Roxy.

I interrupted him. "If good buddy Roddy is so drunk that he

can't find his nose with radar, why did you cancel the limo and choose to play 502 roulette on the city streets?"

Nicky studied me, not sure how to answer. "We both been drunker, okay? Besides, the Rod always prefers being behind his own wheels when he has a hot tootie on his arm."

"A hot tootie?"

Nicky pointed past me to Stella Starlet, who was sounding indecently quiet. "Me, too. Makes it a smoother ride, coming and going as we choose. Sometimes more coming, sometimes more going, you rate?"

Confusion descended on me like a spring drizzle—

How to explain the hot tooties in terms of Roddy's confession to me.

I wanted to push the gay question, but I couldn't. I had made a promise to Roddy. I couldn't assume his best bud here was in on the secret. "Lots of hot tooties, Nicky?"

"How many star fuckers would you guesstimate are out there? Roddy and me, we stopped counting a dozen movies ago."

"The girls with you Monday night. The same ones who were found in his condo? A girl named Hope Danbury. The other—" and I remembered Janie Doe still had no name.

Nicky shot me a look and fondled the bruise growing on his cheek. "Frig no, same as I told the cops when they asked the question." The cops? Steiger or who? I grunted, so he'd know I was paying attention. "We had Miss Hot to Trot Bimbo of 1975 and her sister in slime, Miss Hot to Trot Bimbette of 1977. Extras. Faces in the crowd, the kinds of faces that thin out a crowd. They latched on to us after the wrap. We figured why not? We could always plead temporary insanity."

Nicky leaned back on his hands and briefly memorized the air-conditioning grate. He made a decision. "Okay, so we each of us tooled out from here in our respective wheels with our respective fiancées, figuring the least charity we owed them was a free pour at the Roxy. We're decent that way. Before we could lose them in the crowd, they got hustled off by two black dudes in gold chains and eighteen-carat nose dusters."

"Does Roddy use?"

"What does he say, Pops?" A smug look.

"What do you say?"

"Roddy's afraid of needles." He said it casually, let the message sink in. "Now, here is the part I didn't share with Renko and Belker. You better know it, though." He made sure he still had my attention. "Last time I saw Roddy at the Roxy was in the middle of Maxie's set. I'm grooving up front with my new bride-to-be and he shoots me a high sign stumbling past me, heading for the exit. He's got three women with him, two of them who are helping to keep his face from kissing the floor."

"You mean two women."

"Uno, dos, tres." He counted them off on his fingers. "Who the frig *uno* was beats me better'n my own hand job, but *dos* and *tres* . . ." He drew a finger across his throat. "The same faces as the pictures in the newspaper and the tube."

"You're certain?"

"A baby spot happened to catch them real good when Roddy was on his way out. If you don't tell this to anybody, then neither did I. What they don't ask me won't hurt him." He put a question mark on his face.

The motor home went black. A pair of hands over my eyes. A smell decidedly not Chanel.

Two breasts insinuating themselves against my back.

A flighty, phlegmy voice deciding, "You're a producer, aren't you? Maybe I can help you produce something?"

Stella Starlet.

I peeled her hands away and resisted her efforts to score points below the belt. She didn't like that at all. Nicky sprang up. He grabbed the .38 and rammed it hard against my nose.

Stella let out a howl and ran back inside the bedroom. I heard the door slam and the lock click.

Nicky sighted down his arm and lowered his voice. "How do you feel about dying, not that I assume you have any experience at it." He took a step back. The .38 threatened to blow me a third eye socket while ripping away half my face. He observed the sweat inside my eyes and laughed uproariously. "The line's from my new movie, you turd. This gun? A prop." He gave it a fast study and tossed it over his shoulder. It hit the windshield, bounced off the control deck, dropped harmlessly to the floor. "Another thing I want you to know. Is not the person alive who can mess up my face the way you did and walk away clean; no way. Not here, not now, but I got friends, so you better start watching over your shoulder."

"That a threat, Nicky?"

"What's it sound like, a birthday greeting? Think of it as a promise, and by the way, Mr. Columnist, interview's over."

I thought of it as a threat, and that night I dreamed about it.

In my dreams, the .38 was real.

So were Nicky Edmunds and the punks he led in pursuit of me.

They got so close, I heard the words of derision they mouthed between breaths. The descriptions of the savage death awaiting me. I ducked into an alley and raced for a distant light, my run interrupted by young hookers reaching out for me from darkened doorways; calling my name, making obscene gestures, offering worse than death. The light dissolved into a dead end. I turned and steeled myself for a volley of shots.

I woke up. My pajamas were soaked in sweat. I was glad to be alive. I switched on the lamp. I leaped out of bed. I checked the door locks, the window locks, the lock on the sliding glass patio door. I groped for other light switches every step of the way.

We always survive our dreams, but life plays a deadlier game.

Punks like Nicky Edmunds always seem to know the difference.

Chapter 14

The next time I opened my eyes was to a sense of invading daylight. It took me a few moments of confusion diffusion to remember why I was decked out on the couch. On the AMC movie channel, Jeanne Crain and Jean Peters were no longer reinventing Betty Grable and Carole Landis in a sad remake of *I Wake Up Screaming.* Instead, Gypo Nolan was fleeing for his life through the dreary shadows of Dublin. I moved Wambaugh's new novel from my chest to the coffee table and muted the Sony.

Whatever happened to Saturday as a day of rest?

I worked out my collection of tensions between three loads of laundry, gave the condo its biweekly sparkle, answered correspondence, and returned a few phone calls, starting with Jimmy Steiger.

The story Nicky Edmunds had given me matched one Jimmy already knew, except for Nicky's insistence about a third woman at the Roxy.

I said, "He wanted me to believe he was spilling out of loyalty to his good bud, but Nicky is nobody's fool, Jimmy. He knows there's damage in what he said. He wanted me to know about the third woman for a reason—but not *the* reason."

Jimmy thought about it. "Your security guard, Gustav . . . Gustav . . ." I helped him with the name. "This Ljung guy was pretty definite on his story. Just two women with Donaldson, Hope Danbury and Janie Doe. You suppose, if we locate the alleged third party hearty, we cut ourselves in for a delicious slice of answer pie?"

"If she exists."

"If she exists."

I one-stopped in the lobby for my newspapers on the last laundry room detour.

Sharon has weekends off, but I sensed the rustle of activity behind her office door. I knocked and entered full of good cheer. She gave me a cold eye and shoved some papers at me.

"Glad you thought to drop in," she said. I smiled. Sharon didn't. She said, "Do you mind checking this rough draft? Minutes of the last board meeting."

I rested the laundry basket on the edge of her desk and said, "You're mad at me about something." It doesn't take a genius to sound like a dummy. I didn't need her glare to inform me. I said, "Actually, I'm wondering if you're in the mood for silents tonight. Laura La Plante in *The Cat and the Canary,* Lon Chaney in *Phantom of the Opera* at our favorite picture palace on Fairfax."

"I don't believe so. No."

"After, we could hop on down to Genghis Cohen for some fried rice and fortune cookies."

"I've made other plans for tonight, thank you," she said, as definite as a bee sting.

I took a calculated risk: "Sharon, it's absolutely not what you might be thinking, about Jayne Madrigal and me, I mean."

Depending on Sharon's reaction, I would tell her the rest of it, how I valued her friendship but felt entirely different stirrings when I was around Jayne.

Sharon put her dummy face on display again and said, "I believe you must have me confused with somebody who cares. All I'm thinking is I'd appreciate it if you'd check the rough draft of the minutes. Okay?"

I left bad enough alone.

I tried returning Jayne's phone call again; again had to leave word with her service.

I reached Stevie instead of her machine. We hadn't connected since the Palladium.

"First time Jaynie sees you, you're eyeing some chickie young enough to be your daughter," said the Divine Sarah Bernhardt of the Soaps. "Then, Mr. Hot Breath, you start putting the moves on Jaynie."

"The chickie was eyeing me, not the other way around. She recognized me from the bus cards. You were not the only famous person around . . . Did I observe certain natural endowments the chickie wished to share with the world? Yes. To that I humbly confess."

"In my diary, that's eyeing."

"In my column, that's courtesy."

"I was only sixteen when we met, just a chickie myself. What would you call that?"

"My mistake."

Silence. Then, "The truth."

"Your mistake."

"More like it."

"What'd I call it? I'd call it love at first sight." I heard her rescue a breath. "I was old enough to be your lover, I humbly confess to that, Stevie. You care to try again? I'm game if you are. It's the only kind of gambling I would even think about doing now that I've reformed."

No answer, until, "You make a better friend, honey, for me anyway." Her version of the truth. She was never so defiant defending a lie. "Besides, there's now a Jaynie in the picture.

Tell me about you and Jaynie."

"Nothing to tell."

"Is that the same as nothing you want to tell?"

"Do you also read palms?"

"I tell you everything, most of the time."

I hummed into the phone, briefly. "Jayne seems nice enough. Yeah, she's okay."

Stevie shrieked in triumph. "I knew there was something there. I felt the vibes going every which way between you two while we were taking the pictures for *People.*"

"But you neglected to mention how you plotted to get me there and Jayne and me together." I mimicked her: " *'Oh, honey, it's a disaster thing that nobody else in the whole wide world but you can help me with.'* "

"You think I made that part up?" Her every word sharp and distinct. You. Think. I. Made. That. Part. Up?

"A ruse?"

"Don't use any of your fancy words on me, okay?"

"A ruse by any name."

She hung up on me. I timed my wait. One-thousand twenty-six. One-thousand twenty-seven. One-thousand—

My phone rang. Stevie came on shouting. "It was not a ruse." She pronounced it *rouge.* "I said I was desperate for you to help me and I meant it. There was never enough time to talk about it, although I tried. We kept getting interrupted."

"Try me now."

"It's about Mom. About Juliet."

"Tell me she's not sick."

"Mom? She'll always be the poster girl for healthy. It's this depressing business about Juliet's newest Romeo."

When she'd finished telling me about her mother's latest boyfriend, I said, "What happened to the banjo player your mother picked up at the Palomino?"

"Rex? Tex? Schmex? She caught him plucking the wrong strings. So, now she's found this new one. Where? God only knows. Bernie Flame. Do you believe that name? An actor a hundred years younger than her." Stevie made a sad noise. "My mother gets nuttier by the day, honey. You need to talk her out of seeing this hunk, like all the other times. She listens to you. She never listens to me."

"Juliet never listens to anyone."

"Okay, then. She likes you. Better than me, anyway."

That part was true. Juliet Marriner and I had hit it off the moment we met. Kindred spirits, maybe. She'd gone through her own hurts and misses. We found ourselves talking a common language. She'd blessed our marriage and prayed for me to succeed with her dear Stephanie where she had failed. Later, we also had that in common.

I said, "Juliet likes me better than you like me or she likes me better than she likes you?"

"Neil, I did not call you to engage in word games. Will you or will you not help me to avert another tragedy in the life of my precious mother? If I have ever meant anything to you, even for just one day out of—" She thought about it. "Seven years . . ." Sounding proud for remembering how long we'd stayed married. "Do it for me, honey? Do it for me and I'll owe you one."

"One what?"

"Don't press your luck, Neil. Or is this a new trick of yours? Preying on desperate women."

"You still haven't said. Did it happen by itself or did you work at fixing me up with Jayne Madrigal?"

"Jaynie is not desperate. She's quite lovely, as well as being talented. She seems to like you. You could do worse. Besides, we are no longer discussing that particular topic."

"Answer me or no deal about Juliet."

"You'd do that to me?" I waited her out. "Yes, yes, yes, yes,

yes. I tried to fix you up with Jayne Madrigal. Now are you satisfied? Are you? Are you satisfied, Neil? Can you hear them? My tears. You have reduced me to tears, Neil."

"Bravo. I know where you'll be on Emmy night."

"Hah. Hah. Hah."

"I'll talk to Juliet." Her tears dried up at once. Her gratitude was whelming. I said, "For your mother, Stevie. Not necessarily for you."

The Sheba of the Soaps said, "Tell me something else, honey . . . Do you think Jaynie is prettier than me?"

"Pass."

"Coward."

"Only in the face of your beauty."

Stevie liked that.

Roddy Donaldson had a block on his phone.

Pedro and Maria Elena Cisneros only had time to bless me for calling.

They were racing back to the hospital at the urging of little Pedro's doctor.

"Did he say why?"

"Only that we should be there, Señor Gulliver."

Pearl Danbury's generous voice turned as proud and soulful as a Memphis sax when I told her I wanted to know more about her daughter. She said, "You come to her funeral tomorrow and you'll learn what my baby Hope was really like." I jotted down directions to the church. "You'll see lots of people," she said. "Everyone who knew her loved her. Maybe after, you can write some truth about Hope in that newspaper of yours."

I didn't tell her how big a problem that "maybe" might be for me.

There already was enough grief on her shoulders.

At least, she had something I feared she'd soon share with Mr. and Mrs. Cisneros: closure. *Closure.* What a lousy word.

There's never closure when you lose someone you love. Never. Only memories that make you smile, then bleed, but never go away. Why should they? Isn't love forever? As it should be. *Love.* Now there's a word.

Chapter 15

Shortly before eleven o'clock on Sunday morning, I arrived at the Church of the Righteous Gospel on West Adams Boulevard. The church had once been a synagogue, the same way the black neighborhood had once been predominantly white and Jewish, before the mass population shifts of the fifties and sixties. Evidence remained in the form of a Star of David carved out of the cement belfry, stained glass windows portraying Moses and the Ten Commandments. A sign of new times was gang graffiti on all the walls. Packs of kids in the parking lot were making a business of protection. I gave one a fiver to squat on my Jag's fender and followed the sound of music inside. There weren't enough clouds to mar the warm sky. It was a good day for a funeral.

The choir, dressed in rhythm-and-blue robes, filled the stage behind a large framed photo of Hope Danbury mounted on an easel and decked in garlands of flowers, aiming its highest notes for Heaven while members of the congregation swayed to the pulsating beat of the Staples Singers classic, *I'll Take You There.* The church was crowded, at least three hundred people downstairs and maybe another hundred upstairs in a narrow balcony that was groaning under the weight of shifting bodies. Not all the faces were black. I moved down a side aisle searching for a seat.

Five rows from the front, I caught a hand signal. The corpulent, sweating man in the dignified suit was directing me to a narrow space midway between him and an equally large but older blue-haired woman. He pushed to his right to make the space bigger as I excused myself over shoes and knees and, immediately upon sitting down, regretted his courtesy. It was like being hit by a pair of lumpy battering rams as he and the blue-haired woman gave syncopated responses to the choir, now into a belting rendition of *Rock of Ages.*

There was something about one of the three young women who'd stepped forward to lead the vocals in a choreographed approximation of The Supremes. She was familiar-looking. The more I stared, the more certain I became that I'd seen her before. Recently. Once, I thought I caught her staring at me with a glimmer of recognition, just before the trio finished the song and settled back into the obscurity of the choir.

The preacher was into his opening remarks before he stormed onto the pulpit. He was a large, avuncular sort in a sweeping golden robe and a *basso profundo* voice that hit the back wall and bounced without benefit of amplification.

By the time he had finished describing Hope Danbury and how her hopes and her dreams for a better life were cut short by a tragedy for which there was no accounting, his angry eyes were filled with tears and his words had gone from a mocking confusion over society's deadly forces to confidence in the Lord helping all of us to understand she was an unfortunate, unwilling victim and not the wild child party girl full of evil alcoholic spirits and the devil's drugs depicted on television and by all the newspapers.

Wild Child Party Girl.

The headline description of Hope Danbury to go with the catch phrase coined by Buster Byrd in his latest stories.

The preacher argued that Hope Danbury had survived her senior year at Revere High without yielding to any of the devil's temptations available to her on any street corner within a two-mile radius.

"She willed it that way," he said, his words bouncing off the walls. "Hope willed it that way after watching the lives of so many sisters and brothers end so tragically. She was always guided by the strong hand of a single parent too proud for food stamps, who always managed to find work that gave her ample time to be with her beloved child. You hear me, Pearl Danbury? You hear what I know?

"Your girl child was class vice president, a cheerleader, and an honor student who was heading for graduation and fulfillment of a dream. She was heading for UCLA and her degree in the theater arts. She was hoping the Good Lord would grant her the same kind of successful career that had blessed her role models. Diana Ross. Donna Summer. Whitney Houston. 'Wild Child Party Girl,' indeed! Reckless, soulless journalism is what it is."

The entire congregation was sobbing. Cries of outrage and salvation were coming from everywhere. It was more than emotional bonding. It was a declaration of truth, the same truth Pearl Danbury had spoken to me about. I unashamedly dabbed at my eyes. I wanted to jump up and shout, *Amen, preacher man! Amen!*, but I was pinned in place by two blubbering hulks.

The preacher declaimed, "Hope, don't you care none, girl. We all know better. We know you. We know it's written, 'So for the mother's sake the child was dear, and dearer was the mother for the child.' " Words meant to comfort Mrs. Danbury. Before he got any further, a dreadful howl filled the church. It had begun softly, like a Gershwin rhapsody, and quickly raged as out of control as a summertime riot. It came from behind a black curtain to the right of the pulpit, the mourner's bench where Pearl Danbury was sitting.

★ ★ ★ ★ ★

I slipped the kid in the parking lot another fiver to stay on Jag duty, then fell in step with congregation members walking to Mrs. Danbury's home a few blocks up the street. It couldn't have been more than ten minutes since the services concluded, but people already were spilling out of her small courtyard apartment, downstairs on the right in a well-kept two-story stucco building at the rear of a complex being maintained to high standards in a low-income neighborhood. A pair of one-story buildings ran parallel to a flower garden planted down the middle, bordered by cracked concrete walks and waist-high privet hedges enclosing rose bushes, carnations, daisies, and the occasional child's toy. A baseball mitt. A plastic squeeze doll. Scribbled-on pages ripped from a coloring book and broken bits of crayon.

I worked my way up onto the cement porch and used a shoulder to push through the crowd into the apartment. I searched a maze of trapped bodies and shifting heads for the strong, resigned face I had seen on all the newscasts, enduring with dignity the callous, insensitive slinging of cameras and microphones. Mrs. Danbury was across the room, with the preacher. It took five minutes to reach her. Her eyes began sparkling. She had my hand in hers and was introducing me before I could recite my name.

She said, "Rev. Plantation, this is the newspaper columnist who has come to learn the truth about my baby, so he can tell the rest of the world, Mr. Neil Gulliver of the *Daily.* Mr. Gulliver, I would like you to meet Rev. Ronnie Plantation."

Rev. Ronnie Plantation answered with the look invented by older black men in a less tolerant era and shook my hand too enthusiastically. "Truly honored, Mr. Gulliver." I complimented him on his sermon. He seemed pleased. "Only being the willing messenger for our dear Lord's truth, Mr. Gulliver." He turned to Mrs. Danbury. "Pearl, I feel this is a man who will do justice by you and your dearest Hope." She closed her eyes and nodded in quiet agreement. He sounded ready to launch a reprise of his sermon, but was stopped by a hand tugging at his sleeve jacket, to spirit him away to join a circle in a corner of the room by the buffet table.

We watched Rev. Plantation go, and in the same glancing survey I noticed the girl from the choir who had looked so familiar to me. She was sauntering in through the front door.

She wore her dark, curly hair cropped tight, leaving nothing to distract from the small and perfectly formed, light-complexioned features merging the aura of a young girl with the fascinations of a full-grown woman. Her body moved like mercury under a plain white sheath suggesting more than it revealed. She rubbed tension from her neck while she looked around. It was a motion I knew. I had seen it before. Recently, but where? I shut my eyes and waited for a clue to spring like a miracle from the recesses of my memory.

Mrs. Danbury had observed me studying the girl.

"Her name is Aleta Haworth," she said. Her voice drew me back into the room. I pinned the name on the girl. "She is . . . she was my Hope's very best friend in this world. Only a year ahead of Hope, but, oh my, how Hope looked up to her. Hope, she loved Aleta like an older sister, and Aleta, she always treated Hope the same way. A beautiful, beautiful child, Mr. Gulliver, and on the inside as well."

Aleta was trading greetings and conversation, her eyes darting past them in search of someone in the thick crowd. An older woman, her heavy body sagging under the heat in the room, showed her a camera and pointed to the portrait of Hope adorned with flowers. It had been brought over from the church. She wanted Aleta to move there for a picture.

I had a new sense of memory-jog and shut my eyes again.

Mrs. Danbury's voice sailed over the din. "Aleta, she's already on her way to the kind of success my baby was dreaming about, but she not getting so big-head as ever to forget a friend," she said with pride. "Aleta, she's singing with Maxie Trotter, you know? I don't expect you know about Maxie Trotter, though. Maxie Trotter is—"

Cuh-lick!

Aleta Haworth was "Miss Ovaltine."

The short hair had thrown me. She had been wearing a wig at the Palladium, an intricately woven spider's web of glittering corn rows that spilled to the bare shoulders jutting out from a black vinyl swimsuit. Aleta had shown up carrying a message for Jayne from Maxie, and—

"—and also a great star," Mrs. Danbury was saying. "Oh, Aleta be looking this way. Aleta! Aleta!" I opened my eyes. "Let me get her over here to talk to you for what you'll be writing, Mr. Gulliver. Aleta!"

Mrs. Danbury waved. Aleta smiled and returned the wave, but froze when she saw who was standing alongside her best friend's mother. Her smile stayed rigid while her eyes swept the room. She gestured indefinitely, said hurried words to the lady with the camera, and fled.

Mrs. Danbury made a queer face and started to say something, but I was already shouldering my way to the front door, rudely clearing the path with more pushes than *Excuse me*'s, my mind flashing hot on the possibility that Aleta Haworth was the third woman with Roddy Donaldson at the Roxy last Monday night.

I skirted around a knot in the middle of the room and was grabbed by Rev. Ronnie Plantation, who wanted me to meet his friends. I yanked loose, startling him, apologizing into the air. I squeezed around the sweatshop I'd sat by during the service and kept going.

I got to the front porch in time to see Aleta had reached the street.

I yelled out her name.

She halted long enough to look back and verify it was me, then dashed out of sight. She was gone by the time I got to the sidewalk. It could have been her in the black 560 SL Mercedes hardtop pulling a noisy right turn at the intersection.

Mrs. Danbury remembered Hope mentioning something about Aleta moving to an apartment in Hollywood, but she had no address. She raised the question with Rev. Ronnie Plantation, who summoned his church administrator, Mrs. Gosden, a meek woman wearing a humble white hat and matching gloves.

"Aleta moved out of the neighborhood?" Mrs. Gosden said, like she was hearing a revelation. "I believe our latest records show only her address over on Hillcrest," she said contritely, averting the preacher's scrutiny.

I phone Jayne from a Texaco station on La Brea, near the Santa Monica Freeway.

"Thanks for calling back," she said, making her delight sound real. "When I rang you up this morning and got the machine, I thought, 'Oh, darn, we're going to spend the whole weekend playing telephone tag.' "

"I didn't get the message. I'm not calling from the apartment."

"Oh." She sounded disappointed. Caught herself. Put sunshine in her voice telling me how much Gene Coburn and Knox Lundigan had enjoyed my visit to Stardom House. She let the news sink in, then, "I can't speak for Nicky. He never did check back with me afterward. How'd it go?"

"Better you should hear it from him."

She groaned. "Well, don't say I didn't warn you."

A low rider was cruising the station for a second time. This time it stopped. I got a hard look from the gangster in the passenger window wearing a hairnet and a bad attitude. Nowadays, the streets of Los Angeles are as full of suspicion and fear as traffic; moments like these are often a prelude to a drive-by robbery or target practice.

I hurried the conversation. "I'm not talking about Stardom House or Nicky."

"I don't suppose it was to find out what I might be doing for dinner?" Teasing on the square. I told her why and felt her curiosity even before I heard it in her voice. "Why on earth would you need an address for Aleta? I don't remember introducing you."

"You didn't, but I'd rather not say right now."

"I understand."

"Do you?"

"Maybe I don't."

"I mean, do you have an address for Aleta."

Jayne thought about it before answering. "It will cost you dinner tonight."

"Do you put a price on everything?"

"Not everything. The best things in life are free. Besides, I'm sure I owe you a nice meal for surviving Nick. Eight o'clock my place?"

The low rider's horn tooted a musical message. The vehicle whipped away from the curb and across the intersection, into the left turn lane and onto the freeway.

Relaxing, I said, "I'd feel more comfortable at a restaurant."

"Oh, pooh. Don't turn into such a scaredy-cat. My world famous homemade chili's already simmering in the pot. It won't get any hotter here than that. I promise." She heard me weighing the deal. "Comes with my world famous homemade cornbread."

"If you're going to throw in the cornbread . . ."

"I'm in the tub. Hold on while I get to my Filofax."

I visualized Jayne making the walk. Only once in the years since Stevie lowered the boom on me had the pull of attraction been this strong. Just hearing her voice excited me. I checked my watch to see how many hours it would be before eight o'clock.

Chapter 16

Aleta Haworth lived on a quiet residential street off Beverly and La Brea that was lined on both sides with the type of two-decker, cement and stucco apartment buildings so stylish in the thirties, about three miles from her old neighborhood and just upward enough to leave the past out of focus. The mix is multi-racial, young singles and couples, married or otherwise, who dream big and shop Costco.

The closest parking was around the corner. I walked back to her building with my mind full of homemade chili. The intoxicating aroma was burning inside my nose by the time I climbed the wide stairs to the mailboxes. A row of eight was built into the wall, no names in the identification slots.

I swung the ancient glass door open and was hit in the face by the smell of jalapeno peppers and paprika diluting the smell of time and transience as I stepped into the entrance hall tunnel.

Aleta didn't have a unit number and there were a lot of doors to knock on, but I got lucky with the one by the stairway. It opened a crack, and the pockmarked teenager behind the latch chain, holding an infant howling louder than the sounds of heavy metal raging in the background, knew Aleta by name. He sent me upstairs to 4B in the rear.

I heard the buzzer through the door. No answer. I tried again and after a moment or two rapped a few times. Nothing. I turned the doorknob the way everybody checks for pay phone coins. Surprise. The lock clicked and I pushed the door open.

The place had been ransacked by someone in a hurry.

Her couch and matching chairs bled stuffing, as did the king-sized mattress in her bedroom. Her closets and cabinets had been emptied, clothing shredded, drawers yanked and dumped, collections of record albums, compact discs, cassettes, and videotapes pulled from their shelves, scattered and garnished with magazines, books, and paperbacks, and her sound system and video gear destroyed beyond recovery in an anxious, rambling assault.

I spent the next twenty minutes wandering through the four rooms, careful not to damage the crime scene. Only Aleta's framed posters, mainly rock-and-roll images from the late sixties and seventies, had survived the attack relatively undamaged, except for an artsy, full-length pose of the original Supremes, before Diana was moved to the middle. It was in the bedroom next to her dressing table. An ugly unrepairable gash stretched across three sets of red-sequined bosoms under cracked glass.

The largest and most dramatic poster was a photograph of an oil painting of Aleta's boss, Maxie Trotter, steeped in mysticism and lording over the living room from a place of honor above one of those wood-burning fireplaces with a built-in gas jet. It was inscribed. I moved in closer to see what Maxie had to say: *For Aleta. Welcome to my family. Great to have someone pretty and talented like you so Hot to Trot. Stalk 'em sultry and show 'em smart. Your friend, Maxie Trotter.*

The "Hot to Trots."

That's what Maxie called his trio of backup vocalists.

"Stalk 'em sultry and show 'em smart."

The title of his first hit record four or five years ago and his battle cry ever since.

Something on the mantel caught my eye, a three-and-a-half-inch floppy disk that holds more computer information than the standard five-and-a-quarter size. It was lying flat, partially obscured by a romance paperback that had landed there when the bookcases were tossed. The disk, still in its protective clear plastic casing and unlabeled, was almost as blue as the surface of the mantel.

What made it an especially curious find: There was no sign anywhere of computer equipment. Was that what the burglar took? Computer equipment? Then why not just grab and go? Why create a dump site? Impulsively, I stashed the blue floppy in a pocket.

I was about to call in the burglary when I heard the creak of floorboards behind me. I froze. My eyes did a nervous dance to keep up with my heartbeat. No. Mr. Burglar was in too much a hurry to be staging a comeback now. I hoped. I turned, looked sideways across my body. I saw nothing. I aimed lower.

The scowling, fat-cheeked child in a Raiders t-shirt and hair the color of uncooked spaghetti was four or five and not more than two feet tall. She was standing about ten feet away from me, feet apart, dangling a cloth Cat in the Hat doll in one hand, using the other to point at me accusingly.

"You made a mess," she said, wagging her finger. "You made a messy mess and Aleta's going to be real sore. You made a messy mess." She wheeled around, went running off on her bare, chunky legs, calling, "Mama, Mama! Some man in Aleta's made a messy mess!"

I headed out after the little girl. I took the back stairs two at a time to the first floor and passed through an open hall door, down a wobbly rack of wooden stairs onto a paved one-lane alley. Turning in the direction of the street where I had parked my Jag, I spotted the same black Mercedes I had seen charging away from Mrs. Danbury's home. It was parked in the garage stall marked for Aleta's apartment, 4B.

Had the burglar also stolen Aleta?

I became aware of the classic green Mustang a few blocks after crossing Beverly, when I realized how little I'd had to eat all day and decided to double back to La Brea and Melrose for a refresher course on chili with a couple chili dogs at Pink's.

The Mustang was about five car lengths behind me. When I shifted from the center lane to the right, to make the turn north, the Mustang made an identical maneuver. It was less careful, almost kissing fenders with a Cad in the adjacent lane.

The Pink's lines were short, only a ten-minute wait.

I wolfed down a double with everything waiting for my second doggie, certain Jayne's chili could not possibly compare, and headed back for my car in the lot behind the stand. The Mustang was parked at the end of the row, motor running, facing out for a fast getaway. The driver was at the wheel, but with the canvas top up I couldn't read him in the shadows of late afternoon.

Somebody following me?

Somebody hired by Nicky Edmunds, or . . . ?

I scrambled into the Jag and took off, preferring an old maxim to the idea of a confrontation: *When in doubt, bug out.*

I picked out the Mustang again while turning south onto Glendon from Wilshire, my personal shortcut for avoiding the long traffic waits and turning hassles that were the rule any time of the day at the Westwood and Veteran intersections. I did a sudden stomp on the brakes and waited to see what happened next. The Mustang hung back, suspended in the intersection, until the signal changed, then inched back into the flow lane. I circled the Heathcliffe twice before plugging in the garage gate code and gliding down the ramp. By the time I reached my apartment I had chalked off the Mustang to coincidence.

★ ★ ★ ★ ★

I remembered the blue floppy when I sat down to write my column about Hope Danbury. I inserted the diskette and called it up.

A directory full of names that meant nothing to me filled the screen.

After that, the diskette refused to cooperate, and so to the column.

There are times for every writer when the purest of intentions meet the worst of log jams, and no two words can be made to fit. Other times, thoughts and phrases emerge from hidden places of the heart or mind, and the blank pages seem to fill up by themselves.

I caught myself writing about Hope with immediacy, passion, and purpose, fixed on a glide path stirred by the insights of Rev. Ronnie Plantation.

Hope, a high school girl looking to a future devoid of the mistakes she saw many of her friends making. She didn't touch drugs or alcohol or men. She was an honor student in pursuit of a college education and a career without pregnant pauses. Or anything else the preacher had praised as the hallmarks of the bright, beautiful girl he had watched grow up; who practiced faith, not folly; who had a dream, not a death wish.

That was the Hope Danbury I was sharing with my readers as the monitor filled up on automatic pilot with seven hundred fifty words. In my mind, this was how Hope had to be remembered in more than her mother's memory. I ignored contradictions and questions raised about her by what I'd heard from Roddy Donaldson and Nicky Edmunds.

Before uploading, I read it through twice and did a printout to see how the copy would play on paper. I dropped a few adjectives, added some others, and reluctantly axed a graph that played too rough with public attitudes. I slugged it to be subbed for the Monday piece I had filed yesterday, a memory piece on the old Union Station Terminal.

The column about Hope Danbury wasn't going to endear me to Chet Wilkins.

I didn't give a damn.

Chapter 17

I didn't intend for Jayne and me to make love.

I want to believe she didn't, either.

Not at first, anyway; either of us.

Jayne lived in the valley, the expensive part of Sherman Oaks on the south side of Ventura Boulevard, within walking distance of the Galleria. All the way there I'd driven on the ragged edge of my emotions, promising myself I'd have them under control by the time I arrived or not go in.

"Hi, Scaredy-cat," she answered the squawk box, and buzzed me through.

Most of the townhouse entrances appeared to front an Olympic-sized pool in the center of the courtyard. Her door was one of two at opposite ends of a north side wall I found after passing through an access corridor between two three-tier buildings of brown wood and stucco. It faced on an eight- or nine-foot security fence topped with barbed wire and an empty lot overrun with weeds and wildflowers.

I saw a lot of the usual showy security patrol warning signs and window decals, but no guards patrolling. It was a thieves' paradise compared to the Heathcliffe, where last year I had helped negotiate a renewal with the service that guaranteed us three extra guards for walk-around for a modest boost over the basic fee. Sharon used her usual magic to pull the extra bucks from a couple budget categories. Immediately, our burglary, break-in, and theft rate declined dramatically.

"Right on time, so I take it you had no trouble finding the place?" Jayne said. She was waiting for me in the doorway arch of her unit. Her smile was as warm as a love song. Her insinuating voice had taken on the vitality of a children's playground. One look and so much for keeping my emotions under control. Behind the mask of a stranger was the friend I needed.

"You are as reliable as a Thomas Guide Book," I said. I held out the bottle of Napa Valley red and three dozen carnations I'd picked up in the Village before gliding onto the San Diego Freeway north by the VA on Wilshire.

She acknowledged the gifts and moved forward, but instead of reaching for them she stepped between my arms and surprised me with a kiss. I didn't resist, especially after her tongue found a crevice between my lips and briefly slipped inside.

"Whew," she said, stepping back and fanning her face with a hand. Her lips had been as soft and delicious as her svelte body looked inside the modest cotton granny gown. An enormous cameo framed in gold clinched the high collar at her throat. A fine lace hem about two inches wide stopped just above her ankles. White gym socks added a youthful appeal to the look.

Jayne took the wine and the carnations and searched for fireflies. Behind her, Rod Stewart was singing. She said, "That kiss was not planned, Neil, I promise. I'm on my best behavior tonight."

"I'm relieved to hear that. And me."

Her face was freshly scrubbed, her hair pulled back into a ponytail secured by a large yellow ribbon. She smelled of lavender and lilacs. I recognized I was being allowed to see the child she kept hidden inside the sophisticated businesswoman. The knowledge was flattering.

She started inside, pausing to close the door after I passed by. As she turned, my shoulder accidentally brushed against a breast. I felt an instant electricity. So did she. She made a quiet noise and her nipples began pressing hard against the fabric. I must have been staring at them. She draped an arm across her breasts. A blush illuminated her apple cheeks. She looked like a fairytale princess.

"Welcome to my humble abode," she said. Finally.

I didn't trust my voice. Impulsively, I pressed the modest cleft in her chin.

Our eyes locked.

The corners of her rich mouth flickered, but she said nothing.

It may have been at this moment when we both understood the inevitable.

I cleared my throat and found some safe words: "The chili smells great."

Her smile ignited. "I promised you the best tonight," she said. She swept inside, calling over her shoulder, "There's a pitcher of margaritas in the fridge, or the Heinekens and Diet Cokes. Take your pick, then go take the grand tour while I find someplace to put these carnation beauties and finish setting the table."

Her townhouse was a couple hundred square feet larger than the largest condo at the Heathcliffe. Hardly any wasted space on three levels. This level opened into a living room/dining room combination and walk-in kitchen Jayne had furnished with a checkbook straight out of the pages of *Architectural Digest.*

Eccentric stairs led first to an office half the size of the living room. One wall was lined with bookshelves. Rows of reference volumes. Fiction. Nonfiction. Her taste was eclectic and included titles I knew from the best-seller lists. On the opposite wall was the customary collection of membership certificates, citations, and celebrity photographs in expensive matching wood and metal frames precisely arranged.

I recognized several politicians and one former president in the photos, as well as some of her clients. Jayne hugging Roddy. Nicky hugging Jayne. The producers Buntine and Zipper hugging each other while Jayne mugged for the camera. *Stardom* magazine's Gene Coburn at a microphone, a line of starlets slightly out of focus behind him. Jayne and Stevie mugging for the camera, Stevie half-hiding Jayne's face with her hand; seemingly a gag shot, unless you know Stevie as well as I knew Stevie.

I stepped closer to read the inscription on this year's official portrait of the Sex Queen of the Soaps: *For my dear, darling, precious Jaynie. Like the sister I never had. With all my love, Stevie.* Underlined with a row of circles and Xs. I had to smile and wonder if Jayne knew about the sister Stevie did have, but never talked about.

The computer monitor on the desk was tuned to her modem dialing directory. BBStardom led the list, followed by several names I knew—CompuServe, Nexis, Genie, Prodigy—and others I didn't know. Forty different log-on possibilities.

There was a picture window hidden behind the drawn Roman shade.

She saved the view for her bedroom, one floor up.

It was a cloudless night. A curtain of stars formed the backdrop to an eccentric ridge of the Santa Monicas in the distance.

Dozens of decorative pillows and teddy bears topped her king-sized bed. Neat and sweet. Counterpoint to a mural-sized oil painting dominating the room, a nude inspired by Manet's *Olympia,* her left hand positioned higher to expose a layer of dark, richly textured hair over her pubic mound. Instead of a woman servant, a darkly intense naked man, with lust visible on more than his face. I didn't recognize that Tarzan, but Jayne was the Jayne, more impressive than my imagination ever made her. I felt those dangerous stirrings again.

I retreated through the door across the way and into the bathroom, its design stolen from a mansion in one of those screwball movie comedies of the forties. It was saturated in the same sweet fragrance Jayne had brought to the door with her. Not all the bubbles were drained from a tub built for two. Black silk panties hung over the back of a candy-striped chair at the mirrored dressing table.

I glanced at the door like a kid courting a crime. Then I stepped over and grabbed the panties. I pressed them to my nose, hurriedly, knowing any more thought would make the deed impossible. At once I felt the guilt brought on by the act and by the knowledge of what private history had provoked the act. I replaced the panties and fled to the stairs.

The short passage narrowed some more and dead-ended at a door leading onto a private balcony about ten by twelve feet, furnished with a patio chaise lounge and chairs. Potted greenery added another foot to the safety wall, which stopped at about my waist. The view was broader than from the bedroom. Safer. Monopolized by the intense glow of the three-quarter moon visible high to my right.

My heart rate had returned to normal. I pushed out some air, took a deep and satisfying swallow of Heineken.

Jayne said, "I forgot my margarita downstairs. Mind if I try some of that?" She had crept up behind me and was a foot or two away. I offered her the bottle. She moved to my side. Verified she had my attention before bringing the rim to her lips.

She raised her chin and sipped. She shared an approving look, pushed an inch or more of the neck inside her mouth. She tilted her head back and rotated the bottle inside her grip while she sucked it empty.

She set it down between two planters and said, "May I ask you something, Neil?" I answered her in sign language. "Good. Thank you, because I would like us to be perfectly honest with each other." I nodded. "Do you want to make love to me, Neil?" She read my expression correctly. "Yes. I mean tonight. Do you?"

I struggled with myself for an answer.

She said, "Stop thinking. Do you or don't you?" Her eyes trapped mine and refused to let go. "I didn't want this to happen. I said that already, didn't I? I mean, not tonight, not this way. You had me from the first time I saw you, mister, just the way Stevie predicted it would happen. She understands chemistry, that one. She knows you and she knows me.

"I figured, *Okay, Jaynie, maybe after a while, maybe after Neil gets to know you better.* I meant it when I said 'chili.' I meant for this to be strictly a social evening. I didn't even plan to talk business, for Christ's sake; me. Yes, I want to know everything that went on at Stardom House. Yes, everything that Nick put you through. Why you called to get an address for Aleta Haworth. Maybe that's when it started, why I started feeling as I do now. After we spoke, I couldn't shake the jealousy. I've seen Aleta in action. With Maxie. With Roscoe Del Ruth. I got crazy. Getting crazy is going crazy. My best of intentions went out the window the minute I saw you and that cute face. Your thoughtfulness with the *vino* and the carnations. Too much. The chili was simmering and I was boiling over." She stopped to take a deep breath. "Does any of this make sense to you?"

"Yes."

"Am I talking too much?"

"I think so."

Jayne smiled possessively, no longer the little girl. She no longer tried hiding her erect nipples. "There you go, thinking again." She removed the yellow ribbon, unpinned the ponytail, and shook her hair loose. She dropped the ribbon and the clasp on the grass matting. She unpinned the cameo and set it down carefully on the balcony ledge, by the empty Heineken bottle.

Using a cross-armed movement, she lifted the granny gown over her head and tossed it onto a chair. She was naked underneath. She struck a pose and let my eyes explore her body for another minute, proud to have the attention. Then she said, "Anytime you're ready, Scaredy-cat."

I thought I saw the green Mustang five hours later, when I climbed into the Jag. It was parked on the same side as me, about a half block farther south of Jayne's townhouse. The bright orange flicker behind the windshield caught my eye, glowing like the drag on a cigarette before it dropped from view.

My chest vibrated and I flashed on Jayne and me all over each other, especially the last time, our one for the road before I reluctantly slipped into my clothes and out the door, a brief pause en route for one final taste of her oiled thigh. Her breathing was steady and she didn't move. I wished I could stay the night, but Jayne had insisted on waking up to a busy Monday with only the memory of my scent.

"If you're here, the only thing that will get done is me," she said. "I won't shower. That way, I'll have you all day long." I wanted to argue, but she stopped my lips with a finger and repeated a few of her tricks that had left me speechless and breathless, and did so all over again.

I checked the clock on the dash. A little past three.

I drove around the block. Before rounding the corner that brought me back to the street, I turned off the lights and cut my speed to ten miles an hour, enough to get a good look as I glided by the Mustang, fifty or sixty yards ahead of me. Only, when I got there, the space was empty.

Farther up the street, I saw taillights blink on a car turning right onto Sepulveda.

I popped my headlights and sped after it.

The boulevard was deserted, except for the car trapped at the signal a half mile up and a mini-van crawling in the opposite direction. I jumped two stop signs to reach the car before the light turned green. It was a Dodge Dart. Behind the wheel, a woman about sixty in a nurse's uniform. She caught me staring, mouthed something, and gave me the finger. I picked up the San Diego on Ventura and spent the ride home checking my rearview.

Chapter 18

A message from Gus Ljung, the security guard, had been slipped under my door.

I needed sleep more than conversation, but this was nothing I wanted to put off. I took the elevator down to the main lobby playing with something my crime beat mentor, Augie Fowler, had pummeled into me years ago: *Reality is never what it is, but what you make of it. Things aren't always what they seem to be or who they seem to be, and getting at the truth frequently entails the need to sort the liars from their lies.*

Gus looked up to the sound of my Nikes squeaking on the tile, put down the *Star,* and called my name in the stage whisper people use in bookstores. The lobby was empty, except for us and a couple in UCLA sweats, tangled asleep in front of the big-screen TV.

"Been off sick or I would've answered your messages sooner," he said. "When I called and didn't get an answer, went up and put a note under your door, in case you came home before my shift ends. Don't want to disappoint you some more, sir. Tell me how I can be helpful to you, Mr. Gulliver." He flexed his lips into an insincere smile. I returned one of my own.

Even when Gus meant to sound polite, he came across as insincere and patronizing. Sharon claimed this was not so. She insisted my opinion reflected my dislike for him. She had that part right. It had to do with his eyes. They rarely moved. They were recessed and empty, like burned blue dots on Sylvania flash cubes.

Gus was in his early twenties, a full head taller than me. He carried a boyish load of Nordic blond good looks and easily could have been mistaken for a lifeguard, except for a complexion the color of ice cream, like it never saw sunshine. His shoulders were so broad he had to angle his body passing through a standard door frame. His arms were bought at a gym. His hands were meant to wield a warrior's sword and shield on a Viking vessel under siege, alongside Kirk Douglas and Tony Curtis.

I invited him to join me at the sitting area outside Sharon's office and pushed into a corner of the blue and gold sofa. Gus settled on an arm of the matching chair, at an angle that gave him a direct view of the main entrance. My personal opinion aside, the guy was conscientious.

"It's about this terrible stuff been happening for Roddy Donaldson you want to talk to me?" His English was heavily accented, but better than listening to an Ingmar Bergman movie without subtitles. What made it exceptional was how well he'd learned our language since arriving in America less than a year ago.

I asked him to tell me the story. He launched it without hesitation in the monotone of a memory revisited, adding nothing new to the version I had heard from Jimmy Steiger and later read under Buster Byrd's byline.

The quality and believability of his testimony would be especially critical in front of a jury, because the D.A. had no supporting videotape to introduce into evidence. All the Heathcliffe's surveillance cameras operate on a seventy-two-hour cycle. After every cycle they automatically rewind and the taping stars fresh. The current cycle on the cameras had ended about an hour before Gus came on duty.

On the night in question, while on routine security patrol,

Gus had observed Mr. Donaldson arrive through the south pedestrian gate on the east side of the parking garage. Mr. Donaldson was being supported by two girls, who held him upright by his arms and seemed to be struggling under his weight as they encouraged him to continue walking, in the general direction of the elevator. This wasn't the first time Gus had encountered Roddy in this condition, although never before with girls.

The girls seemed alarmed when they saw Gus, but Roddy greeted him by name. He called him over to meet his friends. He couldn't remember their names and they didn't offer them. All three reeked of alcohol. Gus expected that of Roddy, but thought how pitiful for girls so young to drink so much. He prided himself on being a vegetarian who never drank anything stronger than fresh fruit juices.

Gus asked if he could help. The girls became anxious, telling him it wouldn't be necessary, their words overlapping, redundant, racing a mile a minute, and he wondered to himself if they had been using drugs. He recognized this condition from people at the gym, statues of solitude in the steam of the sauna, cooking the glaze from their eyes and putting the vowels back into their conversation.

Roddy refused his offer. He pulled free of the girls and got two steps away before he tripped over his own feet and stumbled onto the concrete. At this point, Gus took charge. Ignoring Roddy's angry objections, he half-walked, half-carried him to the elevator. Roddy refused to get on if Gus did.

Gus told me, "Was the last time I saw Mr. Donaldson or them girls until it was all over the news on the television, sir."

He responded to my questions in the forthright manner prosecutors love, abetted by body language jurors can respect. His memory was strong, rich in details. I heard the sound of early rehearsal and repetition, but only because he was no stranger to the game. I said, "Do you know Mr. Donaldson's friend Nicky Edmunds?"

A curious look. "Also the movie star. I see him whenever he's coming and visiting, sometimes with girls, but I don't know to tell you their names, these girls, either, or like so. Always different girls. Not same ones like was coming home with Mr. Donaldson. Though sometimes also a limousine."

"Mr. Edmunds was with Mr. Donaldson earlier that night, at a party. He says Mr. Donaldson left the party with three girls, not two." Gus nodded appreciatively. "I thought the third girl might have come back here with them, all of them together. Maybe park the car and then follow her friends inside?"

"Mr. Gulliver, only two be getting on elevator with Mr. Donaldson. Same two I see later on television, only now—"

Gus pulled his thin lips into a tight smile as sincere as a politician's dream, turned his palms to the ceiling, with his cold eyes feeding on mine. He returned his palms to his knees, where his thick fingers resumed a game they had been playing with imaginary lint.

Any suggestion of rehearsal would be gone by the time Gus told his story to a jury. No question Hapless Harris would make absolutely certain of that long before he put Gus into the witness box.

Gus would lock Roddy in time and place and add enough eyeball to the drug use allegation to help make the case stick, although nothing I heard changed my mind about Harris's call for Murder One being media grandstanding.

However, something I heard did make me wonder if Gus was telling the truth. The whole truth and nothing but. I didn't know what, only that it was there in his butterfly voice and his frozen eyes. Whatever Sharon saw in him, I saw something else.

CHAPTER 19

I started Monday morning on scarcely five hours' sleep, my body remembering all the aches and pains induced by my travels with Jayne, to the carnival, the circus, the zoo; to the kind of Magic Kingdom Walt Disney never imagined. To the moon and back. They felt great, memories of a gift that kept on giving. A triple dose of caffeine helped wake me up. So did Mozart on the CD player. The soak in the tub helped soothe the savage beast.

The face staring back in the bathroom mirror looked more smug than usual. I raised my arm, made a fist, and felt my biceps for firmness. Not bad. *Me Tarzan. She Jayne.* I was anxious to hear her voice and charged to the telephone.

Her machine answered on her private number. Trying not to sound disappointed, chipper Neil Gulliver reminded her about tonight and plans for instant replay. I added a giddy afterthought that made me laugh at myself. When was the last time I felt this good? I remembered. I pushed the thought away. This time I knew how to protect myself.

I climbed into my sweats and got the usual morning routine out of the way before calling Henry Bouchey.

Henry and I hadn't spoken much in the five or six years since he'd left the *Daily* to start his own newspaper, and then only a few snatches of catch-up whenever we'd bump into one another at some glamorous event of significance to the readers of his paper, *Trail Blazer.* I told him I had some questions that didn't work over a telephone. He understood at once and invited me over. We picked a time.

I hit the neighborhood early, to pick up a new Cole Porter CD at Tower Records and settle in for a leisurely lunch at the Palm. The place was jumping for a Monday, the usual mixed bag of heavy-hitting movie and music suspects. Gigi the manager smiled and waved away my reluctance to steal one of his booths. He comp'd me to a Heineken and Diet Coke at the bar, ten minutes later sat me at the booth for four under my caricature on the wall. I ordered poached salmon, gorged myself on the bread, picked at the fries and the onion rings until both platters were finger-swept clean, and couldn't stop from thinking how much nicer it would be with Jayne here.

Although the *Trail Blazer* had an editorial staff of forty and its own printing press housed in a modern plant on Santa Monica and Robertson in Boys Town, Henry Bouchey spent most of his work day about a mile away on Westville Avenue behind La Cienega, in a rustic cottage clinging to an era that no longer existed. It was distinguished by a wooden shingle roof painted a florid pink and in desperate need of repair, cubbyhole windows with matching pink shutters, and a front door protected by bars normal for Cell Block Eleven at San Quentin, the last a clue to how dangerous the area had become in recent years.

Side streets in Boys Town nowadays were a major attraction for itinerant hustlers and dime bag peddlers, a hiding place for the homeless and their shopping carts, a hangout for thieves, perverts, molesters and worse monitoring foot traffic coming and going from the jungle of gyms, bars, and boutiques running up and down Santa Monica.

I swung the bar door aside. The massive oak door it guarded also was unlocked. It groaned loudly when I pressed down on the rusted latch and pushed it open, waking up the kid who was stretched out on the tattered sofa. He raised himself on an elbow to check me out. The boy wore tight jeans with torn knees, scuffed Air Jordans, and a gaudy Vanilla Ice tank top. He was fourteen or fifteen, except around his defensive eyes, dark circles of time and trouble. I must have passed his secret criteria. He nodded approvingly and thumbed me to the back, calling out Henry's name in a voice full of phlegm before he settled back down with his face turned to the back cushion.

As I headed down the short hallway, Henry leaned out the last door on the right to check and stepped forward. He engulfed me with extended arms and a wide open, silent mouth, then embraced me warmly and kissed my cheeks like a French general.

Except for another layer of middle-aged chunk, a narrow gold band dangling from his right nostril, and an erratic row of diamond chips decorating his left ear, he looked the same as a year ago, when we traded waves and winks at the Ahmanson, a *Phantom of the Opera* fund-raiser for AIDS research.

Henry wore octagonal rimless glasses and an expression of constant amazement on a mashed-potato face that bore his five o'clock shadow like a permanent stain. He kept his thick strands of auburn hair in a wild style that always made me think of Jerry Lewis as the nutty professor and contrasted sharply with the cheap, neatly pressed suits he favored, their lapels never as wide as the conservative ties he kept tightly pulled at the starched collar of a freshly laundered shirt.

Henry had retired as the *Daily*'s second-string theater critic after the City of West Hollywood took shape, plunging his savings and every dollar he could borrow from banks and friends, even casual acquaintances like me, into creation of a weekly tabloid reporting exclusively on the gay lifestyle. Henry was straight as they come, but he didn't let that get in the way of his concept.

"Show where it's written only fags can profit off of other fags," he said while I was writing him a check for two hundred and fifty bucks. Five months later, Henry sent me his check for the two-fifty, plus a hundred percent interest. His thank-you note advised, *And I didn't have to bend over once.*

Henry took a step back and stared up at my face while he chose his words carefully. "Your column this a.m., about the girl?" He launched his eyebrows and waited to be sure I was listening. "I was moved by it, Neil." His head bobbed like a backseat beaker bird and he got dewy-eyed while waving off my thanks as inconsequential. "Mean it. Tremendously moved. What did you call that precious child? Every mother's daughter? Yes, it was." Said like I hadn't known. "Your call when it came, pure serendipity. It allows me to congratulate you in person."

Henry swiped at an eye. He gave my cheek a playful pinch and guided me into his office, probably the master bedroom at one time, calling over his shoulder, "Timmy, Mr. Gulliver and I are not to be disturbed."

He pointed me to a chair and offered me coffee, saw by my expression what I was thinking, shook his head vigorously while filling two mugs from the coffeemaker buried behind stacks of folders and old newspapers on the filing cabinet.

"No, no, no, no, no. I am still as straight arrow as they come, Neil. Cochise could ride into battle with me. I only rescue them, the dumb fuck kids. Like the brat you saw out there. Timmy. Sweet Jesus, he was trading blow jobs for blow. He picked the wrong alley to suck dick in and was half dead when somebody found him and brought him to me three weeks ago."

Henry apologized for being out of sweetener. I passed on the box of sugar he held up. He aimed the spout at his mug, pouring what may have been the equivalent of six teaspoons. Or seven. I passed on the milk. He took a drink from the carton and set it back down on the filing cabinet.

"Timmy's mom and dad are due in L.A. from Idaho the end of the week," he said, settling onto the secretarial chair behind the scarred secondhand schoolteacher's desk. "All they know is that their runaway had a change of heart. Whatever else they learn will be up to Timmy. I always encourage these brats to lie. It's the kind of truth parents understand best." Henry cleared a space for his elbows and made a triangle with his fingers. "But you didn't come here to hear about Busy Timmy, did you?" He gave me *a let's hear it* hand.

I talked about the national press attention the *Trail Blazer* was drawing lately, due to its weekly front page "outings" of celebrities who kept their sexual preferences private. A month ago, *Business Week* had reported on the paper's spiraling circulation and quoted Henry as saying, "Gay Pride shouldn't stop at the closet door. That's the real drag."

Henry was pleased I'd kept track. "It hasn't made me popular, but it is making me rich," he said.

He crossed to a locked filing cabinet and patted it, as if to say: *Here's where the truth is stored.* From memory he recited the names of film and TV stars and prominent politicians, including a majordomo in D.C. and one closer to home, in Sacramento. All had been outed by Henry and the *Trail Blazer* in the last year.

He looked left and right, as if checking to make sure we were alone, then surprised me with other names that had been in the news recently, a top comic and executives at two of the big movie studios.

He smiled at my reaction. "Next issue for one, next month for the others. There's some documentation I still need. The creeps I sent out spying are holding me up for several thou more than I'm prepared to pay."

I placed my mug on the desk and said, "But you will."

"Names make news and make cash registers jingle like Santa Claus is coming to town. You're not here for a loan, Gully, so what's this all about?"

I put my mug down on the desk. "Roddy Donaldson?"

It was Henry's turn to be surprised. "What about Roddy Donaldson?"

"Between us for now?" I wasn't about to breach a confidence.

"No secrets in this town, Neil, never, especially when it comes to a damned fine newspaperman. That's what I am first and foremost, a damned fine newspaperman, but we'll do it any way you want."

I told him what I'd heard from Roddy.

Henry looked at me like I was the advance man for an invasion from Mars. He pulled open every file drawer in the cabinet and invited me to examine their contents.

"Not a whiff, not a rumor, not a clue," he said, in as forceful a manner as I'd ever heard him use. "If so, and you can go to the bank on this—it would be in there." He had risen to his full height and drawn his arms across his chest. "Tell you something. You come back and show me otherwise and I'll personally go down on the motherfucker. Or take it up the well-known pal canal."

First thing when I got home, I put in a call to the UCLA Medical Center. Roddy was still under guard. No visitors allowed except for immediate family and the lawyers; personal calls permitted. I decided to risk the possibility of a tap on his extension and had the operator put me through.

He answered on the second ring and recognized my voice. "I'd love to chat, Prez, but I have company. Call me back, maybe, or I can call you? In about half an hour or so?" A voice in the background. "Mr. Gulliver, mother." His hand over the receiver. Muffled conversation. Roddy back, clearing his throat. "Mother says to say hello. She thinks it's wonderful of you to call and would like you to tell the homeowners who signed the get-well card how thoughtful and considerate they are." Muffle. Muffle. "And for the flowers. Me, too. They're beautiful, Mr. Gulliver."

A card? Flowers? Sharon's touch. Did she think to add my name? Probably. All the members of the board of directors. Thorough that way. I said, "Just listen, Roddy. It'll only take a minute."

"Yes, roses," he said. "Uh-huh." I summarized the encounter with Nicky Edmunds in a run-on sentence. A chuckle; playacting. "No, long-stemmed. Buds. Yellow well as red, and one or two pinks for contrast. Conroy, but I don't think Flower Fashions would've done it better."

I dropped Aleta Haworth's name and told him about Gus Ljung in verbal shorthand.

A burst of laughter. "News to me. Hold on. Mother, did you know you can now buy flowers with the scent removed, in case you think the patient might be allergic?" A voice in the background. "Mother says she thinks she read that somewhere."

"Roddy, do you know the newspaper the *Trail Blazer*?"

"Uh, yeah. Yes. I do."

"I just got back from visiting with the editor. Henry Bouchey. An old friend."

"So do I. I'd love to see your face, and also Ms. Glenn. It may be my party, but the cops are in charge of the guest list." A Tommy Udo giggle. Widmark had done it better in *Kiss of Death.* "That's a line from *Tough Times Two*, Mr. Gulliver: *It may be my party, but the cops are in charge of the guest list.*" This time trying to sound like Cagney.

"What you and I discussed privately, Roddy? You know what I mean. My friend Henry says it can't be true. If it were true, he'd know about it, he said. What can you say to that?"

I heard a desperate gulp of air, then silence. Then, "You, too, Prez. Thanks again for everything."

And I was hearing the dial tone.

I stuck by the phone, certain he'd call the instant Melba Donaldson left his room.

The call came within the hour, but it wasn't from Roddy.

"Mr. Gulliver? Mr. Neil Gulliver?" I recognized the voice, powerful, commanding, resonant, even before Brian Armstrong identified himself. "I am calling to arrange for us to get together." We'd never met, but I heard in his attitude that he didn't like me. It saddened me.

"About?"

"Details when you get here, Mr. Gulliver." He rattled off directions to Wonderman Towers on the Wilshire Corridor and insisted I repeat them back, even after I advised him that the Wonderman was less than three miles from the Heathcliffe and on my usual route to and from Westwood. Brian Armstrong was a man used to being in charge. I repeated his directions.

CHAPTER 20

I stepped from the elevator directly into Brian Armstrong's penthouse apartment, a fortress of glass on the eighteenth floor with spectacular views of the city and the valley. Past his words of welcome, the evidence of his dislike for me was confirmed on his face. Brian Armstrong had never been that good an actor. Only my hero.

He stood at parade rest, dressed for a country stroll in a brown cashmere turtleneck and coordinated casual trousers, exhibiting a physique that denied the passage of time. His expensive hairpiece, the obligatory wisps out of place at the part, took ten years off his age, which I'd played with driving over and figured at around sixty-five. A light pancake base on top of his tan filled in the rut holes of time and took off another five years, making him into the doomed priest of the mid-eighties, *Fighting Father Jack,* who dies while rescuing his boyhood mobster-pal's falsely accused son, "Kid," played by Roddy Donaldson.

"Thank you for agreeing to see me on such short notice," he said impersonally.

He quit the long, powerful handshake salesmen use to send a message, did a smart about-face, and marched into the room with that broad-shouldered strut everybody knew from *Final Call to Arms, The Bravo Bunch, Viva, Cruz!,* and, of course, *Champion of the Plains,* in which he co-starred with another of my favorites, Sunset Beaudry. The two-inch heels on his suede hobnail demi-boots squeegeed on the parquet floor. He invited me to choose a seat, but elected to stand alongside the antique French fireplace, within reach of a tall frosted glass topped with a small umbrella, a cherry, and a pineapple slice. I recognized him staring down at me from the oil painting in the intricately hand-carved walnut frame, as the best of the D'Artagnans, in *Trail of the Musketeers.*

An overhead caught Armstrong perfectly and made him the center of attention in the dimly lit room. (I could almost hear John Ford ordering the camera to roll.) He may have sensed my feeling that I'd visited here before as I surveyed the room, which was at least fifty feet square.

"Everything you see was gathered up through the years from one or another of my films," he said. "That dear Cary always walked off with his wardrobe when a shoot ended. However, I opt for the best pieces of furniture. I call the nice people from Bekins and have them send the bill on to the studio."

He pointed to the dining-room setting across the room, a plank-top pearwood table surrounded by leather and wood antique Spanish chairs. *"Champion of the Plains,"* he said. "If you know my work, you would recognize it immediately."

"The seduction scene."

Armstrong repressed a smile. "The seduction scene. And the chair you selected?"

I bounced up and made a big show of inspecting the chair. Not necessary, but I wanted to make sure I was right, to impress him, the way he had always impressed me. Seventeenth-century French. Panel back.

"*Fit for a King,*" I said, and quoted his lines back to him: " *'You would murder me where I sit, my dear Morveau, but I promise you this—I will not die. Here or ever. The people will not permit it and I, of course, shall always side with the people.'* "

Armstrong nodded appreciatively. He wrapped one arm

across his tight belly to support his opposite elbow. His index finger stroked the pencil-thin mustache he had inherited in the fifties from Errol Flynn; from the center out, first to one side, then the other. Again, then once more. He studied me quietly for another minute. "How sad when one must destroy the passions of our youth."

I thought about it. I apologized and told him I didn't know the movie the line had come from.

"No need. Not from any movie. I fear it is what I am about to do with you, Mr. Gulliver."

"You're not my type, Mr. Armstrong."

It took him a moment to get the joke. He said, "Does it make a difference to you, my—homosexuality?"

"Not until the day I rent one of your movies and find Zorro wearing a dress."

He laughed heartily. The Armstrong Laugh.

My hero relaxed and for the next half hour told me about his relationship with Roddy Donaldson.

It seemed like sharing the truth with a stranger also obviated any other playacting. The tension drained from his body. So did the starch. He appeared to shrink an inch or two and a slight hunch settled on his back as he toured the avenues of his life that might prove helpful to his young lover.

Their affair had started almost immediately after filming began on *Fighting Father Jack.* By the calendar Roddy was fifteen. They celebrated his sixteenth birthday during the production and, Armstrong insisted, Roddy having been molested as a child made the boy older and wiser than his years.

He said, "I was able to show him how love can be a beautiful thing, particularly when it is mutual."

"You're telling me you seduced him?"

"Hardly, Mr. Gullliver. Roddy seduced me. He knocked on my trailer door, script in hand, wondering if I might help him with his lines. Or so he said, but I saw the look in his eyes, as old as sin itself. He knew, too. *Voilá!* Done! And every day thereafter, thank God." He stared past me out the window.

"You still see Roddy?"

"We still see each other. I have never been one to take my love affairs casually." The Armstrong Stare. "I was not Roddy's first lover any more than I expect to be his last. I'm faithful in my fashion and understand it's his fashion to be unfaithful. At my age, I'm thankful for young favors. All I ever ask and pray is that he be as careful as I have been all my life."

"How do you keep people from knowing?"

"Discretion. A life of discretion." The Armstrong Sigh. "I also taught Roddy. I'm his acting coach, as I have become in my . . ."—a contemplative pause—"my mature years for many fine, young, talented actors. I insist Melba Donaldson, his mother, cast all of my movies; it's a deal-breaker in the standard rider to my contracts. There are ways, you see. As limitless as the imagination—and the need to keep secrets in an evil town that thrives on revelation."

"Mr. Armstrong, lately a lot of discreet people have been all over the pages of the *Trail Blazer.*"

The Armstrong Sneer. "Not fit to line my garbage pail. You mentioned that crass, filthy rag to Roddy, didn't you? When he called, I heard his pulse beating like a Hitchcock drum. He fears our secret is out."

"No. The editor, Henry Bouchey, is a friend of mine." Armstrong's eyes sought refuge. He shook his lower jaw back and forth. "I didn't say one word to him, except to wonder if Henry had ever heard any noise about Roddy, and he had not. He took serious offense at the suggestion. He was prepared to have me read every one of his files just to make the point."

Armstrong drew back into the role of Brian Armstrong. "You

would not have found me there, either, in Henry Bouchey's files."

"Discretion."

"Yes. Sometimes, the Bank of America."

"Are you saying Henry Bouchey can be bought?"

"Mr. Gulliver, the filth-monger is your friend, not mine. Not by any stretch of the imagination."

Armstrong gave me a cold look and his face the rest of the lines. I saw there was no sense pressing him for more of an answer than that. Besides, I wasn't here to inquire about Henry.

I said, "You inferred Roddy has other lovers."

"Yes."

"Nicky Edmunds?"

"No."

"You're that certain."

"I'm that certain."

"Does Nicky Edmunds know about Roddy's . . . predilection?"

"Roddy says not. I believe him. He would have no cause to lie to me."

"Women?"

"No. And if you can't believe Roddy about that, believe me."

"Why should I, Mr. Armstrong?"

He stepped away from the mantel and leaned over me with his hands on his hips, his breath close enough to taste. His eyes disappeared inside two slits. "Because. I. Say. So." He waited for my eyes to absorb every word, then crossed to an antique Welsh burl walnut dresser he used as a service bar and poured himself a jigger of Pinch. He tossed it down. "Sure you won't have something, Mr. Gulliver?"

"Thanks, no." I stood to stretch and did knee bends while Armstrong composed himself over a second shot and put the bottle back on the shelf, careful about the label facing out, like all the other labels. I moved to his spot at the mantel and said, "The last time Roddy was seen out in public was a week ago, last Monday night. Nicky Edmunds saw him leaving the Roxy with three young ladies. Two of them were the same ones who were found dead of a drug overdose in Roddy's apartment two nights later, on Wednesday night."

"I do keep my subscription to the *Times* current, Mr. Gulliver." Armstrong read the line so I couldn't miss the insult. I reluctantly said goodbye to whatever gains I'd achieved over the last thirty minutes. He returned and arranged himself in an antique French wing chair opposite the panel back, where another key light put an upside-down pyramid under his right eye.

I said, "How do you explain the girls?"

"I don't. I don't believe it, either. I've told you. Roddy does not use women. Nor does he use drugs."

"Ever?"

"Never. As long as I've known him. Next question."

"Nobody, including Roddy, can account for the missing hours, between the time he left the Roxy last Monday night and the . . . Wednesday night, when the condo manager and I found Roddy near death in his bedroom."

"I can't help you there, either." He rose. His face went through a thousand changes. Out of the light he showed his age and I saw more truth than he could know. He said, "I forgot to thank you for saving Roddy's life."

"Not necessary."

"Damn necessary. Let me put it this way for you, Mr. Gulliver. I don't like burglars in my life, especially when I must open the window myself, be a willing accomplice. We would not be together now, you and I, talking this way, were it anybody else but Roddy who rang me up. You see, I love the boy.

"I do. I want you to help him."

"I'm trying."

"God bless you, Mr. Gulliver."

He wheeled around anxious I not see him crying.

Brian Armstrong.

The hero of my youth.

Chapter 21

Fired, me?

That's what it said in the lawyer's registered letter that security had signed for and slipped under my door. I spotted it in the middle of a memory battle, swashbuckling in my mind to regain the important piece of my childhood kingdom Brian Armstrong had stolen from me in the last hour. It said:

> *Dear Mr. Gulliver:*
> *At the direction of your employer, our client, we write to advise you that your column, "On the Go," and all related editorial services you presently are contracted to provide to* The Daily *are terminated as of this date, based on your clear and wanton disregard of direction from your superior, Mr. Chester A. Wilkins, in violation of your contractual and professional obligations, as described in detail to management by Mr. Wilkins . . .*

I didn't have to read further. Chet Wilkins hadn't wasted any time. I crumpled the triple-ply custom watermarked bond stationery into a tight ball and tossed it into the round file. Two points.

What now? Tell me, dear D'Artagnan, I asked, do the French have a word for what I'm thinking? Of course, the French do, or they'd have invented one rather than allow their heavy-breathing nationalism to surrender to the English. Shit! A word for all nations. *Mercí, M. D'Artagnan.* Was it worth it, Neil, the column about Hope Danbury in a straight trade for your job? Damn right. In any language.

Would I catch on somewhere else, at the *Times,* maybe? For the moment it didn't matter as much as the story I was chasing.

The intercom buzzer short-circuited my intention of getting on the horn and calling Wilkins to tell him what I thought of his cheap trick.

"Bernie Flame here." The slightly nasal voice of a New Yorker. "Juliet Marriner's boyfriend come to shmooze. I think you already know why, Neil."

I was in no mood for company, but I buzzed him through.

Two minutes after hugging me at the door like I was a long-lost favorite cousin, Bernie Flame was wandering the walls, looking, studying, touching, fondling; putting a new spin on the word *shmooze,* making ours a soliloquy of questions and answers.

Bernie asked the questions. Bernie answered the questions.

He said, "You didn't mind me calling you 'Neil,' do you, Neil? I never been one to rest on formality. I'm Bernard, like in St. Bernard. Was named after my pop's favorite dog. Bernie to anybody knows me and all the regulars at Figaro's, where I hustle tables between acting gigs, which is to say most of the time."

I told him "Neil" would be fine, but he wasn't listening. He was racing his fingers across the rows of books on the bracketed shelves and calling out titles he approved.

Except for his age, Bernie Flame was every guy Juliet ever fell for; better looking than most of them. He was of average height and weight, dressed in the kind of suit actors save for important auditions, a mini-herringbone pattern of tasty browns that flattered his tan. His dress shirt picked up the color and showed off his tie, dignified swirls on taupe silk. Bally loafers with a kiltie tassel completed the look. Layers of Polo clogged the air.

Bernie's head was oval-shaped and gave the impression of

being too large for his body. His features didn't work individually, but came together to create a strong presence. Except for small protruding ears, I was reminded of Michelangelo's *David.* A classic nose. Perfect kisser's lips. Riveting eyes that fixed on you like lasers. When he smiled, which was most of the time, quotation marks formed at either side of his mouth, revealing small teeth filed ruler straight. He carried a sense of laughter that enhanced the serious presence it served.

"Do you know how old I am, Neil?" Bernie restored a Ken Follett to its place on the bookshelf and moved to the picture wall on the other side of the door leading into the bedroom. "I'm thirty-four. You know how old Juliet is? Forty-six her last birthday. Okay. So what's the big deal? I'll tell you what's the big deal. It ain't the dozen years, Neil. That's chicken soup in the greater scheme of things. If The Jewel was thirty-four and me forty-six, Her Royal Pain in the Ass Daughter wouldn't be trooping around trying to break us up. The rule seems to be, *The guy is older? Fine. The girl is older? She is a whacko and he is a weirdo.* Nice picture. That you with the Pope?"

"When he visited L.A. a couple years ago."

"Uh-huh. Looks just like you. This one, too, with The Jewel and her kid. Same big jugs. You had more hair. You do something the way you brush, it would look thicker than it looks. See how I handle the problem?" He aimed the top of his head at me, clamped his thumbs onto his temples, and used his index fingers to push hard on the pompadour rising five inches above his cranium. The pompadour slid backward off his scalp like snow on a mountain and fell behind his head, revealing Bernie's true hairline on a ridge between his ears. The top of his head became a web of gauze. His hair hung from the ridge like a steel helmet.

"You let it grow back there like Rapunzel and then it's all in the way you apply the comb and the brush," he said. "Remind me before I leave. I'll give you the number of my guy, Little

Enrique. Miracle worker to the trade. Did I tell you I'm an actor? I'm an actor."

If he was acting now, trying to win me over, his plan was working.

There was something instantly appealing about the guy and knowing Juliet as well as I did, I understood her attraction.

"You still married in that picture, huh, Neil? I can tell it by the way you got your fingers dug into her waist. Like you never wanted her an inch away from your sight. You are a possessive dude. I know that from The Jewel. She is one wise woman, The Jewel. You think it's only because she's hot I like her. Wrong, my man." He had pulled his hair back into place and was working on the shape.

"When that was taken, Stevie and I were married in name only. We were already running into problems."

Discussing my life with a total stranger?

I cut it off there.

Bernie said, "I know whatchew mean. The Jewel and I ran into one of them old problems of yours a few nights ago, doing dinner at Nicky Blair's." His eyebrows arched. "The bar deep in class ass, like Show Biz was having itself a special bargain sale before Thanksgiving. So, this Romeo, one real Creep City, has some plastic nose dinner hooker in tow and wearing a hard-on where his heart should be. If that's the kind what Stevie thinks is a quality act, I got investment property homes in Bed-Stuy I wanna show her."

"Claes Shattuck."

"Like in Santa Claus?" I didn't realize I had said the bastard's name aloud. Bernie shrugged. "The Jewel told me, but I don't remember. She said it was a name to forget, so I did. Immediately." He snapped his fingers. "She knows these things. She likes you a lot, Juliet, you know? So I come on over knowing I was gonna like you a lot. You seem like a decent dude, even if you gotta do something about your hair."

Bernie couldn't settle down. He would try a chair, like he was testing it, and after a minute be up again. "Fact is, The Jewel got to waiting for your call. Still waiting, only I got tired of seeing her all concerned over the phone not ringing, so I finally said, *Moth, give me your friend Neil's address and I'll go on over and see what gives.* Okay. So she says on back to me, *Flame, relax-ay-vouz. Neil will call me when it's right.*" He acted both parts. "We came close as we ever come to raising our voices. Nothing personal, Neil. I know it ain't your fault. It's strictly because of your ex, her kid, calling and hocking The Jewel six, seven times a day." Acting again. "*Mama, Neil's called you yet? Mama, Neil's called you yet?* Like she's applying for an 800 number for the credit card people, you understand me? I said, *Moth, enough is enough.* Okay. She says, *Call first and see.* I don't talk to machines. You come home to hang-ups? That's me. I lost count on how many times. To make a long story short, here I am, Neil. She wanted to come, The Jewel, only I told her I wanted it to be just me, especially if I was right about what was going down."

"The week, the weekend got away from me, Bernie, and today's not much better. I'm tied—"

Bernie cut the air in front of him with a finger. "Neil, I said already I know it ain't your fault. Stevie, from what she said to her mother to make The Jewel shudder over you calling, Stevie was expecting you to help bust us up. That was it, right?"

"Don't blame her without knowing the history, Bernie. Stevie has seen her mother through a lot of bad encounters." He nodded as if he knew that part. "So have I. I wouldn't want to begin counting."

"Don't add me in, Neil."

I held him off. "Not accusing, so please let me finish . . . It's at a point where Stevie is certain Juliet drops her bloomers on automatic pilot whenever she's close enough to sniff aftershave. I could tell you some real horror stories."

"All she was smelling on me the night we met was good old-fashioned B.O." he said defensively, staring at me so hard I thought I felt the sizzle coming out the back of my skull. His smile neutralized any resentment he was feeling.

"Stevie wanted me to talk Juliet out of seeing you, especially so soon after—well, let's just say it didn't work out with a second-rate musician Juliet discovered at a cowboy bar in the valley."

"Palomino. I seen it in some Eastwood movies, and I also know the whole story. Anyone treats a decent woman the way he treated The Jewel gets a taste of these." Bernie raised his fists alongside his face and shook his knuckles at me. "The guy ever crosses my eyes, I don't wait for no permission to start dotting his teeth."

"You don't have to convince me, Bernie."

"I could tell the second I seen you, but I want you to hear my story anyway, Neil. Because you know you're gonna be getting more static from the Ex-as-in-Hex after today, and I want Miss Stephanie Big Time Star Marriner to understand she got more chances of smelling farts in a tornado than she does of coming between the Moth and her Flame."

Attracted by the Dazzle pattern doing tricks on the computer screen, he sat down and divided his attention between the evolving designs and me, ear resting on knuckles, absent-mindedly using the back of an index finger to stroke the keyboard while he spoke, like Chico Marx shooting the keys on a piano in all the Marx Brothers movies.

"So, I'm playing Polo in Mike Gazzo's *A Hatful of Rain,* you know the show? The part made a star of Tony Franciosa, only he was Anthony then. Gazzo? Also an actor, who aced himself in the bathtub in *Godfather* deuce. I get notices in *DramaLogue* to *kvell* over, Neil. I am the gravy too good for this meatloaf.

"One Saturday night, I'm stepping out of the toilet that doubles as a dressing room in the bigger Equity-waiver toilet that doubles as the Sunset Players Playhouse. There's this old dish holding up the wall opposite. Lean, mean cuisine. Aiming her eyes and her thighs at me like the whole planet is at stake. She announces, *Bernie Flame, I used to be crazy for Anthony Franciosa, and I ain't never been knocked out since until I just saw you tonight.*"

"Juliet."

"Juliet. And it's mutual. One look and it's over for me. Whammo! Go explain. We been inseparable ever since, like the sun from the sky, me and her, going on two months and heading into forever." He read my expression correctly. "Yeah, baby, we got the knot in mind, so I also suppose it's time to start perusing your column regular, seeing as how we are about to be related by a former marriage."

"Does Stevie know that part?"

"Not yet, but I'm thinking of asking her to be my best man." He flashed a smile. "A reason I pushed to barge in today. Comes the weekend, me and Juliet figure to burn rubber to Vegas. Still a secret, so—" He moved his finger from the keyboard and pressed it upright to his lips. "The Moth wants the minister who sings the ceremony like Elvis. Okay by me, as long as he don't mind wearing a yarmulke for the wedding photo, so my family, it won't go bananas."

While I wrestled with the news, Bernie wheeled the desk chair around and clickety-clacked Dazzle off the screen. "You got some fine quality gear here, Neil." Clickety-clack. Clickety-clack. Clickety-clack. His fingers hit the keys like a whirlwind. Concentrating, I can do a hundred words a minute. He was faster. "WordStar. WordPerfect. Word. Speak all the languages. No percentage in losing a temp gig 'cause of being locked into one program only." Clickety-clack. Clickety-clack. Clickety-clack. "Uh-huh. Uh-huh. You got yourself a good program I could beef up for you with modifications, you say the word. Like here's your Solitaire. A little Bernie Flame special magic and you'll never lose." Clickety-clack. Clickety-clack. "I see you're plugged into a pretty sophisticated network."

"My paper. Nonstop service downtown."

Clickety-clack. Clickety-clack. "You got a directory looks like the Whole Earth phone book. You turn out them files the way a turd turns out flies, you should excuse the expression. Hey, some pretty good stuff here, Neil."

"You're reading my files?"

Clickety—

Bernie reached for the ceiling with both hands.

"Just some more code-busting. Sorry. Bad habit I got into. Misdemeanor hacking, never any big stuff like the law keeps busting nerds over, which I can do, of course. IBM. AT&T. The FBI. The Pentagon. All for the grabbing. The trick ain't limited to eight-year-olds, but—hey, hey! What's this? Neil, you aware you been padlocked out of everywhere else at the newspaper?" Clickety-clack. Clickety-clack. Clickety-clack. "Leave us just see about that."

Bernie resumed clickety-clacking, cursed steadily under his breath, until he let out a whoop. "So much for state secrets," he said. He stopped typing, leaned into the screen, and in a moment began laughing. He wheeled around to face me. "Neil, I ain't the only one got a Hound Dog from Hell on his heinie." He stood and, with a theatrical bow, offered me the chair, wandered away in a trail of chuckles to explore other parts of the room.

I found myself exploring Chet Wilkins's personal files, above all a long-term series of confidential emails to the front office that revealed he'd been working aggressively for months to get me canned. My Hope Danbury column had permitted him to accelerate his timetable, as much or more as a series of stern emails addressed to me but never received, not by me anyway, although I'm certain all the front office copies reached their target.

Instead of getting angry, I sense the illicit thrill that always comes from poking around someone's deepest, darkest secrets. I relished the discoveries Chet's file brought, like a junkie thirsting for the needle. I felt embellished respect for my M.E. and for the precision of his strategies.

For me, too, knowing I would not have handled the Roddy Donaldson business any other way. Already there are too many people out there who bend to the slightest pressure and quit what they believe in. How simple to become one. How impossible to be one. For me, anyway. Does that make me a better person? Hardly. *Hardly, my dear Morveau, for I shall always side with the people.*

Bernie was leaning against the kitchen doorjamb, one foot crossed over the other, a baseball grip on the Heineken he had helped himself to, a smart-ass grin glued up one side of his face. That's when I remembered the blue floppy I had picked up in Aleta Haworth's apartment. I retrieved the floppy from the pencil drawer and held it high for him to see.

"Bernie, how good are you?"

He cranked his neck back and sighted me over his nose. "How good do I gotta be?" He put down the beer bottle. He removed his suit jacket, folded it carefully, and draped it over the back of an armchair. He loosened the knot on his silk tie, rolled back his shirt sleeves, rubbed his hands together, and said, "Tell Uncle Bernie what ails ya."

I brought Bernie another Heineken, his fourth in an hour, and looked over his shoulder while he switched between the two horizontal halves of the split screen he'd created on the monitor. He muttered a thank you without dislodging his stare from the multiple rows of curious white symbols and hieroglyphics moving up, down, and out of view at the base of the screen.

He added, subtracted, restored, and made changes that might mean something to another programmer.

No matter what tricks of the hacker trade he tried, the upper half of the screen stayed an empty blue rectangle.

Clickety-clack. Clickety-clack. Clickety-clack.

Waiting for something to happen, Bernie drew deeply from the Heineken bottle and used a finger to wipe away the fresh rim of sweat that had formed on his upper lip.

Clickety-clack. Clickety-clack. Clickety-clack.

There was no point hovering over Bernie as his frustration increased. I used the time to make phone calls, do paperwork, and straighten up the apartment. After another hour, thinking about getting ready soon for the drive to the valley and dinner with Jayne, I suggested he quit.

Bernie wouldn't hear of it. He was determined to bust through the protective shield that kept us from executing any of the files on the floppy. It had become a point of honor. Also a point of concern. He didn't want to chance me reporting to his Moth that her Flame had a mouth that ran ahead of his mind.

I was checking out the bookshelves again, making certain all the spines ran an even two inches from the edge, when Bernie produced a loud musical sound.

He stood up, shook his fists like Rocky, and turned looking for me, his expression a portrait in triumph.

From this angle across the room, I saw a carnival of flashing colors and movement on the top half of the monitor. I headed over.

Bernie settled back in the chair.

He poked a key at random and the screen became whole again.

He said, "Holy Moses, Jesus and Allah!"

Chapter 22

I am no novice when it comes to porn.

The crime beat was an education into the bargain basement of life. I thought I'd seen it all there, live and in person, on film and on tape, the best and the worst, and, too often, worse than that. Stuff that makes you want to puke. Stuff that makes you want to talk serious death for the parties responsible.

I was wrong.

Here on the monitor was the future of porn, a preview of coming attractions; the blue screen turned bluer with a new kind of intimacy. For passive voyeurs or aggressive participation. The computer as sex partner. Fucking technology.

Bernie said, "Okay. Watch now, Neil."

The girl on the screen was entertaining a pair of animals, one of them disguised as a human being. Moaning and groaning her satisfaction. Begging for more. Giving explicit direction and encouragement. Full-picture, shadowbox format delivering scenes as sharp and as well defined as any major studio production. Living color. Stereo sound as good as the relays to my system allowed.

Ponk.

Back to the standard rectangular screen.

Same girl.

Fourteen or fifteen years old. Demure. Dressed for class. Skirt and blouse, the blouse hanging loose, hiding the grown-up body underneath. Brown hair bordering on auburn that once hung in cords of sweat now forming a soft basket of curls, framing a cherubic, freckled face. Cherry blossom cheeks. Chemical glaze now gone from innocent eyes paired to a bluebird voice.

Ponk.

The girl and her collie.

Ponk.

Schoolgirl again, in close-up, telling me about herself and her plans for a career, ". . . a model first or, if I might be blessed by good fortune, a co-star or recurring regular on a hit TV series." Camera on the move, finding ways to keep the scene alive in counterpoint to her anxious drone. ". . . get good grades and study hard, so someday I—"

Clickety-clack.

Ponk.

Another girl. A few years older. Maybe not. Naked on a bed. Her hands caressing her body. Encouraging me to touch her, telling me where. Staring hard into the lens; eyes sending out crystal signals of erotic promise. Stroke gently between her thighs. *Please?* Close-up between her thighs. Her voice imploring: *Now? Please? Promise it won't bite.* Freeze.

Bernie tilted his head to check my reaction, moved on the girl's invitation.

The screen exploded into an orgasm of color.

Her screams of passion mixed with the rocket's red glare, bombs bursting in air.

Fade to blue.

The girl again, with new instructions.

Clickety-clack.

Ponk.

The girl again. She could be a secretary in somebody's insurance office. ". . . and wanted to be a movie star from the time I was a little girl."

I said, "Interactive video?"

Bernie said, "Like I never seen before."

Like I never seen before.

I'd had the same thought. It wasn't that long ago. Where? I juggled my memory, but kept getting thrown off by the images on the screen.

"They got out software now comes close," Bernie said. "Mostly mail-order. Picks up where the computer games leave off. One-ups the hard core in your neighborhood video store. This doo-doo, far beyond any of that."

He ponked the secretary back onto the bed. Raised on her elbows. Her pink tongue doing a slow lube to her lips. Knees aimed at opposite walls. Close view of modest, firm breasts. Scented voice begging one of us to touch her nipples. Either nipple. Both of them erect. Tubular. Gently. *Please?* Ponk. "Like Kathleen Turner, one of my idols, and I have been studying my craft at a school in the valley, where . . ."

Bernie said, "You ring up the right bulletin boards, anywhere in the country, you can get sleaze for the price of a download, you know?"

"I'm aware."

Like I never seen before.

Clickety-clack. Clickety-clack.

Ponk.

"GIF stills. Animated loops from movie porn. People like you and me showing off for people they're never going to meet on the other side of the monitor." Ponk. "Kinkier and screwier than you and me, Neil. This is something else again."

Clickety-clack. Clickety-clack.

Ponk. Ponk.

Clickety-clack. Clickety-clack.

Ponk. Ponk.

Clickety—

"Hold it, Bernie."

"Yeah? What?"

"Go back. Back up."

"Find one to your taste, huh? . . . Jesus, gimme a break, Neil. Kidding. Only kidding."

"No, the one before that one . . . Hold it. Right there."

I had only caught a flash of close-up, but in that brief instant I thought I recognized the woman. It was hard to tell now. Her features were distorted by the cock the naked man in the leather mask had stuffed inside her face. To a wide shot on the shadowbox screen. The woman on all fours, contoured breasts hanging milk-cow heavy. Also taking it from behind from a second lone ranger.

I reached around Bernie and hit the ponk key.

Scenes familiar to me:

The woman in her mid-twenties, who looked like Julia Roberts. A generous close-up on *Murder, She Wrote.* Singing. Soft shoe. An empty stage. A form-fitting white slip. A lousy take on "Maggie the Cat."

TalenTapes. Produced for BBStardom.

BBStardom. Like nothing I had ever seen before.

Like I had never seen before.

"Laraine Dailey," I said, unaware my thought had translated into her name.

"Yeah? Tell me about it."

"I've seen it before, Bernie."

The future, Neil, the future, Eugene Coburn had said.

Two minutes later I recognized two other faces on the monitor.

One belonged to the girl I knew as "Janie Doe."

The other one—

The girl with her was Hope Danbury.

I got sick to my stomach.

★ ★ ★ ★ ★

Bernie stuck with Heineken, but it took a double bromo to settle my stomach and a double Scotch rocks to settle my nerves. When my legs again felt connected to the rest of me, I headed for the bedroom to find the engraved business card Gene Coburn has pressed upon me before I left Stardom House last week.

Coburn had been adamant about my accepting guest privileges on BBStardom, not as any form of payoff for a column, he assured me, sounding like I was incorruptible and the membership was worth its weight in diversion. I'd taken the card to shut him up, never intending to use it. I found it in the jacket I'd worn that day.

Coburn had given me an access number and the code name "Lilliputian," carefully printing them on the back of his business card in a small, precise hand.

Bernie piloted us in.

Animated curtains parted and the BBStardom logo emerged in Cinemascope to a full orchestral accompaniment. He gee-whizzed through the various departments listed in the directory, then went hunting for a trap door, the same way he had gained entry earlier to the *Daily* mainframe. We spent a few minutes playing peek-a-boo with private messages and reading horny references to hopefuls pictured in *Stardom* magazine or on TalenTapes available for play in the BBStardom library, but that was as tawdry as it got.

Bernie's language grew coarser whenever the keyboard refused to obey him and especially because he couldn't locate TalenTapes for Hope Danbury or Laraine Dailey. Close to five thousand actors were categorized by type, like the Motion Picture Academy Players Director, but there were no names. Everyone was identified by reference numbers keyed to numbers alongside photos published in *Stardom.*

Bernie made random choices. Histories and credits recited. Cuts from flickers of opportunity on TV and movie screens. Scenes the way Laraine Dailey had performed her scene from *Cat on a Hot Tin Roof.* Nothing he tried got us the shadowboxed sex we had viewed on the blue floppy.

"Maybe it's not there to find, Bernie."

He scowled. "Only that I ain't found it yet," he said, and began some new game inside the BBStardom system. "Whoever he is put this thing in gear, he knows his high tech."

"I met him. His name is Knox Lundigan."

Bernie thought about it. "Yeah. I seen the name. Got a reputation you could choke a horse with. Up there with guys like Jobs and Norton. Lots of the software people use him as a consultant." He nodded knowingly. "Explains a lot. Tells me more'n we been finding here, Neil."

"Meaning what?"

"Meaning anything. Look, follow what I'm doing here. They went and gave you a Level Seven clearance. That's what every subscriber has. But there's also a Level Eight. That's for people cleared for more other business . . . See here? Like so. If I wasn't here, you never would've known it existed, but it's SOP for bulletin boards nowhere close to being so sophisticated as we got here. Okay. There's a Level Nine for the sysop who runs the board, and maybe he lets sysops around the country log in, who are likewise doing him the same favor. Left hand helps the right hand. With a guy like Knox Lundigan at the stick, could be a million-trillion levels around, easy."

Bernie finished the Heineken, replaced the bottle, and rubbed his fingers over his mouth. I pointed to the empty and he shook his head. "Getting to be that time. The Jewel awaits without. Without me. I wanna be sober for the plunge." He rose and fished his cuff links from a pocket before rolling down his sleeves. "Think Einstein when you think Knox Lundigan. What

I know, this guy is capable of rigging any board into the next dimension. I have to figure he done some of it here and what we been looking for is there. Only we are *here* and we don't know where *there* is."

Clickety-clack. Clickety-clack.

Ponk.

"See that, Neil? A lot of shinola. Enough shinola to tell me right off there's at least a Level Ten on this board I ain't been able to crack. I was too embarrassed to say it before I knew about Knox Lundigan figuring in this. I didn't want to go leaving you behind with the impression Dr. Bernie can't deliver good as he advertises."

I dismissed his concerns and said, "How do we find *there*?"

Bernie fixed his tie and went after his jacket, screwing one arm and then the other inside before tugging at the fit. "We'd have to go *where*, where there's a there, as close to the mainframe as possible and then—" He drilled me with his eyes while playing with his hair.

"And then?"

He moved his hands away from his head and began playing his fingers over an invisible keyboard. "And then we would hack some more," he said.

Chapter 23

"Dinner like my mammy used to make," Jayne announced as I winged through the door with my vintage wine, roses, and praise for the enticing aromas emanating from the kitchen. In an instant, they paled next to her scent.

She let me study her, modeling with the grace of a ballerina. Her eyes flashed back the excitement she saw in mine and challenged me to do something about it.

Her satin evening dress moved with her body as she deposited the bottle and the bouquet on the nearest table. A choker of matched pearls climbed her neck, curtained on one side by a single wave of hair and offset on the other by a single pearl earring the size of a seedless grape.

She closed in on my breath and said, "Dinner won't be ready for another hour." She put a finger over my lips. "I'm ready now."

I followed her upstairs to the balcony.

We attacked one another in a frenzy of mutual need, a wild, clawing, inarticulate, creative passion that left us both in a state of breathless paralysis, a naked tangle of hot body parts on the cold Spanish tile, bathed in the full moon of a warm, windswept, cobalt blue sky and serenaded by the monotonous hum of a police chopper's rotary blades. She waved at the whirly and rolled away onto her back, to give the cops a better view of her breasts.

I said something about exhibitionism.

"I'm proud of who I am and what I am and who I'm with," Jayne said. "How about you?"

How about me? Charging over the 405 I had asked myself the same question and come to no satisfactory conclusions, a victim of my usual contradictions. I'd fallen hard for Jayne, but I didn't know if I could let somebody new inside my life. With Stevie still there, it would be unfair to Jayne, to me, to—

"I asked, how about you, Scaredy-cat?" She leaned over and pinched me. I yowled. She laughed her communicable laugh. I turned on one side, facing her, and rested a cheek on one hand. I cupped myself with the other. "Stevie always makes it sound like she tells you everything, so you must already know the answer."

Jayne sat up abruptly and crossed her legs like a kid at a campfire. "You are not getting off that easy, buster. Stevie tells me what she wants me to hear, except what I want to hear now, I want to hear from you. I want to hear about you. Who are you, Neil? Who do you think you are? Not who Stevie makes you out to be, or my own cockeyed perception. Let's you and me finish what Stevie started. Convince me I am not setting into another fast food and fuck situation. I've flopped with that franchise a few times already. God, I pray, show me this time it's ala carte and elegant."

She was trying to get me to answer her uncertainties and here I was plagued as usual by my own. I didn't know if I'd be able to break the news to her that I'd been fired and there was no column about *Stardom* magazine, and she was lobbying for the kinds of truth three shrinks had been unable to blast loose from me.

"I'm not very good at talking about myself, Jayne. If I'd been better, maybe Stevie and I would still be together. Stevie left. Neil fell apart. He picked up the pieces after a few years, except for a lot of months that rolled under a rug or accidentally got tossed out with the garbage."

"Let's go looking together."

"It's been tried."

"Never with me. If you are not a serial killer, there's hope for us. Can I get you to agree on that?" The tinge of Deep South in her voice became more evident, maybe inspired by the smell of homemade southern fried chicken floating upstairs. The Farberware on the six-burner was full of fresh veggies simmering over low flames. Cauliflower and broccoli. Squash and green beans. Hot muffins in the oven. "Neil, come back, Neil. I just asked you a question." Jayne had caught me trying to hide inside my mind. I took her generous look as understanding. "Make a difference if I show you mine before you show me yours?" I shook my head. "Well, you can't fault a girl for trying."

"You can tell me one thing."

Jayne grinned and rolled her eyes at the ceiling. "I promise there are no other guys hidden in my closets."

"The oil painting in the bedroom. Where does that guy hang out?"

"Only in the painting."

I owed her one. "I think you're wonderful."

"Don't leap before you look," she said, and announced dinner.

We sat naked at the table, the two of us caught up in the intensity of our separate emotions. We talked around it. I gave her small, inconsequential clues to show I cared. I suppose Jayne was doing the same with me, but she was on guard. We remained like that until one of us thought to mention Aleta Haworth.

Aleta had been forgotten until now.

Her name came between us like blessed relief.

I told Jayne about the service for Hope Danbury and its

aftermath, only as far as the wreckage I found at the apartment, careful to avoid getting into any conversation about the blue floppy or what Bernie Flame and I had discovered. Jayne was too close to Coburn. I didn't want to put her in the middle of something, risk anything getting back to him until I knew more.

Jayne thought about what I'd told her. She nodded to some unspoken consideration. She drew back and placed her hands on the dinner table palms down, announcing: "Let's try it again tomorrow. Noon. Meet me at Maxie's recording studio on Magnolia in North Hollywood. Aleta will be there, and the other Hot to Trots. Esther Rae and Darlesque. The rhythm section. We head from there straight to Potomac Junior High for one of the special anti-drug assemblies Maxie has been doing for the LAPD."

"What's that about?"

"Life isn't one giant publicity stunt, fella. You ever hear of public service?"

"Followed by *Entertainment Tonight* and tape at eleven."

"Not on these D.A.R.E. personals. Maxie's in it for the cause, a true believer. One of his brothers died from an overdose of bad shit he got as a gift at his thirteenth birthday party. Another, Morris, is doing bend-over time for dealing. His sister Dionne disappeared on smack, and last the family knew she was doing the streets in San Pete, someplace like that." She emptied the last of the wine. "Dionne had the best voice of all . . . until it went to her arm."

"D.A.R.E. assemblies. Not my image of Maxie Trotter," I said, answering her toast. "I picture Maxie dirty dancing with a leopard on a leash or chewing on a blonde Amazon's elbow."

"We all have a public image to protect."

We fell into silence somewhere between clearing the dishes and Jayne's fresh-made appleberry pecan pie to go with fresh-brewed mocha coffee, as if we had to push the rest of the world aside to hear lyrics Sinatra was interpreting only for us.

She kept staring at me, working her intense hazel eyes like semaphores. I was sure she knew the soul behind her spirit had trapped me. Hogtied and hung me to howl. I didn't mind. Her voice snapped me out of my impulse to tell her a secret. Something. Anything.

"One more for the road, Scaredy-cat?"

I held up the empty bottle. "There's another on ice in the fridge. I'll get it."

"Not what I meant." Her insinuating laughter was irresistible. I leaned forward and poked the cleft in her chin. Touching her was a mistake. She clamped onto my hand with both of hers and held it tightly. Said in a voice brimming with emotion, "It wasn't supposed to be this way, Scaredy-cat?"

I thought I understood, and told her so.

The only green Mustang I spotted after leaving Jayne in the early morning hours was in my dreams. I'd tried convincing her to let me stay the night, but like the last time she insisted on waking up in the morning with a bad disposition she could call her own.

When the phone rang, it was her, calling from Maxie Trotter's studio.

Ten-thirty; too early to tell me I was tardy.

We traded battle wounds before she reported on Aleta:

"A message from her was waiting for Maxie at the switchboard, telling him she was delayed by personal problems, but not to worry. She said she'll catch up with everybody at Potomac Junior High. I called to save you the trip out here." She gave me directions to the school. "Park in the faculty lot. You'll see our limos there. Gangbangers own the streets, so I wouldn't want to come out afterward to four bare axles. Or worse."

"I don't know how I ever managed without you."

Laughter. "Me, too."

Chapter 24

I turned south on Venice and made another right turn a block later, onto Bronson, immediately spotting the parking lot on the corner of Seventeenth and a dime bag deal going down across from the entrance to the junior high, a black kid, thirteen or fourteen, counting out the coins as he dropped them into the palm of a jive-hipped dealer, maybe the same age, who was nervously checking over his shoulders and trying to keep up with the math at the same time. It was almost one o'clock.

A blue sound truck from Studio Instrument Rentals and three white stretch limos in a row obscured the posted No Parking signs on a building about twenty yards from where I pulled in. A couple squad cars were parked across from them. I heard a musical honk, and Jayne emerged from the limo nearest a sliding metal door that was the backstage entrance to the auditorium.

She seemed almost demure in a smartly tailored business suit perfect for classroom use by teachers living on a fixed inheritance. No makeup, except for a dab or two of blush, simple earrings, and a sterling silver lapel pin shaped like a Siamese cat. Hair pulled back and raining down her neck. A shoulder strap purse, Vuitton, as genuine as her smile.

We embraced and she gave me a diplomatic peck on the lips, quickly wiping away any telltale signs. She poked at my sports jacket. "Forgot to tell you not to wear black. It's a gang color. If you get shot I'll never forgive myself."

"If I can survive your Revenge of the Hickies, I can survive anything."

She feigned astonishment. "I don't remember hearing any complaints last night." She twirled me around and herded me toward the stage entrance. "Aleta got here about ten minutes before you. They're all locked in a prayer meeting now. Another of Maxie's rituals. He's a Born Again. Hardly any time before the show, so you won't be able to speak to her until after."

"Does Aleta know?"

"I reckoned it was best to make this a surprise."

"Good reckoning." I stopped to check out the parking lot, scanning for the spiffy black 560 I'd figured Aleta had used for her getaway from Pearl Danbury's apartment. The lot was full of economy cars, mostly Japanese, and a smattering of aging BMWs. The only Mercedes I saw was an early-model four-door, Fairfax cocoa and desperately in need of a paint job. "You see her arrive?"

"Not until Aleta raced past me and downstairs to the dressing rooms. Converted storage rooms, actually, one for the superstar and one for everybody else. I was going over last minutes on Maxie's intro with Sgt. Lewis, the D.A.R.E. program officer in the district. He says he knows you."

"Tommy Lewis?"

"J.T. Lewis. Everybody calls him J.T."

"He knows me."

"He says you saved his life once."

"Some things you never live down."

The door slid open to Jayne's knock. Immediately, she excused herself to answer a flagging hand signal from Maxie Trotter's manager, Roscoe Del Ruth. I remembered him from the Palladium. I watched her walk away and into an animated conversation with Del Ruth, then searched out Tommy Lewis, past some giggling girls who'd somehow managed to get backstage with cameras and autograph books and were huddled in near-hysterics by a cement stairway leading down to the storage rooms. Tommy was sitting on a folding chair by the painted brick back wall of the narrow lane behind the rear drop curtains, parted enough to allow a clear view of the stage. His eyes were closed, his legs crossed at the ankles, and his lips moving to what I suspected would be his words of wisdom to the student population.

I called, "Hey, nigger."

Tommy's eyes exploded open, angry on automatic until he saw it was me.

He cracked his face into a party of delight. "Fuck you, the same way I fucked yo' mama," he said, loud enough to earn a squeal from the overdeveloped teenager in a tank top and hip-huggers heading for her friends at the stairway.

In a flash Tommy had me in his grip, my arms locked to my sides and my feet three inches off the cement floor. He was barely five-eight, having just qualified when that was the minimum height required for a badge, and constructed like a meat locker, but he moved like a sprinter. "You could use some more hair, Bro, but otherwise you haven't aged since whenever it was."

"Three or four years. You neither, Tommy."

"Then your eyes are going, too, my man."

He set me down, took a couple steps backward, arms outstretched, and put himself on full display. If Jayne hadn't said something, I would have needed the name plate on his breast pocket to know him for sure. Tommy's own hairline had declined to his nape, with just enough five o'clock shadow to tell me he was doing a Kojak. The Fu Manchu 'stache was gone, but not so long ago that the ridge under his broad nose didn't seem a tone lighter than the rest of his caramel skin. Thick horn rims had replaced the wire-rimmed specs he'd once favored, and fifty pounds more than he needed made his jowls hang like Christmas tree ornaments.

"Didn't feel like you're packing," he said. He shook his head and smiled falsely, like he owned rental property. He meant the regulation 9-mm Beretta he'd given me as a thank you the morning he was released from County General, Weitzman's slug still too close to his heart to remove. I took to strapping on the 92-F every day, like tying my laces, until the computer made it unnecessary for me to travel downtown to the plant. I check myself out at the Police Academy range three times a year to keep my sharpshooter's ranking, but now the revolver sits in a Nike box in my bedroom closet.

"My contribution to peace in our time, Tommy."

"Killing the bad guys, Bro, that's peace in our time. Taking back the streets, that's peace in our time. Come spend a little time on this tour with me and you'll be packin' and whackin' and ready to nominate old Charlie Bronson for a Nobel Peace Prize."

"That bad?"

"Put it to you this way, Neil. You bailed out my nigger ass so I could be having eight- and nine-year-olds die in my arms, already too stupid gone on stuff to know it wasn't just nap and teddy bear time."

Tommy took off his glasses, wiped a hand across his eyes and over his head, fiddled the frames back into place. His dark eyes had turned flat, like cartoon dots painted on the lenses. I saw more than burnout and wondered to myself who else might know how close Officer J.T. Lewis was to a breakdown.

The gaggle of girls distracted us with new titters of excitement.

A wall of black muscle and bone had materialized at the top of the stairs, his bulges making his Maxie Trotter t-shirt look like a potato sack. The bodyguard's gold tooth caught the light as he surveyed the area. Nodding approval, he gave some hand signal behind his head and stepped aside.

Maxie stepped onto the landing, either half-dressed or half-naked.

His slender frame was covered by a series of tear holes of various sizes, connected by thin, interwoven strands of black silk. The Cossack's hat added six or seven inches to his height and with his two-inch boot heels stacked him at about five-eight. It also made him look like a chocolate Bart Simpson.

The girls instantly surrounded Maxie. Parts of him disappeared behind the taller ones, except for the crown of the hat. He appeared to enjoy the attention, working slowly over each autograph, pausing only to look up on command, a fraction ahead of the camera flash, his gaze always sending out a love signal.

One at a time, band members carrying their axes and an indifferent attitude slipped around the cluster and headed for the stage. The keyboards and drum kits had been preset, along with the sound.

"Today we're doing D.A.R.E. for eleven hundred students or so," Tommy said. "I go out first and do five on the evils of drugs, all the while praying hard nobody falls face down or pulls a piece on me. Then Maxie does two songs, his rap, which comes down to *Just say no shit,* an encore, then gone. Short and sweet."

My eyes followed the two long-limbed honeys in skimpy matching leotards and Cossack's caps dyed blonde who were moving from the stairway to three standing mikes lined up stage right. One had to be Esther Rae, the other Darlesque. Two-thirds of Maxie Trotter's Hot to Trots. Jayne and Roscoe Del Ruth were by the stage manager's podium, still entrenched in conversation, Del Ruth gesturing wildly, Jayne shaking her head. Where was Aleta? She'd arrived barely ahead of me, Jayne said so—probably was still painting on her costume.

Tommy was saying, "The students are polite, Neil, they listen to me, Officer J.T. makin' sweet like *Sesame Street,* but they pay attention to Maxie, sniffing the dude's words like glue. He is one Homes who makes a genuine difference."

The other side of the curtain, I heard the unmistakable sounds of an audience filing in and getting settled. Tommy looked at his watch and figured it was ten or fifteen minutes to show time, depending on how long the principal spoke. He squeezed my shoulder hard enough to leave a bruise and headed off to check last-minute details.

Maxie Trotter's musicians did a little cranking up.

The Hot to Trots bopped lips and practiced their moves.

Figuring a lot of ground can get covered in ten or fifteen minutes, I headed down the stairway to find Aleta Haworth.

Aleta was in the storage room at the end of a passageway that veered left under the stage, behind a door on which had been taped a handmade sign reading "Show." The sign posted on the door across the way said "Maxie" and was decorated with a border of kiss prints.

It was cold and damp down here. I rubbed my hands and massaged my fingers waiting for Aleta to answer my knocking.

When she didn't respond, I called her name a couple times, then inched open the door on hinges that had been greased recently. The room was wider than it was long. Furniture, props, and rolling racks of dusty costumes had been shoved against a wall to clear more space for Maxie's troupe.

Aleta sat with her back to me, at a makeshift dressing table at the far end.

She was studying her face in the mirror like it belonged to a stranger.

"Aleta?"

No reaction.

Her leotard was pulled up only as far as her waist, the straps hanging over her thighs, as if she couldn't remember what to do next. Her arms, rigid, rested by her sides, palms facing in my direction. I glimpsed her exposed left breast reflecting in the mirror. I averted my eyes and started to apologize for the intrusion.

She exploded: "Just get out of here!" The expression on her face was more troubled than I was worth. I identified myself and got as far as mentioning Mrs. Danbury before she interrupted me again. "I said I want you to get out of this dressing room now. Now." Every word was as deliberate as the hardness in her reflection. She stayed as stiff as a statue.

Something was wrong here.

I knew enough to be frightened for both of us. I took a tentative step forward, my hands extended in a gesture of understanding, trying to pick my words carefully, trying not to notice her breast. I caught a flicker of movement, heard the rustle, saw dust flying from a rack of *Our Town* outfits, heard Aleta shouting something, saw the baseball bat charging at me like I was low and on the inside and the slugger was the Babe himself.

Kraak!

He walloped me in the stomach and I doubled over like a rag doll.

Kraak!

The blow landed against my thigh and jarred my body erect. I stumbled backward through the open door and across the corridor; slammed hard against Maxie's door. Vomit began tripping up my windpipe. The Babe stomped after me, wagging the bat up and down in front of him. Any pain was a memory, but the danger was real and I was helpless to stop it as I slid onto the cement floor.

The Babe stepped closer and raised the bat. My eyes clanged shut anticipating the home run he was about to score on my head. An explosive shriek startled them open again.

Jayne, in the corridor.

Her arms crossed in front of her face.

The Babe moving away from me and advancing toward her.

Me too helpless to do anything but greet the descending darkness.

Chapter 25

Jayne's was the first face I saw when I struggled into the light. Her eyes were unfocused and wet, rimmed with worry, and her mouth in constant, nervous flux, doing tricks to her cheeks while her hands squeezed and shaped an invisible mound of dough.

I was on my back on an army cot in the school nurse's office. My body felt like a line from "Ol' Man River." My nose was closed by the puke stink clinging to the cotton knit shirt I knew I'd never wear again.

"Love your new aftershave," she said, searching for a laugh to take the edge off her anxiety. She forced a sharp breath and wiped at her eyes.

I said, "It's called 'Barf.' You can find it in all the better men's shops and selected junior high school basements." My voice was stuck in a hoarse collar somewhere beneath my chin. I wanted to appear macho and witty for her. "You okay?"

"Better than you, although you're one lucky SOB. The paramedics found nothing broken, no internal bleeding." She reached into her purse for a small, brown prescription vial and placed it upright on my crotch. "They said these babies don't kill the pain so much as they execute it."

"The guy with the bat chasing you, he—"

"Pushed me aside and kept going. He must've been afraid my yell would bring everyone running."

"Catch him?"

"A fast disappearing act down the corridor. That was over an hour ago. Everyone's gone. I told Maxie not to send a limo back for me. I'll chauffer you home in your Jag and work something out from there."

"You able to ID him?

"J.T. Lewis asked. I told him all that."

"Tell me."

"He was big. Bigger than you. Wearing slacks and a jacket. A tie. He could even have been a teacher."

"That narrows it down . . . White? Black?"

"White, I'm reasonably certain. The light isn't particularly good down there. I was more concerned about you. I thought you were dead. You didn't move. You sat there like you were dead." A hand cupped her mouth.

"Aleta Haworth. What about her?"

Jayne shook her head.

"Dead?"

"For later, when I get you back to your place. That and something else we have to talk about." Her face had turned hard.

Jayne filled the tub and helped me in after stripping down to a red see-through lace bra and panties and a matching garter bra, explaining it was to keep from getting her outfit wet. She found a sponge, settled onto her knees beside me, and filled in missing parts of the story she'd started at Potomac Junior High.

"Maxie's band was ready to go on, but still no Aleta, I'd seen you go downstairs. I thought you might be the reason she was late. There were also things we had to talk about, so I hurried downstairs and saw what I saw and screamed—"

"Or I might have been dead, if not for you coming along at that moment."

"The band was loud, like it was a freebie at the Institute for the Deaf. Probably why nobody heard me. I made sure you were breathing and ran upstairs to find J.T."

"Tell me about Aleta."

"Nothing to tell."

"Where was she all this time?"

A shrug. "Hiding, maybe? More scared than me?" Jayne squeezed the sponge and rained water on my head. "I never saw Aleta."

"She was in the dressing room."

"Nowhere. When it was over, there was no sign that she'd ever been there in the first place. What do you think? Was the guy after her or did she just happen to be in the wrong place at the wrong time? Some thief after valuables in the dressing rooms?"

"Not if you don't publicize the shows up front, unless you mean it was somebody who belonged on campus. That's too much of a stretch. Aleta taking off while the guy was using me for batting practice, that I can understand."

"J.T. said there were two other ways to get up and down from the basement, so she could have split without being seen . . . Maxie was steaming when he jumped into the limo, giving me the kind of static that said he blamed me."

"For what? For maybe saving my life?"

Jayne gulped a ton of air, held it for a moment, blew it away. "I'm the one who recommended Aleta for the gig. Maxie will want to fire her, but I'll talk him out of it. The subject will be history by tomorrow."

"You were that close to Aleta? Close enough to get her the gig?"

"Not close at all."

"Why the recommendation, then?"

Jayne had been sponging my back and shoulders using little circular motions, a therapy more enjoyable than the pain pills.

She stopped, suddenly quiet; sat down in the middle of the floor with her legs crossed, averting her eyes. When she turned back to me, I saw a new kind of look and recognized I wasn't going to like what it meant.

"Why? So you can write about it in your column? Your daily column, Neil? Your daily column in the *Daily*?"

She knew. It had to be the "something else" she said we had to talk about. I didn't try to bluff. She was better than that. I wouldn't have expected her to buy into it, anyway. I said, "I was going to tell you."

"Hell hadn't frozen over yet? I had to hear it from Roscoe Del Ruth of all people, when he cornered me backstage wondering what you were doing there. He said it was a topic of conversation this morning with his breakfast gang at Nate 'n Al's." I had a strong urge to submerge and test if suicide by drowning was as impossible as they say. "I need to know why, Neil. Why you couldn't tell me last night, so I'd have time to get my story right before calling Gene Coburn and breaking the news in a way that wouldn't cost me a major client?" My gesture meant nothing. "Afraid it would get in the way of some free pussy?"

"That's rude, crude, and unkind, Jayne. You're not being fair."

"We are beyond fair. We are talking about deceit and pussy. Should I guess what your answer will be? You'll say you didn't know how to tell me. Break the news to me."

"Yes."

"So, you compounded a little deceit with a pinch of flattery and earned yourself another loose screw, and now what? What do I tell the client now, this late in the game, when he's already heard it from Roscoe Del Ruth and who knows? *Hey, Gene, look at it this way: We both got fucked.* Sound about right to you?"

"Jayne, I'm sorry. I apologize. I—"

A dreadful noise erupted from her belly and matched the tears spilling down her cheeks. She pushed herself up, yanked her suit off the shower door, and dressed hurriedly. "There's something else I want you to know," she said. "On second thought, there's nothing else I want you to know. Anyway, not now. You're not dead. You're okay. You'll survive. So will I."

Jayne turned to go. I implored her not to leave until we could talk out the problem. She dismissed the urgency in my voice and fled. By the time I'd struggled from the tub and limped after her, she was gone.

I put on my robe, spent the next fifteen or twenty minutes feeling sorry for myself. I threw some Leonard Cohen on the CD, desperate to share my misery with someone who would understand. They do not come any more depressed or melancholy than him. I sank onto the couch and played channel change with the TV remote.

The door chimes startled me.

It was Jayne. Looking miserable.

Neither of us knew what to say.

She held her breath longer than I held mine.

She held up a hand between us. My key ring dangled between her thumb and forefinger.

I said, "Couldn't bring yourself to steal the Jag?"

"Couldn't remember the code that opens the garage door."

I told her.

"Thanks," Jayne said. "Can I come in now?" She dropped the keys on the rug and sauntered past me.

I called at her back, "Sure."

When I awoke the next morning at six, I was alone, except for Leonard Cohen at the same old stand in the front room, telling me things about myself that were nobody's business. Had Jayne stayed the night, still been here sharing my bed, I might have told her things she wanted to hear; things I was anxious to share with her. I might have.

The phone, demanding attention.

I raced for it, praying it was her.

It wasn't.

The caller was Rev. Ronnie Plantation, wondering, "You make it over for a visit, Mr. Gulliver? People here what needing to speak with you."

Chapter 26

I skipped my morning ritual and steered a straight course for the Adams district and Rev. Ronnie Plantation's Church of the Righteous Gospel. The parking lot was unguarded, fewer than a half dozen cars there, but one of them was a classic green Mustang, not unlike the one I was certain had been on my tail. Nevada plates. Top down; nothing on the seats to tell me anything about the driver. I walked around to the passenger side and pushed the glove compartment button. Locked.

Arrow signs got me to the minister's outer office, where the church administrator, Mrs. Gosden, mildly atwitter that I remembered her name, still looking like a bird that's lost its nest, led me back out and pointed to a side door.

"They're waiting for you on the patio, sir."

"Who's they, Mrs. Gosden?"

"Rev. Ronnie and them."

I stepped onto the patio. Rev. Plantation greeted me like a gift from God, declaring, "Too much good California sunshine to waste being inside. Not so, Aleta?" He gestured to my left.

"You say, Rev. Plantation." Aleta was wearing a different wig that did nothing to change her intoxicating look. She was dressed with a shop girl's flair for stylish simplicity on a budget, but no mistaking the drama hiding underneath her dress. It took her another few seconds to recognize me. She gasped and reached across her chest to grab hold of the shoulder of the man standing alongside her.

He placed his hand over hers. "My little surprise, Aleta. I thought it was time you two met."

I didn't know him. He was one of those ageless people who wear their years like diamonds, just enough lines and stray ear hairs to put him in his late fifties, early sixties. A full head of military-styled orange-flavored hair. An unremarkable face, the high forehead topping a seedless chin on its way to pudginess, linked to a lanky frame encased in a set of diplomatic pinstripes.

"How's that table over there for a little chat?" His voice like he was speaking and clearing his throat at the same time. His erect posture and the rhythm to his walk made me think he would fit right in alongside Wilt and West at an old-timers' game at the Forum. "Come sit, Aleta."

She did as she was told.

"I'll just let you people be," Rev. Plantation said, and disappeared back inside the church.

I settled in the chair across from him and said, "I still don't know who you are."

"That's correct," he said. He collected his knuckles under his chin and quietly stared at me, enjoying his little game. "And I know you only by reputation, and some good things people we have in common tell me. Name's Bailey Madison, Neil. I'm with the Treasury Department."

"Why should I care and who do we have in common?"

"A shopping list, you really want to get into it, but it would lead off by your close friend from the *Daily* crime beat, Augie Fowler. Augie is still in rehab drying out, but he said I could swear by you and told me be sure to say hello for him. You need more names than that one?"

"It would break his heart to say I did. What's your game, Madison?"

"Snooping the way you've been doing causes a confusion of the first magnitude, Neil, so I'm attempting to get that problem off the table." He reached over to pat Aleta's hand. "Wouldn't you say so, my dear?" She turned her palms to the ceiling and back to a resting position on the table. Tapped her painted nails on the hard surface. "Neil, she had every right to think you were one of them, one of the bad guys who've been coming after her. You scared the hell out of Aleta."

"One of what bad guys?"

"Chasing after her the way you did. At a memorial service for her dear friend, yet."

"One of what bad guys, Madison? She saw me at the Palladium, at an anniversary party for *Stardom* magazine. We were as close as we are now."

"Don't take this the wrong way, but *you* saw *her*. She is quite beautiful, our Aleta, so how could you help but notice. Mind you, you're not unattractive yourself, but it doesn't automatically make you memorable."

"She might have waited long enough to ask before she ran away from me."

A grunt of laughing. Mimicking. "Excuse me, sir, before I evaluate the need to flee. Do you happen to be one of the nasties intent upon ending my life or, perchance, do I have you confused with some other white face that has no business being here at Mrs. Danbury's today?"

"Very amusing . . . And how do you explain what happened at the junior high, you or somebody using a Louisville Slugger on me."

"Hardly. That baseball bat was intended for Aleta. You happened along at a most fortunate time. No question in my mind you saved our young lady friend's life." His words were as confident as his manner. I associated his accent with places like Ohio, Minnesota, and Pennsylvania, people like Henry Fonda. He let the thought sink in before he cupped a hand beside his mouth, gangster-style. "Neil, the next baseball bat could be meant for you. Or worse. It appears you may have stumbled onto information the nasties are ready to kill for, as they've already shown us they're eminently capable of doing. How do you feel about staying alive, Neil?"

My throat went dry. "I'll admit the concept has always held a great appeal," I said when I could get the words out, faking a courage I didn't feel.

Bailey Madison settled back in his chair and said, "I think it's important that you hear what you've gotten yourself into." He began the briefing lazily enough, but quickly took on the trappings of a distinguished guest lecturer with the need to impress as well as inform. He worked the story cautiously, withholding names. These government people, they also love framing their gab in military terms. It reminds me what I have against war and politics. They feed off each other, like maggots and manure.

He said, "Going back two years, during a routine crackdown on the porno industry that thrives in the Netherlands, Interpol stumbled into evidence that computers were being used as a low-risk alternative to the post office for transporting certain kinds of high-grade porn into the United States and other parts of the globe. Satellites and modems were making it unnecessary to print in one country and ship to others, but the methodology didn't quit at that.

"Last year, when a trail led to Stardom House as a major point of development and distribution, my branch of T was alerted. We were already inside Stardom House, trying to build a drug trafficking case and getting nowhere developing evidence that could stand up in court. I was ready to shut down the operation, until something happened to change that.

"I had an actress with talent to match her failures inside Stardom House, who had never gone beyond minor roles in Equity-waiver plays before she joined my strike force. We had her write a six-thousand-dollar check for a full-color page in *Stardom* magazine. Sign up for TalenTapes. Buy everything Stardom House had to offer. Share in all the fun and games. After her checks turned to rubber, she suggested Stardom House let her work off the debt as one of their career counselors.

"We had my actress running a kid we'd coddled out of a safe house on Hollywood Boulevard and were using as drug bait. She threw the kid into party situations and one of the first names the kid came back with was a young actor from the 'Diapered Dozen' set. During a *Stardom* mixer at a hit-and-run disco on Wilshire, the movie star had yanked the kid into a toilet stall. He stuffed her nose with coke before sodomizing her. The kid didn't care. It felt great, and afterward the young scum-bucket actor tossed her two greenies that put her away in Dreamland for a week."

"Where's this heading, Madison? You have names to share?"

He showed he didn't like being interrupted before converting a silence back into words. "I'll start off with her," Madison said. He scanned Aleta, who had become a hood ornament. She was making finger circles on the table, pausing every so often to nail him with an indifferent look.

This time she shuddered.

Madison described Aleta as a "good soldier." Her fantasy was one I had heard often enough about other Aletas full of show business dreams and ambition in overdrive. Fresh out of high school, she'd landed a receptionist's job at *Stardom* magazine. It led her into a bad crowd, temptation, and a phony bust. A setup. She had no way of knowing she'd been targeted. She was squeaky clean; what they liked best about her.

She had always been too square about church, too aware of neighbors strung out on dope, losers beyond redemption, to get serious about drugs, but her date in the sting was a star making hypnotic promises about getting her through all the right doors.

Down the line he'd be the one turned loose on the kid from the safe house. The star fed her two caterpillar lines from a bottomless stash and, next thing Aleta knew, she was in County detention.

Madison said, "We visited Aleta there and offered her the gift-wrapped opportunity to erase the arrest, like it had never happened. All she needed to do was anything asked of her by her government. It was the answer to her prayers. In time, our arrangement led to a job singing with Maxie Trotter, but it came with a price. Whenever Aleta protested about anything, we leaned hard on her Christian ethic. We reminded her she was helping to save young lives that otherwise might sail off the edge of the earth because of the drug dealings at Stardom House. As I said, a good soldier, this one. She always did as she was instructed. Right, soldier?"

The T-man faked an arm jab at her. There was nothing fake about the contempt for Madison she didn't try hiding. He laughed it off and asked me, "Neil, the name Roscoe Del Ruth mean anything to you?"

I flashed on Maxie Trotter's manager, last week at the Palladium, bald and drunk and living the cliché life, dragging Aleta into one of Porky Pigue's photos. Yesterday, at Potomac Junior High, trapping Jayne in a bottomless conversation, telling her I'd become the former star columnist of the *Daily.* I recognized Madison was about to give me another reason not to like Mr. Baby Cakes.

"We asked Aleta to be nice to Mr. Del Ruth," Bailey Madison began, "in the same manner she'd already been nice to other movers and shakers around Stardom House. Aleta and Mr. Del Ruth became what is called an 'item' in show business circles."

Aleta slapped the table. "I did not want to do it, not ever, but they went and made me," she said, directing the accusation at

Madison, as if he represented a shortcut to the confessional.

He conceded the point with a nod and carried on.

One night, having had more than his usual ten too many, Del Ruth began spilling his words as freely as his liquor. Out to impress Aleta, he told her how fortunate she was to be his exclusively. She just as easily could have ended up like thousands of other hopefuls who'd come to Stardom House looking for a career break, only to be pulled into the kinds of porn games Interpol had reported to Madison.

The business was being conducted on a grand, worldwide scale. It had something to do with fiber optics and a communications satellite, everything to do with the innards of a technology mastered, refined, redefined, and advanced beyond belief by computer Einsteins like Knox Lundigan. It was built around BBStardom and grossing millions upon billions of illegal dollars.

Del Ruth told Aleta how Stardom House telephone numbers customarily given to BBStardom subscribers were domestic, but myriad others drawn from telephone systems throughout the world were stitched together in the satellite, where nobody would think to look. The system allowed dealers in drugs, porn, guns, illegal securities, and more to traffic undetected after logging onto BBStardom using the same basic subscriber phone numbers.

Afterward, using a series of secondary phone numbers and programming codes, the dealers arrived at secret subdivisions located within secret subdivisions, a belly of the beast as broad as the world, including pornography channels operating as "casting couches" for anybody in the Hollyweird–Hornywood mix with an obscene appetite for ordering sex the way some people phone for pizza.

Before Del Ruth could tell Aleta more, he passed out, as he usually did ten seconds to orgasm. The next morning, he seemed not to remember anything. He never brought up the subject again. Aleta's actress-runner told her not to press Del Ruth; it wasn't worth the risk.

Madison said, "I moved my men from drugs to porn at Stardom House. We found Del Ruth's satellite. We got inside it a few times, but were always discovered. The system would shut down before we could locate or download information or pictures, do ourselves some good." He grimaced, showed me empty hands. Spoon-fed me more technology; easy for me to swallow, but hard to digest. "Now, Neil, this is where Aleta's good friend, Hope Danbury, enters the scenario."

Aleta stopped making circles. She dropped her chin onto her chest and assumed an attitude of prayer; hands locked on top of the table, eyes closed; head shaking; struggling with an inner grief.

After Aleta got the job at Stardom House, Hope took to hanging out there once or twice a week. Soon, three or four times a week. Nobody cared. Hope was congenial and knew how to keep out of the way, so Aleta didn't make it an issue. Hope continued to visit after Aleta was hired by Maxie Trotter. She added invitations to recording sessions and Maxie's parties to other invitations that were always floating around Stardom House.

Aleta's eyes flashed open. She glowered at Madison. "Hope was a good girl. She didn't do no stuff. She was just like this dude here wrote up about her in the paper. She—"

"Yes, she was," Madison agreed. He reached out and cupped a hand lightly over Aleta's mouth.

I had a three-quarter view of his face, so couldn't see what else he did, but it made Aleta obedient. I knew what must be running through her mind and heart as Madison told the rest of it, like a TV weatherman working a storm front sweeping over the map from the Pacific Ocean.

Aleta had to be thinking:

Maybe if she hadn't heeded Hope's begging and pleading and let her attend those first Stardom House parties and socials and, afterward, the recording sessions. Maybe if she hadn't presumed Hope would continue to recognize right from wrong and avoid the dangling temptations better than she had. Maybe if she hadn't ignored all the signs after they became increasingly evident in Hope's manner, the way Hope could no longer look her in the face, but always two inches lower. Maybe if she hadn't closed her eyes to the truth and continued deceiving herself that all she was seeing was Hope's usual schoolgirl innocence and enthusiasm mixed in with the special joy that comes from mingling with stars and being able to pretend you're one of them . . .

Maybe.

Hell of a word, *maybe*.

A favorite word among logicians.

Maybe if Hope were still alive she wouldn't be dead.

Makes sense?

Makes sense.

Especially among logicians.

And, maybe, Hope would still be alive if Aleta had not ignored the evidence, had sat on her friend before it became too late; said something like, *Girl, you got to stop it with the drugs before* . . . before Hope, maybe lamenting for the girl she'd never be again, pulled her aside and, stripped bare of the fantasy pride that comes from being desired, confessed about the drugs and a habit that kept her up nights and her mouth dry as seashore rot . . . and everything else.

Aleta appealed to me with her eyes. I tried to make her see she had nothing to fear from me, no matter what Madison revealed. My column was history. I'd memorialized the Hope

Danbury who deserved to be remembered. Aleta studied me for the lie. Apparently satisfied, she resumed making circles.

Madison caught the exchange. He gave Aleta a gentle squeeze on the arm and me a gash of a smile. Clearing his throat, he explained how Aleta tried to comfort her best friend by whispering her own dark secrets to Hope and vowed to help get Hope back to being her mama's little girl. She reported Hope to her runner, who promptly repeated it to Madison, who promised something would be done to help Hope. The T-man raised his hand to show us he'd meant his promise.

He continued, "Earlier on the day of her misfortune, Hope left a phone message on Aleta's machine, saying she'd walked out of Stardom House with proof of the horror stories she'd told Aleta and stories Aleta already knew from Roscoe Del Ruth. Yes, Neil, what you are thinking is correct." A heavy sigh. "Her runner had encouraged her to go looking. Hope didn't say what it was she had, and then it was too late. She disappeared, just as her runner had disappeared a week earlier. The nasties had found out too much. Secrets no longer were secrets."

Madison didn't look afraid of anything. His groomed eyebrows rose like Groucho's and his gaze slid toward Aleta. "Best friends talk. They share their most intimate secrets. Other people find out. Next, you learn your best friend is dead." He splayed his fingers. "Sufficient cause to fear for your own life?" He let the thought soak in. "Your apartment is trashed. A stranger pursues you at a wake. Somebody comes after you with a baseball bat. Any wonder then that Aleta would flee you, Neil? Damn it, man. Put me in her position, I would have done the same thing."

A feeble whimper from Aleta.

I said, "Instead, you tailed me."

"We were sifting through the rubble of her apartment when Aleta got back home from the school, panic-stricken. It told us that Hope may have deposited her proof there before going on to the Roxy. It would have been easy. Hope knew where her best friend hid the spare key. My troops got Aleta out of there. I stayed behind on a hunch that paid off. After you came out of there, I followed you; long enough to learn who you were and where and how you fit. Then I communicated with Augie Fowler, who said you're a man to be trusted." A noncommittal stare. "And here we are."

Chapter 27

I'd done some hard thinking while listening to Madison, certain there had to be a reason he'd fed me so much background. Not everything was in place yet. I said, "Your actress, the runner inside Stardom House—"

"Nobody whose name would mean anything to you."

I remembered what I'd seen at Stardom House and later on the floppy that Bernie Flame had cracked. I said, "Laraine Dailey?" Madison suppressed surprise, not ready to confirm my guess. "And your runaway. That's Janie Doe."

Bailey Madison rearranged himself and stared into the distance, humming an off-key melody under his breath. He propped an elbow on the table, made a horseshoe of his left thumb and forefinger, and ran them from his jawline down his neck to a merger at the perfect knot of his tie.

"Her name was Laurie Ann Bockstatdler," Madison said, sounding almost glad to be sharing the information. "So far as her parents in Boise, Idaho, will ever learn, Laurie Ann died in a freeway accident that incinerated all the occupants of her automobile when it collided with a gas tanker. Give it some thought, you'll appreciate that's an easier tragedy for any mother and father to handle than the knowledge of their woman-child staggering on Hollywood Boulevard, offering up body and soul for a taste of somebody's filthy needle. We cleaned Laurie Ann up. We kept her happy, and she did what we required of her. You know what else? Laurie Ann was happier for it." Poor Madison.

He wanted desperately to believe what he was saying.

"And the 'Diapered Dozen' actor? Roddy Donaldson," I said, fearing the answer.

"No."

"No?"

"Nicky Edmunds."

I was relieved. I'd come close to believing I might be fronting a guilty man. By my reckoning, Hope and Janie Doe were sent to the Roxy to track after Roddy by Laraine Dailey. I told this to Madison.

He said, "Hope was not being used in that manner and Laurie Ann was not working for us that night. Donaldson will be cut loose today, on his own recognizance, because we need him on the outside to keep our investigation on track. The D.A.'s office howled, but our juice flows from higher spigots than Hapgood Harris's juice."

Madison gave me a look to indicate he knew everything about Harris there was to know.

My aches and pains from yesterday were throbbing again. My painkillers were in the Jag. I escaped by thinking about last night and Jayne, the moment I opened the door, saw she had returned to me. Later, an empty space in my bed. What did it take for Jayne to spend the night? The pictured dissolved into a new one, the bed now occupied by Roddy, not Jayne. Roddy with Hope. Roddy with Janie Doe. Both of them. Hope and Janie, who didn't know each other. And what did any of it mean?

As if he had read my thoughts, Madison said, "One more thing, Neil. We suspect everyone connected with the Stardom House operation. Roddy Donaldson is one of them, but the ones who work closest with Gene Coburn and Knox Lundigan, especially them . . ." He let the statement drift away.

I sucked in my breath. I knew who he meant.

"My brains would be stuck to a school wall if it hadn't been for Jayne Madrigal."

Madison shrugged. "You've been spending a great deal of time with Miss Madrigal, and there is evidence she's one of them, Neil. Evidence." He saw how much it hurt to hear, but didn't let that stop him. He kept going, like my pain would help ease his own. "When I tell you your life could be in danger, it's because you may have said something to her in all heat and innocence that puts you at serious risk with the nasties. They're killers and they're prepared to kill again." Madison shifted in his chair. His eyes threw a dark cast as clouds passed, stirring the afternoon light. "Now it's your turn."

I told Madison about the blue floppy.

He listened carefully, especially when I described how Bernie Flame had sat at the computer and burgled us onto the floppy, then tried hacking onto BBStardom.

With amusement, he said, "This fellow talked in terms of eight and nine levels on BBStardom? My troops measured more than forty thousand levels. Forty thousand. And we couldn't crack into a single one. We discovered a second sysop at the hundred-ten level. Whatever is in between that and the system operator at Level Ten is, for now, between Mr. Knox Lundigan and, who? God?" He turned serious. "There'll be leads for us on that blue floppy, Neil. My people will need it."

Madison guided me through our discoveries a second time, cautioning me to stop, skip, jump forward, whenever I got graphic about the sex games Bernie and I had seen, as if to spare Aleta, who'd been listening with stoic resignation, cringing on the parts dealing with Hope.

"You're certain, Neil? No question in your mind?"

"It was definitely Hope."

Aleta averted her eyes and gargled a noise.

"Laraine Dailey?"

"Laraine Dailey."

Madison was not happy.

"Gonna find out what done it and have him done," Aleta said, almost incoherently. She had stopped her finger game to play with her hair. Two strands had come loose from above her ear and she was tugging them through her lips as she spoke. "Have the bastards killed, what they done to my fren' Hope."

She rose abruptly and vanished from the patio.

Madison called after her, but she kept going, on stately legs that appeared ready to collapse at any instant.

Later, I saw her huddled in the passenger seat of Bailey Madison's green Mustang, paralyzed by her memories, visiting Hope, whose death I supposed she blamed on herself. I briefly considered heading over to say something comforting. My Jag was closer than any words Aleta needed to hear from me.

It was the time of day that can't make up its mind.

A red and orange blush illuminated the western skyline. The plump cartoon clouds floating in from the desert were dark enough to make me believe the radio weatherman's talk of a storm front. I found a station that took me back to happier times, but the music couldn't stop me from being my own bad company. I thought about Aleta and Hope and I thought more about Jayne. I shortstopped at the Westwood Ho Market to fill some food shelf holes.

The Heathcliffe garage was too full of shadows for me to identify the one I thought I saw moving after a noise sounding like glass being broken at a Jewish wedding yanked my head around.

It could have been nothing. It could have been one of the "Gones," what the cops call the car bandits who routinely work condo garages, short for *Gone in Sixty Seconds,* like the movie. Only, it was too early for the "Gones," who work the hours when there's less chance of heavy traffic. It could have been one of the nasties Madison talked about. Two of them.

They've already killed . . . prepared to do it again.

I was gripped by a sudden fear. Shoulders hunched, clutching the grocery bag like a football, I took off for the elevator. I whizzed through the widest slots between cars parked in the midway. I thought I felt somebody close in on me as I narrowed the distance.

I hit the elevator vestibule, begging for air, sweat running down my forehead and stinging my eyes, just as the elevator clanged to a stop and the door slid open. Mrs. Sands, Third Floor, South Building, returned my stare. She seemed more frightened than me, but she always seemed frightened. She's the only blue-haired person I've seen who unceasingly shakes from the toes up.

"You okay, Mr. Gulliver?" It was Gus Ljung, his voice close enough to warm the back of my neck. "Just getting here to double-shift and see you taking off like a bat in the belfry. I hurried, case it's being anything at all."

"Everything's fine, Gus," I said, relishing a deep breath in and out on every word. I worked on a smile for Mrs. Sands, who wasn't fooled and kept on shaking. Somebody had signaled from another floor. The elevator door closed with Mrs. Sands still inside and me still here. I turned and looked up at the security guard.

Gus said, "What with the car busters and all, can't be so careful anymore. Doing my duty, Mr. Gulliver." A stage whisper, like he was passing state secrets. A theatrical smile. I half-expected him to salute. His eyes didn't move while he reached around me to insert the elevator key in the call slot.

I got off on three and headed down the hall, knowing even before I turned the key that I was going to be unhappy with what I found on the other side of my door. Or, what I wouldn't find. Call it "premonition." Reporter's gut. It's the same gut cops develop while putting in enough years to qualify as survivors. It comes as a gentle voice disguised as a breeze, talking the language of intuition as it drifts on past.

I parked the bag of groceries on the mail table and tracked a straight course to the computer. The blue floppy was gone. No sign of forced entry. And—

I was sleeping when Jayne stole away from me in the darkness.

There is evidence she is one of them, Neil.

I didn't want to believe it.

I didn't believe it.

I showered the day from my body, but the dirt wouldn't budge from my mind. I played what I knew in combination with what I thought I knew or what was reasonable to suspect. I stepped from the stall cleaner, but not necessarily wiser, choosing the words I'd use to inform Bailey Madison.

I propped the pillows against the backboard and settled onto the bed with a cold Heineken. I began plotting how to crash Stardom House and break into BBStardom. Why? Why not? The more I thought about it, the more it felt like the right thing to do. For Hope. For Aleta. Maybe even for me. Certainly, for me. Most of all, for me. I don't like running scared.

Chapter 28

There was no answer at the phone number Bernie Flame had scribbled for me. Figuring he might be hanging out with Juliet and she would know where to find him, I dialed my ex to get her mother's number. Stevie was into giggling before I could ask, telling me, "You just missed Jaynie." Someone inquired in the background and chatter became muffled momentarily behind a hand on the mouthpiece.

I said, "What was she doing there?"

"The usual usual—being subservient." More giggles. "If you must know, Jaynie was reacquainting herself with Mutt and Jeff. We're going to Vegas for the weekend and Jaynie will be on pet patrol here." Mutt and Jeff were two mongrels who showed up unannounced on Stevie's doorstep last year, unleashed, unlicensed, and, from the sight of them, unloved; a pair of hairy four-legged ribcages. She paused, likely studying their woeful eyes, a fraction of a second too long. "I figure I pay her enough, but she would have volunteered anyway. Jaynie is a love, isn't she, Neil? . . . Neil? I asked you a question. . . . I hear it's really working out well between the two of you, honey."

"So you hear."

"Oh, piffle. You can tell me. If you don't, she will anyway. She's really berserk over you, Neil. I swear. You were here, you would see me putting my hand right on my heart."

"You mean a 34C away from your heart." The words just slipped out. I suppose I needed the comedy relief the way

George Burns always needed Gracie Allen.

"Rude, Neil, rude. I'm a 36C at my most dehydrated. And I'm glad I didn't have to track you down to tell you how spiteful and vindictive you've become."

An educated guess: "Because of this business with your mom and Bernie Flame."

"You have sent my anger into the next state, straight over into Denver, and I may never forgive you."

"Colorado. Denver's the city . . . Listen, Sarah Bernhardt—Bernie just showed up on my doorstep. What was I supposed to do?"

"Of course Denver is the city. I wanted to be sure you were listening. Do? Killing him comes to mind. You do still know people who do that sort of work, don't you?"

"Killing Bernie was Plan B."

"Whatever happened to Plan A, sitting down with Juliet and reminding her of the facts of life?"

"The facts of life have never been her problem, babe. Bernie got to me before I could get to your mother. His story made sense to me. I believe Bernie when he says he's in love with Juliet—"

"The Jewel."

"Sweet, huh? I like Bernie, Stevie. I think he's first-rate. I think he'll be good for Juliet."

An exaggerated Dietrich: "The Moth and the Flame."

"Get off your tight little behind already. Stop thinking only about somebody else coming between you and your mommy. Give Juliet the credit she deserves. Maybe even try giving her the respect she deserves."

The connection broke.

Twenty-eight. Twenty-nine. Thirty. Thirty—

I picked up on the second ring.

Stevie said, "Tell me something else."

"What?"

"Honey, you really think I have a tight little behind?" Uproarious laughter. "Or is that only compared to Jaynie?" More uproarious laughter. "Actually, tell me if you called to wish me bon voyage."

"I didn't know you were bon voyaging until you mentioned it . . . Is this where I'm supposed to ask what's in Vegas? I know better than to think you're a leading candidate for the title of Miss Slot Machine."

"Nothing ever wrong with my slot machine, honey." I blushed. She must have felt the heat through the phone, because she was making like she'd just heard the funniest gag in the world. I heard her teasing back and forth with someone there, then—

"Hold on. There's someone wants to talk to you," Stevie said.

Before I had time to be surprised, Bernie Flame was on the line, yakking like he was hustling a 900 number at a pay booth and about to run out of coins. "Say hey, Neil, wish me *mazel tov.* The Moth and me, just getting ready to elope and Stevie here is gonna give the bride away. I took her bull by the horns and gave her the facts of life, the way you and me talked about and, you know? The *shaineh maidel* come to her senses. Like maybe Bernie Flame ain't such a miserable, low-life sumbitch after all, given a chance to prove it. Like maybe thirty-four can go into forty-six more than one time."

Laughter.

Scuffling for the phone.

Stevie: "He is too a miserable, low-life sumbitch. But as you know firsthand, I've had that kind of personal experience in the family before, so it's no big deal."

More scuffling.

Bernie: "All'n act, Neil. Already she's calling me papa and I'm thinking about adopting her legally. Stevie, cut it out. I'm going to be your papa, for Christ's sake."

More scuffling.

Stevie: "Don't you believe him, honey. Just trying to prove thirty-four into twenty won't go at all. Juliet is having her skin moisturized or I'd put her on to tell you everything. She wants to invite you."

"Does Bernie know you're lying about your age and, sorry, I can't make it."

"You can't make it? Is this a new problem?"

George and Gracie time again. "You'll never know."

"Easy for you to say."

"Are you reading from a *Bedrooms and Board Rooms* script or do lines like that automatically pour from your own bosom of creativity?"

"Why is it, any time we talk, you get onto my boobs?"

"Old habits die hard?"

She muttered something incoherent and passed the phone back to Bernie.

He said, "Don't ever buy the mad act, Neil. Stevie, she's really nuts for you. Just nuts, maybe. So—what's up?"

I gave him the highlights of my meeting with Bailey Madison. He responded with variations on *Uh-huh* until he thought I was finished. "So, this here government guy aimed too high and after that, Knox Lundigan being nobody's fool was lying in wait for them. I guess—"

"There's more, Bernie." I told him the blue floppy had been stolen and what I had in mind.

He waited a respectful moment. "Look, what I think is let's do it, Neil. Tomorrow? You get us into Stardom House and all I need is five minutes. Five minutes max. It'll be my wedding gift to you."

Bernie said it gleefully, matter-of-factly. I relaxed, glad to be reminded that people like him still existed. I believed that Bernie, given the *five minutes max* he needed, could pull off my plan, except—

I didn't have a plan, and—

Breaking into Stardom House and cracking BBStardom definitely called for a plan.

"Call me in the *mañana* and tell me when and whatever, okay?" he said, and handed off the phone to Stevie.

She began midsentence, reporting Jayne was due back any minute and did I want her to call? Or what? She was keeping Juliet company while Juliet had her skin refinished.

"The 'or what' works for me," I said, and disconnected in a hurry, fearing that Jayne might pick that moment to return, and—

What would I say to her? I couldn't trust myself. Not now, wounded, when I might tell her what I'd heard and what I thought. Jayne was entitled to a fairer hearing than that. Yes. She was. Wasn't she?

There is evidence she is one of them, Neil.

I sacked out in front of the TV with the sandwich and salad bar combo I had picked up at the market and did a lot of channel flipping until I scored with an old Alice Faye and Don Ameche musical that didn't take concentration. I developed and abandoned plans that had more glitches than a freeway mile.

Bernie Flame and I had to infiltrate a crowded, off-limits Mission Control where our presence couldn't help but be noticed, especially once he rolled up his sleeves and hacked into BBStardom. I remembered how, growing up, I wanted to be invisible like the Invisible Man, the way all kids do. I wondered how long it had been since I'd checked if somebody had finally invented invisible paint.

I fell asleep dismantling one solution after the next. When the ring went off in my head, waking me up to the millionth screening of *Meet John Doe,* it was not signaling any solution that worked.

Somebody calling.

I checked my watch. Not yet midnight.

There was silence and a hang-up after the machine gave the usual instructions.

Somebody had a change of mind after realizing the hour, or was it the nasties, checking if anybody was home before making an unscheduled visit?

They've already killed. They're prepared to do it again.

Could you kill, Neil, if you had to? Could you, ever again? The first time is the worst time, but—

I rolled off the couch and headed for the bedroom closet. Stacked in a corner are the Nike shoeboxes, about a dozen, in which I store the treasures of a lifetime I can't bring myself to toss, including my Beretta. In a box of its own. Snug in a watch cap, lubed and loaded for action. Sixteen rounds of 147-grain hollow point misery, including the round in the chamber.

I needed it now the way a chocoholic needs his Hershey fix. Madison had spooked me good with his visions of worse than baseball bats.

Get the floppy over to us and steer clear, he'd said. *When this is over, you have the story first. My word about that.*

Of course, I agreed, although I had no home for the story.

Maybe I even meant it.

Probably not.

Maybe only until I climbed back out of the Jag and went over to Aleta anyway and gently prodded her into telling me things Madison had neglected to mention.

There is always a problem hearing the truth, the risk of learning how much it can hurt. I guess if the old adage weren't true, it wouldn't be an old adage.

Trust nobody but yourself.

That's an old adage that has never let me down. I learned it growing up, from my father, before he chose to forget it once too often and lost his way home from the corner drugstore or wherever he went to replenish his bottle of life that night half a lifetime ago.

I returned to the front room and sat with the Beretta in my lap, fixed on the hallway to the front door until my eyes refused to focus and my mind grew weary trying to empty out Mission Control for Bernie Flame.

I know, Bernie, I know: *Five minutes max.*

The mind, like a roulette wheel or a pair of dice, works in strange ways.

I hit on a plan that I just might be able to pull off.

Except, the next morning, Bernie called to cancel.

Chapter 29

The background noise in my ear was unmistakable. A certain jangle accompanies the monotonous hum of people packaged for fun, occasional riffs of joy; in this instance the constant tinkle of ice cubes against glass from a bar close enough to be heard near the lobby phone Bernie was using.

He said, "You know they add a buck to the charge anytime you make a call from the room? So, I come on down here where it's free; anything to keep you from straying too far from the tables is what they do. The Moth'd rather be at the slots than anywheres."

"Bernie, you're not supposed to be in Las Vegas until tonight, remember? We have something we're doing—"

"Jeez, Neil. I don't got enough ways to tell you how sorry I am. The Moth got back from her skin lady pink and glowing like a teenager. She didn't want to wait no more. She said, *Flame, I don't care how much extra it costs to rewrite the tickets.* Tonight. Much as I don't want to let you down, I got an obligation to my bride, y'know? Burbank was fogged in, so we skipped over to LAX and managed to grab two seats on a United one-stopping from Honolulu. Got lei'd more ways than one. You hate me?"

"Of course not."

"I called last night, before Juliet, Stevie, and me shlepped onto the plane. I wanted you to know and I wanted to apologize, but I hung up when all I got was your machine. Some things, they gotta transpire only between real people."

I put my hand over the mouthpiece so he couldn't hear my exasperated sigh. "You'll give Juliet my love, Bernie?"

"Don't count on it. Nothing disrespectful, Neil, but I got my hands full enough as it is. Lissen, what I also mean to tell you is we're only here through the weekend. How about can the Stardom House thing wait until then?"

"Of course it can, Bernie," I said, lying.

He wasn't fooled. "Neil, there's definitely something in the way you say it tells me you got your fingers crossed on both hands. Spill what you got to spill and let's see what we got."

I threw on my jogging outfit to head downstairs and find Sharon, opened the front door to find almost enough floral bouquets to start my own business, the roses alone worth a small fortune, the single card affixed to a spray of Technicolor carnations telling me: *I'm sprung, home and thankful as ever to you for believing in me. Roddy.* In a feminine hand, so probably the clerk who took the order. Nice of the kid. Something to send over later to the City of Hope, brighten up the day for all the kids, everyone there. I'd call Roddy later, thank him, and tell him so, but now—

Sharon.

Critical to the alternate plan I had just worked out with Bernie Flame.

Sharon wasn't in her office. The guard said she should be finishing her rounds in ten or fifteen minutes. It was closer to twenty before she waltzed through the door, punch list in hand. She saw me and stopped short. Instead of the smile that could have won her dentist a blue ribbon, she answered mine with a look that caused a gully between her brows. It was not unfriendly, but conveyed a sense I had already overstayed my welcome. She headed for her chair. I settled down across from her.

Sharon clasped her hands on the desk and waited for me to speak. I did a fast tally. The last time I saw her, two days ago, before playing baseball at Potomac Junior High, she had made a point of staying on the phone while I signed the paperwork she'd spread on the desk. I'd done nothing to encourage conversation, fearful of saying something inadvertent about Jayne, and left her with a wave and her fair share of leftover silence.

I said, "I meant to ask you the other night, but kept forgetting—how was the Sayles movie?"

She recognized I was suing for peace. Her gesture said she was indifferent about the movie. Maybe, about me. She said, "You visiting for a fast game of Siskel and Ebert?"

"Attempting to make conversation."

"Yes, you are."

She was wearing a simple chestnut-colored chemise with military shoulders, two rows of gold buttons and matching epaulets, I had admired a few times before. Her only jewelry the small jade pearls dotting her ears.

She sat like a portrait on a museum wall, proud of its position and indifferent to prying eyes. Her hair seemed to be shorter than I was used to seeing it, casually fluffed to show off the symmetry of her round face. It helped soften everything except her attitude toward me. But for that, I would have said something flattering.

I started to rise, convinced there was no sense in putting my question to her.

Sharon signaled me to stay. "I suppose you already know," she said, engineering her own try for a breakthrough. "Roddy is back. He came home yesterday from the UCLA Med Center." She interpreted my face correctly. "Who told you? Sgt. Steiger?"

"Somebody mentioned something about it in passing."

"Melba managed to duck the press by having an ambulance pulled up in front. She puttered around it, putting on quite a show while the driver and the attendant went about their business in slow motion. At the same time, your friend was already driving Roddy into the garage."

"My friend? Jayne Madrigal?"

"Is that her name, the public relations girl? I can't even remember. I suppose the idea of using a decoy was hers. She strikes me as quite the clever person, who knows how to get things done."

I wasn't biting. "That's her name."

"Melba called about an hour after I got back from lunch at the Greek place. She was hoping I could spare a couple of guards to help Nicky Edmunds get Roddy from the car into his wheelchair and upstairs. I had them waiting and it went off without a hitch. The media was pissed, to say the least."

"Yes." I figured I'd better get down to business before she got back on the subject of Jayne. I drank a gallon of air and leaned forward, resting my elbows on the desk, and made a gesture of appeal. "Sharon, do you think you might be up for doing me a favor?"

She gave me a disbelieving look and searched the room for her answer.

"It's real important, Sharon, and I know I have no right asking you, but—"

"You don't," she said, but curiosity had started dancing on her face and, before she could destroy the moment with the sarcastic remark I sensed building on her lips, I told her what I had in mind.

She thought about it. "Why?"

"I really can't—"

She looked away. "Do you have anything special you want

added to the next board meeting agenda?"

I gestured surrender and explained as much as I figured was necessary. It seemed to satisfy Sharon.

Heading upstairs to her apartment, her main concern was being too old for the role I wanted her to play at Stardom House.

"You know what they call old starlets?" I said.

"What?"

"Zsa Zsa Gabor."

Sharon growled and punched my arm.

At least for the moment, we were friends again.

She settled me in front of the TV with a Diet Coke and half a bag of unsalted tortilla chips, and wandered off to the bedroom. I zapped the sound, got the number for Stardom House from information, and called Gene Coburn.

He picked up immediately, his effusive greeting almost loud enough to dim the curiosity I also heard in his voice.

"I understand you have problems at the paper?" he said.

"Not anymore," I said. "I got gobbled up fast enough over at CNN, so a story on Stardom House still looms on the arrival, only this time with pictures as well as words. You're first on the agenda once I settle in there."

"I appreciate this heads-up, Neil. You're quite the gentleman."

"Another reason, Gene."

"Oh?"

"Someone I'm very interested in personally is excited by what I've told her about Stardom House and begging me to take her over for a look. If it's not inconvenient—"

"Inconvenient? For you, Neil? Scratch that word from our dictionary."

Meeting Coburn at five o'clock was my idea.

It would give Bernie and me the rest of the day to make arrangements.

And I figured five o'clock would be taper-off time at Stardom House, meaning fewer people in the way when it was time for us to make our moves.

Coburn would have preferred an earlier hour, he said, to allow him to guide my friend through the Stardom House process without rushing. "But for you, Neil . . . ?" He laughed, so I laughed. We laughed together. Two little white laughs.

Sharon returned wearing odds and ends she had pulled together. A gold-colored cashmere sweater a full size too small and definitely dangerous to the touch. Painted-on jeans tucked into svelte, flat-heeled satin boots that quit above her calf. Enough bangles to stock a Melrose Avenue boutique. A hint of bangs angling out from a brown felt fedora. Green eye shadow and liner, accentuated lips, and just a dab more color than she usually used to highlight her cheeks.

Her costume was perfect. It took ten years off her and inspired an ambience more relaxed than she'd ever bothered displaying in my company. I praised the transformation, joking, "All you lack is a tattoo."

"Remind me to show it to you one of these days." The way she said it, she could have been telling the truth.

We arrived at Stardom House ten minutes early and met a lot of cars on their way out. Coburn's blazing blue Rolls—license plate GENEUS, so who else could it belong to?—it was parked by the entrance to the main building. He materialized from somewhere less than a minute after Sharon and I were announced. Smile. Wink. Teeth. He released my hands and dwarfed Sharon's, not shaking them so much as making a hand sandwich while he inspected her face. His head bobbed approvingly.

"Your description did not do the lady justice, Neil. You said 'lovely,' but I know there has to be half a dozen or more suitable adjectives in your stockpile. 'Beautiful' would head my personal list. You, young lady, are far more than a candidate for one of my special Publisher's Platinum Pick Pages in the front of the book. We can just make the deadline for the next issue of *Stardom* if we hurry, Miss Griffith."

The salesman, always selling. Sincere. Charming. Confident. Dressed to impress in a hand-tailored double-breasted sport jacket, subtle gray and taupe plaid tracking perfectly onto precisely measured lapels and sleeves. Pinstriped shirt with a white collar. An Ungaro power tie in a floral pattern that probably cost more than my Nike walkers. Shaped brush denims, in the Hollywood tradition. Gucci loafers; no socks.

When he got Sharon's name wrong, I questioned to myself if it was part of Coburn's technique for infiltrating someone's career. And checking account.

She said, "It's Griffin."

"Beg pardon?"

"My name is Griffin, not Griffith. Wanda Sue Griffin. You may have me confused with Melanie Griffith. The one from *Working Girl*? Married to that hunk Don Johnson? A resemblance, people tell me, stopping me in my local Lucky's and all, but I don't see it. Do you, Neilsy?"

Neilsy?

I was "Neilsy" and Sharon was overacting.

Becoming this person "Wanda Sue Griffin" had been her idea, even after I assured her there was no reason she couldn't be herself.

The real Wanda Sue chairs the Heathcliffe Arms Building and Grounds Committee and is afflicted with the stale orange hair that attacks many women who have crossed the threshold to fifty. She hides her age under layers of makeup, on a reengineered face that hints at a lost beauty, but hardly ever bothers to disguise her body, as firm as silicone and daily workouts at the Westwood Sweat Emporium allow. It's routinely on parade in public areas at the building, in a two-piece string bikini as good as any trout lure when it comes to fishing for bed partners, or so the rumors flow. It's said she alternates between members of the gardening and custodial crews, most recently one Chester Fung, whose green thumb is said to extend beyond the impatiens, azaleas, and hibiscus.

I'd told Sharon, "You're far too young and too attractive for that."

"It's Wanda Sue's attitude I'm going for," she said, sloughing off the compliment. She lectured me for three minutes on Stanislavsky and how becoming Wanda Sue would help put her in a power frame of mind. I didn't know Sharon was aware of Stanislavsky. I added that tidbit to the growing list of things I didn't know about her.

"Griffin." Coburn slammed a palm cushion against his high forehead and gestured apologetically. "Of course, of course, of course. Griffin." He used the error as an excuse to throw an arm across Sharon's back and pull her closer to him. He focused on a distant point in the reception area ceiling, reciting, "First thing we'll have to consider is a name change. We don't want that kind of confusion with Melanie mucking up the calls we'll be achieving for you, not to mention SAG and AFTRA and so and so on."

"How about something like Sharon?" I said. "A contemporary name with a warm old-fashioned feeling about it."

He made a face like he smelled something. "The name. Always a big item on our agenda, especially before Wanda Sue's Publisher's Platinum Pick Page goes to press. We get it wrong the first time, it could haunt us for years to come. A rush to judgment would be worse than missing a deadline."

"Gene, about that Platinum Pick Page . . . Wanda Sue understands the process will cost her a few bucks, I made certain when I told her about the opportunities here, but that kind of outlay." I squeezed my face. "A little too rich for her, I think. What's it for one of those pages? Six grand?"

"Neil, please," Coburn said, releasing his grip on Sharon. She quickly inched closer to me as he took several steps backward, wrapped himself in his arms, and drank in a full-length view of her. "Let that be my worry? She is a friend of yours, after all. Let's just say it's a gift, my way of congratulating you on your exploding new career with Mr. Ted Turner and his Cable News Network."

The way Coburn pronounced "friend" made clear what synonyms he had in mind.

"You're very kind, Gene. I'll find a way to repay your kindness once I'm settled at the network."

His response, sincerity sweeter than his cologne, told me Coburn had bought the lie: "Please, write it off to our own friendship, yours and mine. May it ever prosper and flourish."

"Friendship," I agreed. I was tempted to tell him: *No, Gene, I'm not screwing her, but I am here to screw you.* "Thank you, Gene."

He dismissed me with an exaggerated wave. "Now, back to basics. Mind giving me a quarter-turn, Miss—" Smile. Wink. Teeth. "Griffin? That's it, thank you." He framed her in his hands. "Delicious. Your Wanda Sue is absolutely delicious, Neil."

Sharon looked at me oozing Stanislavsky.

"Now without the jacket," Coburn said. He meant an oversized, formless man's-styled green sports jacket she had added to her costume as an afterthought before we left the Heathcliffe. I figured Coburn wanted a better look at those twin treasures in her too-tight sweater.

Sharon hesitated, like she also suspected what Coburn wanted to eye-spy, then made a quiet show of taking it off and, I thought, enjoyed the attention as any budding starlet might.

She draped the sports jacket over her arm waiter style, clamped a hand onto her hip, and turned from the hips—left, right, left again—giving him the display he hadn't asked for yet.

Coburn clapped his hands together and turned, facing me. "Neil, one of my special pages. TalenTapes. A major file on BB-Stardom offered only to those I feel possess the rare star quality it takes to make it in this business." Turning back to Sharon: "You have that star quality, young lady. In spades. Don't tell this to Neil, but I should pay him for having brought you to Stardom House."

He stepped forward, as if planning to embrace her.

Sharon must have sensed it coming. She turned and threw her arms around me, catching me by surprise. She hammered her mouth onto mine and, on the count of ten, pulled back to say, "Oh, Neilsy-Weilsy, thank you, thank you, thank you."

Neilsy-Weilsy.

She was administering a second submarine kiss on me when Jayne showed up.

Chapter 30

Gene Coburn calling out Jayne's name like an oil-slick carnival barker caused me to move my hands under Sharon's breasts and gently push her off, so quickly that she was left with her tongue hanging out. Jayne and I locked eyes. I blushed like a kid caught short in a drive-in. She traded in a puzzled look for an empty smile and advanced on Coburn.

"What an unexpected, pleasant lift to the end of the day," Coburn said, embracing her. They traded air kisses and some lip grazing before Jayne withdrew and turned back to us.

"Mr. Gulliver," she said, acknowledging me for the first time. "Also getting lifted, I see." She stepped over, extending her hand, her expression matter-of-fact; looked at Sharon the way a reader sounds out foreign words, and formed a smile.

I didn't want to show my panic. All Jayne needed to do was identify Sharon and our little game was over. Sharon was already wide-eyed with discovery. I was distressed by the danger I may have inflicted on her. I hadn't shared any of my suspicions about Jayne when I satisfied Sharon's need to know precisely what it was I proposed getting her into, but she was savvy enough to seize on the problem Jayne posed, how Jayne could upset everything.

She moved on Jayne. She shot out her hand and said, "You must be that wonderful Mrs. Madrigal Neilsy keeps on raving over and over about. My name is Wanda Sue Griffin and I'm pleased t'meetcha. Everybody calls me Wanda, though, just plain Wanda, you like, at least until Mr. Coburn decides what my new name should be."

"*Ms.* Madrigal," Jayne said. She let go of my hand, took Sharon's. "Just plain 'Ms.', just plain Wanda."

They stalked each other with their eyes.

"Griffin, Griffith," I said in a hurry. "Supermarket confusion with Melanie Griffith and Gene wants to come up with something different. What do you think?"

I trapped Jayne's eyes. They signaled she had found the clarity in the confusion, but gave no clue to what she intended saying to Coburn.

Before she could say anything, Coburn said, "Jayne, love, the other day when you and I commiserated over the abrupt departure of Neil here from the *Daily,* you failed to say a single word about his joining the Cable News Network."

I answered for her: "I asked your super PR lady to please not breathe a word until it was announced and official. Ted Turner is one of those people who wants the ink dry on all the dots and crosses."

He studied me, his lips slowly inching into a tight smile. "And you were thoughtful enough to tell me before that happened, make me one of the first to know?"

My whole body sang *What are friends for?*

Jayne broke our connection.

She tilted her face at Sharon. Her eyes narrowed. For a moment they stayed closed and her jaw flinched. She said, "Gene, let me tell you about Wanda Sue Griffin." At once, only two out of four in the room were breathing. Sharon and I weren't the ones. "She's no Wanda Sue Griffin, Gene."

We're goners, I thought.

Jayne said, "I can think of several other names to call just plain Wanda without half trying." A conquering look. "You think it would be possible for me to tear you away from Mr. Gulliver and his protégé for a few? Some business we absolutely must discuss."

Coburn sighed melodramatically and sent Jayne on ahead to his office.

He took Sharon by the elbow and led the way to the registration area. I trailed six steps behind, troubled about what Jayne could be revealing to him minutes from now and playing with excuses that would get us past the problems she might create. Out of here in one piece. *They've already killed . . .*

There was a sense of activity winding down. The foot traffic in retreat from the day. Routine noise no louder than the air-conditioning. Less than a dozen chairs occupied by clients waiting to be processed, mostly mothers and kids engaging in stare-offs, like their competition had already started. Most of the rabbit warrens empty.

Coburn directed us to one and returned shortly with a counselor in tow, Ricardo, according to his name tag. He was older than any of the counselors I'd noticed before. His coffee-house threads, pierced ear, and a home dye job that colored his thinning locks, his scalp, and the modest garden of lifeless brown curlicues protruding from his open shirt wouldn't convince a myopic casting director that Ricardo's age was still in leading man territory.

Coburn gave the thumbs-up sign and assured us Ricardo understood how important this consultation was before he retreated for his office, promising to catch up by the time we reached TalenTapes. "I plan to personally oversee your head shots and concept on your video," Coburn said, aiming an index finger at his chest. Smile. Wink. Teeth. Benevolent squeeze to Sharon's shoulders.

I glanced at my watch.

Five-ten.

Bernie Flame expected my call at five-thirty sharp.

Ricardo maintained his glitzy front after Gene Coburn left, like he was auditioning for a spot at the Big Mac counter, but I recognized how much he resented having his shift extended. Or, maybe, Coburn had told him no commission; this one's on the house. In any event, Ricardo was a bad actor. I waited until he was on page two of what looked like the *War and Peace* of questionnaires to inquire after a men's room. As good an excuse as any to disappear for fifteen or twenty minutes, travel time on top of the minimum five for Bernie. Sharon swallowed her lips, aware this was the first critical moment in the plan.

Ricardo showed me he didn't like being interrupted midrap before he provided me with directions. I used his desk to push up from the visitor's chair and asked to borrow the *Daily Variety* and *Hollywood Reporter* on his desk.

"I'm a fast reader," I said. Smile, wink, and all the teeth I could project. None of it mattered to Ricardo, who pushed his bifocals back against the bridge of his broad nose and looked for his place on the questionnaire.

Sharon compulsively latched onto my thigh. "Don't fall in," she said.

I kissed the top of her head. "Since you ask so nicely, I'll even remember to flush." I headed off, at once checking over my shoulders, expecting to hear Coburn chasing after me any second now.

My watch said five-fifteen.

I didn't have a problem until four minutes later, when I reached the corridor door Coburn had used on our tour as a shortcut to the heart of BBStardom.

Following the same route he had taken me on, I charged through the wing where portrait photographers and Betacam crews were wrapping up their last sessions. I moved swiftly past the editing bays and ducked inside the quality control room, where stacks of monitors were performing hard for the handful of technicians still on duty, indifferent to the stranger in a hurry.

For reasons other than Bernie's deadline, I had set a brisk pace and kept my eyes focused straight ahead. Even the best of security steps aside for someone who gives the impression he belongs and knows where he's going. An old newspaperman's trick that works every time.

"Something I can help you with?"

Maybe not every time.

The voice behind me gave me a jolt as I was about to push aside the piano bench blocking the unmarked door with the glass knob. I flicked at an imaginary piece of lint on the linen lilies in the tall ceramic bowl by the bench and straightened up.

"Just stopping to admire someone's handiwork," I said, turning to look at him, my smile signaling peace on earth to men of good will.

Thick, black horn-rimmed frames were the best feature on the kind of face that breeds its own suspicion. His white smock helped me remember him as one of Knox Lundigan's co-pilots. He played with his skimpy mustache, trying to figure out why I looked familiar.

"You don't work here." I shook my head. "Employees only, this section of Stardom House."

"Looking for the loo, actually." He studied me hard. "A john? The head? A terlet?" I held out the *Daily Variety* and *Hollywood Reporter* and gave them a little tambourine shake. "Guess I turned left when I should have—"

He straight-armed the rest of the sentence and gestured for me to follow him down the corridor. It ended at a T. He pointed me to the right. We traveled down fifty feet of old English racing prints decorating the flocked wallpaper, then through walnut double doors onto a section of corridor painted and dressed with framed *Stardom* magazine covers. An exit sign was posted above the double doors at the end of this corridor. Lundigan's co-pilot pointed it out and I figured he was heading me out. Instead, he stopped halfway, thumbed me to a door whose star-shaped identification plate featured a caricature of Sly Stallone. He parked against the opposite wall, arms entwined. I thanked him and pushed my way inside. I locked myself in one of the three stalls, in case he decided to check.

My watch said twenty-two minutes past five.

I pictured Bernie poised over his laptop in his Charade Hotel suite, waiting for my call. Eight minutes to make the connection, or—

That was that.

The men's room door swung open. Footsteps on the tile. The door swung closed. I couldn't be certain if Lundigan's co-pilot was inside or outside. Either way I had to move fast. I had about two inches and thirty pounds on him. If I managed to get in a fast, lucky blow or—

I reached under my jacket and pulled out the Beretta I'd tucked under my belt, in the small of my back. For show. Just in case. In this day and age, one can never be too rich or too careful. I flushed out of habit and because I'd told Sharon I would. Gripping the gun by the barrel, prepared to use it as a club, I stepped out. The john was empty. So was the corridor.

I said a silent thank you to whatever power had sent Lundigan's co-pilot on his way and returned the Beretta to its hiding place. I retraced my steps to the piano bench, made certain no one was watching, and pushed. The door did not respond the way it had when Coburn turned the old glass knob. I noticed a modern Nislow spring lock underneath, no fancier than the Nislows we used back at the Heathcliffe.

Twenty-four minutes past five.

I maneuvered a credit card between the door jamb and the

Nislow. It wasn't the first time I had applied the two-dollar trick taught me years ago by Jimmy Steiger, on a night he had serious reason to demonstrate the preferred police antidote to risking a broken ankle by kicking in a door, albeit not found in any authorized text at the Police Academy.

The card snapped in half. Maybe dry rot from disuse.

I tried my gas credit card.

The lock sank back.

I hurried inside the room. I locked the door and reached out in darkness for a wall switch, the way Coburn had.

The room was in the same disarray I remembered. Crossing in a hurry, my shoulder hit a high rise of cartons. It began swaying. I wheeled around on my soles. Barely managed to prevent it from crashing down. A moment later, I wasn't so lucky. My shoe hit the base of a stack half again as tall as me and built even more unpredictably than the other stack. The boxes took a nosedive, thumped onto the shrouded furniture, and clunked onto the floor, sending out dust clouds.

I sneezed. The least of my noise problems.

I waited for the door leading into Mission Control to burst open.

When it didn't happen, I allowed myself the luxury of a smile and began to believe the room on the other side would be empty. Quitting time came and everyone had punched out. I could stop worrying about how to get rid of them, the part of the plan that never quite got resolved and was still riding out a moment's inspiration, except—

Whenever I get too cocky, something happens to remind me how humility is best saved for the nineteenth hole. This moment was no exception. I knew the instant I opened the door a crack and heard the static hum, sounding the same way freeway traffic drones in the distance. A peek made the news worse.

Chapter 31

Eight of the ten places for co-pilots at the BBStardom console were occupied.

Knox Lundigan's guy from the corridor was seated two to the right of Lundigan, who was dressed for a picnic and just getting up from the captain's seat. Lundigan shook his head and called out casual orders en route to the forward wall of a hundred and forty monitors.

He stopped at a control panel and began manipulating a series of dials and switches with one hand and an auxiliary keyboard with the other. The colors changed. Images came and went. No two images were alike. None remotely resembled what I remembered from the blue floppy.

Twenty-seven minutes past five.

I closed the door and retreated back into the storeroom. I stuck out my chin, eyes shut, lips pursed in frustration, and shook my fists at the air like, maybe, I'd punch a hole through an idea pocket. A second ago I'd seen something. What? I opened my eyes and smiled at the magic of solutions above me—

The sprinkler system.

No time to waste.

Two computer packing cases near the filing and storage shelves were being used for rubbish. I heaved them up onto one of the desks supporting two layers of cardboard shipping cartons, dumped in wadded paper stuffing from some of the open boxes nearby, added liberated rolls of fax paper, some stacks of computer paper, pads, envelopes, and anything else that looked burnable. I emptied in three monstrous bottles of opaque fluid. I found industrial-size bottles and cans of wood panel cleaner and wood and metal polish. I checked the labels for combustibility and poured them in.

I searched my pockets for my cigarette lighter.

I came up empty-handed.

I chided my memory for letting me forget I'd quit smoking last year.

I started pulling out any drawers I could find. Pennies and paper clips. Rubber bands. Staples. Scotch tape. Post-it pads. No book matches. No stick matches. No cheap lighters starring clear-vu nude mermaids or go-go dancers with breasts like watermelons. History will one day record the date when the whole world stopped smoking.

Think, Neil, think.

I thought. I thought some more. I—

—began laughing at the walls, crazy laughter, because I was about to do something absolutely nuts.

Several white smocks were hanging on a wooden coat rack by the Mission Control door. I pulled one off the peg and replaced it with my jacket. The fit was tight, but good enough for my purposes. I ran my fingers through my hair and pulled it up, hoping for a Stan Laurel effect that would oblige Knox Lundigan to think twice if he thought he knew me; same for his co-pilot from the corridor.

I took two deep breaths, entered Mission Control, and slipped into the nearest empty seat at the main console. Lundigan was still working at the control panel and had his back to me. Six other white smocks were between me and the corridor co-pilot, if he bothered to look up from what he was doing and glance over.

No smoking was allowed, so there were no visible clues to play with. I leaned in on the guy to my left, early twenties and so nearsighted his hawk nose almost touched the blue screen while he pumped out commands at a hundred-plus keystrokes a minute.

I said, "Got a light?" No response. This time I drilled the words straight into his ear: "Got a light?" If anybody else heard me, they didn't bother to show it. Hawk Nose turned his head so fast his nose scraped my cheek. He gave me his best show of irritation, adding a onceover and a mild look of curiosity before going back to work. Something else was on his mind. He couldn't be bothered.

I tried the question on the young Asian woman to my left, who sucked her thumb while memorizing the windows on her screen, which she outlined with the index finger of her other hand. She tried both pockets and could do no better than an after-dinner mint in green foil.

I looked over the console at Lundigan and trailed my eyes up to the row of digital clocks telling the time at a dozen international locations. The only time zone of interest to me was this one. The main digits shifted again.

Five-thirty.

I had to tell Bernie something or risk him wandering off figuring something went sour at my end.

I picked up the station phone and felt my heart eating through my chest as I dialed the 800 number for the Charade Hotel.

Somebody picked up on the first ring: "TalenTapes production, Grelun speaking."

I disconnected, took a deep breath, asked the ceiling for forgiveness, and this time punched in a nine first. I was praying

Stardom House used the normal digit that connects to an outside line.

I willed the room to freeze in time and space as the phone rang a dozen times.

A Charade operator come on the line briefly and challenged me to wait, in a raspy voice that provided no options. Tom Jones was singing into my ear how it's not unusual to be loved by anyone, until a different operator volunteered help in one of those start-of-the-shift voices.

The phone in Bernie Flame's suite rang.

And rang.

And rang.

And Hawk Nose stopped what he was doing. He leaned in to inspect my left breast, reared back. He stared me down the way some people examine a fart suspect. He got up, made a show of gathering papers, and headed off.

It had to be the name badge. I hadn't bothered to check it when I traded my jacket for the smock. I fiddled it around so I could read it: EMILY. I checked for Hawk Nose. He was on his way over to Knox Lundigan.

The operator with the raspy voice cut in to ask if somebody was helping me. She cut out before I could answer. Bernie's phone rang another million times or two before a third operator offered assistance. I took a chance. I had Bernie paged in the casino.

Whitney Houston finished singing to me.

Merle Haggard started singing to me.

Somewhere between Tom Jones and Whitney Houston, Hawk Nose had reached Lundigan.

Hawk Nose kept his back to me and may have been waiting for Lundigan to finish what he was doing. I couldn't tell if they were speaking. Lundigan rose abruptly. He looked in my direction. I sank below eye level.

The third Charade operator said in his birdcage voice, "Go ahead, please."

Vegas came alive in my ear.

"Yeah? So?" Bernie. Irritated. Probably for having been dragged away from the table action.

I whispered: "Gulliver, Bernie."

"Can't hear you. Can you talk up?"

I rose up enough to see about Lundigan and Hawk Nose. Lundigan was on the phone. Hawk Nose was staring at me. He quickly turned away.

I raised my voice as much as I dared.

Bernie said, "I still can't—" Came to a dead stop. In the background, an explosion of jubilation. Someone had scored somewhere in the casino. "Oh, Jesus. Holy Moses, Jesus and Allah. Christ. Neil, that you?"

Lundigan replaced the phone and said something to Hawk Nose.

Bernie saying: "They got no goddamn clocks anywheres around this place, Neil, and mine's sitting on the damn dresser upstairs. Gimme five. Ten, make it, and call me back. Okay. Jeez. I am so sorry, man, I—"

Two men hurried into Mission Control through the main entrance and joined Knox Lundigan and Hawk Nose. The dark suits they wore were almost identical. Both looking like they'd be more comfortable in loincloths. One was bigger than the other and both were bigger than me. No doubt security people.

Lundigan said something and pointed to the No Smoking sign, a red circle with a diagonal red stripe through the cigarette. The suit who was smoking extinguished his butt on the sole of his highly polished shoe and dropped it in a pocket.

"You there, Neil? You hear what I been saying?" The suits stood at parade rest as Lundigan identified me with shifting eyes. Their eyes shifted over here. Hawk Nose looked at me like

I'd stepped on his gonads. "Outta here now, man. Up and out, leaving The Jewel to guard my stash at the table. Okay?"

"Okay." I said it loud enough for Bernie to hear me. A few heads turned to stare.

I disconnected and retreated to the storage room. I didn't have to look to know the suits would be clumping after me. I fumbled with the lock on the corridor door, opened the door wide enough to suggest I'd kept on going, and ducked behind a set of double-decker desks shrouded by a blanket. The suits came crashing through the connecting door. They stopped to look around, grunted observations back and forth, and hurried into the corridor. After a moment, as I was rising, I heard a click to my left and froze. Someone shutting the back door to Mission Control.

After another minute, after checking to make certain the corridor was safe, I was about to step out and choose a direction when I thought I heard the suits and pulled back inside. I dropped onto all fours and got under the blankets protecting the desks just as they came through the door. I kept enough face exposed to breathe more than dust and tried not to think about sneezing.

"I ask you again, Randall, why anybody in his right mind would want to play nerd."

"Takes all kinds."

"Now, roosting in a closet and doing some keyhole while the babes show off their tits and ass for the camera, that I understand."

"You've done it often enough."

"I suppose you haven't?"

Mutual laughter.

"You got a light?"

"You just hear Mr. Clean on that subject?"

"That was there, this is here . . . Thanks." Snap. The smell of phosphorous. Burning tobacco. An explosion of light. "Hey!"

"Ohmigod!"

Now the smell was more than phosphorous and tobacco. The suit must have tossed his match into one of my fire boxes.

"—get the fug out of here!"

Fire alarms were going off all over and the sprinkler system was raining.

Hissing noises.

The smell and sizzle of smoke.

A confusion of anxious and frightened voices thundering through the storage room.

Quiet, except for the relentless water shower.

I crawled out from under the blanket and was drenched before I got to my feet. I was fairly certain the downpour would continue until the fire boys arrived. I also knew better than to presume I had time to spare.

Both doors were wide open.

Outside in the corridor, flashes of wet clothing whisked by.

I maneuvered around the rubble of tumbled cartons and boxes caused by the mass exodus from Mission Control, aiming for the connecting door. I banged my legs hard a few times but refused to feel the pain.

Lundigan and his crew had left everything up and running when they charged off.

The sprinklers didn't seem to be affecting any operations.

I already had the phone into my hand as I dropped into Lundigan's chair.

This time it only took me twice as long to connect with Bernie in his suite.

"You know how sorry I am, Neil?"

"For later, Bernie. For now just tell me what to do."

"Got back here and somebody stole my watch right from my dresser. Serves me right. Serves me damn right for standing you up that way."

"Bernie, I'm drowning here."

"Okay, okay. Listen up. I want to hear again what you see on your monitor . . . Okay, good; great . . . Now I want you to hit Escape and see where that puts us . . . Yeah, tell me one more time what it looks like—good. Like I thought. What I want you to do next. I'm gonna try taking us direct to a T-prompt. No, T-prompt. T for *tooches*. I don't need you to get to the C-prompt. You watch the prompt and tell me when—good. You see a new menu box running halfway down the right side of the screen? Read me what it says . . . Neil, I don't care it don't make sense to you. It gotta make sense to me, *farshteit*?"

Answering Bernie was easy so long as he wanted to know anything I could recite off the monitor. I hit commands and keys he called out, never knowing what was being accomplished. The screen would go through tricks too quick to catch, hold on pages lifted from some dictionary of the absurd, and he would inject a cheer for the brilliance of Knox Lundigan. Or for himself, for solving the mysteries of BBStardom. I wiped water from my eyes and did as I was told. I'd quit trying to figure any of it out after the first two minutes. Two minutes after that, Bernie sounded a musical note and pronounced himself satisfied.

"You can get your *tooches* in gear and outta there anytime you like, Neil."

"You're sure, Bernie?"

"Neil, my man, you could bet a million on it." My monitor faded to black, then exploded on again. A sentence appeared mid-screen:

YOU COULD BET TWO MILLION ON IT EVEN.

Fade to black, then Bernie on the phone asking, "Screen like you found it?"

"I think so."

"Same for them wall monitors you told me?"

I checked. "Yes."

I heard Bernie's fingers improvising on his laptop and, after the last keystroke, all the monitors went black. They flashed on an instant later, shorn of their innocence, bass notes in a symphony of porn. One hundred and forty monitors and no two scenes alike. I thought I saw—

Rotted humanity, beyond anything I'd seen on the blue floppy.

That old feeling of bubbling lava in my belly, and—

A face I knew.

Staring back, eyes locked on mine.

I gaped so long I took in a mouthful of water and began choking and coughing. I pressed a hand hard against my chest and cleared my throat and, by the time I was done, Bernie's demonstration was over.

"So, relax, Neil, r-e-lax. We'll all be heading home from Lost Wages on Sunday. Monday bright and early, me and you can finish up the process. It can wait till then?"

"Do I have a choice?"

"The honeymoon's already too short."

The whooping wail of sirens I'd first become aware of as rumors in the distance quit one by one outside Stardom House. I was overdue escaping from here, before some firefighters or worse trapped me and I was obliged to answer the wrong questions.

I hung up.

I felt a hand on my shoulder.

My body grew two inches.

Only the gentleness of the pressure kept me anchored to the seat. My chest closed in like an accordion.

It was Jayne.

★ ★ ★ ★ ★

There was no way of knowing how long Jayne had been standing behind me or what she had seen. I rolled back the chair and got up, not knowing what to make of the moment.

She reached out to touch the ID badge and said, "Emily, get the hell out of here before somebody else finds you."

I opened my mouth to say something.

She stopped me with her hand pressed flat against my lips. "Don't say it."

I moved her hand away. I had to know. "A man named Bailey Madison. He told me you're part of all the shit going down here."

Jayne laughed, a childlike laugh, and stuck out her chin defiantly, "It's not what you think, Scaredy-cat, no matter what you think." The sprinkler system was making a mess of her hair and makeup. Across the room, muffled voices and footsteps in a hurry echoed from somewhere outside the open corridor door.

"Tell me anyway."

"No time now. Later."

When I didn't budge, Jayne said, "I am part of all the shit going down here." She flagged a thumb over her shoulder, in the direction of the storeroom. "Now, get your jacket and the hell out of here."

My emotions didn't know where to begin.

I started for the storeroom.

"Neil."

Jayne's voice turned me around as I was about to pass through the doorway. She brought her fingers to her lips and blew the kiss to me.

I caught it left-handed and said, "Later."

"Later," she agreed.

Trails of black mascara floated down her cheeks and, joined

to a pout that never quite became a smile, made her look like the sad clown's wife.

Charging out of Stardom House past hunting and sniffing firefighters looking for something to break, I made a show of calling for Wanda Sue Griffin. My eyes were red and they stung and my lungs were congested from all the smoke I had eaten, souvenirs of my refusal to flee the premises before making sure Wanda Sue wasn't trapped somewhere inside.

No problem spotting any others who'd fled the building. They were the wet ones, doing their best to towel dry or clinging to blankets that provided some protection from the unusual cold snap of an early evening illuminated by a curious gray translucence that often redefines the Southern California darkness into daylight.

I found Sharon with Coburn and Lundigan, toweling herself off while the partners engaged in animated conversation with a fire marshal. He was an old-timer with intelligent eyes and a handlebar mustache, who wore a dead cigar in the crook of his mouth and his yellow hardhat under an arm as he jotted down their responses onto the report pad in his clipboard.

The two suits were nearby, giving their statements to another marshal. One of them lit a cigarette and immediately had second thoughts. He pulled it from his lips, bombed it onto the asphalt, and ground it out under a heel, all the while checking for other suspects.

I spotted Ricardo the career counselor and Hawk Nose a few feet away from them. They were leaning against a fire department ambulance, chatting like strangers bonded by a common event. I made sure I still had the trades in my pocket, but was not about to hand them over now. Hawk Nose had made enough trouble for one day.

I yelled out Wanda Sue's name as I approached.

Sharon leaped into my arms gratefully. The second kiss was warmer than the first. Her lips parted wide and stayed pressed hard on mine longer than I wanted. She stepped away and I knew by her face that Sharon's concern for my safety had been real.

Coburn excused himself from the fire marshal and joined us with a blanket he had solicited from one of the firefighters passing by with a stack of them. He draped it across her shoulders.

He said, "I can't tell you how frantic your lady became, Neil." Smile. Wink. Teeth. "Whatever goes on in your career, Wanda Sue, I respect the quality of your real emotions."

"Oh, Neilsy," Sharon said, agreeing with him. She let her eyes linger on my face while turning her towel into a turban. I couldn't tell where her acting stopped. There was no disputing the message in the kiss, so maybe her distress wasn't my invention.

Lundigan finished giving his statement and joined us. Coburn reminded him who I was. We shared a perfunctory handshake. He stared past my shoulder and said something, but spoke too softly for me to comprehend his words. If he recognized me, he didn't show it. He exchanged a knowing look with Coburn, then excused himself and started off in the direction of the mansion.

Coburn made a clucking sound and followed him with his eyes. "Surprised Knox waited this long," he said, fiddling with a grin. "Knox has gone to check his systems. The whole damn world could go up in flames and, mark my words, they'd still be operating, the way he has them built." Lundigan altered course, veering off in the direction of the wing housing BBStardom. "Neil, it's the remarkable attention to detail that makes Knox who and what he is. Same for all geniuses, I suppose. That's a point I'm hopeful you'll be able to get across on the Cable News Network."

"Mr. Coburn?"

We both turned automatically at the sound of the voice. Hawk Nose stood a foot away from us. Coburn smeared a patronizing smile across his face and waited for the man to say something. When Hawk Nose didn't, Coburn said, "Just speak up, man." My pulse took off for Jupiter. Hawk Nose let his eyes drift between us as he collected his thoughts. They froze on me. He squeezed them for focus and memory. My pulse made a sharp left turn at Saturn. I caught another breath and retreated behind my Steve McQueen grin while logging a new definition for "identity crisis." Hawk Nose gave the situation another few seconds before casting it aside. He said, "I'm shook up by all this and got a worrying wife at home, Mr. Coburn. You think I might clock out early tonight?"

On the ride home, Sharon stopped chattering when she realized I wasn't listening. A few miles later, she gave up waiting for me to volunteer information. My mind had turned elsewhere after I renewed my thanks and appreciation to her. I had become absorbed with adding today's events to what I already knew.

All the compilation process did was produce a frustrating table of omissions and contradictions, over and over and over again.

Sharon said she understood and didn't press. I was thankful for that.

She turned on the radio and switched FM bands until she got to a classical station sampling familiar themes and making no demands for attention.

She was sleeping when I pulled into the garage, hunched in the space between the passenger seat and the door. Her strong chin rested on her chest. She gripped her elbows in a way that popped her breasts under the damp cashmere sweater and made me think about Sharon as Wanda Sue Griffin in a way I'd never contemplated Sharon as Sharon. I turned on the heater when she quivered a second time, from dampness or from the chill brought on by her own memories of the day.

She breathed evenly through her mouth and, except for an occasional twitch of the lower lip, gave no evidence of the tension and anxiety I read on her face when I found her with Coburn and Lundigan.

Maybe she could tell I was studying her. She roused and drew a close-mouthed smile and let other emotions dance around her face while shifting closer to give my arm a gentle squeeze just above the wrist. Whatever she thought it meant, it made me feel good. Before I figured how to let her know, she was back in her corner, hands cupped delicately in her lap, her breathing regular, and the tilted happy smile still in place.

My thoughts went back to Jayne.

I took my left hand off the wheel and thought about the kiss I had captured from her back at Mission Control. Did she really care about me or was that just part of some act ordered by Coburn? *There is evidence she is one of them, Neil.* I touched my fingers to my mouth and glanced over at Sharon. I experienced a moment of inexplicable guilt.

"Later," Jayne had said.

Later, I'd have more questions.

Later, she might have some of the answers I'd been after since Roddy Donaldson first turned simple confusion into a complex conundrum.

Later, when later finally came, Jayne was dead.

CHAPTER 32

"You were a real champ today," I told Sharon. "Even after I warned you there might be some embarrassment, maybe some risk if I screwed up, you didn't hesitate."

"Maybe it's because I've seen one Sigourney Weaver film too many?" I frowned at her effort to downplay her deed. She said, "I trusted you. You wouldn't have asked me to go with you if I was going to be in any real danger . . . Would you?" She was standing like a schoolgirl, hands clasped, one shoe shifting on its heel; nevertheless, revealing the woman behind the disguise; her eyes eating mine.

I studied the corridor and my shoes, feeling sudden, painful twinges of conscience. What if I'd been found out, and Sharon? *They've already killed.* "If anything had happened to you, I don't think I'd ever—"

"Neil. Please." Her eyes read the wallpaper behind me, on the wall across from her door. "I would not have done it if I did not want to do it. Fact is, you gave me the kind of challenge that has never entered my life." She caught her breath, as if she'd revealed too much about herself.

I said, "You mean you didn't do it for me?" Teasing. Rubbing away the spot I saw she didn't want to be on.

"I did it for me, Neil. I'd like you to know that. It wasn't always that way in my life, but it is now." Sharon turned her eyes back onto me, desperate for—

What?

She and I were communicating at a new level.

"I owe you thanks, Neil, not the other way around."

"Why don't we talk about it later, after a good movie and over a better dinner?"

"And a great bottle of wine," she said, smiling before I could. "But on some other night? Now I think I need to crawl into a hot tub and soak, and send what's left of Wanda Sue down the drainpipe."

"Some other night, and a great, great bottle of wine."

Mutual laughter.

Friendship back on track.

Absolutely back on track.

Felt good. Her kiss, too. Not like her kiss at Stardom House. This kiss said thank you and you're welcome at once, or was that me?

I fast-changed into dry sweats and a warm-up jacket and went back downstairs to find Gus Ljung. He and I had serious business to talk about. A fetching brunette showing off in a Bruins cheerleading outfit was at the entry phone in the outer lobby, bouncing from foot to foot while waiting to be buzzed inside. Gus wasn't at the guard's desk.

I checked my watch and figured him for a Detex tour of the building. We'd added key stations and were running them more often since some new instances of garage and apartment break-ins and vandalism during the overnight shift. Gus could be gone another ten minutes or for an hour.

Still riding an empty stomach and an adrenalin high, I strolled up to the Village, planning to taper down over a monster pepperoni and mushroom pizza and a few tap brews at Janino's Magic Pizza Palace.

The sidewalks were almost deserted, a Thursday calm before the weekend turned Westwood into a bazaar, streets full of high school and college kids crowding curio shops and fast-food joints, lining up for the new movies at what was the greatest concentration of theaters in the country before the advent of those cramped maximulticineplusplexes where screens are smaller and the price of admission taller. The sky was clean. A subdued light; the moon playing games behind a wall of portable clouds being pushed west by the warm winds blowing in from the desert.

Thinking man's weather.

I returned to the Heathcliffe a little after eleven, carrying three slices of pizza in a pie tin and a glow from a third half-yard of beer, won betting a pimply-faced counterman whose metallic voice carried a sheen as greasy as my pepperoni and thought he knew more about Broadway show tunes. He'd be remembering me anytime anyone mentioned Barbara Cook and *Flahooley.*

Gus still wasn't at his station. I left a note on the desk instructing him to phone me no matter what the time, to be certain we caught up with each other before his shift ended and he split. He had no cause to suspect my motives, but I took the precaution of making a reference to "the usual security stuff."

By the time I'd filled the tub and undressed, my eyes were playing tricks on me. I stretched out on the bed for a few minutes. When the phone startled me awake, the digital on the nightstand said it wasn't even midnight, so why was daylight streaming through the window?

"I wake you?"

"Maybe. What time's it, Jimmy?" I squeezed the back of my neck and did a little trick with my eyes that produced a yawn; then, another.

"Almost noon, pard." I moved into a sitting position, my feet on the floor and my back turned away from the light. "Whatever happened to Mr. Early Bird? You get tired of munching on worms?"

I said, "Coming off a day and a dream full of them. Give me an hour to get my act together. I'll call you and spill me guts."

"I'm downstairs, pard. Something happened here during the wee small hours to get me back on the route post haste." He cleared his throat, paused too long for me to fear the best, and gave me news worse than he made it sound. "Jayne Madrigal?"

The south elevator vestibule on the garage level dead-ends five giant steps north of the elevator door, at an impenetrable metal storage room doorway painted gunmetal gray. The interior measures about seven feet in length and five feet wide, undefined spaced used for housing odds and ends that appear to have some value but are routinely forgotten once they're out of sight.

I was inside once, when Sharon led new board members on a full building tour. I remembered now, as I got ready to step inside again, how I had joked about our making a few bucks subleasing the space to the county jail for use as a solitary confinement cell. It might become necessary to give a little on the price, I speculated, because there was only one electrical outlet and no running water.

Now I was hearing how, yesterday, when Sharon did one of her routine punch list inspections, none of the master keys worked in the door. The lock had been replaced since she checked two months ago. She was more concerned than she might be because she had not authorized the change and scratches on the polished surface indicated frequent use.

This morning, shortly after ten, the locksmith who routinely gets the Heathcliffe's business, Harry Weiss, a small, dapper gentleman with impeccable European manners and a discreet mustache, showed up to unlock the door. He also had Sharon's authorization to install a new, tougher lock.

Harry did his magic and the door swung open quietly, as if the fat hinges had been oiled recently. He couldn't find the light switch and the vestibule overhead was no help. He took a small flashlight from his tool kit, aimed it at the far wall, and stepped inside.

Almost at once, he tripped, dropping the flashlight. He leaned hard on his hands and knees and banged his forehead against the sharp edge of something that turned out to be a coffee table. The flashlight clinked to the stone ground. It rolled to a stop pointing at what was, to Harry, the chalky face of a dead man sprawled on the cold cement.

As a young boy, Harry had survived Auschwitz. He had stared death in the face like this many times. Calmly, he closed and locked the door, took the elevator to the lobby level. After learning that Sharon was out running errands until two o'clock, Harry told the guard to call the police. The cops discovered something Harry had not, a second corpse in the storage room. A woman.

When Jimmy Steiger got there, he recognized both corpses well enough to make tentative idents. He had waited until the M.E. and the crime lab team had things underway before calling me.

I got to the storage room in less than five minutes, half-dressed, barefoot, my heart beating loud enough for a marching band, praying it wasn't my cop friend's idea of a lousy joke. Knowing better. My mind wasn't working clearly. I couldn't remember ever talking to him about Jayne and me. I must have.

Jimmy was hanging across from the elevator, trying to keep out of the way of the badge traffic, waiting for the door to let me out, the know-it-all SOB. When he insisted on repeating the story he'd heard from Harry Weiss, I knew it was only to build in some calm-down time for me.

"It's not going to work, Jimmy."

He shrugged. "You don't have to go in there, you don't want."

"I can handle it."

"Not a question of handling." He eased his football body between me and the room. His pallid gray eyes treated me more gently and I knew I'd have to thank him one day, for sharing the hurt on so little information.

"I said I can handle it, Jimmy."

Steiger cocked his head and held up his hands in surrender. He stepped aside so I could join the medical examiner and three other techs working in the confined space.

Somebody had been living down here. The only storage was a chaise lounge and a wrought iron patio table with a cracked green glass top the Board replaced last summer. I recognized several chairs as having been reported missing from various common areas. A floor lamp was twin to a pair in the meeting room off the lobby. Three cardboard wardrobe closets were pushed together against the wall inside the doorway, to my left. Other Bekins storage cartons were piled on top of them.

An electric floor heater. In a corner, a set of barbells and a slant board. On the patio table, a small black and white TV monitor and a portable ghetto blaster. Below the table, two portable video cameras and boxes of unopened tape. Magazines and a stack of books on a chair. SAS posters carefully taped along the wall across from the bed. A dozen or so macho and muscle pinups from fitness magazines taped artistically on the wall above the bed. Wherever there was floor space or a usable surface, car stereos I suspected would match security reports filed on stereos boosted from cars in the Heathcliffe parking garage.

The medical examiner, Doc Cuevas, was on his haunches, alongside the corpus of Gus Ljung.

He looked up like he was getting ready to say something to a grim-faced young assistant hovering alongside when he spotted me. He squinted into the harsh light of two flood lamps lighting the room like a movie set, going for a definite make. A moment later, curiosity left his drinker's face and he motioned a welcome. "Gulliver, you become a bad luck charm or what?" he said, with energy belying his sixty-plus years. "Didn't we just go through this here a week ago? *Verdad?*"

Jimmy was behind me. He called out, "Doc, Gulliver knows one of the victims, remember?" For my benefit, he was trying to cut off any more of the usual crime scene sass.

Doc Cuevas reacted as if he were hearing old news. He made a face and went back to work over the body of Gus Ljung, who looked like he'd been taken out by a single bullet that entered at close range at the left cheek, where Gus Ljung once had an eye. Blood was splattered lightly there, like a Jackson Pollock painting.

Jimmy confirmed it in my ear. Small caliber. Probably a .22, judging by the size of the entry wound and the nature of the damage. Upward projection. Rear exit. The slug lost.

I felt his hands on my shoulders. He said, "It was neater for her, pard." Pressing the button intentionally, treating me like a civilian, knowing the faster he got me through this, the faster we'd be out of here.

Until now, I hadn't wanted to acknowledge Jayne's presence. Something inside me wouldn't allow it. I still didn't, but I could no longer reject the truth of Jimmy's reality.

I fought a surge of nausea forcing myself to look at the chaise, its back tilted at a forty-five degree angle. Jayne could be napping, waiting for the sunshine to break through the ceiling, except for the flaccid posture death brings. Her natural tan had drained away. There was a sunken quality to her face. It would have taken a few more hours here like this to completely distort her beauty.

Sometime between now and the last time I saw her at Stardom House, Jayne had traded her business outfit for a cowl-neck sweater and tight blue jeans full of fashionable holes. Her hair was pulled back into a pony tail and tied with a sage green ribbon matching the sweater. Her makeup was perfect. I couldn't visualize Jayne ever dressed this casually, except times when we were alone.

Jimmy said, "The doc will tell you all the signs point to it happening ten, twelve hours ago, somewhere around midnight. Condition of the bodies and barely any sense of odor—"

"Enough, Jimmy."

All I smelled was Jayne's perfume. Or was I remembering?

I ducked under his grip and moved around to the side of the chaise opposite where two of Doc's people were working. They also knew something and were trying not to let on they were following our conversation. They moved away as I motioned Jimmy to back off. He stayed on my heels anyway.

"Fast and clean," Jimmy was saying, soothing me like one of his children with a boo-boo. "The .22 looks to have been pressed right against her temple. Powder burns. Usual signs. They dug out the slug from the base of the wall behind, so figure she must have been sitting when it happened. Didn't feel a thing. Probably too fast for her to know the shot was coming."

"Jimmy, if I want Dan Rather I tune in Dan Rather."

"Ease up, pard. C'mon. Enough."

"I owe somebody for this, Jimmy."

"No argument from me, okay?"

I leaned in closer for one last look at Jayne. I touched a finger to my lips and moved it to hers, then poked at the cleft in her chin. I heard myself repeating: "I owe somebody for this, Jimmy." Whatever he answered this time was lost on me.

For the first time in God knows how many years, I wanted to kill somebody.

I could.

I could do it.

I could.

I'm not one for mourning. I've seen the apathy happen to a lot of people whose life gets too full of death. The war and the crime beat accomplished that for me. Somebody I know turns off, I do two things.

I check the birth announcements that run every day in the *Daily.* I choose a child's name that appeals to me. I phone a florist's shop and order something expensive, pretty, and potted delivered to the mother, specifying no signature on the congratulatory card. Then, I hole up for three days. I turn off the phones and the rest of the world. I do a lot of thinking about my departed friend. I catalog the good times we shared, how those times may have helped make me a better person. At the least, no worse a person.

Over the years, a few people aware of my habit, who figure they know me well, have asked, *Why three days?* The real story still hurts too much to deal with, so I tell a story a rabbi friend helped me dream up. I tell them how the custom is a carryover from one of the lost tribes of Israel, who celebrated only the first three days of the traditional seven-day *shiva* period, the days for weeping. I always get bobbing heads, a respectful understanding, as if the custom makes sense.

The clerk at the St. John's Hospital gift shop assured me in a voice full of childlike enthusiasm that Mrs. Skolnik would be delighted by the remarkably pretty salmon-colored azalea with white ruffled edges she was eyeing in the display fridge even as we spoke. Mrs. Skolnik had named her new six-pound, eight-ounce daughter "Gislaine Marie."

Gislaine.

As close as I could find to "Jayne."

I did most of my sleeping in front of the television, which I didn't watch. I kept it tuned to CNN, in case humor broke out anywhere in the world. I frequently refilled the five slots in my CD player and kept the music on automatic replay, but caught myself a couple times listening to the same albums over and over. Maybe it was more a case of *not* listening, just being surrounded by old friends; music I'd learned to hum without making a sound.

I took nourishment from the remains of my Janino's Magic Pizza Palace pizza, washing it down with beer and Diet Coke. When the pizza disappeared, I drew from my stockpile of Campbell's chunky soups, eating the chicken and noodles straight from the can. I paced a lot, sizing the rooms, charting new courses when I tired of old scenery. I do my best thinking on my feet, and I was up for the best of my best over the three days. As prescribed by Oscar Hammerstein, I started at the very beginning—a very good place to be—and like the Sondheim on the Sony, put it together—bit by bit, piece by piece.

On their first day at the Police Academy, the future badges learn how solutions in any criminal investigation are derived from intensive, orderly follow-up on known facts; by working from the inside out the way the Method actors like Brando discover the core of the character they intend to become.

The process takes into consideration the accidents of discovery and a whole lot of luck, but generally discounts working possibilities from the outside in, the way Olivier did it. Olivier would first achieve the soul of a character, applying makeup and fixing pieces of a false face until he was satisfied with what stared back at him in the mirror.

Neil Gulliver's "mom and apple pie" approach borrows a little of the best from both systems.

MOM = Motive, Opportunity, Means.

Add a cup of intelligence, a dash of examination, a pinch of interpretation. Some evaluation for flavoring. Stir and bake for three days, and maybe after three days you have yourself a damn fine apple pie.

By Monday morning I was confident I had mine. I could smell the pie baking in the oven, full of apples and answers to most of the questions raised since the night I went into Roddy Donaldson's apartment and all of this began.

I showered and shaved, made fresh coffee, and took my news on the tube.

The killing of Jayne and Gus Ljung had given everyone an excuse to exhume old chapters and verse about Hope Danbury and Janie Doe. A news anchor on one of the local channels displayed the front page of the *Daily,* where a 72-point headline over Buster Byrd's byline read:

MURDER MANSION MYSTERIES MOUNT

There goes the neighborhood, I thought, while attacking a yawn with the back of my hand and reaching for the telephone. I thought: *Keep it light, Neil. Grief only gets in the way.*

Chapter 33

Maisie Scanlon, last remaining vestige of the *Daily*'s old editorial switchboard full of operators and plug holes, was off today. Her machine didn't sound particularly pleased to know I was returning her call. Miss Maisie—she was always "Miss Maisie" around the *Daily*—had made me a special pet early in the game and I could always rely on her to keep me abreast of office politics, but it was usually me who did the calling. Whenever she bothered, it had to be important.

That temporarily handled, I moved on to important calls of my own, starting with Rev. Ronnie Plantation. I told him it was important he find Bailey Madison for me and shared a small taste of the reason why.

"Count on me, Brother Gulliver," the preacher said, like he'd be dialing the minute we were done.

Jimmy Steiger listened hard to what I had to say after dropping the usual come-over-for-dinner invitations and doing a sound check on me. "Your usual three days?"

"To the minute."

"What was the name you picked?"

"Gislaine."

"Sounds French."

"Probably."

"She would have liked that?"

"I liked it for her."

The next three calls were long ones.

I got some of the answers I wanted and dialed Melba Donaldson's office number. That got me Judith at the message center, instead of a machine. Judith had street-corner hustle in her voice, like her mind was already linked to one of the phones ringing in the background. She didn't pronounce Melba's name so much as she auditioned it. I left my name and number and said it was urgent.

Bernie's number didn't answer. I dialed Stevie. Her service picked up on the eighth ring and I found myself talking to Judith again. She slowed to a tap dance when I gave her my name, like she remembered me from three minutes ago and this would advance her to the challenge round.

Her voice embraced a smile. "You're a producer, maybe? If you are, I have some new composites and an updated résumé and—"

Disproving my long-held theory that struggling actors in Hollywood were only allowed to work as waiters and waitresses, the occasional bartender.

I got in another couple calls and was ticking off names on my checklist when the private line rang. I snapped it up, thinking it might be Stevie.

It was Miss Maisie.

After all the plant's communications systems were transformed into sleek marvels of modern technology, she'd been kept on to supervise the phones, ostensibly because of her magic memory. It was said and often proven that Miss Maisie could recite any phone number she had heard during her fifty years with the paper, a career she owed, according to legend, to an affair that began after World War II with the boss, Col. Sam Bixel, who saw more than fragile beauty and an alabaster complexion in the feisty, no-nonsense woman standing an inch or two under five feet, a ring of orange hair, and, usually, thick clouds of tobacco smoke.

When Bernie Flame proposed copying BBStardom onto the *Daily*'s mainframe, I didn't hesitate calling Miss Maisie. I told her what Bernie said he would need, and that took care of that. No questions asked.

This morning, Miss Maisie was in a lousy mood.

"Why I ain't working today?" she said hoarsely. "The whole damned system, it's down. When we rigged it whatever day that was, I wanted to be sure your friend in Vegas got connected okay to the special number, exactly the way he wanted it set up. Everything was hunky-dory, you hear what I'm saying, good-looking?" She cleared her throat and told me to hold on while she lit a fresh Camel. "I stuck around to make sure and it was. Why I was calling when I left you my message, whenever that was, you hear?

"Anyways, the next day you could've sworn terrorists had taken over the building, the way people screamed and carried on. Even your friend, that little weasel Wilkins." She made a sound like she had swallowed a slimy toad. "Like Japan was attacking and he was Pearl Harbor, y'know? I keep hearing something about a virus eating up everything on the mainframe. It don't sound so healthy. Immediately, I start to thinking about what we done the day before with this Bernie Flame.

"I try the special number we set up and not nothing. Nothing. Like the number, it never existed in the first place. Either you're not there or you're not picking up when I call, so I take it on myself to get hold of this Bernie Flame at the Charade. He gets back to me after twenty minutes and he tells me to tell you—I'm reading it right here from my pad—to tell Neil it's a total wash. He says to tell you the virus is probably some unknown flavor of the day and to tell you Knox Lundigan strikes again. He says to tell you you'll know what that means. You know what that means?"

I knew what it meant.

It meant the trip to Stardom House was a failure.

I was getting madder by the minute.

Roddy didn't respond to the doorbell or my knock. I tried the credit card trick and thirty seconds later was closing his door behind me. That was about fifteen seconds longer than I would have liked, because it gave one of the residents time to see what I was doing as he rounded a corner and headed in my direction, one deliberate step at a time.

Mr. Heisinger, a small, frail man in his late eighties with translucent skin and a walker on wheels, resides in a one-bedroom in the east building across the courtyard. Mr. Heisinger disappears on these daily strolls on the average of three or four times a month, obliging Sharon to send out a search party at the behest of his anxious wife. He gave no indication of having seen me. Or anybody.

Except for the smell of hash and some residue in an ash tray, Roddy's apartment hadn't changed since my last visit. When I didn't find what I was looking for in the usual places people hide something, I did my version of Melba on her hands and knees when she snooped under the quilted red satin drape covering the table full of Roddy's electronic toys. I checked a few other spots and again drew a blank. I was halfway back to the door when I noticed the blinking signal on the answering machine.

One caller, about fifteen minutes ago, Judith from the message center, pouncing on the musical tone that followed Roddy's recorded message: "Your mother was calling from her car, Roddy, and said to tell you she was heading out to the Grenedier & Grimm lot. If she does not, repeat, does not arrive before you finish feeding Nicky his lines for his close-ups, you are to tell Winnie in Cleve and Jack's office where she can find you later." A rash of awe in Judith's voice that hadn't been present when she and I spoke.

I gave the front room one last check, to make certain I wasn't leaving any tell-tale signs behind, and headed out.

Melba Donaldson stood in the hallway, key in hand, staring back at me with her insensitive mouth agape, more surprised than me.

I mustered my McQueen grin. It wasn't fast enough or cheeky enough to combat the outrage and suspicion taking charge of her features. She found her voice: "You better have a damn fine good reason for being here or I'm calling the cops."

"I was looking for clues," I said, taking an oath.

"What's that supposed to mean?" Melba was not amused, or as tough as she tried to sound. Her eyes betrayed her qualms and her curiosity.

"Maybe we should step back inside."

"Here will do just fine, Gulliver."

"Have it your way," I said. "Mrs. Donaldson, I know who is responsible for the deaths of Hope Danbury and Laurie Ann Bockstatdler." Her eyes narrowed, adding to the paradox of wrinkles on her face. "That was her name, the girl they were calling 'Janie Doe,' but you've always known that, haven't you?"

I saw Melba didn't want to be here anymore. She exhaled hard. Her breath was sour in my face, from too many years of too much champagne, a stomach varnished by layers of sediment. "If we're going to talk about it, there's a decent bar a lot closer, Melba." I moved aside and motioned for her to enter. "If you're going to call the cops, you know where your son keeps the phone."

Melba trailed me in her Mercedes 420 to The Other Gary Owens, an unobtrusive restaurant with a good bar north of Wilshire, tucked around the corner from the Armand Hammer Museum. The lunch crowd had thinned, and we found adjacent spots in the alley-sized parking lot.

Gary was a small man in his mid- to late-fifties, distinguished by a mustache that could have been clipped off Gene Shalit. He greeted me warmly in an accented baritone, Greece by way of the Bronx, and led us to my favorite booth at the back of the bar. The booth was being vacated by a lawyer-type and a legal secretary–type. The lawyer-type had missed a lipstick smear at the left instep of his generous mouth.

Melba slid halfway in and sat with her back pinched into the corner between the green naugahyde and a wall full of faded caricatures framed in black. She put her satchel purse beside her on the seat and located a pack of Kents, an ebony Gloria Swanson–size holder, and a slim sterling silver lighter. She placed the lighter on the varnished surface of the plank table, drilled a cigarette into the holder, snatched away the lighter when I reached over for it. She stared at me defiantly, sucking in the smoke; turned and pushed the white trail in the direction of the aisle.

A waitress I didn't recognize, a blonde with good legs and a chipper manner, came with the drink orders we had given to Gary, my Heineken and Diet Coke chaser, a pair of double gins on the rocks for Melba. One of the gins was dead before I had my beer hoisted at the front end of a somber toast Melba initiated without warning—

To Jayne.

"I understand you had something going with her," Melba said. It was her first full sentence since we sat down. "Jayne was okay. She did a good job for Roderick and all her clients. Never heard a word of complaint."

"You won't hear any from me."

Melba pushed her rubber nose left and right. She sucked up the air, then moved a hand to the gold cross sitting on top of a harlequin-checked jacket straight out of a Lord & Taylor ad.

The recessed lighting favored her, softening the look and shedding years.

"That takes care of the small talk," she said with an air of finality. "So, just what is it the fuck you think you know, Gulliver?" Her hands appeared to clutch her breasts as her fingers lightly massaged the cross.

I planted my elbows on the table, based my chin on my knuckles, and shared most of the links in a chain of facts that grew longer, even clearer, while I was sitting my version of *shiva,* and took on further dimensions of truth during the phone calls I had made earlier, like the one to Idaho.

Unlike Hollywood, where phone numbers change as often as they're unlisted, the Boise operator quickly found a number for the parents of Laurie Ann Bockstatdler. Only two Bockstatdlers listed, a Bockstatdler, Marvin and a Bockstatdler, Melvin.

Marvin answered, "Bockstatdler Plumbing and Heating." He heard why I'd called and said, "You want my brother, Mel."

Melvin Bockstatdler taught high school English, but was home today nursing a cold. His voice was clogged and depressed. Got worse when I raised Laurie Ann's name.

I told him it was for a follow-up column I was doing on *Stardom* magazine. I felt guilty about the lie, but he seemed pleased to share his grief with anybody. In a moment, he was answering questions before I asked them.

Until the freeway accident took her from them, Laurie Ann called home at least once a week to tell the folks about any progress breaking into the movies. Calling was a condition he and his wife, Lillian, had imposed, if Laurie Ann expected them to continue sending her money to live on.

He said, "You know what a teacher makes here in Boise, sir? I would say there are about three hundred in proximity who make less in a year than one Major League Baseball player. So, sending off those checks to Laurie Ann was not always the easiest for us, but that's what parents do. When she told us about *Stardom* magazine and what it was going to do for her, we couldn't find it in our hearts to deprive her, so we prayed some and then we took out a second mortgage on the house. Well, God bless, she was right. I am looking at her platinum picture page in *Stardom* magazine as we speak, sir. The page got her one of those high-powered managers and some bit part work, making it possible for Laurie Ann to pay us back. Laurie Ann even talked about how she was going on dates with movie stars. Imagine. Our Laurie Ann going on dates with movie stars . . ."

I paused for a shot of Heineken.

Melba looked at me blankly. "What's the punch line?" she said, pushing smoke out her nose.

I said, "The anguish over losing Laurie Ann was too much for Mrs. Bockstatdler. She suffered a stroke three days ago. Mr. Bockstatdler discovered her on the floor in the kitchen when he came home from school. She's in the hospital, in a coma. Not expected to live. Maybe just as well. We can only hope for better for Mr. Bockstatdler when he learns the truth, when he finally makes a connection with a news photo or gets a call telling him 'Janie Doe' was Laurie Ann. He's already on a pacemaker."

Melba shrugged. "Your idea of a punch line is not very funny." She studied her cigarette holder.

"Then let me give you funny, Melba." I plucked the holder from her fingers and extinguished the cigarette in what was left of her second gin. "You are one first-class bitch, Melba."

She got back the holder and traded her distaste for my disgust. "A job's worth doing, it's worth doing well."

I signaled the waitress to bring us another round and took a deep breath. "Laurie Ann's father told me the manager she signed with was Roscoe Del Ruth."

"Then she must have shown Roscoe something. He doesn't

take on just anybody."

"Mr. Bockstatdler gave me the names of the three movies Laurie had bits in. They include *Tough Times Two,* which you cast, and I'm willing to bet, when I check further, I'll find you also cast the other two movies."

"If they were important films."

The waitress arrived with our drinks and replaced the bowl of peanuts that had been on the table with a full bowl. We waited for her to clear the table and leave. Melba used a finger to stir the ice cubes, maybe to take warmth from them. I tried the nuts.

I said, "Nicky Edmunds was among the movie stars Laurie Ann told her father she was dating."

"He's an animal, that one. Not just on the screen. To get into Nicky's pants is like a badge of honor for these groupies."

"Melba, until I spoke with Mr. Bockstatdler I was so caught up in what I heard I wasn't taking into consideration what I didn't hear. You've ever read Sir Arthur Conan Doyle, you understand what I mean."

"Doyle?" She seemed genuinely puzzled. "He ever do any movies, or just books?"

I ignored the question. "Del Ruth knew who Janie Doe was. Del Ruth managed her. You knew. You got her work. Nicky Edmunds knew. Yet, none of you identified her to the cops. You let her go on being 'Janie Doe.' Why?"

She considered the question. "You check the credits, you'll see I was calling her Laura Bach. Roscoe wanted to name her Amelia Earhart. He said he liked the way she went down on him, you imagine that, the horny bastard?

"Why didn't you inform the police, Melba?"

"Maybe for the same reason as you? Anywhere in the news today, she's still 'Janie Doe.' You think you know something, tell me. You said you know who killed her and the other one, the black girl, so you tell me. Tell me now."

"You did."

I let it slip out. Nothing melodramatic.

She thought about it, looking for the right response among the ginless rocks of the glass she had just drained. She would look up in a minute and challenge me to back up the accusation, the way they do it on television; bet. Putting me in the position of sharing my montage of fact and guesswork. I decided to beat her to it. If I got lucky, she'd start filling in the blanks I couldn't figure for myself—the way they do in real life.

I said, "You and Gus Ljung."

CHAPTER 34

Melba Donaldson turned her face to the wall and shifted her eyes back to me, weighing the accusation. I said, "The two of you were making it, weren't you? You and Gus? Getting it on? Or just how do they say it nowadays?"

"Fuck you!"

"Some things never change."

She fumbled with a fresh Kent.

"I doubt it was your original intention, Melba, involving Gus. Involving Roddy."

"If you know so much . . ." She waved for the waitress to bring her another. She was six slugs into the gin already, on top of her champagne slings, but still seemed in control. I pushed the bowl of peanuts closer. She ignored them.

I said, "Try this for a scenario, Melba. Hope and Laurie Ann weren't at the Roxy to party with Maxie Trotter. They went to hook up with you, on whatever pretext was cooked up by you and your pals at Stardom House. It was probably panic time over there for all of you. Hope had revealed a lot during one of her drug binges. You'd learned Laurie Ann was part of a government sting to flush out your drug and porn traffic. What didn't you know? You had to find out.

"Let's suppose you told Hope and Laurie Ann the person you wanted them to meet, a producer or some other big shot, had been detained, but you'd arranged to catch up with him later. So innocent. Nothing to raise suspicions. Besides, by now the two girls have a few under their belts? A popper and some toot? They're ripe for anything. Easier to handle. Except for one minor complication—Roddy.

"When you arrive at the Roxy, you discover they've stumbled into him. Sure, you can pry them loose, but darling Roddy is completely blitzed. What's a mother to do? You want to get him into his limo and send him home. He tells you, *Sorry, mommy dearest, no limo. I drove myself from the studio.* You are not about to let the boy drive anywhere else, not in his condition. With help from Hope and Laurie Ann, you manage him into his car. They pile in, too, when you tell them it'll take ten minutes to get Roddy ready for beddy-bye and then the three of you can go straight on to your meeting. When you—"

"More nuts or some chips and dip?" The waitress was back with Melba's drink. I told her we were fine and rinsed my teeth clean with Diet Coke until she was gone.

"My guess, Melba? You called ahead to Gus Ljung before leaving the Roxy, so he would be waiting for you when you drove into the garage. He helped get Roddy upstairs. Afterward, the two of you talked Hope and Laurie Ann into Gus's secret apartment near the elevator. Maybe you had them wait there for you, in case you were noticed by a resident. It wouldn't be the first time Mama asked a friendly guard to help get her Roddy home. Is that how you met Gus in the first place?" No answer. "Gus Ljung's little love nest or whatever it was supposed to be, besides a great way to beat paying rent. That's where the girls died, isn't it?"

Melba's sandpaper laugh carried over my head and caromed off the bar walls. She toasted me and said, "Fascinating, Gulliver. You're definitely wasting time with a column. You should be writing screenplays." There was a distinct burr to her words, the last stop before the slurring starts. The gin was winning. "Go try it sometimes, Gulliver, whyn'tcha? And I'll arrange for you to sit down with Steven Spielberg."

She wasn't fooling me. I told her so.

Melba used the cigarette holder like a baton and wagged it between us. "You're so damn smart, explain why I did with 'em, me and Gus, for two days 'efore you found—?" She tilted her head and worked her mouth into something resembling a triumphant smirk.

"I was hoping you'd tell me."

That laugh again.

Gary's bartender, a towheaded kid in a Michael Jackson t-shirt under his UCLA Bruin letterman's sweater, looked up from the textbook he'd been poring over and made a face, but it was going to take more than her noisy laugh to get a reaction from the rotund drunk in the cheap suit occupying the stool next to the service rail on the counter. He had followed us inside by a few minutes and now was asleep, wearing his bald head on his arm while his free hand protected a brandy snifter.

"Le's suppose a min, Gulliver. Le's suppose what you're saying is . . . truthful?" Her head shook to contradict her words. "Me and Gus . . . Everything . . . Happens way you say it happens." Her speech was slowing down. Not so much talk as manufactured words. The booze was closing in fast. "I say—" She thought about it. "I say . . . Tell me."

"Tell you what?"

Melba smiled and shook her head in agreement. "Why, if that way you say, why I go and do not do it first place in Roderick's? Why I later take him, them, up so look like—"

"So it looked like Hope and Laurie Ann died in Roddy's apartment and Roddy was somehow responsible?"

"Hah!"

"I'll take another guess."

"Hah!"

"I'll guess you started out looking for answers and then things got out of control and you had two bodies on your hands. You are a bright woman, Melba, intelligent and resourceful. You did some fast thinking and came up with an ingenious scheme. You and Gus managed to get the bodies into the elevator and into Roddy's apartment undetected. Maybe the two of you had assistance? A call to Gene Coburn, maybe? *Hey, Gene, baby, we have two stiffs on our hands.*"

Melba's head shook back and forth vociferously.

I turned my palms to the ceiling. "Only guessing, remember?"

"Hah!" At some point, she'd put her Gloria Swanson prop on the edge of the table. She reached for it and the cigarette holder fell onto the floor. She didn't try retrieving it.

I said, "You and Gus set the scene, then left, knowing it would only take a phone call to Sharon Glenn to set the discovery process in motion. Sharon is always so pleasant and obliging when it comes to checking up on Roddy for you. How many times has that naughty boy come home so swacked it takes two or three days for him to sleep himself back to normalcy? It couldn't have worked better. I know. I was there."

"Didn't do it, Rod . . ."

"Of course he didn't. And you counted on the police figuring out that part in a hurry. You'd pumped enough stuff into Roddy to raise the question, the same way you jammed a needle into Hope Danbury. You were supremely confident the police would decide the deaths were the work of someone else, parties unknown, because your Roddy doesn't do drugs. In fact, he's scared witless of needles. There'd be plenty of witnesses to testify to that if, God forbid, it ever got that far."

"Forbid."

"The overdose was not meant to happen. Isn't it only the black widow spider that kills her own? You lucked out there, didn't you, Melba? Another hour or so and you might have had the next James Dean on your hands."

I paused, ostensibly to take a long swallow from my Heineken. I wanted to be sure Melba understood what I had told her so far, maybe got a sense of where I was heading. I wanted her to squirm. Her eyes were moist, either from the gin or the thought of Roddy dying from an overdose inspired by Mama. She played with her hair, pulling strands of strawberry behind her ear, wrapping them underneath a lobe punctuated with a glittering diamond too big to call a chip.

I said, "Suppose it did, an overdose? You always had your ace in the hole." Melba gasped for air, in anticipation. "Any sexual activity wouldn't point back to Roddy. To Gus, maybe, but there was nothing to connect him to the murders. He'd be off sick somewhere, far removed from the scene. If that wasn't enough, as a last resort you were ready to pull a skeleton out of the closet, Roddy, too; let the world know your son the movie star is gay."

Tears broke over Melba's lower lids. They traveled in all directions, depending on where they fell in her spider's web of wrinkles. "Not . . ."

"Roddy doesn't think you know he's gay, Melba. I know better."

She abruptly raised her arms between us, like she was defending herself from Stephen King's imagination. "Crazy, you . . ."

"Brian Armstrong. Name pull a chain? Roddy's longtime gentleman friend; off and on, so to speak. I wouldn't be surprised if it was your idea to put them together in the long, long ago. Career jumpstarts for you as well as your son. I visited Brian. He explained how a fifteen-year old boy abused as a child and hurting for affection seduced *Fighting Father Jack*. How, ever since, Melba Donaldson and only Melba Donaldson casts his movies. Is it reciprocity or something as naughty as blackmail? A small enough price to pay for keeping secrets?"

"You fuck!"

I ignored her outburst. "What Brian Armstrong told me about Roddy went against what I'd heard from the publisher of *Trail Blazer,* an old associate of mine named Henry Bouchey. I believe you know the name, Melba. Henry denied Roddy was gay. Swore up and down he would know it if it were true, would *out* Roddy the way he *outs* other famous closet dwellers. I knew someone was fibbing. I thought about it. I remembered how Brian Armstrong said he'd paid off Henry Bouchey to keep his name out of the paper. I phoned him to double-check my memory, then phoned Henry. Henry and I had a lovely chat and when he was finished making the same denials as before, he dropped the truth on me."

"Not supposed . . ."

"Of course not. Henry is not supposed to publish the truth about Roddy, because he's paid a handsome sum every month to look the other way, same as he does for Brian Armstrong. And often, Henry gets slipped the names of other stars leading double lives, a bonus for his continuing good will. My friend Henry was a hard case, but I got him talking, telling me everything, after I threatened to break the truth through the tabloids. There is no newspaperman alive on earth who likes to lose an exclusive. You were going to break the truth, too, if it came to that, with the cops and the D.A.'s office. No drugs. No women. No case against Roddy. Not enough evidence to beat a motion for dismissal by your lawyers. Roddy would walk and the law would be left with another open case on the books. Not the Black Dahlia, but not bad, either."

Melba's eyes grew wetter and homeless. She gripped her upper arms against a chill I wasn't feeling. I couldn't tell if she felt unhappy for Roddy or herself, when a voice from nowhere said, "Sorry I'm late, baby."

★ ★ ★ ★ ★

I turned in the direction of the voice. Whoever he was, he loomed over the table nourishing a thin-lipped smile that said nothing, displaying the cigarette holder that had fallen onto the floor. "Got held up in canyon traffic, then Sunset going through Beverly Hills. Some days. Go explain."

Melba knew him. She reached toward him. He moved her purse from the seat to the table, slipped the cigarette holder inside, and slid into the booth alongside her. He gave her arm a little poke with the edge of his fist, then pinched and shook her cheek playfully. He took her hand and massaged it in his. "You're cold, baby, and you been crying. What's this *bollo* been saying to you?"

He had four inches, forty pounds, and a few years on me, so taking offense at his calling me a prick was not the best plan. He was a Latin, to go with the word; attractive in a slick sort of way. Coal black eyes and Elvis lips the main attraction on a lean, chiseled face. Hollow cheeks. Pitch black hair slicked back tightly and culminating in a pigtail two inches long and tied with a rubber band. His suit of lights was burnt orange. A brown shirt picking up his natural tan. A splashy tie pulling it all together.

"If Mrs. Donaldson wants you to know that, it's Mrs. Donaldson's place to tell you," I said, keeping it cordial.

"He making new trouble for you, baby? Tell Che and we see about it." Che's voice had the studied roll of a drive time disk jockey.

Melba shook her head again. I could almost hear Judith, she of the message center, on Roddy's machine talking about Melba calling from her car. It explained how Che knew where to find us.

He noticed the empty glass in front of her and nodded knowingly. "You can blow a fortune with her, a place like this," he said, disgust swimming in his breath. The waitress was heading for us. Che signaled her away. He leaned closer to Melba. "Baby, I want you to stay behind and after we go have one more for the road. You sit here and you wait while I go deliver our package and catch up with you later. What you think? You hear what I'm saying? You think you can manage that?" When she didn't answer, he tugged at her hair.

"Yes." Barely a whisper.

I said, "Why do I think I'm your package, Che?" His expression answered for him. "What makes you think I'll leave Mrs. Donaldson to go with you?"

"For openers?"

"For openers."

Che motioned with his head in the direction of the bar. Sitting on the stool directly opposite us was another Latino, arms folded across his chest, two enlarged eyes staring at us behind thick wire-rimmed glasses, a pencil-thin mustache decorating the wide span between his flat nose and his lip. He was also in his late teens, also well dressed and groomed, but smaller and darker than Che, who was about the color of sweet chocolate. Probably more Indian blood than Che.

Che said, "One sign from me, Willie will pull your arm out of its socket, the same way you would pull the wings off a fly, and it will give him pleasure." His smile an open invitation to disobey before he flashed Willie a hand signal. Willie replied in kind.

"Okay, no more flies." I started to raise my right hand, but withdraw it fast when Willie bounced off the bar stool. His high-tops squeaked loudly hitting the hardwood floor, rousing the drunk at the end of the bar.

The drunk mumbled something to a customer who'd come in since the last time I had glanced over there, lanky and predisposed, a life insurance salesman–type, staring at the mirror behind the bar like it contained answers to a quiz he was scheduled to take later. The customer answered and made a toast with his bottle of Evian. That satisfied the drunk, who resumed napping.

Che said, "You are one wise guy, *bollo.*" He squeezed Melba's arm. "Baby, you called it right on this. I begin to understand why. It's a shame I didn't punch his ticket that day downstairs at the school." Melba muttered something unintelligible.

I said, "You usually bat left-handed?"

Che smiled. "Only when I got to. Both of you would've been home runs, you and the nigger girl, except you showed up to save her and then Mr. Coburn's girlfriend shows up and stops me from knocking you out the park."

I flashed on Jayne.

Che showed some teeth. "Right now I got a gun aimed at you under the table, ready to perform *bicho* surgery you don't do what I ask. It's a .38, *bollo.* It blow your balls away and build you a new asshole size of the Second Street tunnel." The thought excited him, hurried his speech. He licked his lips in anticipation.

"Between you and Willie, I assure you, you have my full and complete attention."

Che approved. He fished a capsule from a jacket pocket, pushed it across the table, and told me to take it. "Goes down real smooth with the beer," he said, like a TV pitchman. The capsule looked like one of those extra-strength Tylenol capsules before they were pulled from the marketplace and reemerged as caplets; full of tiny white, green, and blue pebbles. He seemed amused as I bounced the capsule in my palm, weighing the possibilities. "Won't kill you, *amigo.*"

"If it does, what can I expect from you? An apology?"

He rolled his eyes upward. "Man's a joker. Look, you swallow it and in a minute you're going to get tired. In two minutes you're going to get weak in the knees. Then, me and Willie, we can take you out from here without worrying about you doing something stupid. *Comprendé?* We make our special delivery the way they want and that way you get to live longer. Right, baby?"

Melba didn't respond.

Che gave her a peck on the cheek anyway.

I said, "Do you count backward from ten or something?"

"Just swallow, asshole."

I popped the capsule.

Che motioned me forward. He ordered me to open my mouth and raise my tongue. He said, "This time swallow or, I swear, me and Willie will be delivering damaged goods." He pointed to the Heineken bottle.

I took a hefty swallow.

Thirty seconds later, I felt my brains draining. The bar began spinning clockwise, like an English carousel.

"You need help with him?"

I had a sense of the life insurance salesman stepping over as Che and Willie navigated me out the bar and past a clucking Gary Owens.

Che assured him they could handle the situation, in slow motion explained the obvious: "Got a serious drinking problem, our *amigo.*"

The life insurance salesman said something in a foreign language. The three of them shared a good laugh before he wandered on ahead of us into the parking lot and climbed into what appeared to be a green Mustang.

Or was it one of James Mason's Afrika Corps tanks in *The Desert Fox*?

Did it matter? Did it—

I was Chicken Little and the sky was falling.

★ ★ ★ ★ ★

Fingers pry open my eye. A thread of brightness eats into the gray light, blinding me. "This dickhead's still in Dream City." The voice, male, cold as the room, a hollow quality to it. "Maybe another half hour, hour most." Not Gary Owens's. Someplace else. Stretched out on my back. Tight space. Raw ass on what? Feels like a canvas cot. Since?

A second voice: "Her, not so better. Good thing next time is the last time. Bitch's had it." Also male. Syllables in flight. Don't recognize it either. Across the room from me. Five, six feet. "One whipped pussy."

"Amazing how long she lasted already."

"Braggart." A snort. Shared laughter. A calloused hand finds my cock, strokes it. "Wouldn't mind kick-starting this one myself." Snigger. "Remember to wear a condom." Snicker. "Cold or glow in the dark?" Snigger. "Something in a nice gangrene?" Laughter. A comedy store for creeps. He abandons my cock when it refuses to respond. I want to reach up and grab his throat. I can't get my arms to function. Can't move my hands. Can't move my fingers. Can't—so tired. Eyes weighted by tire irons. Think about it later.

Floorboards respond noisily to tramping footsteps. A door opening and closing. A slab of light comes and goes on the ceiling. A rush of warm air, bringing with it the stale smells of history in a bottle. Key turns in a lock. Muffled voices. Steps fading down and away from the creak of wooden stairs. One. Two. Three. Four. Quiet, except my breathing. I hold my breath. Press lips tight. Listen hard. Force my head in the direction of the sound. A pull in the shoulder, pain at the base of my neck. My eyes fighting to read the dim light, helped by an intense red glow outside a window with panes painted over.

A figure huddling in a corner.

Twitching in a back bay of reality. Naked. Trembling. Seeming beyond fear in the bothersome light.

Do I recognize her?

I call over, identify myself.

My name means nothing to her.

Can't be certain she's heard me.

She appears to be functioning in some other world.

Moments later, she inquires with a tourist's curiosity: "Do you want to die? I have to kill you, you know?"

I know the voice. "Why do you have to kill me?"

"So you won't kill me." Sounding surprised I had to ask. "I have to kill you so you won't kill me. How they play the game."

The game?

I press my palms against my thighs. Cold to my own touch. I dig down with my fingernails, scrape against my flesh. Deeper, harder; trying to inflict pain.

Wake up, Gulliver. Damn it. Wake up.

Ask Aleta about the game.

Chapter 35

I heard the cuh-lick of a light switch and a voice wondering, "So how are we doing, Neil?" My eyes crawled open to burning brightness. I squeezed them shut again, opened them a fraction, and began adjusting to the golden light, wondering how long I had been asleep. A figure emerged, grew, took shape. Smile. Wink. Teeth. Coburn. "Please don't get up on my account," he said, full of charm and chuckles.

He pushed down on my chin to get my mouth open wider, deposited a small yellow pill on my tongue and played with my throat until certain I had swallowed. "Sorry, a safety precaution," he said solicitously. "My safety." A smug, precise burst of laughter. "Not as potent as the one Che fed you. Works as quickly, but a shorter duration."

"Thanks for small favors." It was a struggle speaking. The words didn't want to cooperate with my throat. "Where am I, Coburn?" I glanced over to the corner where I'd seen Aleta Haworth. Empty. No evidence it had ever been otherwise. I thought: *Tough it out, Neil. Tough it out.*

Coburn said, "You might call here a way station between fantasy and reality, Neil." He crossed the room in a few steps. He was impeccably dressed in half of Rodeo Drive. He carried a metal bridge chair to a place alongside my cot and arranged himself comfortably. "You're in a dressing room on stage two of the historic Grenedier & Grimm Studios, lost to prying eyes on the back side of the property."

Besides the cot and the chair, I made out a dressing table and a mirror with hinged flaps and a border of light bulbs. Cotton stuffing was visible through time holes in a tufted chair that matched the pink color of the table skirt. The table surface was full of the usual clutter, abandoned cosmetic jars and tubes, powder puffs, empty bottles, soda cans, a stack of magazines. Buster Keaton stared down from a framed movie poster for *Sherlock, Jr.* The three-by-five on the wall next to me had pasty-faced Harry Langdon shyly offering daisies to an actress I didn't know.

Coburn was saying, "It's a relic from the past, before talkies came along, the only working stage with the original glass skylights intact . . . The open wood beams for hanging lights . . . Catwalks . . . No sound insulation, obliging us to do a lot of looping back at Stardom House. I understand Pickford did some of her finest work here, before running off to form United Artists with Griffith and the boys, Charlie and Doug. A year or so ago, Cleve and Jack negotiated a long-term lease with the people at Metropolitan, who were happy to take the income and run without investing in restoration. We're careful how and when we work and, given the usual courtesies of a movie lot, nobody ever bothers us; knock wood." He looked around and, settling for the floor, leaned down and knocked twice. "We take all our first-time players here, to give them a feel for the *real* Hollywood. A sense of at last being on the way to stardom and a fulfilling career."

Smile. Wink. Teeth.

I said, "Is the cost of the coke and the heroin and all the other shit built into your budgets or is it taken out of their paychecks?"

"Dear me, no; from petty cash. You'd be amazed, Neil, simply amazed, to learn how small a percentage of our talented, aspiring young actors needs any encouragement whatsoever. For anyone to believe otherwise is to treasure naiveté as the national pastime."

"Why am I here, Coburn?"

"See what I mean about naiveté?" A sly grin crawled up one side of Coburn's face and he wagged a forefinger at me. He moved it down the length of my chest and used his thumb to snap the finger against my dormant cock. The sharp, stinging sensation hurt. I made a noise and my eyes began watering. My discomfort pleased him.

"If Melba hadn't stumbled into you, we would have found you someplace else soon. Trust me on that one. Clearly, you have gleaned too much about our day-to-day operations for us to ignore you, hoping you'd simply go away. So, we're going to help you go away."

"The same way you helped Hope Danbury and Laurie Ann Bockstatdler go away."

Coburn disagreed. "With less fanfare or discovery, Neil. The way we dispose of others who can cause us trouble. Matters with those two got out of hand before we could apply our usual discretion." He made a meaningless gesture. "The best laid plans . . . ?"

Smile. Wink. Teeth.

Coburn was confiding in me like I was already dead and, however unintentional, he was sending me a message I didn't entirely understand. Something in what he said, the way he said it, screamed out that the murder scenario I had shared with Melba Donaldson was wrong. To further complicate matters, Coburn's yellow pill had started turning my brain into mush.

I said, "Aleta Haworth. Cops would have written her off as the victim of a petty thief who panicked; a schoolyard junkie prowling for drug money; something like that."

"You catch on fast. Something like that. Not unusual for the neighborhood. I recall correctly, it was Cleve Buntine's inventive idea. Or maybe Zipper's. From one of their old movies. Effective nonetheless. We won't have to go to as much trouble now for the devious Miss Aleta. We found her shortly before we found you, but you know that already."

"Nothing inventive about Jayne Madrigal or Gus Ljung." Coburn answered me with a queer look. "Lot about their murders was plain sloppy."

"Well, Neil, I don't know how to answer you on that." Coburn gave it thought. "Gus Ljung was always proving himself a nuisance. I was sick of the problems Gus was causing us." He thought again. "Jaynie? I loved Jaynie. Not in the way you yourself were veering, but, Christ, man—Jaynie was one of us and she pulled her own weight."

He invited my comment, but I couldn't speak. I could hardly think and, right now, it was more important to listen. Coburn's trumpet was sounding loud and clear. I didn't want to miss the brass bassoon.

He said, "After the ugly business with the dead girls, I wanted to purge ourselves of Gus. Jayne urged patience. Jaynie said he could be useful in helping us get a certain floppy disk from you. She was right. Once Jaynie managed to locate the floppy in your apartment, it became a matter of Gus finding an opportune time to get inside using a pass key. Stupid as he was, he was sure to get that part right. Jaynie also contemplated using Gus's help after you led her to a certain portable computer, which we still must talk about."

"Portable—?"

"No time for coyness, Neil. The one and same damn T-980 Melba has been crazed over for weeks. And, may I add, driving me and everybody else crazy, but—"

"Eugene?" A familiar voice outside the dressing room door.

"In here, Knox."

A moment later, Knox Lundigan was standing alongside

Coburn. He wore rust-colored slacks and a windbreaker over a Vanilla Ice t-shirt; dirt-stained Reeboks; a Dodger cap set back on his head; shades. He bent forward, studying me the way a biology student examines a frog.

"You know you could've really damaged something?" he said, speaking as quietly and as noncommittal as the first time we'd met. "You could've really crashed something, knowing as little as you do." He looked to Coburn for reassurance. Coburn gave him a few friendly pats on the thigh. "Would've meant hours and hours on top of what you've already put us through. You deserve to be punished, you truly do."

"Relax, baby, please," Coburn said. "We'll be playing the game with Mr. Gulliver. You know that."

The game.

The two words didn't sound any better now than when Aleta had used them.

"When?" Lundigan was adamant.

"Shortly. Mr. Gulliver and I are finishing a pleasant chat. Five minutes, maybe?"

Lundigan checked his watch. "Better'n he deserves." He slapped my face, turned on his heels, and stalked off.

I had been close to falling asleep. The pain woke me up. I wanted to put my hands where it hurt, but I lacked the strength to follow the impulse. At least Lundigan had stayed away from my cock.

Coburn waited until certain his partner had gone before slipping into laughter. "You should have seen the boy before I managed to calm him down, Neil. Knox doesn't cotton to anybody playing with his toys. I, of course, don't like anything that makes Knox unhappy. He gets dreadfully sulky. It tends to interfere with business for days at a time. Like now." Unfolding himself from the chair, Coburn stepped to the mirror and examined his pock marks, rubbing and patting to smooth them out. "I don't suppose you were ever in porno before today, were you?" He spoke to my reflection, nodding approvingly. "They're bound to be a big hit on the circuit once we add them to the TalenTapes library. We'll blur your face in post, just enough to keep subscribers guessing; nothing as extreme as the big dot they did for the rape trial. More like that famous old X-rated film they say was Marilyn Monroe. Is it or isn't it Neil Gulliver, the famous columnist? Doing *what*? No, come off it. You would be amazed at the large number of subscribers who don't want to know. They absolutely adore guessing, and Neil Gulliver missing and presumed dead will add to the fun of the speculation in their perverted imaginations. It's destined to become one of our most popular loops."

Coburn studied my reaction and took pleasure watching the emotions scramble on my face. He dug his thin, bony fingers into his hair and used his palms to push the dense white laces tight against his head and back over his ears, then returned to the chair.

"So, what were we discussing before Knox came calling?"

He played with his tie and waited expectantly for me to say something.

I felt the muscles constricting in my throat and heard my heart beating inside my eardrums as my eyeballs probed the insides of my lids. I had hung on best I could. Now, I couldn't hang on any longer.

Wherever? Not alone. Hearing voices. Feeling presence. Spread-eagled under a panoply of lights; third degree bright; Malibu hot; blinding; sweat gluing my naked body to metal slab; Frankenstein Monster model; inclined. Wrists, ankles clamped. Helpless. Body under siege. I try calling out. Hey, stop—Hand slaps down over my mouth. Hard. Stings. Hand moist. Smells like strawberries; nicotine. Under attack. Too hard to resist.

Resist. Fight it. I stare past my belly to a bald head retreating. Baby Cakes. Miss Ovaltine. Nude. Full-bodied. Arms protecting breasts. Aleta. Frightened eyes beg forgiveness. For Hope. For herself. For who? Meaty hands gripping her by the shoulders, pushing her into a prostrate position on her stomach; on top of me.

Willie from Gary's bar. Hairy. Sweaty. Barrel-chested. Grunting. Instead of wire-rimmed glasses, wearing shiny, wart-infested dildo size and shape of Florida. Willie mounts Aleta. His weight oppressive, difficulty breathing. Her eyes grow, explode. Her mouth exhausts putrescence. Her screams, loud. Louder. I feel the trickle of her terror and the collapse of her soul. Applause. I hear applause. Someone, somewhere calling: "Cut!"

Chapter 36

Jack Zipper, Jr., apologized again.

"It wasn't our desire to throw you into those scenes, Neil. If you know our movies, you know Cleve and I have far too much class for schoolboy pranks, but Knox the Lox just goaded and goaded and goaded. Finally, Mean Gene had no choice but to go into the Cave and ask Cleve if he'd mind just this once. Cleve figured, what the heck, besides, it would give him a chance to read you for the lights, so you'll look your best when we tape you for the game."

We were seated in canvas-back chairs about five or ten feet behind the central video camera setup. There were two other setups, one on each side of the simple portable set that was wheeled into position in the middle of the soundstage, after the set I had been on was pushed out of sight. Fifteen minutes ago? Keeping track of time had become an exercise to keep from passing back into Dreamland.

My set had been the kind of torture chamber where Boris Karloff and Bela Lugosi used to hang out. The one being adjusted now for the preset lighting was straight out of a low-budget talk show, two Eames chair knockoffs, a cheap white plastic end table between them, a patched black curtain for a backdrop.

I counted a half dozen crew members working swiftly and efficiently. Most in t-shirts or windbreakers silk-screened with the names and logos of movies I knew, faded denims, and sneakers.

The baseball caps also carried movie advertising.

Dressed otherwise, they could have been Stardom House counselors. I decided they were. There are only so many jobs for waiters in Los Angeles.

I remembered my credits: Zipper was the writer half of the writing-directing team. A few years ago, he and Buntine had parlayed a low-budget fright flick made on a dime into a series of high-grossing major league productions.

Zipper was in his mid-forties and had the style of face assigned to the back rows of church choirs, oxidized by the rigors of a cruel business, where forty is already too old for those who had missed the brass ring. Dark half moons were a permanent fixture under tired eyes magnified behind dated frames. A wart the size of a June bug was lodged just below freshman jowls. He wore an ageless double-breasted suit in a tan windowpane design. A blue shirt for contrast. Silk tie with brown and blue triangles afloat on gold. Brown, wing-tipped, tasseled Ferragamo slip-ons.

I was still naked, as were several people milling about the periphery of the action indifferent to anyone else's body parts. I was trapped in the chair by leg cuffs, using both hands as a jock strap; consciously trying to keep my sphincter disciplined. I ached without pain, except in my head. I kept pushing to work off the effects of a needle applied between fetid scenes I didn't want to remember and would never forget.

Not only Aleta Haworth and Willie.

People.

And things.

I thought I spied Lundigan slipping and sliding up to eye level a few times, but it may have been my imagination, sent winding up stairs and down cellars by the magical injections. I didn't see Aleta. The last time I saw her, Aleta was unconscious and being carted off like a sack of skin by two crew members.

Zipper patted my arm for attention and pointed to the set, like something was about to happen. A crew member gave the table a final adjustment. Satisfied, he took a .38 or .45 caliber automatic from his hip pocket—I couldn't tell which from this distance—and placed it on the table.

A voice echoed from on high: "We're just about ready to go, boys and girls. Peter Cottontail verifies the sound levels are fine. Che, if you'd see to it that our two stars take their places, I'll be a happy camper."

Zipper leaned into me, his hand tipped against his mouth, and whispered, "That's Cleve." He pointed across me to the large, silver-colored motor home isolated against one of the soundstage walls. "He works inside there; calls it the Cave. Knox the Lox rigged it so Cleve's board automatically keys to Knox the Lox's board back at Stardom House. You would be tremendously impressed learning what it means for the final quality of our work, not to mention the economics."

Willie emerged from somewhere. He was flanked by two young girls, neither more than fourteen or fifteen. He was clothed now. The girls were naked. I didn't want to look, more embarrassed than either of the girls seemed to be, but Zipper took hold of my chin and pulled my face forward.

"I wanted you to see how the game is played, Neil. That's the reason you're sitting here, before it's your turn. Aren't they an inviting pair, those two, a genuine sight for sore eyes? Add their ages and I bet my better half still has a good dozen years on them. Ummm-yum." The bastard fortified his words with vitamin D, as if expecting me to be in his debt forever. I'd have added him to my personal list—the one headed "Get Even"—except he was already on it. On spec. The same way most Hollywood writers work. Son of a bitch that he was.

The girls had difficulty walking. The fragile-looking Asian stumbled once or twice heading to the set, while the strawberry blonde only just beginning to burst through her baby fat kept trying to veer away. Willie used his meaty hands to keep them on course and helped settle them onto the Eames chairs.

Zipper said, "A pill, the same one you got, and just enough powder to keep them functioning on low beams."

Cleve Buntine's disembodied voice: "Mr. Edmunds, I'm advised we are ready for you if you are ready for us, you devil, you."

Laughter.

A voice whispered in my ear: "You remember I told you about watching over your shoulder? So, here we are."

With that, Nicky Edmunds rushed forward and leaped onto the set.

He was wearing crimson briefs barely bigger than a g-string and brandishing a glittering *papier maché* pitchfork, which Nicky pumped up and down like a barbell to a smattering of applause and appreciative hoots and whistles. He did a few turns, then stopped, faced the girls, and performed a courtly bow. Both girls reached for him. He responded with chaste kisses on their foreheads.

Nicky pretended to discover the automatic and held it up to the light for study. Satisfied, he returned it to the table. I exhaled. I had not appreciated how tense I'd been since the gun appeared. Now, figuring it was the prop from my earlier encounter with Nicky, I could relax. Whatever the sexual horrors, the game was back to being a game.

More applause.

Buntine: "We're rolling tape, Nick, so anytime it feels good to you . . ."

Nicky's face had been painted red and his eyebrows darkened to the same shade as a painted-on Adolphe Menjou mustache. He raised and lowered the brows, then turned his back to us, facing the girls. He played Zulu warrior with the pitchfork. He declared, "Show time." Applause. "Let the game begin." More applause. Hoots of enthusiasm.

Zipper said, "Neil, I want you to understand about the dialogue. None of it, not any, is mine. Conceptually, the game is mine. Dialogue is something else, although you know if you've seen any of our movies that mine is extremely good. Sharp. Incisive. Nailing all my characters bare to the bone. The dialogue for the game is all improv, created by the actors, moment by emotional moment; captured for all time by Cleve, amazingly, on one take and on tape, for Christ's sake, although film is the medium Cleve knows best. He's a filmmaker, not a tape maker, but also a chameleon when it comes to creativity, that one; always knows where to place the camera to get the best from any scene. Always. Watch, you'll see."

Nicky said, "I crave love, you fresh little bitches, so tell me how you think you can satisfy me."

The strawberry blonde went first. The vulgarities of her response to Nicky worked on me like saltpeter, but Zipper's breathing had become labored once she started using her body as a blackboard. A glance confirmed the private game he was playing at his crotch.

The Asian launched into a speech that could make a drunken sailor squirm. It caused Zipper to suck in his lips and yank out his cock. He came, caught the cum in his hand and wiped it off on a patch of shirt inside his jacket.

Nicky thanked both girls profusely. He wandered the stage in a tight circle, hands clasped behind his back, as if troubled by the decision he had to make. The two girls had leaned back into some neutral world, each smiling at secret thoughts.

After another minute, Nicky turned to face the center camera and said, "Ruby."

The girls became troubled.

Nicky feigned dismay.

"Dumb old me," he said. "You're both named Ruby, aren't you?" He found a mark between them and a few feet forward, and swayed back and forth. Finally, pointing: "You." The Asian girl smiled broadly and flicked her tongue. "You lose," he said, withdrawing his finger. The Asian burst into tears.

The other Ruby let out a whoop.

Without hesitating, she reached for the automatic. She took it in both hands, took careful aim—her tongue jutting out one side of her tight mouth—closed her eyes and blew apart the Asian Ruby's head. The recoil kicked her out of the chair and backward, off the set and onto the stone floor of the soundstage.

Fresh laughter mingled with the applause.

Zipper nudged me and said delightedly, "Nick sure fooled me this time. Usually, he goes for the hot case of yellow fever."

CHAPTER 37

I was on the set, one leg cuffed to the Eames chair, when the slaps whipping across my cheeks startled me. "It's your wakeup call," Nicky Edmunds said, cooing at me like a lovebird, his eyes on top of mine. He smelled of booze, his sweat and his breath sweet and sticky; cognac and what else?

The scraping noise was being made by crew members working over remainders of stain in the foreground with scouring brushes. The squeaking sound by the new backdrop being hoisted, this time the curtain velvet and dark blue.

I supposed Che or Willie, someone like that, had carried me over here. The last I remembered was the Asian girl's face exploding like a *piñata,* Zipper saying something stupid. Me screaming threats at Nicky Edmunds and struggling to pick myself up; tearing at my shackle.

Someone, maybe Zipper, grabbed my hair from behind and jerked my head back.

Somebody else pulled down my jaw by my teeth and hit my tongue with a clear plastic tube the size of a breath mint dispenser.

The tab of liquid was tasteless.

At once, my mind exploded into a world of distorted rainbows and illusions.

Now, no watch to tell me the time, when that was; before; what happened. Mick Jagger, "Jumping Jack Flash," breaking up the sound system. I hear every instrument, every note separate and distinct, dissolving into soaring symphonies I don't want to hear. Listen. Important. Important I regain control of mind and body. Important.

A guy with stained eyes and a manufactured tan working over my face. Dabbing my cheeks, pat-pat-pat, pat-pat-pat; rubbing; smoothing. Doing something to my lashes. Brows. He pulls back, likes what he sees. Disjointed smile. Teeth twisted and nicotine-stained. Masonic ring. "Had to restore some color to your face, mate. You were whiter'n a spade's worst nightmare. Ta." He steps aside, gone, and I make out Aleta settling into the other chair.

Aleta leans forward, hands on knees, indifferent to the world around her; breasts displayed confidently. She briefly studies me for recognition, shakes her head, allows her eyes to go lost in a fog.

I probably remember her words to me better than she does. *Do you want to die? I have to kill you, you know?* Her words turn into sand castles. Her words melt with the next wave. *I have to kill you so you won't kill me. That's how they play the game.*

Knuckles rapping on top of my head. Che. Leaning over my shoulder. Showing me my Beretta. Had it packed inside my belt at Gary Owens's place. Che must have taken it. He's the devil now, not Nicky Edmunds. Makes sure I'm watching as, with a flourish, he places the Beretta on the table between Aleta and me. Bows and begs off, Arab-world fashion.

Mick Jagger, over and out. Buntine's voice replaces his: "Waiting on you, Gene."

A crew member helps Coburn onto the set. Smile. Wink. Teeth. Finger salute. He adjusts his million-dollar suit and circles an arm overhead.

"Tape rolling, Gene. And five, four, three . . ."

"Miss Haworth, Mr. Gulliver, tell me the best secret you

have, something you're certain will please me. Miss Haworth, dear—ladies first."

Aleta lowers her shaved head and rubs the insides of her eyes, absent-mindedly scratches a nipple with the fingers of her other hand. She aims her face at Coburn, touches a finger to her lips, roams her eyes. "Laurie Ann Bockstatdler and Hope Danbury . . . Spying on you."

"I know that, dear. You told me that once before." Aleta pouts. Tears form. Bald head shakes. "Because you've always been such a grand sport, I'm going to permit you to try once more."

Aleta is happy again. She shoots a stream of urine that catches a thigh and spills down a leg. Canary yellow. Turtle soup green. First time I see someone pee for joy.

Coburn repeats himself: "Tell me the best secret you have, something you're certain will please me. Miss Haworth, dear—ladies first."

Buntine's voice: "Gene, you mind giving me the line one more time? Not you. The mistake is with me in the Cave; on the wild track."

Coburn obliges. Aleta uses the extra time to press her thoughts. She has difficulty. She bookends her head with her hands, like the girl in the Munch painting.

My world is settling down again.

I try my fingers. They work. My toes, numb, but the wiggle touches ground, not grass. My Beretta is normal size, not the cannon that minutes or a million years ago puffed out clouds of candy-striped smoke. My arm, no longer plastic and I can no longer reach it to light the fuse with a flick of my nails. I can't get to the Beretta without dragging my chair along.

Aleta gives me a mean look before she falters over her words, telling Coburn: "Laurie Ann Bockstatdler and Hope Danbury spying on you."

"My dear, didn't I just say—"

"And Aleta Haworth," she says. She extends her hand for a reward.

Coburn shifts his head left and right. "Yes, and you, too, dear. I already know that from you. Laurie Ann and Hope *and* Aleta. Is there some other name you have to share?"

Aleta shakes her head and sinks down in the chair. More tears. Coburn administers words of encouragement. He reminds her that Mr. Gulliver is yet to be heard from. Turns away from her to me. "Do you remember the question, Mr. Gulliver?"

"The blue floppy. I got it."

"Heavens, Mr. Gulliver. I know that part already. I know you have the blue floppy. Surely you can do better than that?"

"From Aleta Haworth. Got the blue floppy from Aleta Haworth."

"Yes, I know. What else, Mr. Gulliver, what else?"

"What else?"

"Think carefully. What else, Mr. Gulliver?"

"Portable computer?"

"All right. Yes. A portable computer to go with the blue floppy you got. Good for you. What about the portable computer? It's beginning to sound like a very good secret."

Coburn was smiling again. I smiled back and shifted it to Aleta. Whatever they'd fed her, she didn't appear to be pulling out of it as well as me.

Get a grip, Neil.

Fight.

I seesawed my head, as if thinking over Coburn's question. Buying time. As much as I could. Getting the last of the boulders out of my brain. I was also buying time for the man who had stepped out from behind one of the video cameras and into my sightline. It was the bald drunk in the cheap suit from Gary Owens's bar. Once sure I'd recognized him, he began stretching his hands like he was pulling taffy. Telling me to buy time.

Coburn said, "We're running out of time, Mr. Gulliver. You know how the game is played. Do you want me to declare Miss Haworth the winner? Is that it, what you want? Or do you want to share your very good secret?"

I dug my teeth into my lower lip and did a survey of the sound stage.

Smile. Wink. Teeth.

My smile. My wink. My teeth.

I said, "Maybe he can tell you."

"Who can tell me?"

"Him." I pointed to Coburn's left, to the central video camera. "Over there."

Coburn turned to look. "Jack Zipper? How would Jack know where—?"

Before I could tell him I meant the man by the canvas chair next to Zipper, the one I'd been sitting in, I heard the gunshot. I saw the hole a 147-grain hollow point makes when it tears into a person's back, between his shoulder blades, and ruins his suit and his health.

Coburn stumbled forward, dove face down off the set.

I snapped my head in the direction of the sound.

Aleta was in a shooter's stance, her legs spread, my Beretta gripped in both her hands, sighting down the barrel at my chest.

"Aleta, don't."

"He was going to like your secret better than mine. He was going to like your secret better than mine."

Another shot exploded.

The bullet caught Aleta in the neck.

She dropped the Beretta and, as her eyes contemplated the reality of the moment, she tried plugging the hole with her hands. Blood gushed through her fingers and formed a slim tributary down the right side of her mouth. She stepped forward. Her foot caught against the tubular metal leg of the chair, causing her to stumble and reverse direction. She banged into the table, slanted over it, and plunged out of sight.

"You next, *bollo.*" Che had shot Aleta at close range, at a little better than arm's length, with the .22 now pointed at me. It's a compact weapon meant for women, kids; up-close accuracy. Not necessarily lethal at the distance between us. I had a better chance than Aleta, who'd had no chance at all.

I pushed hard against the side of my chair and it fell over, taking me with it. I felt the heat of the bullet whiz past my ear and heard my leg cuff clang against metal as Che screamed something in Spanish and advanced on me.

The Beretta was between us, two or three feet away. I inched over and strained to reach it with my left hand. My fingers touched cool metal and I knew in an instant I would have a solid grip on the Beretta and blow the bastard away, because I was on a movie set; I was the good guy. That's the way it works in the movies, and so what if I wasn't a leftie?

A bigger question: Could I bring myself to shoot?

Kill again?

I framed a picture of Jayne in my mind.

Che moved like a cat. He kicked aside the Beretta with the edge of his brightly polished Ballys, like it was his movie, not mine, and hammered the top of my hand with his heel, cracking my knuckles like they were walnuts.

He crouched and pressed the mouth of the .22 between my eyebrows. "This is for making miserable my woman's life. I want you to know that. *Comprendé?* For making my baby cry, asshole."

I closed my eyes.

I heard thunder.

The whimper of dying had an accent to it as Che fell away from me.

The .22 scraped across my forehead before it popped aimlessly a fraction of a second later.

Detective Sgt. Jimmy Steiger, serving and protecting, had beaten Che to the trigger. He had abandoned his spot by Zipper to the bald drunk and stood grinning at me from the edge of the riser. He called over, "Does that make us even or do I still owe you one?"

The voice calling from on high, from Cleve Buntine's Cave, interrupted my answer. It was Bailey Madison, announcing how many feds and locals were present to make certain nobody fled. Citing charges. Reminding them of their rights.

The bald drunk was cuffing Zipper. Zipper was giving him an argument.

Less than a minute had passed since Aleta Haworth had killed Eugene Coburn.

CHAPTER 38

Zipper didn't have the leg iron key. Instead of fishing it off Coburn, Jimmy Steiger pressed his Detective Special against the chain, made bullet magic to free me, and sent one of his men to hustle up a robe for me. The badge returned with a black silk hostess number he'd found among dozens piled on a nearby table. The robe stopped just above my knees. It was a size too small, and I was barely able to tie the matching sash around my waist. "It's definitely you," the chubby cop assured me, smearing a lecherous grin across his moon pie face before lumbering back to business.

Jimmy said, "Manville stores his taste buds up his fat behind, pard, so I'm afraid we still have you on indecent exposure." I told Steiger what I thought and, first checking to be certain my legs worked as well as my adrenalin, went searching for my Beretta. I dropped it into the pocket of the robe. Jimmy said, "Suppressing evidence?"

"It's mine."

He held out his hand. "I'll see you get it back."

"Need it for the duration." Jimmy gave me a look. Without asking, I snatched the department badge hanging from his handkerchief pocket and flapped it on my sash. "Also, this," I said, and got away before he could object.

I went looking for Nicky Edmunds. I had not spotted him in the sweeps happening all over the soundstage. Flashing Jimmy's badge got me out of there; the robe got me a few wolf whistles from Jimmy's guys.

I pretended away the hurt in my swelling left hand and ignored the attacks on my bare feet while I wandered the lot in search of Nicky's trailer. Except for a sailing moon, the light wasn't much better than my sense of direction, but I found the trailer five or six minutes later.

Willie was sitting guard outside the trailer door. He appeared to be sleeping, his chins hanging on his chest, arms using his belly for a table. I stepped off the gravel path and out of view against the tin wall of a tool shed. I considered my options. The robe did not offer much protection from a rising chill that kept me alert and modulated the pain in my swelling hand. Would my knuckles ever be the same again?

I was over the urgent need to punish Nicky for what I'd seen him do to those two girls. Not the desire or the passion. Or the look on the Asian Ruby's face when Nicky made his choice. I figured the look was going to be with me forever, along with—

Willie.

Sitting there now in the gliding light with an ugly face full of mean wishes.

I would remember him as the two Rubys' escort. How many kids before those two? I owed him for Aleta and I owed him for me. Aleta was dead and I was not dead. He was a hairy toy with a slick mustache, a scum snake on another scum snake's payroll.

I demanded of myself: *Leave Willie and Nicky to the law.*

Like hell.

Willie made it easy when I stepped out onto the path again. Alerted by crunching gravel, his hand rose with his chins, one eye opening wider than the other to get a better focus. A chunk of moon dodged the clouds and I caught a glint of the gun he'd held out of sight, tucked under an armpit, seconds before I squeezed the trigger. Maybe, seconds after I squeezed the trigger.

My shot caught him in the gut. I heard the crack and Willie's brief anger, smelled the graphite, watched Willie rear backward in his chair, heard the chair clang against the side of the motor home.

Too easy.

I experienced a brief shame.

I verified no pulse, parked the Beretta in the pouch pocket of my robe, and pried the .38 from Willie's hand before stepping to the door and opening it a slice. The trailer reeked of grass, the smell heavier than last time, like the place was being fumigated.

Nicky responded the second time I called his name. He invited me inside. There had been enough noise to make him aware this wasn't a social call. I took the metal steps cautiously. I groped for the light switch above the kitchen service counter, ducked, sinking below Nicky's sightline with my left shoulder pressing hard against the exterior wall of the counter.

I thought I caught a glimpse of him at the end of the aisle, in front of the bedroom door. I filled my lungs with atmosphere and got an instant lift. Working out my next move, I told Nicky what was happening inside the soundstage. When he didn't answer, I said, "I thought I'd head on over and see if I could save the law the time and trouble of finding you, Nicky."

"You're some Boy Scout," he decided, in a voice that said he'd be halfway to the moon if not for the trailer roof. "Come on up. You got the gat, Homes. All I got is what's left of a good time."

"More lines from the movie, Nicky?"

"The only lines we been doing here led us through the doorway of a thousand delights, Pops. Tell Pops it's so, Ruby." After a silent moment: "Tell him it's so, Ruby."

"It's hurting this time."

"I said to tell him . . . Hey, Pops, I'm doing her in the ass while we talk and Ruby says it's hurting. Tell me, it's so? You're an authority on the subject now." Ruby let out a scream. "*Pendona.* You don't do what I say, you pay." Something small hit the lush green carpeting, in my line of vision. "Babes don't really need their second teat anyways, do they, Pops? Two sets of lips fine engineering, but one teat works for anybody's mama, excepting twins."

Ruby screamed.

"Let her go, you bastard."

"What movie *you* acting in, Pops?" He repeated my words. "Now you going to go dishing out dialogue, that's how the line should've read. Or this—" Nicky said them again, changing the cadence and the inflections. "Think you can remember for the next time?" I didn't answer. "Pops, Pops, Pops, let me hear from you, Pops. It ain't a game now, so you don't have to worry about winning or losing. Nobody wins here."

I looked at my broken hand. It was turning purple and the misshapen fingers had frozen at curious angles, but I didn't feel the pain I knew must be there. Much of anything else either. Snorting the boo clouds had done that for me. My head kept expanding with the universe. My thoughts were made of elastic. Logic had become a luxury and common sense a disaster.

I uncurled myself from the stairwell and stepped onto the aisle. Nicky and Ruby were at the other end, more naked than when they'd played the game, she in her emotions, while Nicky had lost his crimson briefs and the pitchfork. His face paint appeared to have been licked or sweated off. He leaned against the bedroom door using her as a shield. She was unconscious. Her slender arms hanging limply at her sides. He had her gripped tightly under her breasts with his right forearm. Ruby's right breast was the one he had sliced the nipple from. There had not been as much bleeding as I'd have imagined; barely a trickle.

Nicky's left hand gripped the pearl handle of a switchblade about eight inches long. The sharp edge nested against her throat. My eyes dropped down to a fresh slash mark on Ruby's taut stomach, a horizontal red gash below the belly button.

"Here's the deal, Pops. You hand over your gun and I hand over the space cunt."

"Otherwise, you kill her."

"Right on, Homes. You must know this scene by heart." He indicated with his chin. "Just set that beauty on the table over there and the cunt is out of here."

I thought about it: The .38 goes on the kitchen table. Nicky inches forward, keeping Ruby between us until he can get a safe grip on the gun. He pops me and Ruby, because it's how his mind is working. Off-balance and unrelenting.

Plan B: The .38 goes on the kitchen table. Nicky inches forward, keeping Ruby between us. As he reaches for the gun, I go for the Beretta in the pocket of my robe. I'm not as gone as he is. Besides, I have an Expert's rating.

With any luck, I don't kill Ruby for trying.

Nicky's pinwheel eyes appeared to follow my train of thought. "What you got down there, cowboy?" Was this nutcase also a mind reader? *That bulge under your robe a Beretta or are you glad to see me?* Mae West, young man, Mae West. "You carrying a cop badge? A dick's badge for a dickhead? You Dick Fucking Tracy or is that the genuine article or—?"

"On loan, Nicky. I needed a hall pass to get to you." He nodded before pulling the switchblade hard enough against Ruby's throat to draw a trace of blood. Her mouth opened to exhale a whimper. I said, "The gun is coming." I stepped forward and placed the .38 on the table. Nicky told me to push it closer toward him. I did.

"Now your pocket," Nicky said. "I also want the piece in

your pocket, Pops. Unless Willie went and shot himself with his own gun, you're carrying two of 'em, Pops."

"Maybe I'm glad to see you."

"What's that supposed to mean?"

I threw away the remark with a gesture and said. "Nicky, you're thinking pretty straight in the head for somebody as fucked up as you are."

He liked that. His lids appeared totally shut, but he saw enough to smile as I drew the Beretta from my pocket. I studied it before I started to place it alongside the .38. On a second thought I pulled the gun back.

Nicky turned the switchblade upward, so that it touched Ruby under her chin, and warned me about tricks. I told him he had no worries. Maybe he didn't appreciate the way I had said it. He said, "Back off."

Everybody in Hollywood wants to direct.

I backed off.

Nicky stepped closer to the table. He tried holding on to Ruby, holding on to the switchblade, and taking control of the .38, but he kept coming up a hand short. He solved the problem in a moment that went on forever. In what I read as a single move, Nicky slit Ruby's throat, dropped her and the switchblade, got two hands on the gun, and fired at me.

The impact of the bullet threw me onto my back. I lost my grip on the Beretta, but managed to hook my index finger around the trigger guard before the gun could fly away.

Nicky took a few stuttering steps closer. He worked himself into a sharpshooter's stance. I got off my shot in front of his. His shot went into the carpeting. My shot wasn't much either. It hit Nicky just below the shoulder, good enough to cost him the .38, twist him around, and drop him to the ground face first.

I waited, ready to fire again, then I crawled over to him,

climbed aboard his back, and planted the mouth of the Beretta behind and just below his right ear. Nicky was still breathing. I was leaking from somewhere, painting his backside as red as the paint on his face and his Adolphe Menjou mustache had been, not sure I could hang on until someone showed up to check out the gunshots or, maybe, just because Jimmy Steiger had missed me long enough.

The pain was intense. I sucked up more cloud through my nose, through my mouth. I was still ordering the contact high to hurry when my eyes quit celebrating an early Fourth of July.

The world was closing in on me.

I felt my life shutting down while trying not to hate Nicky Edmunds more than I already did. This was a time calling out for mercy and forgiveness.

Nicky flinched.

I fired.

And forgave myself.

Chapter 39

Knox Lundigan. Cleve Buntine and Jack Zipper, Jr. Roscoe Del Ruth. Melba Donaldson. The bust led by Bailey Madison and Jimmy Steiger had landed them on a variety of charges, leading off with Murder One. Others who'd been caught in the net Monday night at Grenedier & Grimm Studios were falling all over themselves trying to cop a plea bargain with the D.A.

BBStardom shut down within seconds after Aleta Haworth killed Eugene Coburn. Knox Lundigan had run commands from his control station that also instantly wiped clean everything taped by Buntine. It meant the D.A. probably would have to deal. Worse, that BBStardom was far from being out of business.

Me, I was sailing a bed at Good Samaritan, duration yet to be determined. Nicky's bullet had missed any vital body parts during its brief visit through my body and doctors were conjecturing that the combination of drugs I'd ingested had helped save my life, by putting a clamp on my system and slowing down blood loss before the Emergency Rescue Team got to me.

I had to fight the ERT off for a few minutes. I wasn't through dictating copy to the *Daily,* some kid on rewrite until his cracked soprano disappeared, replaced by the acerbic tones of Buster Byrd, reminding me, "You don't work here anymore, Gulliver."

"Just take it down, Buster," what I remember saying, operating with the rush that any newspaperman gets from an exclusive of this proportion. Any proportion. I might see Buster Byrd's byline over the story, but I'd know—and so would he—who the real reporter was. I could live with that. Could Buster?

I opened my eyes who-knows-when to find Jimmy Steiger dozing in a metal chair by my bedside. He caught the vibe and popped awake, his face exploding in a carnival of relief. "Now I can believe the doctors," he said.

I think I said, "This can't be hell, not with you here, Jimmy." The words made sense in my mind, but my speech sounded asleep, a slow-motion drone pulling every syllable to the max.

"My turn here," he said. "Greetings from some of your other fans who've kept the vigil, especially your ex."

"Stevie?"

"Her home away from home here. They've had to drag Stevie away to do her soap stuff. After all these years, I still don't understand you two."

"Love at first blight," I said. "Tell me something else, Jimmy."

"Doc Cuevas's post turned up as lethal a combination of street drugs as known to man and his dealers inside Nicky Edmunds. We're talking meth, flake, noise, maryjane, monkey dust, opie, sunshine. Nicky was a pharmacy on ten toes, capable of floating more junk than Michael Milken did on his best day. He was in the process of shutting down on automatic pilot when you mercifully and in infinite wisdom took the load off his shoulders, pard."

"Meaning?"

"Doc is logging the cause of Nicky's demise as a combined and cumulative drug overdose. His official report will say Nicky was dead before you discharged your weapon in a further act of self-defense, same as it already says in my crime scene report about how you dispatched Nicky after protecting yourself against Guillermo 'Willie' Flores y Garcia. In other words, you're off the hook, hero. Almost."

"Almost." My lips were dry. The word came out as a croak.

Jimmy fed me some water through a bent straw before continuing: "The one and lonely assistant D.A., Hapless Harris, has been making noises about asking his boss to charge you with involuntary manslaughter, same way the dumb SOB went flying off the hook after Roddy Donaldson. I've reminded Harris that, absent other evidence, Mr. Neil Gulliver is the D.A.'s only eyeball witness on Murder One and accessory to charges at the Sodom & Gomorrah Soundstage . . . That's what the *Daily* and Buster Byrd called Grenedier & Grimm when they busted the story and since. The Sodom & Gomorrah Soundstage. It's been adopted by the media all over the place."

The news called for a smart remark. I didn't have the strength or interest. I said, "Ruby? The Asian kid?"

"Lola Chen. Her real name. Sixteen her next birthday. Honor student at Le Conte Junior High in Hollywood until she got stars in her eyes and talked Mama into buying a page in *Stardom* magazine. The family shelled out more than ten gee on the deal."

"They lost more than the ten gee."

Steiger gave me a look. "One bullet and you've gone sentimental on me?"

"Doing it to myself . . . Roddy Donaldson? Maxie Trotter? Tell."

"Madison and me, we don't have anything that would tie either of them to any of this. Donaldson spent last Monday night dining and playing party games with—you ready for this?—Brian Armstrong. Into the wee, small hours. Maxie Trotter and his band were at a rehearsal hall, SIR, over on Sunset, by the old Columbia lot, getting ready for a concert a week from Saturday night at the Forum. For charity. Sold-out for weeks."

"Been thinking, Jimmy."

"Will miracles never cease?"

"I was wrong about something and Hapless Harris was right."

Jimmy gave me a look and faked a trembling hand, which he elevated upward. "Let me get a doctor in here. You're definitely beginning to sound like your brain's on backward again."

I signaled for more water and washed it around my mouth.

"Roddy did kill Hope Danbury and Laurie Ann Bockstatdler," I said, struggling with Laurie Ann's last name. "Roddy also murdered Gus Ljung and"—saying her name was hardest of all—"Jayne Madrigal."

Jimmy eased back on the chair. He studied my eyes for the gag. He saw how serious I was, and got serious himself. "Proof? You know, as in 'Proof, the Magic Dragon'?"

I shook my head.

He directed an inquiring gesture at the peeling paint and plaster of the ceiling and locked onto me with a hard stare. "Pard, tell you what I'm thinking. I'm thinking that your thinking might not be the strongest kind of evidence to sway a jury." When I didn't answer, he said, "A jury will be more inclined to believe Mrs. Melba Donaldson when she gets up on the witness stand and says she's the one what done the nasty deeds."

"You planning to tell me that eventually?"

"Eventually."

My detective friend described how Melba had volunteered her confession to him during the booking process. The story she told him coincided with the story I had laid on her at Gary Owens's bar, except for the part about Roddy. What Melba had to say about her murdering Jayne and Gus was a logical extension of the story.

Gus Ljung was her protégé. She and Gus were lovers. She caught Gus with Jayne, and it answered suspicions she had been harboring for weeks. She went for her .22.

"Her story holds together," Steiger said, as if deciding for both of us. "There's Gus living and loving his life away in his secret castle. It would take someone who knew about it to find him there, and it would take someone he knew and could trust for him to open the door and invite that someone inside so easy."

A lingering passion for sleep surrendered to the adrenalin of the news. "You're like every cop who ever worked backward from a notion, Jimmy. If you were Gus Ljung, how anxious would you be to open your secret door and usher in your lover while your secret girlfriend was stretched out there?"

He thought about it out loud. "You're saying Mama Lion protecting her cub? Why not, especially now when she's looking at Goodbye City anyway, on accessory or worse?"

I said, "Given the dearth of diamond-quality evidence, she gets to cop out. She does a few soft years growing fruits and veggies at Sybil Brand. Writes her autobiography. Sells it for lots of zeros to the movies or TV. Gets sprung in time to cast it. Now, both mama and son can live happily ever after."

"Okay, Roddy Donaldson, but he's still a notion, only yours this time. What's it the old lady used to say on the commercials, pard? *Where's the proof?*

"Where's the beef?"

"Yeah, right, and my beef is with no proof."

Jimmy Steiger had me there.

The story stayed page one, under Buster Byrd's byline at the *Daily.*

The *Enquirer* made it worthwhile for a night nurse to steal a few candid shots of me with the pocket Canon they provided. He apologized when I caught him at it, but I let him go ahead anyway. Everybody has to make a living and Christmas was approaching, tied to a recession the president refused to acknowledge.

I said no to the television shows. *A Current Affair* and *Hard Copy* were prepared to sweeten the pot for exclusives, but I'd have had to shave.

I filled time sending off potted plants to new parents in the Good Sam maternity ward, off a list I got from the administrator's office. Most were charity cases that could stand some bonus beauty in their lives. Most had foreign-sounding names, getting me to wonder if accents are genetic. What other reason for accents? It was me thinking silly to offset the wounds that are inflicted on the soul by the deaths of people with whom you crossed lives.

I tried restricting my thoughts to those I had liked and those I would never have an opportunity to like, but there had been too much death for that: Laraine Dailey; Lola Chen and the other Ruby, identified by Buster Byrd as Heather Frane. Heather Frane, only fourteen going on fifteen, whose parents sat on a couch in their Bell Gardens living room comforting one another and barely making sense to the TV field reporter.

There wasn't time or opportunity for the quality think time I covet and was lacking. Far too many interruptions, some more welcome than others, like Augie Fowler, finding a phone from wherever he was drying out; repeatedly calling to satisfy firsthand that I was making progress.

Jimmy, reporting back on the flashes of inspiration I asked him to run down for me. He could tell I was on to something. After the first time, he didn't have to ask what and played out the story my way. He brought get-well drawings from his kid and reminded me a couple times how upset Margie would be if I didn't get over for a meal the instant the doctors set me free.

And Aleta Haworth came to visit.

★ ★ ★ ★ ★

Aleta had survived Che's shot. She appeared to be in better condition than me when she was wheeled to my bedside by the bald-headed drunk from Gary Owens's bar. His name was Ray Shannon and he was one of Bailey Madison's people.

After Jayne disappeared, he had been put on Melba Donaldson's tail, the same way Madison played tagalong with Che and Willie. Or I might well have become more Brand X doggie dinner at the Grenedier & Grimm Studios.

Aleta was wearing a heavy wool jogging suit under a hospital-issue white terry-cloth robe and tired running shoes. A red and gold *papier-mâché* flower was pinned to the robe. Her shaved scalp was disfigured by an eccentric, multi-colored hairpiece. Her neck wound was buried inside a thick round of bandage. Che's .22 slug had spilled a lot of her blood, but missed kill points like the carotid artery and neck bone.

"She's well enough to be going home today," Shannon said, "but she insisted on saying goodbye to you first." He told me what I already knew from Jimmy. The shot had somehow affected her larynx. For the time being, until doctors probed some more, Aleta was voiceless.

No matter.

Everything she had to say to me was written on her face.

It wasn't necessarily "Thank you."

I read Aleta's embarrassment over what we had been through together. I sensed an enigmatic bond based on something else we were sharing: the murder of people we cared about. I told her this. Tears welled in Aleta's eyes. She reached out for me. We gripped one another tightly. She cried. I wanted to, but I couldn't.

I considered telling her what I thought and was quietly working on with Jimmy; promising her I wouldn't let Roddy get away with murder; that I owed it to her, to Hope Danbury and her mother, to—

Bailey Madison's man said something about the hour and wheeled her backward away from me onto the aisle. Before he turned the chair in the direction of the exit, Aleta gave me a look I had not seen before. I was satisfied she understood my unspoken promise. I smiled away in pain.

Sharon sent flowers and came around, too. She brought greetings and get-well cards from Heathcliffe residents, including many I didn't know by name. Gossip and jokes, and a few good laughs whenever she caught me feeling sorry for myself, like Wanda Sue Griffin charging into the office yesterday, hollering that Chester Fung had to be fired immediately for "insubordination and breach of gardening."

Sharon even brought greetings from Roddy Donaldson, who had not quite made it here past sending an avalanche of flowers that smelled prettier than Roddy smelled to me. His card thanked me again for believing in him and hoped I understood the pain he'd been experiencing since his mother's confession. It looked to be written by him, signed as if it were an autograph to a fan, *Very Truly Yours.* As if it could be a courtroom exhibit further indicting his mother, further distancing him from the murders. The little prick.

Sharon saying, "Roddy's invited me to be his guest at Maxie Trotter's concert next week at the Forum. A star-studded fundraiser for Maxie's anti-drug crusade, being telecast live by MTV. You, too, if you're out of here and up for it by then."

"Thoughtful of him."

"Front row seats. Roddy says it's a token. Him trying to show his appreciation for the part you and I played in saving his life."

"Thoughtful," I repeated, thinking how confident Roddy must be feeling about the net result of Melba's confession.

Do the Crime. Have Mama Do the Time.

Sharon said, "It'll be Roddy's first time out in public, something Jayne Madrigal set up for him after his release from custody. He'll be introducing Maxie and the band."

I thought: Publicity stunt. Jayne finding daylight in the disaster. That was Jayne. She was always good at what she did—great at fooling people.

Stevie returned my call from the *Bedrooms and Board Rooms* set. Before I could tell her why I'd called, what I needed, she was shedding real emotion and concern for me, the kind she usually reserves for herself. This time she also had concern for Jayne, when I brought up Jayne's name and she fathomed my doubts creeping into the conversation.

She said, "Honey, take my word for it. Whatever else you think about Jaynie, she was bonkers for you. From the get-go. She made the segue from curiosity like I've never seen before. She wanted to do it right, make sure she won you over, even though I told her she could get more satisfaction from a good douche."

"Thank you."

"Kidding, puss, you know that. Jaynie called to find out all your fave foods, your fave books, your fave faves. Everything but your fave positions. The first night you went to her place for dinner, remember what music was playing?"

"Rod Stewart. 'You're in My Heart.' 'Tonight's the Night.' "

"When she called me to ask, I told her how you were deep certain to get off on Rod Stewart, because of your being a sentimental slob and our having gone to see Rod Stewart in concert at the Forum the next week after you picked me up at the Imagine That! Festival for John Lennon."

"It was a Bee Gees concert at the Forum."

"What'd that bullet do, honey? Blow a hole in your memory?"

I wanted to share my worst fear with Stevie, that Jayne had brilliantly applied the feminine science of trappery with ulterior motives that had absolutely nothing to do with romance. I had something it was her job to find and get away from me—the blue floppy.

I said, "I'll always remember Jayne for what she was and what she came to mean to me. If she were here now I'd tell her: *Jayne, it was the Bee Gees, not Rod Stewart.*"

Stevie hung up, was calling again within twenty seconds, to say, "You just can't stand it, ever, when I'm right and you're wrong, but you're in my heart anyway." Added some off-key lyrics.

"And mine, so maybe you'll do me a favor?"

"Tonight's *not* the night, honey, if that's what you called about, although a hospital bed would be a first for us."

I told her what I wanted her to go home and look for.

A few hours later, she called to say she'd found it in her closet.

Bernie Flame brought it to me at the hospital Saturday morning: Proof. Or the next best thing.

Chapter 40

Saturday. Bailey Madison joined us about an hour after Bernie Flame arrived at Good Samaritan. The blue floppy disk was slotted for action in Roddy Donaldson's sleek portable, the one everybody had been so anxious to find. Bernie had the computer set up facing me, on a bench table he'd sweet-talked away from the nurses' station. I elevated the bed to forty-five degrees and gave the thumbs-up sign. Bernie closed the privacy curtains, giving us our own screening room, and apologized for slow reflexes.

"Been up half the night programming macros and the other half the night extending my honeymoon with My Butterfly," he said. I gave him a questioning look. "The Moth, but not anymore. She's My Butterfly now."

He hit a key on the numeric pad. It took a few seconds for the command sequence to run, producing Laraine Dailey. And Hope Danbury. And Laurie Ann Bockstatdler was "Janie Doe" again. Again, those nightmarish images of rampaging sexuality played out on the LCD VGA display. Backlit. High resolution. A sound level barely loud enough for us, but nothing to share with anyone else in the ward.

Whenever I opened my eyes, it was to glance at Madison. He was leaning against the back wall by the shelf of body monitors, shoulders hunched, wrestling with himself. He gave away nothing by his expression, but his jaw never quit working as he clamped down hard on his back molars. He spoke in isolated words, incomplete sentences garbled and lost inside his mouth. Finally, he swiped at the air to signal he had seen enough, but Bernie and I weren't finished.

At my command, Bernie keyed another macro.

The screen piggybacked and leapfrogged.

When it finally settled at the opening menu, I said, "I believe this is what you really need to see, Madison."

The menu on view was not the one subscribers routinely found after they'd logged onto BBStardom. It resembled an airline schedule at LAX; flights in, flights out. Some of the designations led direct to the sex and drug channels, within easy access to those who'd paid the price and knew the passwords, other designations to other levels and new menus, where different codes were required.

Another macro carried us deeper inside the mysteries of the ugly world Knox Lundigan had created. We sampled the sex play produced and distributed by Stardom House. In shorter takes when it got grittier, more violent. Never a second time after the first murders, snuffs that revealed Lola Chen as one of the lucky ones when she'd played the game.

Codes and trip keys, increasingly complex the deeper the destination. Confidential messages back and forth spelling out deal terms, code numbers, code names. The Stardom House code bank, one of the wonders of an access level Lundigan and his dead partner had never intended for anyone else to see.

I was in awe.

Madison, when he finally regained his voice, his head swinging sideways in disbelief, said, "It's far, far more than I imagined. You have done your country a great service, Bernard."

Bernie couldn't suppress a smile.

He looked like he'd just solved the riddle of the Sphinx.

I said, "The light show isn't over yet, Madison," and gave

Bernie a high sign.

Bernie returned it and squatted in front of the keyboard to transmit a series of commands. Madison's eyes narrowed and wandered between us. He was not the type of person who appreciated being on the outside of secrets.

Bernie also noticed. He said, "Neil told me what to look for or I never would have found it. Personal codes. Lundigan must've done his homework on Chinese boxes." He hit the Enter key twice, and—

We were seeing Roddy Donaldson and Gus Ljung partying with Hope Danbury and Janie Doe.

In the procession of vignettes we sampled, Roddy and Gus became increasingly aggressive. They conferred on camera regarding what games might come next. Every so often, the girls shared uncertain looks. One would start to say something, and—

Cut.

When the picture was restored, the two girls would be happier; robust with a newfound energy; a widening hollowness in their eyes; incrementally enslaved by the notion of obliging their hosts. Ugly, all of it. Especially the last minute or two. Neither Hope nor Janie Doe stir. They're lifeless dolls. Roddy and Gus push and prod. Probe. Reality intrudes. They ponder the truth of the hour in psychobabble, and—

Cut.

Madison said, "They were loyal soldiers who believed in the cause and fought the good fight. There are casualties in every war, Neil, and we mourn them."

"The way Laraine Dailey was a loyal soldier?"

He thought through his answer. "Yes, of course. Laraine, too."

"And you mourn her, as well."

"Yes. Of course."

"And Jayne Madrigal?"

No response.

When I'd reached Madison with an invitation to be here, he had wanted instead to send one of his men over to pick up the portable and the blue floppy, but I had insisted he come to Good Samaritan. I was determined to look in his face when I asked the question about Jayne.

It's not what you think, Scaredy-cat, no matter what you think, she'd said to me.

Later, she had said, she would tell me *later.*

Only *later* became *too late* and I'd had to work it out for myself.

"I said, Jayne Madrigal, Madison. Her? Are you also mourning her?"

Madison turned away from me. He turned back, now browsing me to see what I thought I knew. He remembered Bernie, who understood the look the T-man gave him. Bernie mumbled something about taking a healthy piss, tuned the menu on the screen into a vivid blue emptiness, and disappeared through the privacy curtain. Madison adjusted the curtain, buying another minute. We measured each other with our eyes.

I said, "When we were at Rev. Plantation's and you told me about springing Roddy on his own recognizance, about needing Roddy loose to keep your investigation moving, you forgot to mention Jayne was on top of that aspect, correct?" Madison wasn't going to help. "You were so busy covering up, convincing me Jayne was one of the nasties, you forgot to mention it was a role Jayne was playing. She was acting. Jayne was one of your bad-ass guys, another soldier in Bailey Madison's army."

"Need to know, Neil. It was not information you needed to have." The sharp edge was missing from his response.

"I'd like to have it now," I said.

Madison assumed an at-rest position and pushed the back of

his head against his shirt collar. After a deep breath he said, "Jayne did not want you to have it, Neil." He let me be mystified for a moment. "I was ready to tell you the afternoon we met. Our mutual friend Augie Fowler had said you could be trusted, I could swear by you. Good enough for me, coming from Augie. Especially it coming from Augie. Otherwise, you think I would have brought Aleta along? However, Jayne already was on record."

"Did she say why?"

"Jayne feared you would think her interest in you was professional, that she had come on to you amorously as part of her assignment."

"Wasn't that the case?"

Averting my stare. "Briefly, maybe."

"How brief?"

Shrug. Quietly: "Very briefly. By the time I sensed what was happening and told her to stop, it was too late. She would not hear of it. She assured me she could handle it. She assured me she could handle you and she could handle her job without one getting in front of the other. I knew better, but she had this way, Jayne did." The edges of his mouth twitched in and out of a smile. "Do you care to hear more, about her running to your rescue at the school or, later, jeopardizing our operation by tracking after you at Stardom House? I can—"

I signaled Madison to stop. "Getting me out of Stardom House, she blew me a kiss, Madison. I knew what the truth was when she blew me the kiss."

"How?"

My turn to smile. "Need to know, Madison?"

Madison shook his head. "No need, Neil. I've been there a few times myself." For a moment I thought he wanted to tell me something. It slipped past his gaze and, instead, he said, "When you spoke with Augie Fowler recently . . ."

"I did. So?"

"You told him you had proof Roddy Donaldson did the killings, my three soldiers and Gus Ljung."

"I did."

"What you have shown me here this morning, while exceptional, is not proof. Is there more to this than met my eyes?"

"I have theories."

"Need to know, Neil."

I put my new scenario together for Madison the way I'd put it together for myself after I recognized Gus Ljung performing on a screen at Stardom House, when Bernie was showing off how well we had penetrated BBStardom.

It wasn't Melba Donaldson who had been paying off Henry Bouchey to keep him from outing Roddy. Roddy was doing the shelling out, money, sometimes a fresh name, through his boyfriend Brian Armstrong. That was something Jimmy Steiger pinned down for me on one of the errands I'd sent him on, visits with Armstrong and Bouchey.

Roddy had told me the truth when he said his mother didn't know he was gay. I was the blabbermouth who'd let Melba in on the secret, when I smugly introduced the subject at Gary Owens's bar. She may have confessed murder to the cops in order to protect her meal ticket, her beloved Roderick, but she didn't kill anyone.

I believed the part where Melba was doing Gus Ljung, the way I was prepared to give odds she'd boffed Che and a casting couch of thousands, but unlikely she suspected Gus was doing her son at the same time. I didn't suppose Brian Armstrong knew, either.

Madison gave me a two-handed *More* gesture.

I said, "Melba gets Roddy back home from the Roxy with Hope and Janie Doe. Gus Ljung is waiting. Roddy has had travel time to get ahead of the booze and whatever else he and Nicky Edmunds were putting into their systems. Roddy sees Gus. Sees his mama. He panics, fearful she saw him hugging Gus. Or, maybe, a smoochy-smoochy look traveling between Gus and him that she shouldn't have seen?

"He needs to show her something else. He needs to show her macho-macho man. He plays grab-ass with the girls. He does some titty-pinching. They get him upstairs where he insists he's not through partying. Melba can't persuade him otherwise. Melba reluctantly splits, unhappy about leaving Roddy and her boyfriend with Hope and Janie Doe. Roddy can relax now, unload the girls, but Gus is too horny to let this opportunity pass him by.

"Gus goes for Roddy's stash. Whatever grows, Roddy blows. Roddy, the chemist's best friend. He had learned years ago from Brian Armstrong how to find true happiness without using the needles he fears so much. Jimmy Steiger confirmed that on his visit to Armstrong, whose own jones is that old reliable Hollywood staple, opium. He smoked it out flashing an old Armstrong booking sheet Brian Armstrong's high-powered lawyers had managed to keep wrapped all these years: puffs and peckers in Westlake Park.

"On top of Roddy's drugstore, Gus hauls out Roddy's portable computer, the one they use whenever it's the two of them playing there—and his video camera. The computer has been retooled and reconfigured by Knox Lundigan, the way it's done for subscribers to the TalenTapes library. Gus plugs into the camera and logs onto BBStardom. He does not insert a floppy. Maybe he can't find a floppy in his hurry to get their show going. For now, the show can stay on the computer's hard drive. It helps explain why I couldn't find disks when I broke into Roddy's apartment to search for the missing computer, disks, anything tied to TalenTapes." Madison's eyebrows jumped at that bit of revelation. "I figure their party went on for the better part of three days, otherwise there'd have been a death stench when Sharon Glenn and I went to check on Roddy and found the bodies. They were still relatively fresh.

"Everybody presumed sex and focused on the drug angle to make the case against Roddy work. Based on other things I knew, I also let it slide, until the other day. I asked Jimmy Steiger to push the M.E. for another battery of tests, given the new prominence of Gus Ljung in the investigation. Semen traces in all the usual places, including those that never matched Roddy. It's why I'm betting the D.A., Hapless Harris, gave in so quickly when you negotiated Roddy's release. This time, the semen came up matching Gus."

Madison slapped his hands together.

He said, "The rest becomes obvious. Gustav Ljung set it up to look the way it did to distance himself from the truth. He sneaked out of the apartment with the portable, the camera, the drugs, any possible link to him, and left Donaldson to OD. Left him for dying alongside the girls. Donaldson survives and is still exploding with rage when he gets out of the hospital. His need for revenge overtakes good judgment. He picks an appropriate time to drop in on Ljung."

Madison seemed pleased with himself.

I changed that soon enough, reminding him, "The portable was not inventoried on the Ljung murder scene. A lot was, stuff that made me believe Gus often spent shift time breaking into residents' apartments. The portable was too big to get overlooked. It's not the kind of sticky-fingers item badges are prone to take as their own. Maybe you should stake out Harry Weiss, the locksmith who made the discovery?"

I didn't give Madison a chance to answer.

He looked like he didn't want to answer.

I knew he was covering up again—

For her.

I said, "Tell me, Madison . . . Jayne Madrigal just happened to be in that hideaway with Gus when—"

"I suppose." Not anxious to hear the rest.

"Why? Why was she there, Madison? How did Jayne know to be there?" Vertical frown lines formed and deepened in his forehead. "Tell me, or should I tell you?"

CHAPTER 41

The corners of Bailey Madison's mouth twitched before he gestured me to continue.

I said, "The night Melba brought Roddy and the girls back to the Heathcliffe, Jayne was with them. Her heading for the Roxy after canceling Roddy's limo at the Grenedier & Grimm Studios would be in keeping with her role as the complete PR professional. Melba can leave her boyfriend with Roddy and the girls, because Jayne will be like a chaperone.

"Jayne gets a sense of the relationship between Roddy and Gus Ljung. Maybe it's confirming her earlier suspicions. Maybe Jayne pops a couple highboys as her excuse for doing a number on Gus. She joins in the fun and games long enough to see the camera and the camera operating. She knows it's Exhibit I stuff, possibly more so than the blue floppy, and that's how she reports it back to you, Madison.

"When Roddy in the hospital wants his computer and she and Melba can't find it in his apartment, Jayne realizes who must have it. Gus isn't quick to admit it or hand it over to her, because what's on the hard drive can link him to the two deaths. She's patient, our Jayne, figuring to work her way into his confidence through his pants. When she spends the night with me, she comes across the blue floppy. It's no big deal talking Gus into using his set of security keys to waltz in and out of my place. She thanks him in her special way down in his hideaway, and leaves with the computer as well as the floppy. She's not able to pass it to you immediately, and this whole business has heated to the point where she's not comfortable keeping the computer at her apartment . . ."

Madison's head was swiveling in disagreement with what he was hearing from me, but I was too inspired to stop.

"My ex-wife, Stevie Marriner, unintentionally provides Jayne with a solution," I said. "She's on her way to Las Vegas for Bernie Flame's marriage to Juliet, Stevie's mom. Jayne will be running back and forth to her place to feed Stevie's pooches, Mutt and Jeff. Jayne buries the computer in Stevie's closet, with the blue floppy snug and safe in the disk drive. Not likely anybody will think to look there. After her death, when Steiger confirmed the computer was not on the inventory of Jayne's apartment, I played my Stevie hunch. It was the best guess, short of Jayne having passed it to you."

"Finished, Neil?"

"Almost . . . Roddy is discharged from the hospital, free and clear. He confronts Gus, who manages to romance himself back into Roddy's affections. Roddy recognizes the issue with Jayne. What she saw. What she might tell Melba. And—the computer. Missing. If Gus doesn't have it, Jayne must. Gus understands what Roddy is now suggesting is safety first, for both of them.

"Roddy gets Jayne to the Heathcliffe on a ruse. Maybe Jayne has second thoughts about going, but he's still her client and she still has a part to play for you, Madison. She winds up in Gus Ljung's hideaway, and—" I aimed my invisible finger gun at the T-man and squeezed the trigger. "Gus, too. Roddy's revenge, or a case of his wiping the slate clean. Roddy may already have owned the .22, direct mail or over-the-counter; it's the fashionable weapon of choice. Steiger hasn't located it yet, but he plans to keep hunting."

I signaled Madison it was his turn again.

It took him a few minutes.

"Proof, Neil, proof. You continue to distribute The Next Best Thing. I have heard nothing from you yet that puts Roddy Donaldson in his room, the hideaway, with Gustav Ljung or Jayne Madison."

"The coroner's report," I said. "It could have been before Jayne got there or . . . later. Roddy and Gus did some celebrating. Inside Gus's mouth, the throat and the esophagus, the M.E. found semen matching Roddy's blood type. A sliver of hair in Gus's mouth was also a match. It times out right."

"Why didn't the coroner find it earlier?"

"A backload on bodies. This is Los Angeles, where death never takes a holiday. Doc Cuevas and his department already had the one plus one. Even without Jimmy asking, they eventually would have scored the two."

Bailey Madison lost himself in his own mindful evaluation. He puttered around, organizing the dishes and containers on top of the roller table. He straightened out a stack of newspapers and magazines on the medicine table. He decided, "Still won't wash, Neil. Any trace of the coroner's report will be gone within eight hours. Detective Sgt. Steiger will be discouraged from investigating any further. You will find only frustration if you continue trying to conjure up proof."

"Do I need to know why?"

"I'll tell you anyway. The brass I answer to would not let me reveal as much as would be necessary to bring Roddy Donaldson to trial successfully. There's still too much at stake globally for the drug and porn task force to risk it coming out in a courtroom. For now, it remains extremely important to have those people thinking Jayne Madrigal was on their side. Don't say it, Neil, what I know you must be thinking. What you just heard is the truth. That's the way it is in real life. For now, it will be good enough if we can put an end to Stardom House."

"Good enough for who? For you, maybe. I'm going public

with the story, Madison, even if it has to be through that nitwit at the *Daily,* Buster Byrd. I owe that much to myself and a lot of other people. Do you want me to list them for you? Or just the ones that aren't on your own list?"

Madison waved me off.

"When we're finished with you, Neil, nobody will buy your story."

"Maybe they will, when they see the proof."

"The Next Best Thing."

"Proof. Bernie didn't want to lose his good work, the way he had once before, so he ran copies of the blue floppy before heading over here today. Bernie also ran copies of the game Roddy and Gus played with—"

"I would be saddened to know you're telling the truth."

I didn't like what I saw staring back at me. I didn't mind being a hero for myself, but I didn't want to gamble with Bernie Flame's life. "Just kidding, Madison."

"Neil, promise me you won't kid that way again."

"You have my word."

"Then you have my word on something. In a week I'll have resolved the Roddy Donaldson affair to your complete satisfaction. Can you wait the week, Neil?"

"Why?"

"Why a week?"

"Why at all?"

"Because you're right to remind me of the people who are owed. Because I have as deep a personal stake in this as you. Because Jayne Madrigal—" He took a deep breath and held it for eternity. "Because Jayne was my daughter, you see? She was my child. My only child." A fireball of horror streaked across my mind. "When I say we mourn them all, I did mean it, Neil. In Jayne's case, most of all."

Madison seemed to be begging my forgiveness. The moment

was brief. It passed. He managed a smile. And for an instant I felt closer to that flag-waving son-of-a-bitch than I had to any man in years.

Chapter 42

The doctors sent me home after the weekend. I still ached and pained, but they'd decided nothing was so serious I couldn't take care of myself. Besides, Good Samaritan was short on beds.

By the following Saturday, Bailey Madison's week had come and gone.

Nothing had happened.

So much for his word.

My depression over Jayne deepened.

I spent most of my waking hours, which had become most of my hours, trying to sleep. When the door chime finally registered on me, it took me a minute to understand where I was. On the couch, in front of the TV, north by northwest of another nightmare.

At the door, Sharon, drawing me back to reality, insisting she'd been pressing the chime for at least five minutes.

"I was about ready to order up security," she said, her troubled face examining my sleepy-eyed confusion. "Neil, you are okay, aren't you? Maybe I should call your doctor?"

I thanked her for her concern and dismissed the idea. "Can't believe I fell asleep," I said. I checked my watch. It was verging on three-thirty. "Had to be all your chicken broth for lunch. A heavy meal does that to me." I rubbed my stomach, impulsively began to rub the top of my head at the same time, in the opposite direction.

Sharon laughed. Her mood brightened at once. So did mine. The way it did every time she checked on me, always with an excuse like chicken soup, but also an unexpressed need to be positive I was healing.

I suppose I was.

Physically, anyway.

"I wanted to remind you about the MTV broadcast before I run off with Roddy, in case you change your mind about not tuning in the show," she said, almost apologetically. "It starts at five, because of going out live to the East Coast."

Maxie Trotter's concert.

That explained Sharon's outfit, an oversized scoop neck sweater over stonewashed jeans and penny loafers, sleeves pushed to the elbows. The barest touch of makeup. Tinker Bell earrings; a larger version around her neck. Her hair running wild, casual, challenging her wardrobe. Her cologne not too sophisticated.

I'd let her know days ago I had no interest in going to the concert. Now, I made an exaggerated show of shaking the Tinker Bell pendant on her sweater. Her smile gleamed. I said, "You never mentioned a date with Roddy was part of his front row offer."

She lost the smile and pried my fingers off the bell. Satisfied I was serious, she said, "It's not a date. None of your business, but still not a date. Roddy is going in a limo and he offered me a ride, that's all this is. A ride. Beats fighting the freeway and dueling for a decent parking place."

"He's a wonderful human being is Roddy Donaldson."

As if on cue, Roddy materialized, heading for us from the direction of the elevator.

He was also dressed for rock-and-roll. He called out for her with boyish deference while tapping the face of his gold Rolex with an index finger.

"I have to walk out on stage for the intro five o'clock straight up," he said, acting as if Sharon were alone in my doorway. "We need to get a move on, in case the San Diego is shlogged with commuter traffic this early."

"Never too early for shlogging," I said under my breath, determined to keep my rage a silent prisoner.

Sharon squeezed my hand and turned to go. Roddy turned so he didn't have to look at me, but I wanted him to look at me, damn it. I called his name. When it failed to get his attention, I struggled up the corridor behind them. At the elevator, I yanked him around by the shoulder.

His eyes were full of bitterness.

I hoped he noticed the hate in mine.

I choked on my temper and headed back to my apartment, picturing what might have happened if Sharon hadn't been there, if Roddy had thrown a punch, given me some other excuse, any excuse, to wrap my anxious hands around his throat.

I laughed at the thought of killing again and how easy it gets once it starts, the same way I smile at a child's innocence; a knack never lost.

I screamed at the ceiling, "There's a murder among us, Madison. He walks free and your word is shit. It's been a week and your word is shit."

Curiosity got the best of me a couple minutes after five o'clock, once I had caught enough of the next movie in the Movie Channel's "Boston Blackie Marathon" to know it was one I had already seen. I clicked to MTV.

Roddy was stepping a couple feet to the right of the mike center stage. Whatever he had just said had the crowd on its feet and cheering madly. He had his arms raised over his head and was shaking his clenched fists in a passionate gesture of victory.

The director cut briefly to a close-up of his enticing face and the famous grin, the adorable cheeks, the dimple deep enough to store a dime inside. A giant spot bathed him in stardom, while another kept up a vigil for Maxie Trotter, who was yet to join his band on stage. The speakers on my set vibrated to the high end notes of "Sparkle Plenny Enny Momen'," Maxie's latest single. It was impossible to turn on a rock station without getting an earful.

The camera cut away to Maxie's Hot to Trots, already into it, oohing and aahing with gospel fervor in the kind of outfit churches had banned five or six hundred years ago. Esther Rae. Darlesque. A new Hot to Trot, Aleta Haworth's replacement.

A whump and a duhmp and you sparkle penny enny momen'.

Put a rum to the whump and you sparkle plenny enny—

Roddy moved to the music, giving it enough body to earn new roars of approval from the couple thousand fans packed SRO into the Forum. His eyes squeezed shut. Lips mouthing the lyrics.

He was unaware of another Hot to Trot, a fourth member of the trio, who'd stepped out from behind a framing curtain stage left and was heading toward him with determined steps.

Aleta.

Her neck still protected by bandages.

A spot reflecting off something she gripped decisively in her right hand, obscured from the camera's eye by her body.

Another angle.

I can see Aleta is holding a .25 automatic.

So can the director.

He stays with the angle as she moves in on Roddy.

Behind her in the wings, indistinct in the shadow light of backstage, Madison's man, Ray Shannon, bouncing in a way that effectively albeit not obviously blocks off several people who've just taken notice of Aleta.

Roddy, with the music:

Pump the rump to a dump and you sparkle plenny enny momen'.

Eyes closed. Mouth selling the lyrics.

The screen fills with a view from a camera at auditorium level, at the foot of the stage. Aleta angles the .25 upward at the base of Roddy's spine. The shot lost under the music. At that angle, her shot would catch him in the medulla oblongata. A big target. A certain target.

A different consistency to the crowd noise as Roddy lurches forward in puppet steps marked by certain death.

Another angle before the screen goes black and silent.

Bailey Madison.

He is a visible, fleeting presence in the wings, a day late on a promise, but I know I don't have to be concerned for Aleta.

I snap off the TV and head for the fridge and a cold brew, putting my rump to the dump, wondering how long before I'll sparkle plenny again; wondering how long it will be before *later* becomes *now.*

I hear myself laughing.

I like the sound.

It's almost genuine.

ABOUT THE AUTHOR

Robert S. Levinson is the best-selling author of twelve prior crime-thrillers: *The Evil Deeds We Do; Finders, Keepers, Losers, Weepers; Phony Tinsel; A Rhumba in Waltz Time; The Traitor in Us All; In the Key of Death; Where the Lies Begin; Ask a Dead Man;* and the "Neil and Stevie" novels *Hot Paint, The James Dean Affair, The John Lennon Affair,* and *The Elvis and Marilyn Affair.* His short stories appear frequently in the *Ellery Queen* and *Alfred Hitchcock* mystery magazines. Bob is a Derringer Award winner, won *Ellery Queen* Readers Award recognition three times, and is regularly included in "year's best" anthologies. His nonfiction has appeared in *Rolling Stone, Los Angeles Times* Magazine, *Written By* Magazine of the Writers Guild of America West, *Westways,* and *Los Angeles* Magazine. Bob's plays *Transcript* and *Murder Times Two* had their world premieres at the annual International Mystery Writers Festival. He served four years on Mystery Writers of America's (MWA) national board of directors. Bob wrote and produced two MWA annual "Edgar Awards" shows and two International Thriller Writers "Thriller Awards" shows. His work has been praised by Nelson DeMille, Clive Cussler, Joseph Wambaugh, T. Jefferson Parker, David Morrell, Margaret Maron, William Link, Jeffery Deaver, Heather Graham, John Lescroart, Ed Gorman, Wendy Hornsby, Doug Allyn, DP Lyle, Michael Palmer, James Rollins, Thomas Perry, Joseph Finder, Paul Levine, William Kent Krueger, Christopher Reich, and others. Bob resides in Los Angeles with his wife,

Sandra, and Rosie, a loving Besenji Mix, who thinks she rescued them. Visit Bob at www.rslevinson.com and on Facebook.